BLOODLINES

THE LEAGUE OF TWELVE
BOOK I

Mirador Publishing
10 Greenbrook Terrace
Taunton
Somerset
UK
TA1 1UT

Bloodlines

The League of Twelve
Book I

N. Fishfish & K. Matthews

~~~~

To everyone who has the courage to look past what they see, to find the secrets that are only revealed to those who believe in the extraordinary.

~~~~

1 - THE FIRST OF TWELVE KEYS

Marcus Shea knew the layout of this upscale suburban neighbourhood better than he cared to. Although not much had changed, when he was a young boy, a park sat where three new homes stood.

He parked his car and walked confidently toward the house he had called home so long ago. Soon he would take what should have been his. Dressed in a black, long-sleeved shirt and brown cargo pants, he made no attempt to hide his face. The thought that he would be recognized was of no concern; he was his brother's identical twin.

The cool night air blew in a gentle breeze through his hair as he pressed on toward his brother's house. He stopped for a moment to look up at the full moon in the sky, well aware of what his brother and nephew had done earlier that night. It had been the first time Sebastian joined the other members of The League of Twelve to open the portal between Earth and the planet Eyras in the Andromeda galaxy. His eyes narrowed as he thought of his brother. Jacob was always dutiful, the preferred brother, the chosen one. Marcus clenched his teeth and flared his nostrils. This would be the day Jacob finally lost.

He quickened his pace as he approached the house directly behind the Shea home, anxious to get to his prize. He kept to the shadows as he made his way through the yard behind Jacob's home.

From the neighbour's yard, his brother's home appeared nearly vacant, save for the smoke that rose up from the chimney and the dim light that shone through one of the bedroom windows. Marcus, however, knew the family was home.

He advanced toward the window in the den; he knew that his brother usually left it unlocked. After he removed his gloves from his back pocket, he put them on before he unsheathed his dagger and sliced through the mesh screen. Just as the midnight hour began, Marcus lifted the heavy window and crept into his brother's home unseen, thanks to the large bush between the window and the house next door.

~~~~

The Shea family were creatures of habit. Jacob's wife, Maxine, always showered at 11:00 p.m. and was in bed by 11:30 p.m. On many occasions as Marcus watched the Shea home in preparation for that night, he caught glimpses of Maxine through the upper bathroom window as she prepared to bathe, unintentionally offering him a taste of what he could have had.

Maxine was the secretary at her husband's law firm, Shea and Partners, LLP. She was the perfect wife, the perfect mother who provided her husband with two beautiful children. In Marcus' mind, she should have been his, not Jacob's. He wondered if the children would look the same had they been his. The same DNA should, in theory, produce the same results.

Marcus shook his head and turned his thoughts back to his mission as he quietly walked through his brother's dark house.

The youngest Shea child, Marianne, was twelve years old. She had her mother's beauty, porcelain skin, and soft brown eyes. He was certain he would find her in her room, door shut as she texted her friends. The big question was where would Sebastian be? Marcus knew Sebastian still lived in the family home, as all potential league inheritors did. He also knew that Sebastian had just inherited Jacob's ring and key two weeks prior.

At six foot two and muscular, Sebastian's build nearly mirrored that of Marcus. He could prove troublesome but Marcus knew that the only advantage Sebastian had was his youth, as he himself was in top physical shape.

A corporate attorney at his father's law firm, Sebastian had followed in his father's footsteps like most league children did but unlike Jacob, he did not like to follow rules.

The blood moon lunar eclipse this night meant that Jacob would not join his wife in bed at the usual time. He would have accompanied Sebastian to the City and Marcus was certain his brother and nephew would both need time to unwind.

Marcus found Jacob in front of the fireplace in the Great Room, drink in hand, mesmerized by the intense flames as he contemplated what had taken place earlier that night.

As he quietly walked through the open frosted French doors, Marcus thought, *Knowing how much you coveted being in The League of Twelve, I am surprised you gave up your position so soon, Jacob.*

Silently, Marcus inched his way to stand directly behind Jacob and with little effort, covered his brother's mouth, and ran the blade across his throat. His blood spilled onto the rug beneath them. Marcus watched as Jacob brought his hand up to his neck and tried unsuccessfully to speak.

The metallic scent of blood wafted through the air. Marcus inhaled deeply. He wanted to absorb every bit of his brother's last moments, to have them imprinted on his memory. He felt his twin's throat open, felt the pain and shock but knew it was worth it. Throughout his life, Marcus could sense his twin's feelings. He breathed a sigh of relief with the knowledge that he would no longer be so intimately connected to his brother. As Jacob's last gasp of breath escaped, his glass of scotch fell to the floor. *Pity wasting this Chivas Regal*, Marcus thought. He raised one eyebrow. *At least the League's choice of liquor was unerring.*

He stepped away from his brother and let him fall to the floor before he walked to the side table and helped himself to the open bottle of scotch. He picked up a napkin from the side table and wiped the blood off his blade as he walked to the fireplace. He tossed the napkin into the flames before he exited the Great Room.

With no lights on, he turned his head slightly and listened to make sure no one had come down to the main floor before he walked to the double staircase. He quietly ascended the stairs so as not to alert his sister-in-law or her progeny to his presence as he made his way to their bedrooms.

In the master bedroom, Maxine slept like the dead. Marcus stood beside her for a moment, his blade still in his hand, a peaceful look on his face as he watched her sleep. He liked the way her light brown hair was strewn across the pillow. His lip turned up in a sneer as he thought about his brother. Jacob always had the best of luck. He sheathed his blade and grabbed Maxine's head. With one quick turn, her neck snapped. No blood. Marcus looked at her, gently stroked her cheek, and whispered, "Were you mine, things would have been quite different."

He pushed sentiment aside and turned his attention toward the large statue on the pedestal in the northeast corner of the bedroom, the statue that was designed especially for his family's astral key. Made of a solid blue-grey marble, the statue was intricately carved in the form of a dragon with her wings extended beside her whelp. A ring of orchids forged from steel around the base of the statue provided the perfect concealment for the Shea key. Marcus had seen his father place his key there on many occasions. He walked across the plush, ivory coloured carpeting to the marble statue, reached between two metal flowers, and removed the key he coveted for so long. He looked at the key and smiled before he placed it in his shirt pocket.

As a small child, Marcus was aware that his father's astral key was special and needed to be kept safe and hidden. When he was told that either he or his brother would one day inherit their father's key and position in The League of Twelve, it became a prize to be fought for and won.

With the first of the twelve astral keys in his possession, Marcus exited the bedroom. Two inconveniences remained and Marcus was certain the young girl would be easily dispatched. He headed directly across the hall and stood in front of the door to his niece's bedroom. With his ear to the door, he listened for any sign that Marianne may be awake. He heard nothing. Quietly he opened the bedroom door.

Marcus walked toward his sleeping niece. He mumbled, "They are making this too easy."

He grabbed one of the frilly pillows at the end of her bed and held it to her face. She flailed her arms and legs and knocked her lamp off the nightstand.

Insolent child, he thought as he tossed the pillow aside.

Marianne had a mere second to scream before he quickly twisted her head. Her neck snapped as easily as her mother's. He snickered as he thought, *The king, queen, and princess Shea have all been dethroned.* He then picked up the fluffy pillow and dropped it beside her head.

With his mouth full of disdain, he whispered, "Sleep well, sweet child."

In his bedroom at the far end of the hall, Sebastian sat in front of his computer as he drafted a document for a client, headphones on as music played. He heard a sudden noise and rose to investigate. He looked out into the hallway and found his sister's bedroom door was open. She never left her door open.

He walked to Marianne's room, peeked in, and saw who he thought was his father beside his sister's bed. "Dad, what's going on?"

When Marcus turned around, shivers ran down Sebastian's spine. The full moon's light shone through the window and highlighted the scar on Marcus's cheek. He had come face to face with his Uncle Marcus, his father's identical twin. His mind raced with the stories his mother had told him about Marcus, how malicious and vindictive his uncle was, how he had tried to keep her and Jacob apart, how he left home, and how bitter he was that the league had chosen Jacob.

Sebastian growled. "Why are you here?" His heart pounded in his chest as he looked from Marcus to his sister; Marianne was still. He called out to his sister. She didn't respond. He shouted her name as he kept his eyes on Marcus.

Marcus spoke, derision evident in his voice. "I'm afraid she won't answer you."

Sebastian ran at Marcus. His shoulder crashed into his uncle's chest. As they landed on the floor, Marcus rolled and pinned Sebastian beneath him.

Marcus grabbed his throat with both hands and squeezed.

Sebastian reached up with one hand and grabbed Marcus' wrist to relieve the pressure of his uncle's hands around his neck and with the other, he jabbed his fingers into Marcus' eyes.

Marcus grunted in pain and threw his head backward. He brought one hand up to remove Sebastian's fingers from his eyes and shifted his centre of balance.

Sebastian then had enough time to swing his right leg up and push Marcus off him. He rose and sneered. "I thought you'd be dead by now, Marcus."

Marcus' arrogance was apparent. "Not yet, nephew. I'm not as weak as your father." He spun and kicked Sebastian's midsection.

Sebastian landed hard on his back. He rolled backward, scrambled to his feet, and stood defensively as Marcus walked toward him.

Marcus tilted his head left and then right. He stepped closer and closer to Sebastian, then punched high at his jaw.

Sebastian quickly raised his hand to block and simultaneously delivered a blow to Marcus' midsection with his other fist. As Marcus doubled over, Sebastian raised his knee and connected with Marcus' chin and throat, knocking him backward.

Marcus landed on his back and coughed. He rolled and was on his feet in seconds as his hand rubbed his throat.

Sebastian taunted his uncle. "You're a little out of shape, Marcus. That's what happens when you can't train in the City of Radiance." The smug look on his face divulged his enjoyment of the adrenaline rush.

"I will be there soon enough." Marcus licked blood from his lips, then wiped his mouth with the back of his hand.

The moonlight shone on the double-claw-shaped sigil of the Cancer astral key that had fallen out of Marcus' pocket and caught Sebastian's eye. He saw Sebastian look intently at the floor, so he turned his head, and caught sight of the key.

Sebastian lunged toward the key. He had to get to it before Marcus did.

Marcus hurled himself into Sebastian and forced him to the floor before he reached the key.

Sebastian grabbed the fallen lamp and threw it at Marcus' head.

Marcus lost his balance and staggered backward.

Sebastian rose and charged at him; he delivered a series of blows to his ribcage.

Marcus reached behind himself for the dagger he had secured to his back, gripped the hilt tightly, and quickly removed it from its sheath before he plunged it into Sebastian's side.

Sebastian gasped as the dagger penetrated his flesh.

Marcus pushed the blade further inside his nephew and blood began to pool around his hand.

As Sebastian fell to his knees, Marcus removed the blade and thrust it in once more.

Marcus looked down at Sebastian in arrogant superiority as his nephew knelt before him. He knew that once Sebastian was dead, his brother's bloodline would be as well; the continuance of the Shea bloodline would be left to him and his descendants.

After one final blow to Sebastian's head with the hilt of his blade, he watched his nephew fall to the floor. He tilted his head, looked at Sebastian as he lay on the floor, and spat the blood from his mouth onto the carpet beside him.

He growled. "Out of shape, my ass."

Marcus sheathed his blade and watched as the blood flowed out of his nephew's side, watched as Sebastian closed his eyes and breathed one last breath. He crouched down, checked Sebastian's neck for a pulse, and found none.

As he rose, he saw the Shea ring on Sebastian's finger, covered in blood. "I coveted that ring for so long, now it can be buried and forgotten along with you."

Marcus reclaimed the Cancer key, tossed it in the air, and caught it. He whistled as he walked toward the master bedroom. He knew that if he took a few baubles and trinkets that it would lead the police to think that this was a burglary gone wrong. He placed the Cancer astral key back in his shirt pocket, patted it, and smiled.

Marcus didn't so much as glance at Maxine as he opened her jewelry box and took a few pieces before he left. "There, just your average everyday home invasion."

He walked into Sebastian's bedroom, the one that had been his so long ago. He pulled at the ledge at the bottom of the window and found it was still loose. A smile crossed his mouth and he lifted the ledge to reveal the space beneath. "Right where I left it."

He removed the box, blew the dust off the lid, and opened it. Inside were the treasures he had hidden in his youth - money he had taken from his parents, gemstones and rings that he had stolen from the league's African faction jewelry store, and underneath it all the most nostalgic item in the box.

Marcus removed his gloves and placed them in his back pocket. With the letter in his hands, he remembered the day he received it as though it were yesterday. He opened it and silently read the first paragraph.

Marcus,

I don't even know how to put into words how what you did made me feel. You claimed to be my friend. I tried to trust you even though everyone else told me not to. They all told me you would do something and I would see what kind of person you really are.

The memories of that night so long ago filled his mind. He narrowed his eyes. "You made your choice and I made mine. Yours was the wrong choice."

He placed the letter back in the box.

Once he replaced the ledge, he used the bottom of his shirt to wipe his fingerprints from it before he exited the room. He tucked the box under his arm, placed his gloves back on his hands, and left.

As he descended the staircase, Marcus spotted the antique Katana on the wall in the foyer and walked to it. He examined it and appreciated the rich, brown leather hilt and sheath. "Beautiful."

He admired the craftsmanship. He unsheathed the blade and touched its edge. It was dull.

Marcus sighed and lowered his head. "Oh, Jacob. Really? Such a beautiful blade and you can't even keep it sharp, yet *you* were the one chosen. Foolish immortals and their bad decisions."

Before he headed out, Marcus took a few other trinkets with him, along with the Katana; he thought it would look perfect on the wall in his penthouse. Once he was home, he would plan how to obtain his second astral key.

~~~~

As the grandfather clock in the hallway chimed 2:00 a.m., Sebastian opened his eyes and inhaled deeply. He tried to sit up and groaned at the pain. He winced, brought his hand up to his head, and felt a slight bump near his left temple. He tried to get to his feet and wondered why he wasn't healing, why his ability to self-heal had failed.

Pain shot through the left side of his body as he began to rise only to slump back to the floor. He brought his hand to his side and felt the dampness of blood. He got to his feet and stumbled toward his sister.

He touched Marianne's neck to check for a pulse. Unable to find one, he screamed in anguish. His next thought was of his parents.

Sebastian staggered to their bedroom where he found his mother. She appeared to be asleep. As he got closer, he realized she was dead as well. He sat beside her on the bed. The pain in his side seemed to vanish as he shook his mother's shoulders. "Come on Mom, wake up. Don't be dead. Please, you can't be dead."

He leaned forward and kissed her forehead as tears escaped his eyes. He silently swore to make Marcus suffer.

As he turned to leave his parents' bedroom, Sebastian winced at the pain in his side. He stopped in the bedroom doorway and wondered where his father was.

He held his side as pain shot through his midsection as he searched the other upstairs rooms in vain. "Dad! Dad!"

With his shouts for his father unanswered, Sebastian returned to his bedroom and picked up his cell phone. The low battery indicator flashed. He then dialed his father's number and listened to it ring as he made his way downstairs. His father did not answer. He dialed again and this time, he heard his father's ringtone just before his own battery died.

He walked in the direction of the sound. "Dad! Where are you?"

Again he called out to his father as he stumbled through the main level of the house. He found his father in the Great Room, dead on the rug, blood pooled around his head.

Sebastian dropped to his knees. He leaned forward, his head in his hands and screamed in despair before rage set in. He lifted his head, a look of malicious determination on his face.

With his hand on his left side, he rose and set out to John's house. Self-preservation and revenge were foremost in his mind as he stumbled across his neighbours' yards and through the empty streets as he made his way to the Evans' home.

He hoped that together, he and John could make it to the City of Radiance in time to heal his wounds.

2 – THE CITY OF RADIANCE

Earlier that night under the full blood moon, John Evans and his father, Michael, walked outside into their backyard.

Michael looked at his son and saw himself at that age. Father and son both stood nearly six feet tall and shared the same dark brown hair colour but where Michael's eyes were deep green, John's were hazel.

Michael had groomed John from a young age to one day assume leadership of The League of Twelve. The league consisted of four members from North America, four from Europe, and four from Africa, with locations chosen for the latent energies they emitted along their ley lines.

Michael, the Gemini member and current leader of The League of Twelve, felt that his son was ready to take his place and so they conducted John's Ring Transference. Passed down from one league member to his or her successor throughout the generations, a league ring carried the family name of whoever wore it. The Evans Ring was a solid white gold band with an oval blue star sapphire in its centre. Though the band had been changed many times over the years, the stone remained the same.

Tradition dictated that a Ring Transference take place outdoors and must be private, with only the current ring holder and the one who was to receive the ring in attendance. Rings were only passed during significant lunar events and that night most definitely qualified. Not only was the moon full, but it was also a blood moon, a harvest moon, a supermoon, and a lunar eclipse.

Michael walked ahead of his son, placed his hands in his pants pockets, and turned to face him. "John, I know you've wanted my ring for a while now. Since your mother's death, I felt I needed to throw myself into league business. With so many rings being passed down, and a new league taking shape, I needed to make sure everyone was prepared for a new leader. I feel you're ready now and I want you to know that I believe you can lead this new league and make the tough decisions."

John listened intently, feeling a nervous excitement as his father spoke.

Michael glanced eastward in the direction of the entrance to the tunnels that led to the City of Radiance, with John by his side. "As you know, I'll be staying in the City tonight and plan to spend a few years there, so the house is yours now. I've made arrangements for Dr.'s Chan and Bloom to handle a few of my responsibilities at the dental clinic and I've also asked your brother to take over some of my patients. With you now leading The League of Twelve, he has agreed to assume more of my workload to leave you free to deal with league business."

He looked at John and placed his hands on his son's shoulders. "You know I will always be here for you if you need me and I will come back from time to time."

Michael turned away to hide the tears that began welling in his eyes. "I believe you and your brother can handle things here."

He looked up. "Just be careful. Tonight's moon is bringing about a darkness that I can feel."

As the Earth began casting its shadow over the moon, Michael turned back to John. He removed his league ring and placed it in John's hand. The gemstone began to glow.

John looked at the glowing ring in his hand, placed it on his finger, and felt a surge of power run through his body as it bonded with him and his innate ability began to surface. His eyes opened wide, their hazel colour glowing in the light of the full moon as he held his hand up and stared at the ring on his finger.

Michael smiled and raised his eyebrows. "It's quite a feeling, isn't it?"

John was awestruck. "Yeah. I had no idea I would feel anything let alone whatever that was."

"You know that all potential members of The League of Twelve are born with abilities that only surface once they wear a league ring. But..." Michael smiled, "what you don't know is that the gemstone in the ring bonds with its wearer's DNA. The stone in each ring was spelled by an Eyrasine enchantress at the time the league was formed to bring these abilities to realization, as well as for the astral key to recognize you as its new holder."

Michael handed John the Gemini astral key. "This is a secret known only among league members and cannot be shared, not even with your brother."

John looked at the ring on his finger, the key in his hand, and then at his father. "I will make you proud and keep our legacy strong."

Michael put his arm around John's shoulders and together they walked to the garage. "You know, after I get a few things settled in my apartment in the City, I'll be back to take you out to celebrate your inauguration."

John smiled as he and his father continued to the garage. "Celebrate? I was kind of hoping there would be more than just you and I getting together in the backyard."

"You're also going to have to make time to look through the Central Archives, spend a day or two getting familiar with what was done in the past. I've got a book of contacts that I need to give you, but we can take care of that later. Let's get you to the City."

Inside the garage, they found John's brother, James, getting out of his vehicle. James had just returned home having remained late at work to give his father and brother the privacy they requested.

John and Michael walked toward Michael's car as James walked toward them.

James punched John's shoulder lightly. "Congrats, bro."

"Thanks. We're headed to Jayded Ink. Do you want to come to the City with us?"

"Thanks for the offer, but I'm going to log into the dental clinic and look over a few of dad's patient files. I need to get familiar with his patients since some of them will be mine soon. Good luck tonight." James headed into the house.

~~~~

John and Michael drove to Jayded Ink, a tattoo shop in downtown Niagara Falls, that housed a hidden doorway behind which were seven tunnels. The tunnel on the far right was the one that led to the City of Radiance, situated at the centre of the Earth in a parallel dimension.

John reflected on the significance of the moon, the equinoxes, and solstices, and how they corresponded to portal openings. The veil that separated dimensions was always thinnest during significant lunar events.

As he and his father walked toward the Hall of Gates, John thought back to the first time he entered the City of Radiance. He had stood in awe of its grandeur and how something so huge could be so close to the rest of humanity, yet just out of reach.

Accessible by only three gates, the City was a beautiful hidden paradise with a sky-blue crystal dome that surrounded the entire city and radiated power throughout.

Three shops on the Earth's surface, each owned and operated by league families, contained hidden doorways. Behind these doorways were stairs that led to interdimensional tunnels from which the City of Radiance was accessed. One tunnel led under Niagara Falls, one led beneath Stonehenge, and the other led below The Great Pyramid of Giza.

Michael turned to John, raised his eyebrows, and tilted his head slightly downward. "No goodbye, no see you soon, agreed?"

John smiled. "Agreed."

"Go." Michael gestured toward the Hall of Gates. "Find the rest of your league. I sent them each a text to meet a few minutes early tonight so that you could have some time to talk with each other before you get down to business, since tonight will be your first portal opening."

"Thanks, Dad." John nodded and turned to find his friends. While he was curious as to what innate ability his league ring would grant him, John was confident in his own earthly abilities and knew the rest of the league well enough to also be confident in theirs.

Michael watched his son walk toward the Grand Temple and he smiled as a sense of pride washed over him. He knew that the North American faction of the league, and the league itself, would be in good hands with him as their leader.

John made his way to the Grand Temple, located in the middle of the City of Radiance. Two tiered levels, each approximately two city blocks wide and five feet high, encircled the cylindrical Grand Temple. He walked past the shops, parks, and gardens found on both levels. Constructed of a silver coloured stone, the exterior of the Grand Temple was adorned with jewels that reflected the light from the huge blue dome and glistened like rays from a sun.

John walked between the two pillars found on each side of the four open entrances, into the Grand Temple. The entrances were situated true north, true south, true east, and true west, just as the corners of The Great Pyramid of Giza.

Inside the Grand Temple along its perimeter were the Healing Chambers, Council Chambers, Training Arena, Laboratory, and Forge. The Hall of Gates, John's destination, stood at the very centre. This was where the members of The League of Twelve first met after entering the City of Radiance. He approached the Hall of Gates where he found Sebastian and another North American league member, Ann Johnston, had already arrived.

Sebastian raised an eyebrow. "So John, tonight is a first for both of us."

Ann jabbed Sebastian lightly with her elbow. "Ahem."

She looked at John, her expression playful. "Congrats on the promotion, John. Just don't expect me to start calling you Mr. Evans!"

"Sire will be just fine," John jested.

Ann and Sebastian looked at each other and smiled.

Sebastian closed his eyes and shook his head.

Ann, the Taurus league member, leaned into Sebastian, flirting but trying not to be too obvious. "You guys are in for a ride. Opening the portal is an awesome rush."

Sebastian felt Ann's soft hair against his arm. He looked down at her as she spoke with John. Her smile, the excitement in her eyes, made him wonder what she...he stopped and realized he was smiling.

Ann noticed that Angeline Flynn, the Capricorn member and European faction leader, had arrived. She headed toward Angeline. "Gotta run, boys."

Emerging from the Training Arena, Conor Rivait, the North American faction Aries member, ran his fingers through his messy blonde hair as he walked over to converse with John and Sebastian. "Are you guys free next weekend? I was in the Armory earlier and there are some new weapons I would like to try out. Interested?"

John and Sebastian looked at each other and nodded. "Sure," Sebastian answered.

John's expression turned serious. "Before we head into the Hall of Gates to open the portal, I thought you should know that my father said he sensed a darkness brought about by tonight's moon."

Conor furrowed his brow in curiosity. "Anything more specific?"

John shook his head. "No. He just said a darkness."

Sebastian looked over Conor's shoulder and saw Ann and Angeline headed their way.

Angeline was tall with unruly dark brown curls and was a perfect contrast to Ann's petite frame and her long, straight, chestnut brown hair.

Sebastian asked, "Where is the rest of the UK gang, Ange?"

Josh grinned. "Turn around, mate."

Sebastian turned and saw Josh Morrison, Amber Price, and Ethan Wells, the Pisces, Aquarius, and Sagittarius members of The League of Twelve respectively.

While Angeline walked to John with Ann to congratulate him, Sebastian turned to speak with the European faction members.

"Hey guys, it's been a while. How's the bangers and mash?"

Ethan's bright blue eyes filled with mischief. "A mite better than your burgers and fries."

Josh piped up. "'Bout bloody time you and John got your rings and keys! Don't fret none. Seeing how it's your first time, we'll be gentle with ya." His tone was deep and provocative.

Sebastian turned back to John. They looked at each other and both raised an eyebrow.

John retorted, "You had your first time at the Summer Solstice," he paused, "and who says I like it gentle?"

Josh put his hands up in surrender. "Point taken. Now, I can see Seb liking it rough, but you, John? I'm rather impressed!"

The friends all laughed.

With a muscular physique and above average height, Josh was a striking man. His dark skin complimented his dark eyes, eyes that gave his looks a hint of mystery.

Najeeb Cham, Dalila Saliba, and Mariam Chahine, the Leo, Virgo, and Libra league members, along with their faction leader, the Scorpio member Zayne Nader, arrived together and moved to rendezvous with the other league members.

"Hello!" Mariam shouted.

Her wavy black hair bounced as she walked; her ample hips swayed with each step. "Since we have an entirely new league, perhaps we will see more of each other. Now that we hold the keys, we can come and go as we please."

Angeline smiled sincerely. "I would like that very much."

Dalila chimed in. "As would I. I would also like to spend more time in your family's restaurant, Ann. When I close my eyes, I can still see that incredible cake you made for my brother last year. When I concentrate, I can taste it as well!"

She licked her lips. "It was absolutely decadent!"

Ann gushed, "Aww, thank you Dalila. I do love making memorable dishes and you are welcome anytime."

Zayne spread his arms wide. "Assalam alaikoum."

With a deep, booming voice and a height of slightly less than six feet tall, Zayne seemed daunting. However, those he allowed into his circle of friends knew him as a loyal, sincere man.

A hyperpolyglot with the ability to speak and understand any language, Angeline spoke with her fellow faction leader in Egyptian.

Najeeb smiled and nodded his head in approval of Angeline's perfect Egyptian intonation.

Ann was also able to converse with her Egyptian counterparts in their native tongue by borrowing some of Angeline's energy and using her own ability to mimic supernatural gifts.

Conor yelled from behind. "English, please!"

Zayne laughed as he walked to John to offer his congratulations. He also wanted to discuss the eerie feeling he had felt earlier that day.

John called to Angeline and the three faction leaders moved off to the side to talk privately about the darkness that John's father had mentioned; Angeline and Zayne had both felt it as well.

"I don't know what my dad meant by 'darkness'. Have either of you seen or heard anything that we need to be wary of?"

Angeline shook her head. "I haven't. Have you, Zayne?"

Zayne narrowed his eyes. "I have not. Although it is nearly daylight in Cairo, I will let my crew know to be extra vigilant."

Angeline nodded. "And I will bring my gang up to speed."

John, Angeline, and Zayne returned to join the rest of the league.

"Let's do this, boys and girls. If we don't open our end of the portal on time, I'll have the Council of Seven breathing down my neck and I do not need that on my first day. If I go down," John paused and looked from Angeline to Zayne, "you two are coming with me."

Angeline and Zayne looked at each other, both of them wide-eyed.

Angeline clapped her hands together. "Chop chop, we haven't time to waste!"

The others laughed.

All twelve league members went to their respective doors, as was tradition before each portal opening. There was a round port at the centre of each door where a key, shaped in the key holder's zodiac sigil, was to be inserted. Each key could only be used by the league member who was born of that astral sign, as their keys were activated with their DNA.

Each key's sigil lined up with only one notch in the port and once aligned, the sigil extended into the lock, was pushed in further, and turned clockwise. Once the key was removed, the door slid into the floor and after the league member had entered, it rose to shut silently behind them.

They each entered the Hall of Gates, constructed through the axis at the centre of the Earth, and prepared to activate the portal. On the floor inside the Hall of Gates was the Celestial Circle. Evenly spaced around the portal in the centre of the room, inside a one-foot wide ring of silver, were the twelve circular gates, each inscribed with one of the astrological sigils. Each sigil was etched in beautiful detail on bright white marble that matched that of the remainder of the floor. The sigils were each coloured the same as the stone in the ring that the corresponding league member wore. The walls were a luminescent pearl white colour and the ceiling resembled a clear night sky with millions of stars shining above. Only when all twelve keys were in place and activated around the Celestial Circle could the portal between the worlds be opened.

~~~~

Upon entering the hall, the league members each took their place behind their sigil.

At the start of each portal opening, the leader of The League of Twelve was charged with ensuring the readiness status of each key holder.

As each league member held their key above their sigil, it detected their presence and the marble cylinder on which it was etched rose out of the floor.

From the moment he placed the Evans Ring on his finger, John had been anxious to run his first status check. Once everyone was in place and their sigils had risen up to meet their keys, John began. "Alright, go or no-go, starting with Aries in North America. Conor."

Conor pushed his key into its port. "Aries, go."

One by one, the others followed suit as John called out their names.

"Ann."

"Go for Taurus."

John inserted his key. "Gemini is a go. Seb."

"Go on Cancer."

John nodded. "Next, African faction, go or no go starting with Leo. Najeeb."

"Leo, go."

"Dalila."

"Virgo ready to go."

"Mariam."

"Libra, go."

"Zayne."

"Scorpio is a go."

"Lastly, European faction, go or no go starting with Sagittarius. Ethan."

"Sagittarius is good to go."

"Ange."

"Capricorn is a go."

"Amber."

"Go on Aquarius."

"Josh."

"Pisces is good to go."

"Alright, we turn our keys on three. One, two, three."

As each key clicked into place, the hall filled with a resplendent light that shone like thousands of crystals in moonlight. A feeling of euphoria washed over everyone in the room as the interdimensional portal transported the Eyrasines to Earth.

After several minutes, the light started to diminish and the people from Eyras were seen standing in the centre of the circle.

With their duties fulfilled for the night, Conor opened his Aries door to let the Eyrasines into the Grand Temple. He led them to the Healing Chambers, the City's hospital. There, medics stood ready to examine them for any trauma resulting from their journey through the portal.

Once the Eyrasine people were out of the Hall of Gates, Ann smiled and looked from John to Sebastian. "So guys, how cool was that?"

John and Sebastian both smiled and looked utterly flabbergasted. Neither one expected the intensity of what they had just felt, an intimate feeling of ecstasy. They felt as though every cell in their bodies were pulsating with the energy of the universe.

Ann laughed at their reactions.

After she removed her key, Ann walked to John and Sebastian. "Did you guys notice anything dark out of the corner of your eyes when the portal was opening?"

John looked from Sebastian to Ann. "I did notice some shadowy figures. It happened so fast I couldn't really say what I saw."

Sebastian agreed. "It *was* fast but I saw them as well."

John looked back at Ann. "I know that every time the portal opens some geist slip through but this seemed like a lot."

"It did seem like more than the last time." Ann placed her hand on her hip and narrowed her eyes. "Why does it have to be beings that steal DNA?"

"We should talk to the others and see if they saw or sensed anything. This could have something to do with the darkness my dad was talking about." John sealed his gate.

He walked toward the exit and thought back to the first time he saw a geist's soul mist. He and every league member knew that in mist form, a geist needed only a small opening in order to move between solid objects. This was how they were able to exit the Hall of Gates and leave the City of Radiance. On Earth, they were seen only as a dusky mist until they stole a sample of DNA from a human or animal and replicated them. It was this process that each of the league members was shown prior to being inducted into The League of Twelve.

John remembered seeing The Council of Seven bring a geist into the Training Arena and kill its physical body to allow its soul mist to escape. He had watched the geist replicate a volunteer by brushing its soul mist against her flesh and recalled feeling amazed and concerned all at once. After the new body had formed, John saw one of the Immortals place a biostentium cuff around the geist's wrist. Later he was told it was in order to be able to distinguish her from her host donor.

John recalled thinking that the way the body formed was fascinating. He was awed by the short amount of time it took for a new being to manifest.

The geist told him that the replication process also allowed her to retain some of the memories and knowledge of her host so she would be able to blend into society.

With that sobering thought, he turned and exited the hall.

Once everyone was out of the Hall of Gates, Jacob Shea walked over to the league members, who waited nearby. He looked at Sebastian and John, and grinned. "Well, how was your first time?"

"You were right, dad. It's a rush you just can't put into words."

Jacob smiled. "Come on, boys, drinks are on me tonight."

John looked at Jacob. "Thanks, but I think I'll stick around and talk to the others before I meet up with my dad. Some of us saw quite a few dark shapes come through. Since this was my first time opening the portal, I'd like to get an idea of what the others thought. What exactly did you see, Seb?"

Sebastian narrowed his eyes in thought. "I can tell you I saw something that I can only assume were geist mists but the light from the portal made it difficult to say for certain. I could ask a few people down here in the City if they saw any geist mist passing by but from what I understand, they can spread their mist out and seem nearly invisible."

"It's alright, Seb. I'm probably just overthinking it." John furrowed his brows. "I just keep thinking about the darkness my father mentioned earlier."

"You sure I can't talk you into coming for a drink with us?"

"Not this time."

Jacob put his hand on Sebastian's back. "All right, then. Oh, and John, congratulations. If you're anything like your father, the league is lucky to have you."

"Thank you, Mr. Shea. I have some big shoes to fill."

Sebastian quickly nodded his head. "Okay, I'm out of here."

He left the Grand Temple with his father, not knowing that the euphoria he felt earlier would shortly be surpassed by grief.

3 – HEALING BODY, SPIRIT AND MIND

Back home, John saw his brother, James, seated at the large oak kitchen island as he looked intently at his laptop. He walked to the refrigerator, took out two beers, and passed one to James before he joined him.

James looked up and leaned forward. "So...how was it? Was it as cool as Dad always made it out to be?"

John couldn't help but smile. "Even better. It's hard to describe but it was really amazing. It didn't take long but the wave of exhilaration that I felt...it was so intense."

James always knew that John would be the next leader of The League of Twelve. He was happy for John but still felt a slight bit envious. "It sounds like your first time was good. Congrats."

John drank some beer. "Thanks. A few of us are going to the Training Arena next week. Do you want to come?"

"Sure!" James enjoyed a good workout in the City's Training Arena.

The Evans boys were tall. James was slightly taller at six feet and both were muscular with short dark hair; there was no mistaking that they were brothers.

John told James about the newest arrivals from Eyras while they drank their beers. "Twelve people came through the portal, then Conor brought them to the Healing Chambers. It was so well organized, it seemed to take no time at all."

"Sounds like it went smoothly."

After he finished off his beer, James got up and stretched his arms before he headed to bed. "Just shoot me a text with the day and time," he said through a yawn.

"Okay."

While the rush from the night's events still pumped through him, John got up and walked around his home, slowly sipping his beer. In the den, he walked to the fireplace and ran his fingers along the ledge near its top. He fondly recalled the many times his mother had told him not to sit so close to the fire.

His mother had furnished the house in a classic contemporary style, with leather sofas and glass top tables in both the den and living room. John liked the hardwood floors laid throughout the house and the cathedral ceiling, but he decided some changes needed to be made to make it his own. He looked around the room. A family portrait, framed in a gold coloured wood hung above the wood burning fireplace; this he knew he would keep. His mother looked so happy and alive that he couldn't believe two years had passed since she had died.

John continued his walk through the house. He entered the kitchen and placed his empty beer bottle in a bin beneath the kitchen sink. He reached over and opened the window above it to let the cool, fresh air in as he peered out into the backyard. As he breathed in deeply, he saw something move at the far end of the yard. He walked to the switch beside the back door and turned on the backyard floodlights.

Sebastian staggered a few steps then collapsed as John watched.

Before he ran out the door, John shouted, "James!"

At the urgent sound in John's voice, James ran down the stairs. He saw the door that led to the backyard open and ran through it. Outside he found his brother helping Sebastian to his feet. He hurried to Sebastian's side, grabbed one of his arms, and helped John carry him inside. "What happened?"

Sebastian's legs buckled beneath him and he fell to his knees as John and James tried to steady him. They laid Sebastian on the kitchen floor as blood sputtered out of his mouth.

Sebastian struggled to speak. "Marcus is back." His eyes closed and he lost consciousness.

John looked at his friend's torn and bloody shirt and grimaced. He lifted it and saw the stab wounds in his side.

He looked at James, fear and concern evident on his face.

John exhaled loudly. "James, phone Conor. Tell him we're picking him up to go back down to the City. These wounds must be beyond Seb's ability to self-heal."

~~~~

Conor waited at the end of his driveway, medical bag in hand. He hoped his transference healing ability would be enough but was prepared in case it wasn't.

When James pulled his car up to the curb, Conor hurried into the back seat. Once he shut the door, James sped away.

Conor lifted the blood-soaked towel John held against Sebastian's side and then quickly replaced it. "How long has he been like this?"

"He collapsed in our backyard about fifteen minutes ago." With wrinkles of concern across his forehead, John looked down at his hands covered in his lifelong friend's blood.

Conor lifted the blood-soaked towel, placed an entire roll of gauze over both stabs wounds, and pressed. "This is bad. Get to Jayded Ink. We don't have much time."

James sped to their destination, grateful for the empty streets.

Once James had parked the car behind Jayded Ink, John hurriedly got out, unlocked the back door of the shop and held it open.

James and Conor carried Sebastian from the car into the shop.

At the rear of the tattoo shop, in the back of a storage closet, a hidden door concealed stairs that led to the secret tunnels. Motion sensitive crystals intermittently embedded in the ceiling and walls of the entranceway illuminated as John walked beneath them.

Close behind, James and Conor carried Sebastian to the tunnel entrance. At the mouth of the tunnel they positioned themselves and Sebastian on the raised platform and John passed his key over the one stone that initialized it. Once activated, it shifted them interdimensionally to the far end of the tunnel, many miles beneath the Earth's surface. The stone lit up and a silent five-second countdown began before it transported them to the City's entrance.

What appeared to be an ordinary stone wall, the City entrance had a notch at its centre two inches deep where an astral key was to be inserted, pushed, and then removed. This caused the stone wall to slide back and to the left into the tunnel wall, behind which was a metal door.

James and Conor supported Sebastian on either side as John pushed his key into the stone wall.

Once in the City, John procured the nearest transport pod.

James and Conor eased Sebastian inside and sat him next to John who held him steady.

With everyone onboard and the door shut, a disembodied male voice requested instructions. "Please state your destination."

"Grand Temple, west entrance, top speed." Conor then sat beside Sebastian as the pod rose to reach a height of fifteen feet above the main floor level and sped off.

The transport pod landed softly just outside the west entrance. Conor got out and ran ahead to the Healing Chambers to inform the medics that Sebastian would soon arrive in need of surgery. A physician himself, he knew what information the medics would need.

John and James were not far behind Conor, as they carried their unconscious friend.

~~~~

Hours later, Sebastian awoke groggy; his blurry eyes struggled to focus. He saw John, James and Conor around him and tried to sit up.

"Easy, Seb." Conor eased Sebastian back down in his bed, one hand on the back of his friend's head and the other placed on his chest. He raised one eyebrow. "Those stitches in your side are a work of art and I don't want you ruining my masterpiece."

"Yeah, whatever." Sebastian groaned and closed his eyes as his head sank into the pillow. As the previous night's events came rushing back, he turned his head to the side.

"They're dead. My whole family."

"Whoa! What?" James was astounded. "Back up, your whole family is dead?"

"Marcus was in my house. He took my Cancer key...I should have kept it with me." Sebastian succumbed to the timed intravenous morphine drip connected to his arm and again lost consciousness.

John worriedly ran his hands through his hair and paced at the foot of Sebastian's bed. "Seb's blood is going to be all over that house. If the police find his blood they'll suspect he…"

He took a deep breath. "James, get Rafe to clean Seb's blood out of his house."

"Rafe?" James questioned.

John quickly searched through the contacts on his phone before he texted Rafe's number to James. "He's the Eyrasine forensics specialist. I'm sending you his number. Let Rafe know what's happened and he will know what to do. Also have him trip the alarm when he's done to get the police there."

Thinking on his feet had been part of John's training before he became the leader of The League of Twelve and his mind had switched to crisis mode. "If anybody asks, tell them Seb was with us at our house drinking all night, and James, tell Rafe I would like a copy of his report."

James nodded his head and moved off to phone Rafe.

John left Sebastian's room, cell phone in hand. He sent a text to Angeline and Zayne as he paced. *Seb is badly wounded. Meet me at the Healing Chambers right away.*

~~~~

Angeline and Ann remained in the City after opening the portal. They sat in Brewed and Steeped Cafe sipping coffees as they discussed the latest arrivals from Eyras.

Height, weight, hair, eye, and skin colour of the Eyrasines varied, much like the human residents of Earth, with one striking difference being in the colour of their eyes. Eye colours in pure Eyrasines were similar to primary and secondary colours and were not subdued as they were in most humans; blue eyes were as bright as blue sapphires, and green eyes as intense as green emeralds.

"Did you see the woman with that wicked tattoo on her leg?"

Angeline had a smile on her lips. "I did, and I want one!"

Angeline dug through her purse for her phone to schedule a visit to Jayded Ink and saw a message from John. "There's a message from John. I wonder what he wants."

"You won't know 'til you open the message."

"Don't be cheeky." She glanced sideways at Ann before she read the message aloud.

Wide-eyed, the two women looked at each other for a fraction of a second, then raced to the Healing Chambers.

Ann was panicked as she arrived. "Where's Seb?"

John pointed toward the back left side. "First recovery room on the left through the doors."

Ann raced past him to get to Sebastian as her heart pounded in her chest.

Angeline stayed with John. "What happened?"

John ran his fingers through his hair and closed his eyes. "Seb showed up at my house with two gashes in his side. Just before passing out, he said that Marcus was back."

"Marcus? What...why would he come back?" Surprise and dread filled Angeline.

"I don't know. But Ange...Jacob, Maxine, and Marianne are dead and Marcus took Seb's key."

"What?" Zayne had just entered the Healing Chambers.

~~~~

With the intravenous morphine no longer attached to him, Sebastian slowly opened his eyes and saw Ann in the chair beside his bed. He looked at her, felt her warm hand on his arm and stared into her eyes. As she sat beside him, he knew she had no idea how he felt, that he wanted more than just friendship from her.

"Hey Seb, I hope the other guy looks worse." Ann joked as she looked at the goose egg and bruising on the side of his head. She hoped to get a smile out of him.

"Where's John? I have to tell him..." He tried to sit up only to be overcome once again by the pain in his side; he slumped back down in the bed.

"You don't have to do anything but heal." Ann placed a hand on his arm. "What happened, Seb?"

"Marcus. He was in my house."

She opened her eyes wide in astonishment.

He closed his eyes and rubbed them. "He...killed them. My whole family."

"Oh God, Seb, I am so sorry." She leaned over and gently hugged him.

"I'll be alright."

The look on his face told her that he was far from alright.

She then rose to her feet, filled with anger. "Do the others know? We have to do something!"

"I told John."

As they spoke, a medic entered the room. "Could you please step out of the room for a moment? I won't be long."

"I'll be back later, Seb."

Sebastian simply nodded.

Ann headed out to join Angeline and John.

~~~~

Conor returned from the Laboratory with a poultice of medicated Eyrasine herbs and found John, Angeline, Ann, and Zayne outside of the Healing Chambers.

Ann walked to him. "Mind if I join you inside? They don't need me out here and I'd like to keep Seb company, if it's alright."

"Absolutely." He held the door open for her. "After you."

"Oh, how very chivalrous, doc. Thank you." While she seemed outwardly calm and collected, inside she was worried about Sebastian and incensed that Marcus had nearly killed him.

She and Conor walked to Sebastian's room. "How bad is he, Conor?"

"His self-healing ability is helping him." His voice divulged how impressed he was with Sebastian's gift. "Honestly, if he didn't have it, I'm not sure he would be alive."

He looked at Ann and saw a few tears had welled in her eyes. "Seb is a fighter. With that and his ability working together, his wounds don't have a chance. Hell, I think he was half healed before he got here."

"Yeah, as if a few scratches could keep him down, right?"

Once they were in Sebastian's room, Conor held the poultice container toward Ann. "Hold this please."

"Sure."

Sebastian looked at them, his eyes half open.

Ann smiled. "Hey, Seb. We're just here to check up on you."

Conor removed Sebastian's bandage and exposed the half-healed wound that he and Vretiel, the chief medic, had stitched closed not long ago. He next removed a medical spatula from the drawer in the bedside cart and scooped a healthy portion of poultice. "This shouldn't hurt. This is just a mix of Eyrasine herbs and some aloe. In layman's terms, it's more slimy than gritty."

Conor applied the poultice then examined the bump on Sebastian's head.

Ann watched as the brownish green paste covered the wounds in Sebastian's side. She saw his chest muscles tighten as he quickly inhaled. Her eyes wandered over his body searching for other wounds and found that she felt more than just concern.

Conor shone a light into Sebastian's eyes. "It doesn't look like you have a concussion, or at least you don't have one anymore. Just be sure to eat enough to replace the energy you're using to self-heal."

Sebastian placed two fingers over his brow in salute. "You got it, doc."

Conor placed his flashlight on the stand beside Sebastian. "Now it's time for some light therapy."

He wheeled Sebastian's bed into the Solar Plexus Alcove, with Ann again by his side. There, another medic positioned Sebastian under the phototherapy lights and handed him a small cup of liquid.

Sebastian lifted the cup to his mouth, grimaced at the smell and turned his face. "What is in this?"

"Just drink it. It will help the lights heal you faster."

Sebastian complied and then sneered at Conor.

Conor took the cup with a smug smile, tossed it in the trash can and walked to the monitor connected to Sebastian.

John entered the room and saw Conor speaking with the medic. He changed direction and walked to Ann, who stood near the back of the room. "Hey Ann, how's our boy?"

Ann tried to keep her voice steady. "It's just a scratch. He'll be back in fighting form in no time."

John moved to Sebastian's side. "Until you're one hundred percent healed, you are staying at my place." The look on his face was almost fatherly.

He tossed a key to his house onto Sebastian's bed. "As for your alibi, you were with James and I last night, got drunk, and crashed on our couch. We can talk tomorrow once you're feeling better."

"What? You think it will take me a whole day to heal? I'll be out of here by supper time." Sebastian closed his eyes and relaxed as the morphine, Eyrasine poultice, and phototherapy lights worked their magic.

John, Conor, and Ann headed out of the Healing Chambers.

While John moved off to speak with Angeline and Zayne about their next steps, Ann stayed near the Healing Chambers doors. She leaned against the wall, worried about Sebastian and wondered if anyone suspected her feelings for him.

Angeline leaned slightly forward with her fists on her hips. "Marcus wouldn't dare try to come into the City after killing his brother. He must have help. How many people are we looking for, John?" She was concerned about the immensity of the threat they faced.

John shook his head. "We don't know if he has help or if he's working alone." He, like the other league members, had heard stories about Marcus and knew that he was not well liked, nor was he missed.

John rubbed his face. "You can be sure that whatever he is up to, it isn't good. Until we know what he is planning, we all have to be on high alert. Sebastian is not an easy guy to take down and yet Marcus killed his whole family and nearly killed him. We have to be ready for anything."

Zayne folded his arms. "We need extra guards at each of the entrances to the City. Since Marcus has Seb's key and his father's DNA, we can't afford to be lax with security."

John nodded. "Agreed. Zayne, Angeline, get the rest of your crews. We need to have a meeting. Tell them to meet us in the Hall of Gates right away. In the meantime, I'll let the Immortals know that Marcus has returned and that we would like extra guards at the City entrances and then I'm going to speak with my dad."

~~~~

After speaking with Celeste and Jael, two of the Council of Seven immortals, John pulled his cell phone from his pocket and sent a text message to his father. He was certain that Michael would be his best chance at getting the intimate information he needed to fight Marcus as his father had a personal relationship with him for many years before he left town.

Michael walked toward his son who sat on a bench not far from the Hall of Gates. "Hey John, what do you need? Miss me already?" He chuckled. "You know, I'm going to need your help moving some more of my things down here. Not much, mind you, but a good bottle of scotch would be nice."

John looked sombre as he stared at the floor. "Sit down, dad."

Hearing the serious tone in his son's voice, Michael sat beside John, worried about what he was about to hear.

John closed his eyes and propped his elbows on his thighs. "Marcus is back. Seb's family, all of them, they're dead,"

"What? They're dead? Are you saying Marcus killed them?"

Grief visible in his eyes, John looked at his father as he recounted what Sebastian had told him. "Marcus stabbed Seb as well and left him for dead. He lost a lot of blood but he's in the Healing Chambers now so he'll be fine but Dad, we have to find a way to stop Marcus."

Michael's hands clenched into fists in his lap and he stared straight ahead. "When did this happen?"

"Right after we opened the portal. Seb left with his dad and I stuck around for a bit. Later, when I got home, I found Seb staggering in our backyard. We don't know what Marcus is up to or why he's here now. You know him from way back, what can you tell me about him?"

Michael rose. The Marcus he knew was an arrogant, self-important jerk. He hadn't heard anything about Marcus for so long that he wasn't sure how much help he could be to his son.

"Open the door. Let's see what the Central Archives has on him first."

John spoke wearily. "Not bad for my first day, huh Dad?" He rose and walked to his Gemini door on the Hall of Gates.

Lines of concern crossed Michael's face. "This is a bit much for anyone."

He wanted to be able to help but also hoped the Central Archives would reveal the information that Michael himself had never wanted to divulge.

John unlocked his door and he and his father walked to the Gemini sigil on the floor. Once it rose up to meet his key, John brought the Central Archives to life. A holographic image appeared and waited for John's instructions. "Access all information on Marcus Shea."

The screen went blank and then the requested information started scrolling, only to stop a few seconds later.

"That's it? All we have is his name and an address from thirty-five years ago? Glad I wasted my time!" John tore his key from the sigil port in front of him. He walked to his Gemini door and smacked it before he turned and leaned against it.

Michael turned and looked at John, his voice dire. "There are some things you should know. I had hoped that I would never have to tell you but Marcus coming back changes things."

So much had happened so quickly that John was not sure he wanted to hear more bad news. His first days as leader of The League of Twelve were more eventful than he ever thought possible. He placed his hands in his pants pockets and braced himself for the worst.

Michael paced around the celestial circle in the Hall of Gates, his hands clasped together behind his back. He knew that what he was about to tell his son would weigh heavily on him.

"Before Sebastian was born, Marcus and Jacob had a falling out. They both wanted their father's ring. They both trained, both did everything they could to make themselves look like the right choice. Jacob was chosen because Marcus was unstable. His anger and his jealousy just weren't something the rest of the league wanted. Every member chose Jacob, so when the Immortals made their final decision, it was unanimous. Marcus resented Jacob for this and to get back at him...he slept with Maxine pretending he was Jacob."

John's eyes widened in astonishment.

Michael changed direction and continued pacing. "There's more. Jacob went to Maxine's place that night and found them in bed together. Maxine had no idea until Jacob showed up that she had been with Marcus. Jacob attacked Marcus. That's why Marcus has the scar on his face. Jacob nearly killed him. That's when Marcus disappeared. No one knew where he went and really, no one cared. He was always a thorn in the league's side anyway, so no one questioned his leaving."

Michael walked to John and looked directly into his eyes. "Marcus is not here for fun. If he took one key, you can bet he's going after the rest. And John...Sebastian can never know."

John closed his eyes and ran his fingers through his hair as he tried to absorb all of this information.

While John and Michael searched the Central Archives for any further information on Marcus, Angeline removed her cell phone from her purse. "Let's make those calls, Zayne."

"I'll get us some coffee." Ann left the Grand Temple and headed to Brewed and Steeped; she was glad for the distraction.

Angeline and Zayne walked through the Grand Temple. They paused in front of the massive sapphire tablet embedded in the wall just inside the south entrance, where Ann found them upon her return. Etched on this tablet was a brief account of the Eyrasine exodus to Earth, as well as the laws that were meant to govern the City of Radiance, written in the ancient Eyrasine language. On the wall next to the tablet, was a computer screen from which any Earth language could be selected to translate the inscription.

Omm, the Supreme Ruler of the planet Eyras, sought the counsel of his advisors. With the inevitable collision of Andromeda and the Milky Way, extensive research had been conducted and it was determined that Eyras in Andromeda would not survive the collision. In order to ensure the continuation of his people, Omm needed to evacuate Eyras.

Omm's advisors, a group of immortals, all agreed that those of the royal bloodlines needed to be the first to leave Eyras. After much searching, a planet suitable for habitation was found: Earth in the Milky Way. After Omm had completed making the twelve gates and the portal that would transport his people to their salvation, he journeyed 2.5 million light years to Earth.

In the centre of the Earth, Omm created an interdimensional city that he named the City of Radiance. He designed it to be a fully self-sufficient city where his Eyrasines would live; a place where they would age slowly, living to almost two hundred years. He created twelve gates mirroring those on Eyras around a portal through which his people would travel between Eyras and the City of Radiance at the Earth's core.

Having found their queens on Earth, King Alexander and the other eleven each started a family. With the bloodlines secured, the kings formed a league to protect the portal.

Each king wears a ring: four kings wear blue sapphires, four wear emeralds, and four wear diamonds. These rings are to be passed down to their successors, with the band changing as necessary and the stone remaining.

The firstborn blood descendants of the kings in every following generation will each be endowed with great responsibility and great power, as they must one day assume the role of league member. They are The League of Twelve, the guardians of the gates."
~ The Exodus to Earth, as told by King Alexander, first son of Omm ~

As they looked at the tablet, Angeline reflected on the importance of the league as protectors of the City and each of the families who trusted and relied on them. She turned and looked at Ann and Zayne. "Shall we?"

Together they began walking toward the Hall of Gates to wait for the others to arrive.

~~~~

In the Hall of Gates, with everyone except Sebastian present, John stood over his Gemini sigil with his father by his side and explained the situation. Grief, shock, and anger resonated throughout the room.

"With Marcus here and the Cancer key gone, we need to step up our game. We have until the Winter Solstice portal opening to get Seb's key back. We don't know what Marcus is planning or what his endgame is, but his timing can't be an accident. First, my dad and Seb's dad are the last of the previous league to pass their rings and keys, then there's the blood moon, and now, at this last portal opening, all of us saw more geist slip through than we expected there to be. There has to be a connection somewhere that we are just not seeing."

Ethan stood with a look of disbelief on his face. "So, Marcus killed Seb's family, took his key, and did all of this on his own? How could he manage to slay an entire family by himself?"

John had no answer. "We don't know if he's got help or not. Seb only knows that his family is dead and Marcus was the only other person he saw in his house."

Mariam sincerely wanted to believe that this was an isolated incident. "Perhaps Marcus just wanted his brother's family out of the picture so he could try to take his place in the league."

Michael once again paced through the room. He felt both sorrow and anger. "The Immortals would never allow him in the league. There is a reason why he wasn't chosen. Marcus is seriously deranged. Knowing him, he's got an ulterior motive. If all he wanted was revenge, he would have just killed Jacob's family and not bothered with the key. He's after something, like John said. You all need to figure out what."

John glanced around the room at his friends, his fellow league members, the people he had to lead. "We all need to train harder now. Marcus isn't going to be easy to take down so the old ways of doing things are no longer going to cut it. Until we get Seb's key back, we meet here once every month, on the first Saturday. I know the meetings used to be quarterly, on the solstices and equinoxes, but we need to keep each other informed. If anything seems off, anything at all, let your faction leader know."

John looked at Josh, the league's funeral director. "Can I count on you to make the funeral arrangements?"

Josh nodded. "Absolutely."

John ended the meeting as he felt he had said all there was to say. "We're done here. I'll be with Seb if anyone's looking for me." He exited the Hall of Gates through his Gemini door and headed to the Healing Chambers with his father following behind him.

Michael also wanted to check on Sebastian. He was as much of a son to Michael as his own boys.

John found Sebastian trying to get out of bed with two medics restraining him. "Seb! What the hell? Get back in bed!"

"I'm fine!" Sebastian snapped. "I need to find Marcus. He has to pay for what he did!"

With his tall stature and muscular physique, he usually appeared intimidating, but in that moment, Sebastian looked utterly menacing.

Knowing what Sebastian was going through as his wife's passing was still a fresh wound on his heart, Michael sat in a chair next to Sebastian's bed, clasped his hands together in his lap and said, "Seb, I am so sorry about your family. Jacob was like my brother and I will feel this loss for a long time. Listen, you will need to be in top form to take down Marcus, so stay here until you are completely healed. If you fight Marcus while you're still injured, you will not get through it alive."

As Sebastian relaxed a bit, the medics backed away.

John tried to reassure his friend that he would make things right. "Family is important. We weren't born brothers but we are blood brothers. As soon as you're well enough, we'll take Marcus down together."

4 – THE ALIBI

John returned home and found James cleaning Sebastian's blood from the floor in their kitchen. He walked toward him and stopped as he recalled last night's events, his fists clenched at his sides. He took a deep breath. "James, let's do this later."

"I'm almost done." James looked up and yawned. "You look awful, by the way."

"Thanks. I wish I felt that good." John rubbed the back of his neck.

"Does Seb know about his alibi?"

"Yeah, I told him when I gave him a key to the house. I'm going to bed."

John left the kitchen and climbed the stairs to his bedroom. He was confident in his abilities, yet concerned he may not be ready for such a big threat. The entire league was his responsibility and he was already feeling the weight of such a great authority.

~~~~

John laid in bed but had trouble turning his mind off. Marcus. Geist. Murder. Revenge. So many thoughts flowed through his head.

He turned onto his side and heard a light knocking at his bedroom door. "James, what do you need?"

When the door opened, he saw Ann. Confused, he furrowed his brow as he watched her approach him. She sat on the bed at his side and smiled.

"Ann? Couldn't whatever you want wait until morning?"

John sat up. Ann had no reason to be in his house, in his bedroom. He became concerned. "Did something happen?"

Still smiling, Ann placed a hand on John's leg.

His concern turned to uneasiness.

"What are you doing?" He waited for an answer, for Ann to say something.

She remained silent.

"Why are you here, Ann?"

Ann looked up as a black fog filled the room. It swirled and encircled her as red bolts of lightning began to strike from within the fog.

John jumped out of his bed. "Ann! Where are you?"

He looked around his room and before he could take a step, a bolt of lightning struck him and threw him against the wall. His head struck the wall and he slumped to the floor.

John quickly opened his eyes and sat upright in his bed. "What the hell was that?" He rubbed his face and groaned. He got out of bed, grabbed his cell phone and headed downstairs to get a drink.

"That is one dream I will be keeping to myself," he mumbled. He entered the den, headed to the table next to the fireplace and reached for the decanter of whiskey. He poured some into a glass and placed his cell phone on the table. He finished his drink in one swallow before he left the den and walked toward the kitchen where not long ago, Sebastian had lain near death.

~~~~

In his room in the Healing Chambers, Sebastian reached for his cell phone, and called Ann. He knew he could count on her to help him out and not ask too many questions.

"Ann, hey, I need a favour. Are you still in the City?"

"Yup, I'm with Ange. You had everyone pretty worried."

"Yeah, sorry about that. Can you bring me a T-shirt and sweatpants? I'm getting out of the Healing Chambers and I need you and your key to get me out of the City. I can meet you at the west entrance."

"Sure. I'll be right there."

Ann placed her phone in her purse and looked at Angeline with surprised relief. "Seb's out of the Healing Chambers and needs a key to get out of the City. You coming with?"

"No, you go ahead. I'm going to head home. Give Seb my best."

"Will do."

Ann made her way to the Grand Temple after she obtained clothes for Sebastian from a shop in the City. She saw him near the west exit wearing his blood stained pants and ripped T-shirt. She quickly walked to him, placed her hands on her hips and narrowed her eyes. "They didn't let you out, did they? *You* let yourself out!"

"Technically, yes. Can we go now before the medics spot me?" Sebastian smiled sweetly, his eyes pleading.

Ann let out a loud breath and pursed her lips. "Fine. But you owe me."

They boarded a transport pod and sat next to each other.

Ann gave the pod its instructions. "North American exit, medium speed." She handed him his clothing. "I hope these fit."

"I'm sure they're fine. Thanks Ann." He grabbed the collar of his torn and bloodied shirt and when he pulled upward, he winced in pain as the stitches pulled in his side. "I thought I would be healed by now."

"Here, let me help." She placed her hands in one of the holes in his shirt, pulled, and ripped it up to the collar before she eased it over his head.

Sebastian raised an eyebrow. "That works."

Ann picked up the shirt in Sebastian's lap and handed it to him. He fought through the pain to get the shirt on then stood up and began to unbutton his pants. Overcome by a feeling of lightheadedness, he fell back onto the seat.

"Seb!"

He snapped, "I'm alright." He was angry and frustrated that his body hadn't healed itself. "What did Marcus do to me?"

"You've never had wounds as bad as this before and you've only had your ability for a couple of weeks. It'll take time for your body to adjust."

Sebastian squeezed his eyes shut and lowered his head. "I know," he replied, his voice soft and low.

Ann took the pants from Sebastian's hand, rolled them into a pillow, and stood up. She leaned over and placed the pants behind his head.

While Ann adjusted his makeshift pillow, he slowly opened his eyes and caught a glimpse of her generous cleavage.

"Rest, Seb. Just close your eyes until we land."

Sebastian took a deep breath and closed his eyes. His lightheadedness began to fade as he rested.

After a few minutes, the transport pod landed softly in front of the North American exit.

Ann lightly touched his shoulder. "We're here, Seb. How are you feeling?"

"I think I'm alright. Closing my eyes helped." He stood and exited the transport pod.

Ann picked up the pants Sebastian had used as a pillow and followed him out. Once she reached the exit, she inserted her key in the metal door and they stepped onto the platform.

The interdimensional shift through the tunnel had Sebastian feeling nauseous. He placed both hands on his stomach. "I'm not sure what they gave me in the Healing Chambers but I'm sure it won't taste any better coming up than it did going down."

"We'll be at my car in a few minutes. We're almost through."

Her voice was stern but her expression was sympathetic. "There will be no getting sick in my car. None. At all."

"Just get me there, and I'll be good, I promise."

As they exited through the backdoor of Jayded ink, Ann eased Sebastian into her Porsche Spyder. She placed her hand on the top of his head. "Watch your head, big guy. We don't want to add to your injuries."

Once Ann had taken her seat behind the wheel, she tossed the pants she was holding into the back seat and saw Sebastian smile.

"I forgot what a sweet ride you have, Ann. I'll have to take it out for a spin some time."

She glanced sideways at him. "Yeah, sure…but for now, how about you concentrate on healing yourself?"

Sebastian had spent so much of his energy healing himself that it left him feeling drained. He closed his eyes and leaned his head against the seat rest as Ann drove.

She pulled into the circular driveway at John's house.

Sebastian thanked her for the ride with a gentle kiss on her cheek that seemed almost reflexive. He exited the car and walked up to the Evans home, leaving Ann speechless.

He reached into his pocket for the key John had given him and unlocked the front door. The few minutes he spent relaxing in the transport pod and then in Ann's car had him feeling better physically. Emotionally, he wanted nothing more than to drink that night out of existence even though he knew it could never happen.

Inside the house, John returned to the den to retrieve his cell phone. He picked it up, began to walk out of the room and noticed a shadow move in the foyer. He placed his phone in his pocket and walked silently to the gun cabinet. He removed a shotgun and loaded it quickly. Quietly, he exited the den and aimed his shotgun at the front door.

Sebastian raised his arms. "Whoa!"

John felt a rush of adrenaline course through his veins. "Damn it, Seb! I could have shot you!" He lowered the shotgun and narrowed his eyes. "There is no way the medics let you leave."

Sebastian lifted a shoulder and shrugged. "Like they could stop me. I just left. Ann dropped me off."

James, awakened by the loud voices downstairs, jumped out of bed, ran around the corner and down the staircase, taking two steps at a time.

He saw John in the foyer with a shotgun. "John! What the…" His voice trailed off as he saw Sebastian. "Seb?"

"Told you I would be out before supper. Pour me a drink, John. The chamber water tasted like ass. I need something to get that taste out of my mouth."

John shook his head and walked into the den. After he unloaded the shotgun and returned it to its case, he poured Sebastian a full glass of whiskey. He watched Sebastian walk across the den, grab the decanter and drink straight from the bottle.

Sebastian didn't stop until it was empty.

James returned from the kitchen with three beers and handed one to each John and Sebastian.

John took the beer from Sebastian's hand. "Seb, why don't you get some food, sit down and relax."

"I'm fine, John. Look." Sebastian lifted his shirt. Two faint marks and stitches were all that remained where just hours ago, there were two deep stab wounds.

His tone was cocky and one eyebrow was raised. "I did most of the healing on my own but I'll give the Eyrasines some of the credit." He wasn't willing to tell John he had felt lightheaded and nauseous on his way to the house.

John walked to the armchair beside the gun cabinet and sat. "Yeah, you were in no shape to heal yourself, Seb. It blows my mind how quickly Eyrasine medicine works."

Sebastian could see the exhaustion on John's face. "I slept in the Healing Chambers but you look like you need to sleep. Go to bed, John." He placed his hand over his heart. "I promise I'll be good. I'll just watch TV for a while and probably head up to bed myself."

John pointed his finger at Sebastian. "Promise me you won't do anything stupid, like go after Marcus alone."

Sebastian smirked. "Yeah, yeah, I'll wait until I'm fully healed...and maybe I'll wait for backup."

John shook his head, got up and walked out of the den. He climbed the stairs, hoping his mind would slow down enough so that he could sleep and be functional at work in the morning.

~~~~

John managed to sleep a few more hours before he headed to the shower. As the water poured over him, he placed both hands on the wall behind the stream of hot water and hung his head, his heart heavy at the loss of his friend's family.

The warm water cascaded down his body and felt good. He wished it could wash away the turmoil inside of him.

He didn't want the rest of the league to see him emotional; leaders had to be ruled by logic, not emotions, if they were to be effective.

After he toweled off and dressed, John went to the kitchen for a cup of coffee. He saw James, already seated at the kitchen table, full coffee mug in his hand.

James yawned. "Where's Seb?"

John reached for the freshly brewed pot of ambrosia and rubbed the back of his neck. "Still sleeping in the spare bedroom."

"I don't know how he managed to sleep at all." James sipped his coffee and thought about Sebastian finding his family dead, what that could do to a man psychologically.

John filled a travel mug with coffee. "Keep an eye on him while I go to the clinic to check up on things. I'll see you tonight."

James watched his brother walk toward the garage. He could see that the recent events had taken their toll on him.

John entered the garage and walked straight to his fully loaded, black Cayman Porsche. He sat behind the wheel and pressed the button on his garage door opener. The engine roared to life as he turned his key in the ignition.

Once on the road, he lowered the windows; the speed and wind felt good against his skin and he breathed in deeply. He needed to feel something other than grief and worry.

Arriving at Dr. M. Evans, DDS and Associates, John entered the clinic. The interior structure was designed by Michael and his fellow dentists, Dr. Bloom and Dr. Chan, but they had left the choice of colour scheme and decor to Michael's wife, Yvette.

She loved decorating her home and when Michael offered her the opportunity to decorate the interior of their office, she jumped at the chance. Yvette had left her mark on the dental office with her choice of decor before she passed.

Michael, John, and James were reminded of her every time they went to work.

One of the secretaries, Jessica Smith, sat behind the semicircular reception desk. She looked up and smiled as John approached her. "Hello, Dr. Evans. All of your scheduled appointments have been confirmed and there are some files on your desk for you to look over."

John thanked her and continued to his office. He phoned home. "James, stick with Seb and take him where he needs to go. I don't think he should be alone today."

"That's the plan." James replied. "He's sleeping right now but I'll go check on him."

"Thanks, James."

~~~~

Demons plagued Sebastian's sleep. He tossed and turned as he dreamed of faceless monsters and his family lying dead. He awoke abruptly; his heart pounded in his chest and his body was wet with sweat. He sat up and looked around. When he saw he was alone, he sighed with relief. In a matter of hours his life had been turned upside down. He heard a knock at the door. It opened and James appeared in the doorway.

He looked at Sebastian, concerned. "Is there anything you need?"

Sebastian rubbed his face with both hands. "A drink. The stronger, the better."

"Help yourself to anything. Our home is your home." James leaned against the door frame. "You know, even with the Eyrasine medicine and you healing yourself, you still need to rest. When you're up to it, I can take you where you need to go."

"I can't take it easy, James! I have to make funeral arrangements."

"Josh will take care of everything. All you need to do is show up."

Sebastian slowly got out of bed and put on the pants he had left in a pile on the floor. "I should phone Josh. There are a few things I need to go over with him."

As he pulled his cell phone out of the pocket of his pants, Sebastian noticed the message light flash. He scrolled through the list on the screen and shook his head. "The police phoned. They're going to want me down at the station to let me know what happened."

He closed his eyes and exhaled loudly. "How am I going to act surprised to hear about my family's death?"

"We'll go to the station first." James placed a hand on Sebastian's shoulder. "We can head over to Josh when we're done. I'm just going to grab something to eat. I'll meet you downstairs."

After a quick shower, Sebastian dressed and headed downstairs. "I just need to borrow a jacket, if you don't mind."

James left the kitchen and headed to the garage. "Yeah, help yourself."

"Thanks. I'll meet you in the car."

Sebastian walked to the closet, chose a jacket, then walked to the den. He grabbed a small bottle of Jack Daniels, took a long swig, and put the bottle in his inside jacket pocket before he joined James.

~~~~~

Marcus sat on a bench in the park across the street from the police station, a magazine in his hands as he waited for one of the three geist he had employed. He looked up and saw Sebastian and James exit their vehicle. "How did you survive?"

His fists clenched around the magazine.

Uvall approached him in the form of a lanky, blonde man. "What do you need me to do?"

Marcus recognized Uvall from the picture text he received after he had acquired his latest body. After seeing Sebastian alive, he altered his plans. "Follow the two that just went into the police station, but keep your distance. The Charger parked out front is their vehicle."

He saw Uvall nod his head as he walked back to the vehicle Marcus had provided him with. "Hopefully this geist will prove useful."

Marcus got in his car and drove to his downtown penthouse.

~~~~~

Just as James parked his car in front of the police station, Sebastian reached into his jacket and took one more long swig of whiskey before he went inside.

"Seriously, Seb?"

Sebastian shrugged his shoulders. "You know I can't get drunk with my self-healing ability."

James shook his head. Both he and Sebastian got out of the car and walked to the front door of the police station.

Inside, James tried to appear nonchalant as he spoke with the officer at the front desk. "We're looking for Constable Fields."

The officer didn't look up from his computer. "Name?"

"Sebastian Shea. Constable Fields phoned me earlier and left a message asking me to come down to the station."

"Have a seat. I'll let him know you're here."

After a few minutes, Constable Fields, a man in his mid-fifties with a salt and pepper crew cut and mustache, walked straight to Sebastian, his hand extended. "Mr. Shea, we need a statement from you. I have some news."

Sebastian stood and shook Constable Fields' hand. "What is this about?" He hoped the constable wouldn't see the grief in his eyes.

Constable Fields pointed to a door at his right. "We can talk about that in the interview room. This way, please."

James watched through the door's window as Constable Fields informed Sebastian that his family was found dead. He saw Sebastian lower his head and cover his face with his hands before pounding the table in front of him with both fists.

Sebastian raised his head and James saw his mouth form the words, *Who did this.* He watched Constable Fields pace the room as he continued to speak with Sebastian.

"The perpetrator was shot and killed on the scene. We found the murder weapon on him so there's no doubt we have the right man." Constable Fields hoped to ease the sting of the news.

Sebastian's brow furrowed in confusion. He knew it couldn't be Marcus. Any blood or fingerprints he may have left were likely gone as Rafe must have thoroughly cleaned any traces of him. There was no doubt in his mind that Marcus had a hand in placing blame on someone who surely was an innocent bystander.

After he gave his statement, Sebastian walked somberly back to the waiting room with the constable.

"One further thing, Mr. Shea. We will need you to identify the deceased before they can be released. There's an officer at the hospital waiting for you."

Constable Fields looked at the notes he had taken while speaking with Sebastian. "James Evans."

James replied hesitantly. "Uhh...yes."

"Come with me, please. I need a statement from you as well."

"Sure. What's going on?"

"We'll get to that. Follow me." The constable led James to the interview room.

~~~~

Once inside his car, James started the engine and looked at Sebastian who was finishing off a bottle of Jack Daniels in the passenger seat beside him.

Sebastian tossed the empty bottle into the back seat. "The officer told me they caught someone, James. Who could they have caught? You know it wasn't Marcus."

James asked, "Was there someone else in your house?"

"I have no idea but I'm going to find out."

Sebastian's thoughts turned to his family. He let out a long breath. "I need to identify them, James."

"Alright. We'll go to the morgue and then head to the funeral home. I'll phone Conor and let him know we're on our way. Why don't you phone John and let him know that we've talked with the police."

"I will, right after I speak with Josh. I'm also going to need to swing by the office. I have to let them know what happened."

No matter how much he drank, Sebastian could not seem to retain enough of the alcohol to take away the pain he was feeling. Up until this point, Sebastian felt his self-healing ability was a blessing but now, he thought it seemed more like a punishment.

~~~~~

In the dental clinic, once John received the call from Sebastian, he walked to the reception desk. "Jessica, please have Drs. Bloom and Chan take my appointments, as well as James', for tomorrow if they can, otherwise cancel them. We have a funeral to go to."

John's heart was heavy as he told Jessica about the Shea family. The last time he informed her that there was a funeral to attend, it was for his mother.

"Oh, I'm so sorry Dr. Evans. Mr. and Mrs. Shea were wonderful people and their daughter always had a smile on her face whenever she was here. Please pass along my condolences."

"I will."

"Would you like me to arrange to have flowers delivered to the funeral home?"

"Yes, thank you. I'll have Rachel give you the details."

"Of course." Jessica nodded before she turned her attention back to her computer screen. She had worked for the Evans family for nearly twenty years, unaware of her employers' secret lives.

John walked back to his office and found Rachel Rivait, Conor and Jayde's sister and the hygienist with whom he worked closest. He gently took her arm, pulled her aside and informed her of Sebastian's family's murders.

Rachel put her hand over her mouth. "Oh no." She too had known Sebastian's family for her entire life and was shocked. "How did this happen?"

"It was Marcus. We don't know anything more so please don't say anything to anyone just yet. With everything going on, I'm going to have James covering most of my appointments for a while after the funeral. We have to get some things under control in the league right now."

"No problem. I'll make sure things go smoothly for him." Her voice was sorrowful. "I guess I'll see you at the funeral. I can't believe this happened."

"Neither can anyone else." John placed a hand on her shoulder. "Thanks, Rachel."

~~~~~

After Sebastian identified the bodies, James drove him to the funeral home. Inside, they found Josh with the funeral home director.

Josh made the introductions. "Sebastian, this is Shane Aslo. Shane, this is the son and brother of the deceased."

Shane stood with his hand extended. He took Sebastian's hand and offered his condolences. "Mr. Shea, I am so very sorry for your loss. Rest assured, your family will be treated with dignity and respect."

"Thank you. I'm here to advise you that Josh Morrison has the authority to make any and all decisions regarding my family's funeral arrangements." He handed Shane his business card. "If you need something signed, please send it to my office and they will make certain that it gets to me."

Sebastian walked closer to Josh and spoke quietly. "I want a small, private ceremony, with all of our families and only the senior partners from the firm in attendance. My parents wanted steel urns, in sapphire blue, but dad wanted his to have a blue sapphire embedded in it. Other than that, the details are up to you."

He nodded in thanks and walked to the exit.

Before he left with Sebastian, James turned to Josh. "Thanks Josh. Seb wouldn't have been able to do this on his own."

~~~~

Shea and Partners, LLP, occupied the top three floors of an eleven-storey, circular high rise building located in the downtown core of Niagara Falls.

After entering the building, Sebastian and James walked straight to the elevators, which were located on either side of a large central water fountain in the middle of the main floor lobby.

Just as he called the elevator, James' phone rang in his pocket. He looked at the display and saw John's name. "Hey, John, I'm at the law firm with Seb, what do you need?"

"I phoned Ann and she said if Seb wants any particular food or drinks for the wake, to stop by the restaurant today."

"Okay, I will let him know." James placed his cell phone in his pocket as the elevator doors opened. "Seb, after we finish here, how about we head over to Ann's restaurant and let her know what you want for the meal after the funeral. Besides, we could use a bite."

"Fine. I should probably eat something." He turned to face the elevator doors and leaned against the back wall. The ride to the ninth floor was a silent one.

The elevator doors opened to the lobby of Shea and Partners. Sebastian walked to the reception desk and told the secretary, Eve Carter, what had happened and that he would be taking some time off.

She gasped and placed her hand over her heart as she listened to Sebastian. The newest employee at Shea and Partners, Eve been hired by Sebastian's father a few weeks before.

"Drew Johnston is to handle my clients in my absence."

"I will have your files brought to Mr. Johnston's office this afternoon. I am so sorry for your loss, Mr. Shea. Your father will be greatly missed."

It was evident to Sebastian that her words were sincere. "Thank you, Eve." He walked to the far end of the office to inform the senior partners and speak with them about distributing his father's workload.

After he spoke with the partners, he and James left the law firm, unaware that one of Marcus' geist sat in a parked car down the street, watching them.

James drove toward Transcendence and Uvall followed with enough distance between them so he wouldn't draw their suspicion.

Sebastian's stomach began to growl as they arrived at Ann's family's restaurant.

"I guess your body wants more than just alcohol, buddy!"

"Shut it." Sebastian's mouth curled into a slight smile.

James noted that this was the first time Sebastian had smiled since Marcus had murdered his family. He also knew the pain of loss. His own mother's passing had left him bitter and distant for quite some time.

Just before he got out of the car, James punched Sebastian's arm lightly. "Let's see what Ann's got on the stove."

"Whatever it is, I hope there's a lot of it." Sebastian realized he hadn't eaten anything for nearly twenty four hours, other than what was provided in the Healing Chambers.

~~~~

John phoned Vivian and Jake, Ann's parents, to let them know that Sebastian and James would stop by the restaurant shortly after Sebastian had given his statement to the police.

Vivian walked through Transcendence. The oak hardwood floors had been polished and the crystal chandeliers had been cleaned; she replaced their usually bright bulbs with those of a softer white light. She had known Jacob and Maxine Shea for so many years and felt as though she had lost a brother and sister.

The elegant dark wood tables and black leather chairs in the main dining area were set in a semi-circle around a large round table upon which Vivian placed a sapphire blue tablecloth. An area that ordinarily accommodated upwards of two hundred and fifty guests was arranged in such a way that even with the open concept, high-domed ceilings, it had an intimate feel. Rustic stone walls in earthy tones and shades of cream, added to the serene feeling of the restaurant. Much like many other league buildings, this upscale dining establishment had been remodeled many times, yet some of the original architecture remained. Along the bar to the right of the entrance, champagne flutes sat in crates ready to be filled for tomorrow's guests.

With James close behind, Sebastian walked into Transcendence toward a large circular table. The blue colour of the tablecloth prompted Sebastian to look at the ring on his hand, the one his father passed down to him not long ago. He looked up at the sound of Ann's voice.

"Hey, guys. John said you would be coming by. I've got some minestrone soup and a fresh loaf of garlic bread that I just made in the kitchen. I will be right back with a bowl for each of you." Ann knew how her friends loved her cooking.

Sebastian and James sat at the bar as Vivian came out of the kitchen, her light brown hair tied back in a bun. With her petite, shapely frame and hazel eyes, she could have passed for Ann's sister rather than her mother.

Vivian walked to Sebastian and softly hugged the man she had known since his birth. "Oh, Sebastian. If you need anything at all, please let me help."

"Thanks. I will."

Vivian placed her hands on Sebastian's face, framing it. "You're not alone, hon. You are never alone."

Ann came out of the kitchen as Vivian walked back in. She placed the soup and bread in front of Sebastian and James and watched as they ate as though they had not eaten in days. "Now, I know my prowess in the kitchen is, well, legendary, but can you guys even taste what you're putting in your mouths?" Her voice was dramatic but inwardly, she was pleased that Sebastian felt up to eating.

"Delicious as always, Ann. Listen, with Marcus being back, I think it's a good idea for you guys to have some extra security here, maybe put up a few cameras. You know how I would hate it if anything happened to my favourite diner." He winked at Ann.

Jake emerged from the storage room behind the bar. "You are right."

Ann's father Jake was nearly the spitting image of his son, Drew. Jake wore his brown hair short, drawing attention to his steely blue eyes. A man of few words, Jake usually let Vivian take the lead in conversations, however, knowing what Marcus had done to Sebastian's family, he did not feel the need to hold back.

"Marcus is a vengeful bastard and he is not above hurting any one of us. The first time I met him, he told me he would be joining Vivian after the next time the portal was to be opened and that I shouldn't wait up for her. Promise me that when you find him, you'll let me get in a few punches as well." Jake's disdain for Marcus was evident in each word he spoke.

Sebastian got up to leave and spoke with his back to the others. "Trust me, if I find him first, there won't be anything left for anyone else to take a swing at."

He turned to Ann. "Thanks for the food, Ann."

"Is there anything special you would like us to prepare for tomorrow?"

"I'm sure whatever you make will be fine." With his heart still heavy, he was not concerned with the details of the wake. He walked toward the front door, his mind flooded with thoughts of revenge. The pain and anger at the loss of his family was the only catalyst he needed to rid the universe of Marcus Shea.

James quickly finished his meal and ran after Sebastian. "We'll see you tomorrow."

"James, I need to swing by my house and grab a few things. It shouldn't take long, but you don't have to wait. I'll just meet you back at your place."

"Not a chance, Seb. I'll help you carry your stuff down. Remember what Aunt Viv said? You're not alone."

"You're not going to kiss me are you?"

"You'd like that, wouldn't you?" James chuckled.

~~~~

James parked his car in front of the Shea's garage, not really wanting to go inside, but not willing to let Sebastian enter alone.

The bulk of the Shea home was built hundreds of years ago, with additions made by each generation who lived there. The inside had been gutted and redone a few times, but parts of the outer walls were the original stone.

Sebastian walked to the front door, straight through the police tape and tore it away; they hadn't removed it. He didn't need a reminder of what had happened. With James behind him, he walked upstairs toward his bedroom and passed his parents' and sister's rooms. He could not stop himself from looking inside.

James saw Sebastian clench his fists and placed his hand on his shoulder before he continued down the hall.

Inside his bedroom, Sebastian packed enough clothes for the next week and chose a suit from his closet to wear to his family's funeral. "I need to get out of here, James. I can't stay here while I'm waiting to find a place closer to the firm."

James leaned against the door. "You can always just keep your room with John and I."

"Thanks. I'll stay until I find something." He went downstairs and headed straight to the garage. On most days, the sight of his BMW i8 lifted his spirits - the sound of the engine, the richness of the leather interior. That day, however, he wanted to test the limits of his car, to race down the road and outrun the grief that followed him.

He just needed to get through the funeral. Seeing his family for the last time was going to be the most difficult thing he had ever done.

~~~~~

Sebastian felt numb as he walked into the funeral home the following day. This was not supposed to happen; not yet. He thought about how Marcus' reappearance changed so many things. A rage built up inside him and he drew in a deep breath and saw that John and the rest of the league members were already there.

Ann had paced in the funeral home's lobby as she waited for Sebastian to arrive. When she saw him enter through the large double doors, she walked to him and hugged him tightly. "Seb, we will get through this. We're all here for you."

"I know. You guys are helping me keep myself together."

At the far end of the lobby, the funeral home attendant opened the doors to the room where Jacob, Maxine, and Marianne lay peacefully in their coffins. Everyone stepped aside to allow Sebastian to enter first, to give him a moment alone with his parents, his sister, and his grief.

After a few minutes, he watched as everyone filed into the room. He was touched at the outpouring of love and friendship from people he had known, some since his birth. He always knew that league families took care of each other, but that day, he could feel it.

The minutes turned to hours as he listened while people shared stories about their time with Jacob, Maxine, and Marianne. With the senior partners from the law firm in attendance, everyone was careful not to mention geist, Eyras, or their abilities.

He placed his hand over his heart. "I appreciate it, more than I can say, that you have all come today. Your support and friendship mean so much."

Once the room had emptied, Sebastian walked to the coffins.

First, he approached his mother. The night he pleaded for her to wake up filled his mind. He leaned forward and kissed her forehead. "Rest, Mom. I love you."

He walked to his sister's coffin. Memories of the day she was born swirled through his mind. "You should have had more time, Marianne. I am so sorry I wasn't there to protect you." He touched her hand and gently squeezed it before he walked to his father.

Jacob was his mentor, father, and friend. Sebastian looked at his father, lifeless, and he couldn't believe that this was the same man who only a few days ago, was laughing and drinking with him, talking about the first time he would be opening the portal. "Thank you, Dad. You were the most amazing man I have ever known."

Sebastian left his family and saw John, Conor, Ann, Angeline, and James. The league families were a tight group, but Sebastian and these five were the best of friends.

With tears in his eyes, he walked to them. No words needed to be spoken.

~~~~

In the restaurant across the street from the funeral home, Marcus sipped his martini. He had thought that killing his brother would satisfy his need for revenge, but he was wrong. He wanted everyone in the league to die a slow, agonizing death once he had procured their keys.

~~~~

Inside Transcendence, Sebastian picked up a glass of champagne and walked to the back of the restaurant, acknowledging further condolences along the way. He found Ann and Vivian near the kitchen entrance.

Ann spotted Sebastian and walked to him. "Hey, Seb. Would you like me to put a plate together for you?"

"You really outdid yourself. Everything looks great."

"Mom wanted to make today special for you."

While they stood in front of the food tables, Ann filled a plate for Sebastian and handed it to him.

He looked at the plate in his hand, pleased. "Chocolate trifle?" He smiled. "How did you know this is my favourite dessert?"

"I know everyone's favourite foods." She returned his smile.

Sebastian looked at the tables filled with everything that his parents and sister loved to eat. He saw the salmon mousse and raspberry cheesecake his mother loved next to a beautifully arranged tiered platter of butter tarts that his sister would have claimed as her own.

On the far end of one of the tables was a Boston cream pie, the only dessert that his father could not refuse.

He looked at the incredible effort that Ann, Vivian, and Jake had put forth. He had always known that Ann was good at making sure everyone felt special, important, necessary.

Ann looked up at him. "Is there anything else you need?"

"You've done more than I could have asked for. I can't thank you enough." He grabbed her hand and squeezed gently as Vivian approached them.

Vivian placed her hand on Sebastian's shoulder. "Is Ann taking care of you, Sebastian dear? Do you need anything?"

He held up his plate. "Thanks Aunt Viv, but Ann's been great." He spooned some chocolate trifle into his mouth before he set the plate down on the table.

Vivian saw the way Ann looked at Sebastian and excused herself.

"This is really delicious, Ann." Sebastian looked around the room at the people who had come to pay their respects to his family. "Guess I should get this over with, eh?"

Ann touched Sebastian's arm lightly. "You've got this."

He looked at her hand on his arm; it felt warm and right.

He raised a glass of champagne. "Thank you all for your support and comfort. You are all family to me and I know my parents felt the same. To Jacob, Maxine, and Marianne. You are loved and you will be missed."

Everyone raised their glasses in a silent tribute to Sebastian's family.

From across the room, Dr. Yvonne Rivait, Conor's mother, could see the exhaustion on Sebastian and walked to him. "Sebastian, you look absolutely exhausted. Go home, hon. Get some rest. Doctor's orders." She winked before she kissed his cheek and moved to rejoin her husband.

Sebastian shrugged his shoulders and smiled.

"We can wrap things up here." Ann could see Sebastian's exhaustion as well.

"Alright. I just need to speak with the firm's senior partners then I'll head out. Thanks for everything." Without thinking, Sebastian leaned down and kissed Ann's cheek before he moved to join the senior partners.

John looked at Ann. They both had a look of bewilderment on their faces.

John smiled. "Would you like some help, Ann? I can put the tables and chairs back where they belong or whatever you need."

Ann grinned. "We're good here, John, but thanks."

"Okay. I'll see you later. Everything was great."

Sebastian walked back to John. "Would you mind coming with me to the funeral home? Shane phoned me and said that I can pick up…" His words stuck in his throat.

"Absolutely." He knew exactly what Sebastian was going through.

~~~~

As Shane Aslo brought out the urns that contained his family's ashes, Sebastian's thoughts drifted to the night of their deaths. He wondered if they had all been together, would they have been able to defeat Marcus? Would they still be alive?

Shane walked toward Sebastian with three urns and a large envelope on a rolling cart. He picked up the envelope. "This contains the death certificates and a copy of the obituaries. Again, I am sorry for your loss, Mr. Shea, and if there is anything else we can help you with, please do not hesitate to let us know." Shane offered his hand for Sebastian to shake.

Sebastian accepted his hand. "Thank you."

He picked up his father's urn and walked to his car with John carrying the other two. "If it's alright, I would like to keep their ashes at your place, just until I find something of my own."

"Absolutely. No rush finding a place, though. Let's just get through tonight and take it from there."

With the urns secured in the back of John's car, Sebastian and John drove away, each in their own vehicle.

Sebastian's thoughts turned to Ann. She always knew what to say or do to make him feel like there was hope. He hadn't really thought about it before, but he realized she had always been the one to help him through rough times.

Sebastian's stomach started growling. "Yet something else to put Ann in my thoughts."

~~~~

Sebastian entered the Evans house and headed to the den.

John arrived only moments before and saw Sebastian. Suspicious, he followed him.

Sebastian walked straight to the whiskey. While everyone else had imbibed at Transcendence, he didn't find time to eat very much, let alone drink.

John entered the den. "There's pizza in the fridge if you're hungry."

He wanted to help Sebastian get his mind on something other than the loss of his family. "How about first thing tomorrow morning we go to the training arena? Nothing says we have to wait until next week. I really think your liver needs a break from booze."

"Don't forget who you're talking to." Sebastian lowered his head. "It takes me ten times what you can drink to even begin to feel anything."

"Still, you're lucky you didn't end up back in the Healing Chambers after what you drank yesterday! Your self-healing may stop you from getting drunk but sweating it out in the arena would be good for you."

"Fine, grandma, but don't think I'll go easy on you."

John chuckled. "I would expect nothing less."

5 – MARCUS

Marcus walked through his penthouse and thought back to the night he had taken his brother's life. Killing Jacob had been too easy. He was almost despondent that his brother had not put up a fight. A smile formed on his lips as he thought, *That son of his sure made up for it.*

His nephew, Sebastian, was a tall, muscular man, not unlike himself.

Over six feet in height, with piercing, deep blue eyes, Marcus was a striking man. Although he was middle aged, he seemed much younger if you overlooked the grey in his light brown hair.

He stood and faced the mirror above his fireplace mantle. *There may be a few wrinkles on my face, and a few extra pounds tacked on since I was young, but I do like the scar*, he thought as he stroked his cheek. *Women don't seem to mind it either.*

As he walked toward the kitchen, his cell phone rang. The lobby attendant informed him that a pizza delivery person had arrived. "Please unlock the penthouse elevator so that my food may be brought up." He walked to the elevator and waited.

Once the elevator doors opened, Marcus said, "Please, come in." He directed Uvall toward the kitchen. "I have been looking forward to your report."

Uvall, who had been assigned to surveil each of the North American faction members, had much to report. He followed Marcus to the kitchen and placed the pizza on the counter. Before he gave his report, he handed Marcus a piece of paper.

"Each of them was at the funeral home and then at their restaurant. I followed one back to her apartment, so now you have all four addresses..."

When his computer signaled an incoming video call, Marcus raised his hand to interrupt Uvall's report. He opened his laptop and accepted a video call from Oriax, the geist he had assigned to watch the African faction league members. "What have you discovered?"

"No one in Egypt seems to do much, other than their jobs, family things, and visiting the jewelry store you mentioned. None of their homes were empty long enough for me to have a good look for a key like you described." Oriax hoped this information would be good enough. Egypt was hot and he was accustomed to the cool chill of the geist world, Celesol.

"I had been hoping more would come of your time there. I would like you to keep watching them."

Oriax, turned, flared his nostrils and inhaled deeply before he turned back toward his monitor. "Alright. I'll let you know when I have something."

~~~~~

Ganga had yet to report.

She had sneaked into Eyras hundreds of years ago through the portal Omm had placed on Celesol, her home planet.

Omm had sent his immortals to investigate the planet. When they realized that the majority of the geist were hostile, they abandoned Celesol. Unbeknownst to them, thousands of geist had discovered the portal and in mist form, escaped through it to Eyras before the portal was sealed.

Once on Eyras, Ganga was forced to stay in mist form so as not to be discovered.

When she found out the portal on Eyras led to another planet, Earth, she and a few other geist covertly joined the Eyrasines and made the journey with them. She eventually encountered Marcus and agreed to work for him.

Assigned surveillance of the London faction members, Ganga had chosen her form rather poorly. In the body of a petite florist, she worked out of a small shop in downtown London. While she found arranging flowers to be tedious, she preferred it to bowing to Marcus.

Why should I be his bitch, she thought.

Ganga reached for her cell phone. It was time for her to phone Marcus. He wanted a report on the London league members and she had little to give him. She dialed his number and when she heard his voice, she rolled her eyes in disgust at his arrogant tone.

He pressed the speaker button on his phone. "Ganga, how good of you to finally check in. I was wondering if you had been injured or killed."

She gritted her teeth. "You needn't worry about me. I'm just putting in my time until you satisfy your part of our deal."

"Always the realist. That's why I like you, Ganga. You tell it like it is."

"No sense in telling it like it isn't, now is there? Do you want your account of what they're up to here, or not?"

"Of course I do!" His condescending smirk was nearly audible.

"They go to jobs. They go home. They go into the antique store and stay in there for a long time so I assume they go to the City of Wonderful like you said, and then they come out." Ganga's report sounded as though she read a prepared statement.

"City of Radiance, Ganga. And..."

"And what?" Ganga interrupted defensively. "That's what they did. You said to watch them, so I watched."

Marcus released the speakerphone button and placed his cellphone against his ear. "Don't think you can't be replaced, Ganga. Choose your words and your tone carefully."

The power he held over his geist was intoxicating. Marcus loved being in control and believed he made a great leader. As long as they were paid and the promise of reopening the portal to their world was still on the table, he knew the geist would continue to do whatever he asked of them. He had found his true calling.

The League of Twelve didn't want him. His grown son didn't need him. These geist, however, needed him and this fueled him.

Oriax heard the conversation between Marcus and Ganga and he chuckled. "Too bad Asmodeus isn't here. He could take care of your league problem."

Uvall harrumphed. "There's no way to get him out of his tomb. Stolas was there. He was helping the league back then. He told me everything."

"Now that information is useful, Uvall. Is there anything more you can tell me? Where his tomb is located? Even the smallest detail that Stolas revealed may play a great part." Marcus needed to know more.

Uvall narrowed his eyes and tapped his head. "This brain is like a steel trap." Excited, he rounded his back and continued with his story.

"So, he told me the league guy and his friends dragged him to these tunnels and it took all of them to throw him in and get the lid on. Then, the league guy took two metal things out of the sides of the tomb. Stolas said he put them inside something that looked like rock statues before he left. He said the statues fit together kinda like bulky puzzle pieces."

Uvall used his hands to mimic the action of his words as he looked from Oriax on the computer screen to Marcus.

Marcus thought he looked more like a fool trying to open an imaginary jar of jam. He rolled his eyes and breathed deeply while Uvall continued, but with this latest information, he knew where to find Asmodeus. There was only one set of tunnels that the league used and Marcus knew just where they were.

"Then, no, wait, *before* he put the pieces in the statues, Stolas said the league guy used the things, kinda like keys I guess, to tighten the lid, to close it up good, right before some witch sealed it. She put a spell on it while she held the guy's hand." Uvall wiggled his fingers and opened his eyes wide, then made a slashing motion. "She cut it with a knife and let the blood drip onto some kind of picture on the top of the lid. Said only his blood could open it."

Uvall shrugged his shoulders. "That was years ago though. The guy has to be dead by now."

Marcus was pleased. "Ah, but his blood would have been passed to his descendants.

If I am not mistaken, the league only ever worked with one coven, and they worked out of a little shop called Crimson Spark. What we need to do is get someone from this coven to tell us which league member's blood was used to seal the tomb. Once we know whose blood we need..." Marcus' tone turned dark. "Well, we can drain it from their corpse."

He placed his elbows on the kitchen island and clasped his hands together. "Simple, really. Honestly, I had completely forgotten about Asmodeus. With him by my side, the league doesn't stand a chance.

"Uvall, you never cease to amaze me! Do you know where Stolas is now?"

"He's here. I saw him a week ago. He was buying a hot dog from a guy on the same street as that law firm."

"It's like my destiny is finding me!" Marcus smiled as he raised his hands. He turned back to Uvall. "Find Stolas. I need to know every last detail of what he saw. Let him know he will be well paid for his information."

He rose and walked to his bar to pour himself another glass of wine.

Uvall shrugged. "I know someone who might be able to find Stolas, but I'm going to need some cash. This guy won't even talk to me for free."

Marcus pulled out his billfold as he walked toward Uvall. He removed four hundred dollars and held the cash out to Uvall but retracted his hand before Uvall could take it. "Tell your informant that if his information leads me to Stolas, he will get more."

He once again held the cash toward Uvall.

Uvall reached out reluctantly, then quickly snatched the money.

Marcus turned his back to Uvall and stroked the stubble on his chin.

Uvall wrinkled his brow. "So if I'm looking for Stolas, who's going to find your witch?"

Marcus turned his attention to his phone. "Ganga, I will arrange a plane ticket for you to come to Niagara Falls so you can find this witch. You will be on the next flight."

"Sure, just tell me when." She was more than willing to leave London. Surveillance was not something she enjoyed.

Marcus dismissed Uvall, ended his phone call with Ganga, then terminated the video call with Oriax. He paced through his penthouse. *This is all falling into place rather nicely*, he thought as he sipped his wine. He decided that as soon as he had confirmation of Ganga's plane ticket, he would indulge in some well-deserved downtime. He eased back into his sofa and his thoughts drifted to what his life had been like after leaving Niagara Falls so long ago.

Rejected as a league member, Marcus had left home. He took what he knew he could easily liquidate, loaded up his Corvette Stingray, and vowed to return one day to claim the destiny that was denied him.

The West Coast appealed to him and he decided to make it his home. Once he purchased a house and settled in, he began his new life.

He earned his degree in robotic engineering and was free to travel as a contractor without commitment, until he met Madeline.

A manufacturing firm hired Marcus to supervise the design of a robotic system that would improve their overall output. Madeline Walker was the receptionist he saw at the start of each day. Her long, blonde hair framed her face but his attention was always focused on her bright, blue eyes. Full, perpetually pouting lips had him fantasizing, more often than not, about how they would taste.

While she was usually seated at her desk, Marcus was occasionally treated to the sight of Madeline's broad hips that swayed as she walked. He believed that delicate women were for weak men. He much preferred a woman who could match his enthusiasm and stamina in the bedroom.

The day that Madeline's car battery died was a day he remembered quite fondly. He offered her a ride home and she accepted. Their relationship blossomed and proved to be a welcome distraction for him. The hatred for his family that he held onto so tightly was no longer in the forefront of his mind, and it wasn't long before he proposed. The knee-jerk instinct to claim what was rightfully his still had its hold on him.

Five years into their marriage, Madeline gave birth to a healthy boy. Marcus was certain that his son, whom he named Kyle, would one day work by his side to help him exact his revenge against The League of Twelve.

He then realized that the five years he spent with Madeline before Kyle was born, had been a distraction from his plans for revenge, the distraction of being wanted...and sex.

The day he found out his wife was a geist, Marcus had been watching his son while she was out. He had just put Kyle in his playpen when he saw something he could not explain; Kyle had morphed his face into that of a character on the television. After a few seconds, his face returned to its original form. Marcus knew he himself had no such ability, which left only Madeline.

Throughout his entire marriage, he had thought his wife was an ordinary human. Not once in the past five years had she mentioned to him that she was an exceptional being. He wanted to be angry but the gift she had given to him in this tiny child was too incredible.

When Madeline returned, he was sitting on the floor with Kyle.

"My love, is there anything you have neglected to tell me? Anything about yourself you have held back?"

Madeline looked puzzled. "I don't think so. Why?"

"It seems you have given me a rather unusual child. Surely you have noticed his amazing abilities more than once, having spent so much time with him."

"I have noticed he's an amazing boy. He has his father's eyes and his mother's pout." She hoped Marcus would not see the worry in her eyes.

"But Madeline, have you seen this?" Marcus turned his son to face her.

Kyle had taken the visage of another character he had just seen on the television.

Madeline gasped. She saw that Marcus' expression was not one of surprise and narrowed her eyes. "You don't seem to be upset by this."

He simply stared at her.

She exhaled loudly, sat down, and began to explain. "I wasn't even sure I could procreate with a human. I was hoping I would be able to live here, unnoticed, unremarkable, and that I would never have to tell you what I truly am."

Marcus stood and placed his son in his playpen. He walked to Madeline and grabbed his wife by her arms.

She steadied herself for what might come next. She was well aware of his temper but he had never hurt her. As she looked into his eyes in that moment, she was unsure of what to expect.

He pulled her to her toes and kissed her deeply and with more passion than he had exhibited since she gave birth to Kyle.

Confused, Madeline opened her eyes wide. "Okay, you're not mad. But you don't know *what* I am. It's not something easily explained."

"You would be surprised at the life I lived before meeting you as well," Marcus confessed. He took hold of Madeline's hand and walked toward the couch with her.

When they sat, he turned to face her and kept her hand in his. "You are not the only one with secrets."

Intrigued, she crossed her arms and turned in her seat to face him. "Alright. You go first. Let's hear your confession, Mr. Mysterious."

"I have a twin brother. An identical twin. We look the same but we are each most definitely our own person. I am descended from a king not of Earth. This king came from a planet called Eyras."

Madeline's expression changed from curious to shocked. "You know about The League of Twelve?" Her voice was low and her expression was filled with surprise. "I haven't seen anyone from the league for a very long time." She scrunched her nose and continued. "I suppose I should tell you that I am a bit older than I initially confessed to...a few hundred years older, actually."

She rose and began to pace. "I am of a race called geist. When I first arrived on Earth, it was a time when the league was known for killing geist without discretion. Geist were the enemy and the enemy was destroyed. Since then, I did my best to avoid them. That's why I came here, far from the league."

Marcus rose to join her. He grabbed her around her waist and spoke in a most seductive tone. "So, I married an older woman, did I? How very modern of me."

She laughed as he nuzzled her neck, then moved to cover her mouth with his. She loved this man, more than she had ever thought possible. She took Marcus' hand in hers and walked with him back to the couch.

She stroked his hand. "We come from a planet very few beings know of, and a place most of us want very much to never see again."

He brought his hand up to her mouth and ran his finger across her lips. "I have known of the geist my entire life. I was raised by a league member. My brother *is* a league member. We both wanted to be in the league but I was not selected. The smug, self-righteousness my brother exuded was unbearable and so I left them and have not been back."

As she lifted the chain around his neck revealing the medallion she gave him so long ago, she looked into his eyes and hers welled with tears. "You never questioned it when I was so adamant that you always wear this."

She ran her finger over the brushed metal and told him of the power it contained. "This medallion was enchanted by a witch. As long as you wear it, you will be able to sense vibrations when you are with a geist and should a geist ever kill you, that geist would transfer some of their essence to you. The witch told me that a few hours after your death, you would be resurrected. You would be as our son is."

Madeline turned away from Marcus, rose and began to pace. "She also told me that this magick is unstable; it's dark magick so there could be consequences and there is a chance that it may have unwanted side effects or may not work at all. This spell had never been done before; the witch created it for me and destroyed it after she spelled your amulet. She only agreed to do it because she owed me. I saved her life a few years ago and this was her repayment.

"I gave this to you hoping that you would never need to know its purpose. I just needed to have some kind of insurance that you would be protected from those of my kind who don't feel as I do about humans."

"Am I right to assume that this would be the reason I feel vibrations when I am with you and certain other people?" He then realized that he had been living among geist for quite some time.

"Every geist can sense other geist through their body's frequencies. When I had your amulet spelled, it enabled you to sense them as well."

Madeline kissed Marcus playfully and sighed with relief. She felt as though a fog that had surrounded her for so long had finally lifted. With her past no longer hidden, she felt truly free.

She felt certain that the small bit of her essence that the witch placed in Marcus' medallion would keep him safe should he need it, as a part of her would always be with him.

Marcus' phone rang and brought his thoughts back to the present.

"Hi, Dad. I'm here."

Marcus smiled. "Kyle! I'm so glad you're here. I'll have the attendant let you up."

It had been over a week since he left a message on Kyle's phone, asking for his assistance. When he received no response, Marcus believed Kyle did not want to help him. With his son in the lobby, he was certain that all those years of grooming had been well spent.

Kyle leaned against the back of the elevator as the doors opened. A large duffel bag hung from his right shoulder. "Hey, Dad. It's been a while."

Marcus walked to his son and hugged him. He stepped aside to give Kyle and his large satchel enough room to exit the elevator and raised both hands. "Come. My home is yours."

6 – THE TRAINING ARENA

In the circular Hall of Gates each league member stood at their respective sigil on the floor as John began. "Ange, would you mind?"

Angeline tilted her head slightly. "Not at all." She held her astral key over her Capricorn sigil and it rose to meet her key. With a quick turn, the 3D Central Archives sparked to life. "Begin recording."

The Central Archives began its panoramic video recording of the room.

"First monthly meeting of The League of Twelve. John Evans presiding. All members present. The floor is yours, John."

"Thank you, Angeline. As this is our first monthly meeting, I can't imagine we have much to discuss so I'll just go through what has happened since my father stepped down." John cleared his throat and continued. "We all know what happened to Seb. We know more geist came through the portal than we had expected. We also know that during the last portal opening, the celestial events far outnumbered those of previous openings. Now we just need to figure out how or if all of these things are connected."

John looked at each of his fellow league members. "We don't have much else happening here in North America, so, Angeline, Zayne, have either of you got any information to share?"

Angeline addressed the room. "We've not got much happening in London, at least not anything of concern to the league."

Zayne stood with his arms crossed in front of his chest. He thought for a moment. "Egypt has been quiet. Nothing out of the ordinary has happened as of late."

John looked from member to member. "Does anyone else have anything to add?"

No one spoke.

"I know everyone has busy schedules, but when you get a chance, if you haven't already done so, I'd like each of you to take a look at what your predecessors recorded in the Central Archives. Knowing what happened in the past could help us in the future.

"Alright, now that our first monthly meeting is over, let's meet in the Training Arena in," he checked his watch and continued, "twenty minutes."

Angeline took hold of her astral key in the port. "Meeting concluded. End recording." She removed her key and the port slowly retreated back into the floor.

~~~~

After they placed their belongings in one of the lockers that lined both the walls inside the entrance to the Training Arena, Josh and Ethan headed to the Weight Room. The various training rooms were situated along the perimeter, leaving a large space in the centre, padded with thick mats, for sparring and hand to hand combat training.

Dumbbells, kettlebells, weight plates, and bars lined the walls of the Weight Room.

Josh picked up a press bar. "Eh mate, grab a couple of the forty pound plates for me, alright?"

Ethan teased, "Sure thing. You need a spot, yeah?"

"Only if you bring forty kilo plates instead of forty pounders!" Josh retorted.

Ethan grabbed two forty pound plates and handed them to Josh before he retrieved two for himself.

Josh and Ethan were close in age and had grown up the best of friends. They trained together nearly every day since they were told about The League of Twelve and that they would each, one day, take their place as members.

Mariam stood with her hands on her hips as she scanned the selection of protein shake mixes available at the Hydration Station. She decided that after today's workout, she would make one that tasted better than the mango and boysenberry concoction she made last time. She shivered as she recalled the taste.

Zayne and Najeeb walked into the Training Arena together. Najeeb headed straight to the Current Pool. He had spent his morning under a tent in Cairo and felt his muscles needed to be gently worked before he sparred with anyone.

Staffs, blunt training swords, and wooden daggers hung from racks mounted to the wall between the Current Pool and the Archery and Knife Throwing Room at the rear of the arena.

"Enjoy, Najeeb." Zayne turned into the Archery and Knife Throwing Room. He had always excelled at hand-to-hand combat, but even at a young age, throwing a blade and hitting a target in the distance seemed more exhilarating to him. He approached the displayed knives and selected a set of twelve with ornate wooden handles.

With the knives lined up in front of him, he expertly threw knife after knife, until all twelve had been thrown. He looked at the target at the end of the room and found he hit close to the centre with eight of the twelve blades; the other four blades had been lower and to the right. He tilted his head to the left. "Not bad."

Dalila opened the door to the Archery and Knife Throwing Room. "Zayne, care to join me in the Shooting Range? Your marksmanship makes you the perfect critic of my technique."

60

"I will join you if time permits," Zayne replied.

"Thank you!" Dalila continued to the Shooting Range.

In the main area of the Training Arena, Ann and Angeline walked to the fighting staffs and took two down.

Angeline snickered. "The two of us with big sticks in our hands? Ha! Oh the damage we could do!"

Ann stretched her arms. "Did you warm up, Ange? I warmed up at home."

"I am ready to go."

"Alright, let's do this." Ann lightly thrust her staff toward Angeline.

They assumed their stances and Ann led with a cross strike. Angeline lifted her staff to block as Sebastian walked past to spar with John.

"Hey ladies, save some of that energy for your fight with me." Sebastian winked. Spending time in the arena was invigorating and his heart felt lighter than it had in days.

"John!" Sebastian yelled. "Gloves or swords?"

"Gloves." John shouted from across the arena. "I'll grab the mouth guards, just in case."

Once their gloves were on and their shirts were off, John punched his gloves together. "Let's dance."

They circled each other. Sebastian led with a jab, then dealt an uppercut, which John blocked easily.

John knew Sebastian would be distracted. Marcus was not going to go easy on him. "Come on Seb, get your head in the game." John pushed Sebastian with his gloves to provoke a reaction.

He lunged at John, pummeling his midsection with a series of powerful blows.

John locked his arms around Sebastian's head. *This is more like it.*

Not far from John and Sebastian, Angeline's next move had Ann on the floor.

"Ann! What the bloody hell?"

"Sorry." Ann breathed heavily, as she looked toward Sebastian. "I was a little distracted."

Angeline followed Ann's line of sight and saw a shirtless Sebastian sparring with John. "Really, Ann? Is there something you're not telling me?" Angeline hoped Ann was finally ready to admit the feelings she had for Sebastian.

Ann's tone was defensive. "No. No! I was just…distracted."

Angeline helped her off the floor. "Come on, Ann, focus."

She grabbed Angeline's outstretched hand and pulled herself up to her feet. "It won't happen again."

Across the arena, Amber saw Sebastian take off his boxing gloves and walked over to him. "Nice sparring, Seb. Think you could take me on?" She hoped her question wasn't too vague.

Sebastian chuckled. "Amber, I would flatten you."

"You think so? Let's have a go then, yeah?"

Amber, the smallest and youngest league member, didn't present much of a challenge for Sebastian.

He raised both eyebrows. "Just remember, you wanted this."

"Let's get on with it." She was anxious to have Sebastian touch her, regardless of the circumstance.

He didn't want to hurt her, but he also knew she would face far worse than he could ever do. He let Amber lead with a jab to his right side and allowed her to connect.

"Not bad. But can you block?"

Sebastian swung at her, an easy jab, which she blocked well.

"Good!"

"Is all that all you've got?" Amber looked into his eyes. His eyes locked with hers and she smiled.

"You want more, eh? Alright." He swung at her, a hook punch he expected her to block but instead, he connected with Amber's jaw.

She lost her footing, landed on her backside and let out a rather undignified yelp.

Sebastian knelt down beside her. "Oh God, Amber! I'm sorry! Are you okay?"

"I'm sure the stars I'm seeing will pass shortly." She tried to giggle through the pain and humiliation.

John walked to Amber and helped her off the floor. "Marcus isn't going to give you the love tap Seb just did. We all need to put more time into our training."

Amber smiled, but felt mortified. Being singled out for correction wasn't new to her.

John turned to the others in the arena. "It's time to pair off. Let's move to the centre."

As Ann watched Sebastian with Amber, she turned to Angeline. "What's Amber's deal?"

Angeline pulled Ann to the side. "Love, you're a brilliant fighter, but your subtlety needs some work. You should just let Seb know how you feel."

Ann hugged her. "I never could hide anything from you."

As Angeline started to move away, Ann hugged her tighter. "Wait. Remember when I dropped Seb off at John's place? He kissed my cheek before he got out of the car."

Angeline leaned back to face Ann. "And you let him stop there?"

Ann laughed loudly. "This is why I love you, Ange. Oh! He also kissed me at the wake. That makes *two*!" She smacked Angeline's rear end as she walked away.

Angeline gasped. "You cheeky girl!"

Everyone stood in the middle of the arena. "Alright, today we're just practicing with the daggers, not our abilities." John pointed at Ethan. "This means you!"

Ethan laughed. "Yeah, alright. Wouldn't be much of a fair fight if I vanished."

John nodded. "I'll bet! Okay, Ethan and Najeeb, right corner. Amber and Josh, left corner. Seb, you and Ann take the left wall. Right wall, Ange and Zayne. Mariam and Dalila, centre stage ladies. Conor, you're with me. Conor and I will be handing out the wooden practice blades."

John thought that once he became the leader of the league, his friends whom he had known his entire life, may not fully appreciate his transition from peer to one of authority, let alone still maintain a friendly relationship with him. He was glad to see that he was wrong.

He found that leadership came rather naturally and wondered if there was something bred into the Gemini bloodline to make it that way, or if it was just that he had been groomed since a young age for that position. Either way, he found that he fell into his new role quite easily.

John walked among his friends. "You cannot be afraid to hit hard or play dirty. Marcus isn't going to hit to wound; he will be aiming to kill. We are going to be fighting for our lives, so fight like you mean it."

He and Conor finished distributing the practice daggers and moved to the side to begin sparring with each other.

On the other side of the Training Arena, Sebastian knew that he should not go easy on Ann. If she had to fight Marcus, she had to be ready.

While he was contemplating what to do or not to do, Ann crouched down and with a low spinning sweep kick, she knocked Sebastian to the ground.

"Seb, that was just embarrassing. Something on your mind?" She hoped it was her.

"Well, what I wasn't thinking was that I would be on my ass right now. Think you can help me off the floor?" He reached up for her hand.

She smiled smugly. "I guess it's the least I can do, since I'm the one who put you there." As she reached her hand down, Sebastian reached up and quickly grabbed it. He pulled her on top of him, rolled her over and pinned her to the floor.

Ann laughed and struggled to break free, but with Sebastian weighing nearly twice her own weight, she found she was unable to remove him. "Alright, big boy, let me up."

He leaned in close, his cheek touching hers. "And if I don't?"

Ann stopped laughing and her breath caught in her throat.

John tilted his head slightly to the right when he saw Sebastian on top of Ann. "Okay. Do you two have something to share with the rest of the class?"

They smiled, and together said, "No, sir, Mr. Evans."

John laughed and shook his head.

~~~~

The league members sparred for nearly an hour, switching partners every five minutes to give each of them the opportunity to spar with every other member. After they showered off, they each went their separate ways.

Angeline and Ann walked to John, Sebastian, and Conor. "Ann and I are heading up to Transcendence. Would you care to join us?"

"Thanks, but Conor, Seb, and I are going to try out some of the new weapons our doc here mentioned," John replied.

Ann shrugged. "Your loss boys. I've got some honey sesame chicken in the slow cooker that's been simmering all morning." The two ladies headed to the North American exit.

Teasingly, Angeline elbowed Ann as they walked. "So...I saw you got yourself some physical contact with Seb."

Ann laughed. "Not enough."

While Ann and Angeline headed to Transcendence, John, Conor, and Sebastian walked toward the Armory.

The Armory was a single entry room which was locked at all times. Access to this room was only available to league members and the Council of Seven.

As they walked, Conor said, "I saw a few guys from the Forge bringing in some really oddly shaped guns, so I stopped one of them and asked what they were. One was...I think it's better if you see it yourself. They posted instructions for each of the new weapons on the wall above them."

Sebastian looked at Conor. "Weapons we need instructions for? I know those Eyrasines in the Forge are brilliant, but what could they make that we would need instructions for?"

"I guess we will find out." John inserted his astral key and unlocked the Armory.

In the centre of the room was a large, round table with twelve chairs around it, where the league members could place their weapons and any ammunition.

Hung on the left wall of the Armory were many weapons used by past league members. These battle worn weapons served as a reminder that The League of Twelve had protected the City of Radiance, and all those with Eyrasine blood, for a very long time.

Along the back wall, bows and arrows, spears, longswords, short swords, pistols, and rifles were displayed.

The right wall was reserved for all newly forged weapons.

Conor pointed to the weapons he had seen earlier. "Here."

Sebastian walked past Conor. "I'm certain we don't need instructions."

Conor looked over his shoulder. "Just read them, Seb. I don't want to have to heal you because you shot yourself."

"Nah, the Healing Chambers are close by. They can patch me up if I need it," Sebastian joked as he examined one of the guns.

While Sebastian and Conor talked, John picked up a watch and its instruction sheet. With its cuff strapped to his wrist, he read the instructions. He was impressed. "Guys, check this out!"

John pressed two of the knobs on the watch simultaneously and metal hidden under the watch face extended outward and formed a blade eight inches in length.

"Impressive, but can it keep time?" Conor asked, sarcastically.

"Who cares!" Sebastian and Conor moved closer to John to examine the weapon on his wrist.

John held out his arm. "Even with the blade being so thin, the sheet says it is indestructible because it is made entirely of trichromiel."

He smiled as he pressed the two knobs to retract the blade. "This, I like!"

"Try this." Conor tossed Sebastian a folded throwing star, designed to look like a hair clip.

"What is this?" Sebastian turned it over in his hand.

"It's a hair clip. Put it on!" Conor smirked.

"I think it would look better on you!" Sebastian joked. "I wonder if Ann would like this," he whispered to himself.

John turned to Sebastian. "What, Seb?"

He looked up from the hair clip in his hand. "What? Oh, nothing." He tossed the folded star back on the table, picked up one of the two guns and loaded it.

"Read the instructions, Seb," John told him.

"Yeah, yeah, it's a gun. I've loaded plenty of guns." He placed the bullets inside the gun's chamber. "It loads like a small frame revolver. What could the instructions say that I don't already know?"

"Fine." John held up both hands up. "Just go to the Shooting Range before you start firing it."

Sebastian headed out of the Armory toward the Shooting Range. He turned the gun over in his hands. "It's a gun. It doesn't look *that* much different than any other revolver I've ever seen."

John looked over the instruction sheet Sebastian should have read, and hung his head. He growled through gritted teeth before running from the Armory to find Sebastian.

He shouted Sebastian's name as he ran toward the Shooting Range. "Seb! Stop!"

Sebastian turned around and looked at John with his eyebrows raised. "Uh, yes?"

"The bullets are spelled. They're truth bullets."

"Truth bullets?"

"The bullets are spelled to make whoever was shot with them speak the truth until their wound closes."

"Okay, I guess I shouldn't waste these on target practice."

Conor had followed John out of the Armory. "If Angeline were here, she would have ripped up one side of you and down the other! You know how she is about making sure everything is done properly."

Sebastian harrumphed. "Yeah, yeah. You guys hungry? I passed Cor Pizza on my way here and it smelled really good."

"Probably not as good as what the girls will be having, though," John said. "But pizza sounds good to me right now."

Conor agreed and slapped Sebastian lightly on his back, as he was feeling rather hungry himself. "Let's go. I'm not due at the hospital for hours so I have time."

"I'll meet you there after I put this gun back." Sebastian walked to the Armory.

~~~~

As they entered Jayded Ink, Angeline saw an opportunity to do some window shopping.

She and Ann walked into the main shop from the back room.

The black counter atop a glass display case held the cash register and impulse buy items, such as incense sticks and holders. Inside the display case were earrings, rings, and body jewelry. Sample books were stacked neatly on the far end of the counter.

Angeline picked up one of the sample books Jayde had put together and browsed through it.

Ann grabbed a few Skittles from a dish beside the cash register and popped them in her mouth.

"Ann, I need this!" Angeline exclaimed. She pointed to a tattoo that looked like an intricate wood carving. "It's rather similar to the marking we saw on the Eyrasine woman during the last portal opening."

"Ooh! That is nice! Leave Jayde a note."

"I believe I will." She picked up a pen and a sheet of paper that was tucked under the cash register.

Angeline recited as she wrote. "Ahem, Dearest, darling, Jayde. I beg you to please find time for me to pop in and get this brilliant marking straight away. I swear to you, I will name my first child after you. Ange."

Ann groaned and rolled her eyes. "How can she possibly resist that?"

"Oh, shut it! I was doing my very best to sound desperate! Let's go. I'm ravenous!"

They left Jayded Ink through the back door and walked the few blocks to Transcendence as the day was mild and the sky was clear. Once it was in sight, Angeline sighed. "Thank goodness! I wasn't altogether certain I wouldn't faint from hunger."

The two women entered the restaurant and headed toward the kitchen.

Vivian looked up at the sound of the door opening. "Hey, girls."

"Hey, Mom." Ann selected a mint from the dish of candies placed on the bar.

"Auntie Viv, is there a bowl of that divine chicken dish Ann prepared this morning with my name on it?" Angeline placed both hands on the bar and tried her best to look as though she was famished.

Vivian performed her best elegant curtsy. "Oh Angeline, of course there is. It's sitting in the slow cooker waiting for you to set it free."

Vivian walked to Ann and kissed her cheek before turning to leave through the front door. "I'm heading out. Lock up out back before you two leave."

"Got it, Mom."

"You pour the whiskey and water. I'll grab our food." Angeline walked around the bar and through the swinging double doors into the kitchen.

Ann rounded the bar and selected a bottle of honey whiskey.

These two had their own traditions outside of the league and honey whiskey was their drink of choice ever since they were in university together.

Angeline returned from the kitchen and placed two full plates on the bar then sat down while Ann poured them each a shot and a glass of water. After they clinked their glasses and finished their first shots, Ann filled their glasses a second time.

"Since we have a private moment, I have some news of my own," Angeline bubbled.

"Oh my *god*! I know that tone! What's his name? When did you meet him? Why am I only finding out now?" Ann blurted out as she leaned across the bar.

Angeline played with one of her earrings. "You know that Josh's sister Faith is the concierge at the Aemetta Suites, right?"

"Yes...and?"

"Well...Faith handed me a note with a bloke's name and room number, saying he had seen me and asked who I was and such. When Faith told him I was the Event Planner for the hotel, he said he wanted to arrange a Christmas gathering for his staff and would very much appreciate me ringing him up when I found a moment."

"Okay...so you phoned him...keep going."

"His name is Aidan Temple. He is the Chief Executive of Temple Technologies. His company is apparently filled with the hardest working people in all of Europe, according to him, and so he wanted to treat them to an extraordinary party. An approximate guest list of four hundred people. Some nice, light canapés and a more hearty meal, perhaps. I thought I would ask your opinion, since you know more about food than I do." Angeline knew that Ann was bursting to hear more.

Ann grabbed Angeline's arms, in anxious anticipation of a juicy story. "I don't care if he's feeding them bits of carpet and lint! Did you meet with him? What does he look like? What colour are his eyes?"

"Oh...well...I did bring one of your catering menus to his room. He was..." Angeline looked up. She acted as though she had to think hard to recall his appearance and demeanor.

No longer able to control her enthusiasm, Angeline blurted out, "Oh to hell with it! He is absolutely fantastic! He has dark brown hair with a bit of a wave, and deep, dark brown eyes that I nearly drowned in while I was speaking with him."

Angeline turned in her seat, crossed her legs, and placed her elbow on the bar. With the back of her fingers beneath her chin, she continued. "He asked me to supper, I accepted, and I have seen him twice since. For now, I'm keeping him at arm's length, but I find I'm thinking about him much more than I should. Now really isn't a good time for me to be away from the league."

Ann pointed her fork at Angeline. "There is a New Year's Eve party that I believe is being held in *your* hotel! Ask him to be your date! Sounds like he wouldn't say no."

"Enough of Aidan. You, Seb. What's happening there?"

"I think you're up to speed. Seb kissed me in the car and at the wake, and pulled me on top of him in the Training Arena, and yeah, that's it." Ann threw her head back and sighed. "Ange, it was all I could do to not throw my arms around him and kiss the hell out of his gorgeous mouth!"

Angeline wrinkled her nose and smiled. "He is rather dishy."

"Yeah...dishy. And hot." Ann turned her head and looked at Angeline sideways, a mischievous grin on her lips. "Did I mention hot?"

The two friends laughed.

Ann raised her shot glass. "To us. These guys don't stand a chance."

"Cheers, love. Here's to these blokes realizing they had better just give in to us," Angeline said with a wink, before they clinked their glasses together and finished their shots.

Angeline began to eat. She opened her eyes wide and placed her hand in front of her mouth. "Oh my, Ann! This dish is fantastic! I believe I may recommend this to Aidan for his Christmas gathering."

"Aww, thanks Ange," Ann replied coyly. "It is delicious, if I do say so myself."

The two girls ate until their plates were empty.

"I'll get these dishes to the sink then we can head out." Ann walked to the kitchen with their plates. Inside, she saw a bag of trash her mother hadn't put in the bins and shouted over her shoulder, "Ange, I'll be just a minute longer. There's a bag of trash I need to put out back."

"Right then, best get to it. Chop chop." Angeline placed two more shot glasses on the bar and filled them.

Wanting more water than what Ann had initially poured, Angeline walked behind the bar and refilled their glasses. She searched for lemon and finding none, she walked to the kitchen where she was certain there would be some in the refrigerator.

~~~~

In the alley beside Transcendence, Uvall paced impatiently.

Minutes later, Nybbas arrived and nervously glanced around as he approached Uvall. "What do you want?"

As one of the geist who worked for Azroth in Solar Flair, Nybbas was privy to many secrets whispered by the intoxicated patrons. If the price was right, he was always willing to sell this information.

"I'm looking for Stolas. I heard he was in town and I need you to find out if anyone at Solar Flair knows where he is, for old time's sake." Uvall grinned and handed Nybbas a thick envelope.

Uvall had worked with Nybbas selling information in the past and knew he wouldn't say no to the amount of cash he was being offered.

Nybbas opened the envelope and liked what he saw. He leaned against the restaurant's alley door and placed the envelope in his jacket pocket. "When do you need this information?"

"Yesterday." Uvall handed him a paper with Marcus' phone number written on it. "Call this number the minute you have the information. You'll get another payment if your information is good."

Nybbas heard someone unlock the door he was leaning against and quickly ran down the alley and around the corner.

Uvall climbed on top of the large steel garbage bin behind the door with a dagger in his hand. He had been watching the restaurant for nearly an hour before Nybbas showed up and knew that the only two people inside the restaurant were both league members.

Not expecting to encounter any geist, Ann was knocked to the ground as Uvall jumped at her.

With his blade in hand, he sliced Ann's shoulder.

A burning sensation shot down Ann's arm. She rolled over and jumped to her feet to face her attacker. She saw the black aura; she jumped and spun, kicking him in his face.

After he staggered backward, Uvall managed to regain his balance.

"Ange! Help!" She quickly scanned her surroundings for anything she could use as a weapon and picked up an empty wooden crate.

At the urgency in Ann's voice, Angeline dropped the lemons she had selected and ran through the kitchen. She knew there was no time to get her Soul Dagger from her purse on the bar and so, on her way to the back door, she grabbed a cast iron pan and a knife.

As Uvall raised his arm and threw his knife toward her, Ann held the crate in front of herself and blocked the blade, mere inches from her face. She rushed at the geist with the crate still in her hands. Her low hit took his feet out from under him.

He landed on top of her and brought his arm back to punch at her just as Angeline came through the door. Seeing Ann underneath a strange man with a black aura, she raised the cast iron pan and hit his head.

Uvall fell, unconscious.

"Where did this geist come from?" Angeline asked.

"No idea." Ann pushed Uvall off of her. "Help me drag him back into the restaurant."

After she removed Uvall's knife from the crate, Ann and Angeline dragged him through the kitchen and sat him on a chair next to the bar.

Ann went back into the kitchen and secured the back door. On her way back to the bar, she grabbed a few aprons hanging on the wall and ran them under the tap.

"Here." She walked out of the kitchen and tossed a wet apron to Angeline. "Help me tie him to the chair."

Once they had the geist secured, Angeline phoned John.

"Are you still in the City? Good. Grab the Dagger of Truth and get to Transcendence. We have a geist to interrogate."

Angeline placed her cell phone on the bar and retrieved her crystal needle from her purse to stitch up Ann's shoulder.

The Council of Seven had created a needle of indestructible crystal capable of healing a minor wound within a few hours, leaving only a hint of a scar. A translucent thread, not unlike the silk spun by spiders, was produced when the needle passed through flesh.

"Since when do geist hunt *us*?" Ann emphasized.

Angeline frowned. "I am beginning to think there is more going on here than just Marcus being back."

Ann saw the concern on her friend's face as she stitched her wounded shoulder. She looked at the rip in her shirt and wrinkled her brow. "Aw, Ange! I liked this shirt. We need to do some shopping."

Angeline laughed. "Only you, love, could think of shopping after being attacked."

7 – JAYDED INK

Kyle Shea, well over six feet tall, shared his father's strong build, blue eyes, and light brown hair, but otherwise, his appearance favoured his mother. His temperament was also much like his mother's, as her influence played a major part in his upbringing; his father was more of a side note.

Marcus placed his arm around his son's shoulders. "Your room is the first door on the right past the kitchen. You will find a key on the nightstand so that you may come and go as you please. Why not settle in, then we can talk while you eat. There is not much in my refrigerator, but you are welcome to whatever you can find."

Kyle picked up his duffel bag, found his room, and threw it on the bed. "There. All settled."

He looked around the room, bare except for the bed, a nightstand and a five-drawer chest. On his way back to the kitchen, he noticed a katana on his father's living room wall.

He chuckled. "Are you some badass Samurai now, Dad?"

"There is a lot you don't know about me, Kyle."

"Business first or should we get something to eat?"

"I will talk while you eat. There is a lot I need your help with."

"Alright." Kyle continued to the kitchen. He walked around the white and grey marble-top island surrounded by black seated stools and opened the refrigerator.

Kyle and his father were always at ease around each other and seemed more like friends, rather than father and son. When Marcus was home, he always made sure that Kyle was a priority. Their time together was always spent engaged in activities that were fun, yet served a purpose.

Marcus was certain he had an ally in Kyle.

He sat on the arm of his sofa and crossed his legs. "Do you remember the stories I told you when you were young? The stories about people that came from Eyras and made their home on Earth and how they continued their bloodlines here?"

Kyle closed the refrigerator and looked at Marcus. "You said they hunted people like Mom, right? You said if they knew about her, they would kill her."

"Exactly. They can sense somehow whether a being is geist, like your mother was, or an ordinary human, and all geist are killed. What I didn't tell you is that I have a brother, Jacob, and he was one of these people." Marcus clenched his fists. "I tried to protect you and your mother from my brother by keeping you both as far from him and the rest of the league as I possibly could."

Kyle looked at his father, confused. He was always told to be careful who he allowed into his life because league members were indistinguishable from everyone else, and now his father told him that his own brother was a league member.

"Okay, so...what exactly are you saying?"

Marcus lowered his head and cast his eyes upward at Kyle. His voice low and deep, he said, "I know where they are. I have an opportunity to eliminate this league and take their keys, but I need your help."

"Whoa! You want me to help you kill a bunch of people?"

Kyle's shock was not what he had hoped for.

"Not people, league members," Marcus spat out angrily.

He now realized he had to change tactics.

"And I don't mean to kill them, just replace them with those I can trust. It is this League of Twelve, that hunt and kill geist here on Earth. From an early age, they are taught to hate geist and told that they need to be eradicated. They are the reason your mother had to hide far away from Niagara Falls, where the league is based."

Marcus knew he had to control his rage. Kyle may be his son, but he also had his mother's kind, gentle heart.

"Mom is dead now. There's nothing we can do to change that. This league didn't kill her."

Marcus hoped that what he said next would sway his son to his favour.

He walked slowly toward his balcony and stared out into the evening sky. "I did not want you to know, but I see now I have no choice." He kept his back to Kyle. "Not long ago, my brother's son tried to kill me."

Kyle felt a wave of anger rush through him.

"His name is Sebastian Shea, the Cancer league member, and he is every bit as loathsome as his father."

He saw Kyle grit his teeth and clench his fists. He felt his son was ready to hear what role he would play. "I need you, Kyle, to push that hatred down and get the league to befriend you."

"I can't pretend to like this Sebastian knowing that he tried to kill you! You can't ask me to do this!"

Marcus' voice was stern. "I can and I have."

He paced through his living room, his hands clasped behind his back. "There is only one way to bring down the league, and that is from the inside. You are only part geist. The human in you masks the part of you that they can sense." As he said it, he wondered if that were indeed true.

He turned to face Kyle. "This is why I need you. As my son, your blood is also part Eyrasine. You could help me take their keys and create a new league, one that will protect geist. Can I count on you?"

Kyle snarled. "These people made it impossible for us to have normal lives and if they're as malicious as you're saying, yes, I will help you."

Marcus was pleased. "I need you to infiltrate the league. Let them get to know you, trust you. Once they let their guard down, I will let you help me end their reign."

"What do you need me to do?"

"There is a tattoo shop downtown called Jayded Ink. The entrance to the tunnel that leads to their secret City of Radiance is located somewhere in that shop and I want you to find it for me."

Marcus knew where the tunnel entrance was located when Roy Rivait ran the motorcycle repair shop that concealed it. Now that it was a tattoo shop, he knew the doorway would stand in the same location, however, he needed to know whether or not Kyle was truly on his side and he felt that this test of loyalty would do just that.

Marcus could see the focus on Kyle's face. "I need you to befriend the girl who works there. Her name is Jayde Rivait. She has long black hair, many tattoos, and piercings. She rather stands out."

"Okay, so I get this girl to trust me, then what?" Kyle listened intently.

Marcus had raised his son to fear the league and he was certain that helping to eliminate them was going to be Kyle's shining moment.

"You should be aware that her brother, Conor, is a league member. Just don't reveal too much about yourself to Jayde. She can't know your last name or that I am your father. You will most likely end up meeting your cousin Sebastian. You *must* control yourself. You cannot let him know how you feel about him."

He saw that Kyle was sufficiently angered. "Let's take this one step at a time." He handed Kyle a paper on which he had written the address for Jayded Ink. "First, get the girl to trust you. Then we can plan our next move."

Kyle believed that his father was a good man and that his cousin, the cousin he had never known, had tried to kill him. He felt that helping his father was the right thing to do. "I'll head to Jayded Ink once I've finished eating."

Marcus was gambling on the fact that Kyle, being only part geist, had an aura that was undetectable. If he was discovered, Marcus hoped his son would have enough sense to quickly get away.

~~~~

Jayde sat with her back to the door etching an image into the forearm of a rather unfit man.

The man under her needles licked his lips. "You do good work, Jayde."

She could spot a dirtbag from a mile away and when she saw this man walk into her shop, she was prepared for what would surely be a colourful conversation.

She didn't look up. "Thanks. I do my best."

"Really, I mean, you are so beautiful and talented."

"Ha! If you think flattery will earn you a discount, you are sadly mistaken."

She heard the bell on the front door chime as Kyle walked in.

"Take a seat, grab a magazine, and I'll be with you in about ten minutes," Jayde said, without turning around.

"No rush." Kyle felt confident that he would have no trouble getting this girl wrapped around his finger.

He walked slowly through the shop. There were tattoo designs and some sketches framed in black on the plum coloured wall behind Jayde's workstations. As he got closer to them, he noticed a signature on the bottom and realized that Jayde herself had designed these tattoos; he was impressed.

He stopped for a moment to watch Jayde work. Her focus was as impressive as her artwork.

Kyle then walked past a row of five chairs in an eclectic mix of colours with a coffee table set in front of them. The decor in the shop followed no set pattern and he was unable to discern anything about the woman who worked there. He picked up a binder from the coffee table in front of him, then saw something that most definitely made an impression.

As Jayde put the final details on her customer's tattoo, she felt his hand on her breast. She kept one hand on his forearm and didn't look up as she calmly placed her equipment on the table. With her other hand, she made a fist and quickly hammered it into her customer's mouth. She twisted his arm and rose to pin it behind his back.

"Get. Up," she shouted.

As she forced her customer to the exit, Kyle walked ahead of her and opened the door. She walked through it with her customer's arm still pinned behind his back.

"If you dare show your face here again, the bottom of my boot will be the last thing you ever see!" She then shoved him onto the sidewalk.

Still fueled by the audacity of her customer, Jayde walked back through the door that Kyle held open. "Thanks."

She was glad that she got a larger than usual deposit upfront from this customer.

Her tone was a little sharper than she intended when she thanked the man who held the door open, but if that scared him off, she was fine with that. She wanted to close up early and get something to eat anyway.

"You handle yourself pretty well. I have to say, not many people are quite so capable." He saw that Jayde's customer was most definitely in no shape to fight back. When Jayde stood, he could see that her body was solid muscle. At five foot nine, he thought she was as tall as she was beautiful, and apparently knew how to take care of herself.

Jayde raised her eyebrows and lowered her head. "You don't know me. Did you see anything you like?" She was unaware of the double entendre in her words.

"I just arrived in town and I spotted your shop. Thought I would stop in and see what you have to offer. Although, I may have seen more than you would have liked." Kyle raised an eyebrow asking a silent question.

"Nah. Just another day. Some guys see big tits and think with their dicks." She began to close up the shop.

Kyle nodded. "I'm Kyle, by the way. If I promise to keep my hands to myself, will you let me look around?"

"You have a few minutes. I'm closing up early. This girl needs some food!" She patted her stomach.

Kyle saw an opportunity. "I could use a bite myself." He walked to the counter, placed both hands on it and leaned forward. "Tell you what, I'll treat you to some food, then when I come back for my tattoo, you give me a deal. Sound fair?"

Jayde found she wasn't quite able to read him. He was gorgeous, but she felt that gorgeous men were, more often than not, arrogant self-righteous douchebags. She had far too much self-respect to consider a relationship with that sort of man.

She sat on the stool she kept behind the counter, crossed her arms, and looked directly at Kyle, still trying to size him up. "Well, that depends."

She decided that she wanted to see what this guy was made of. "Since you're new around here, I choose the place. Sound fair?"

Realizing Jayde had just used his line, he answered, "Of course."

Jayde stood up and grabbed her coat. "Cool. There's a great place a few blocks over. Do you like Italian?"

"If it's not moving, I'll eat it."

Jayde chuckled. "Okay, I'm parked in back."

"Hummer? Metallic grey?"

She glanced at Kyle. "Yeah. You're parked out back?"

"I'm parked beside you. Red mustang."

She walked to the front of her shop and locked the door. "Follow me out the back. If that asshole is still around, I will most likely finish him off, end up in prison, and need you to post bail."

Kyle was no longer confident in his abilities to sway this woman to his favour. She was talented, confident, and obviously held no punches.

As he followed her to the rear of the shop, he scanned everything he passed, taking note of what was where. He couldn't see a door that looked in any way special, but that didn't mean it wasn't there. His father knew this door existed and his first priority was to befriend Jayde and discover its location.

Once in the parking lot, Jayde got in her car and lowered the window. "The restaurant isn't far. Try to keep up."

Kyle smiled. "I'll do my best."

He walked to his car and sent a text message to Marcus. "At Jayded Ink. No doors look suspicious."

~~~~

When the text from Kyle came in, Marcus smiled. With his son's part of the plan underway, he phoned Ganga to inquire as to whether or not she had visited Crimson Spark.

Ganga groaned. "I'm heading there now. I'll text you when I'm done."

After the call ended, she punched the steering wheel. "Every step I take he wants a damn report!"

~~~~

Crimson Spark was a small, family-owned establishment that sold all varieties of herbs and teas. For anyone who knew how to ask, ingredients and incantations for innocuous magick spells could also be purchased.

A member of the Crimson Trad Coven, Maeve Zorida had been surrounded by magick her entire life and she was highly skilled in all aspects of white magick. She was, however, also fairly accomplished in the art of black magic, but the price for these spells and incantations was much higher and only available to a few select customers. These spells she kept secret from her mother and the rest of the coven.

Inside, Maeve waited on a customer.

Maeve was a petite woman with copper coloured hair that looked as though it were aflame. Her dark brown eyes accentuated her flawless porcelain skin.

Dressed in a cream coloured dress that hung in layers to her knees, she wore tight knee-high black boots with three-inch heels which gave her small frame a longer look.

She placed her customer's goods in a bag and accepted the money. "Enjoy." She then walked into the back room to get herself a cup of tea.

As the customer walked out, Ganga walked in.

Maeve suddenly sensed something in the air, an imbalance. She looked through the two-way mirror between the back room and the shop and saw Ganga. She huffed and rolled her eyes before she returned to the main room of the shop.

She forced a smile. "How can I help you?"

"Marcus sent me. He needs information."

"Marcus? I don't believe I know anyone with that name. Please, look around and let me know if you need help with anything." She smiled politely and hoped her discomfort wasn't obvious. She turned and began to walk around the counter, away from Ganga.

Ganga moved closer to her. "He said you would know about a witch that sealed a tomb and where to find it."

Maeve looked around her shop to make sure no one else was there. "Come." She quickly walked to the front door to lock it and changed the sign to read *CLOSED*.

With Ganga following, she headed to the back room. Maeve shut the door. "What do you know?"

"All I know is a witch sealed a tomb with Asmodeus in it and Marcus wants him out."

Maeve stood silent, her eyes wide. She knew who Asmodeus was. She also knew that Marcus was not a man who could be trusted. Cerra, her grandmother and the coven's high priestess before she died, had warned the coven about him years ago. He was the unstable twin of The League of Twelve member, Jacob.

Maeve also knew that each league family was wealthy. "Magick like that does not come cheap. What is he willing to pay?"

With one finger over her lips, Ganga looked up, cleared her throat and rather than using her own English accented voice, she altered her tone to match Maeve's Irish lilt. "Well, I believe Marcus will kill you if you don't and he will probably let you live if you do. Other than that, you'll have to ask him."

Maeve shook her head and exhaled loudly before she walked to her work desk to retrieve her business card. "Set up a meeting. I will go to him. Phone me once it has been arranged."

She let Ganga out through the back door then sat down at her work table, somewhat unsteadily. Her mother had told her about Asmodeus and the artifacts that were used to keep him entombed. She knew that Eric Turner used his blood to seal the tomb and that he died many years ago. Maeve's mother, Siobhan, had inherited her mother's grimoire and having read it herself, Maeve knew it held the sealing spell used to entomb Asmodeus. She also knew it held the incantation, as well as all necessary steps, to reverse the sealing.

She sat at her work desk in the back room, her hands clasped together on the desk in front of her. She had never performed such a complex spell before. This one needed blood, and blood magick was the most intense, the most depraved of all magick.

She left the sign on the front door reading *CLOSED*, and headed upstairs to her bedroom. Maeve and her mother lived together above the tea shop, finding it both convenient and practical.

On the way to her room, Maeve passed her mother. "I've got a booming headache, Ma. Would you mind tending the store for a bit? I think I need a wee lay down."

"Poor darlin'." Siobhan moved to touch Maeve's forehead. "You haven't a fever, have you?"

"Don't fuss, Ma," Maeve snapped as she moved away from her mother's hand. "I just need two aspirin and to lay my head down."

She continued to her bedroom and without turning around, said, "I turned the sign on the front door to read *CLOSED*. You'll be needing to change it."

Maeve entered her bedroom and locked the door behind her. She went immediately to the cedar chest at the end of her bed and unlocked it.

When Siobhan inherited Cerra's grimoire after she died, Maeve showed such interest in it that Siobhan agreed to let her keep it. She wanted her daughter to be well versed in all manner of magick; to know the difference between white magick and black magick, and to practice only magick that would do no harm.

She opened the cedar chest and removed her grandmother's grimoire to acquaint herself with the unsealing spell. She wasn't sure Marcus would pay her price, but decided that she would not help him unless she got everything she wanted - enough cash that she could leave town and start over somewhere far away, somewhere neither Marcus nor The League of Twelve could find her.

~~~~~

In Marcus' penthouse, Ganga handed him Maeve's business card and described her. "Her hair was the colour of fire and she had a dress that looked like it was made of rags."

"Interesting." Marcus looked at the red, sparkly card in his hand. "Phone Ms. Zorida and inform her that she is to meet me at The Rogue Bistro tonight at 7:30 p.m."

Ganga nodded before she walked to the elevator, all the while wanting to smash Marcus' smug face into his kitchen counter. She phoned Maeve as instructed and left a voicemail message.

Once Ganga was gone, Marcus had a few hours to himself before he was to meet with Maeve. He showered, dressed, and sat at his kitchen island, stroking the medallion around his neck.

While he was married, he had lost his focus and now, his future was clear.

~~~~~

Marcus entered The Rogue Bistro at 7:15 p.m. and was greeted by Cynthia, the stunning hostess, who wore a tight, short, royal blue dress, and matching stiletto heels.

Having patronized this establishment many times since his return to Niagara Falls, he was well acquainted with Cynthia. He kissed her cheek, and whispered, "Your beautiful smile could brighten even the dullest of days."

"Flattery won't be able to get you a table better than what we keep reserved for you." She picked up a menu. "Follow me."

He found Cynthia's sway hypnotic. Her curves and the smooth way she seemed to glide across the floor turned his thoughts to a meal that wasn't on the menu. He knew that he could have Cynthia fall victim to his charms with little effort, however, he had business to attend to.

As he slid into his corner booth, he ordered. "Please have a waitress bring me a glass of your best scotch, two fingers, neat. I am expecting a young woman with fiery red hair to join me shortly. Escort her to me as soon as she arrives."

Cynthia tilted her head in acknowledgement and walked toward the bar. She knew full well Marcus' eyes followed her every move.

Once his scotch arrived, he sipped it slowly and watched the restaurant's servers bustle about, tending to their patrons.

Maeve entered the restaurant precisely at 7:30 p.m. and stood for a moment just inside the doorway. She could sense nothing.

Cynthia approached her and saw her bright red hair. "Are you meeting an older gentleman tonight?"

"I am." Maeve narrowed her eyes.

Cynthia smiled. "Follow me, please."

At Marcus' table, Maeve remained standing.

"Cynthia, please bring my companion a glass of red wine."

Maeve turned to Cynthia. "I'm fine, really. I won't be here long."

"Nonsense. Sit," Marcus commanded. "You know why I've asked you here, correct?"

After Cynthia was far enough away, Maeve, still standing, placed her hands on the table and leaned toward Marcus. "I've not come here to socialize. You want something. I want to know what you are willing to give me."

"Well, that depends. What would you like? Money? Protection?"

"Money is a good start. And your word that nothing I do can be traced back to me."

"Done. Name your price?" The corners of his mouth curved up into a slight smile; he had thought the witch would ask for more.

Surprised at Marcus' pleasant demeanour, Maeve relaxed and took the seat across from him. She had expected him to be more detestable based on the stories about his past with The League of Twelve.

She pulled a pen from her purse, grabbed a napkin from the table, and wrote a number, certain that Marcus would never agree to it.

Marcus looked at the number then stared at her. "You set your sights high. I admire that. We have a deal."

Her price accepted, Maeve leaned toward Marcus and whispered, "Cerra had written that the tomb is found in a secret tunnel. She made no mention of where this tunnel is located."

Marcus smiled. He knew where the tunnel was. With Maeve confirming what Uvall had previously told him, he felt confident that he had the correct information to find and release Asmodeus.

Maeve glanced around the restaurant, making certain that no one was close enough to hear. She leaned across the table and spoke in a soft, low voice. "You must know that before you can open the tomb, there are two artifacts, stone statues, which you must first acquire. They were entrusted to the league the day the tomb was sealed, though they do not know their purpose. They were told to keep them far from each other. Where they are now, I do not know. I do know that the blood of Eric Turner sealed the tomb and it must be blood from a direct descendant of his, one who is currently a member of The League of Twelve, to open it."

"My dear, your information is exactly what I had hoped for." Marcus raised one eyebrow. "I will get in touch with you to arrange a day to exchange your services for my cash."

Marcus knew exactly where the artifacts were because he had seen them many times in Wells' Antiquities and Al Jawhara. More than once he had asked his father why there were two statues, one in each of the two stores, that were so similar and each time his father would tell him that they were special to the league. His father never elaborated and Marcus had assumed that it was just one more secret that only the league members were privy to. He now realized that his father offered no explanation because his father was unaware of their purpose. So many secrets were kept in the league, and it also appeared that some were kept *from* the league as well.

He removed an envelope from his inside jacket pocket and placed it on the table. "A small retainer. The remainder of your requested fee will be paid upon completion."

Relieved that their meeting was over, Maeve picked up the envelope and stood to leave.

"Will we not seal our deal?" Marcus held out his hand for Maeve to shake.

She brought her hand up to meet his and he grabbed it, pulling her to him. "If you try to double-cross me, I will kill everything you have ever loved while you watch."

Maeve jerked her hand out of his grip and glared at him before she left. When she left her shop to meet Marcus, the thought crossed her mind to turn her car around and inform the league about what he intended to do. She had been warned of the consequences of betraying The League of Twelve, but had never been told of anyone who suffered at their hands. With Marcus, however, she could see in his eyes that his threat was genuine.

Marcus remained in the restaurant to finish his drink. He was well aware of who Eric Turner's descendant was, her name was Ann Johnston. Ann's mother, Vivian, was a Turner when he first met her.

This latest bit of information was proof that he was on the right path to fulfilling his destiny. His thoughts turned to his son and he wondered if he was having the same good fortune.

8 – DAGGER OF TRUTH

Inside Transcendence, John, Conor, and Sebastian headed straight to the geist that Ann and Angeline had tied to a chair. Sebastian used every ounce of strength he had to punch the still unconscious geist and knocked him and the chair over.

John reached for a glass of water on the bar and poured it onto the geist's face.

Uvall awoke, coughing. He saw John and Sebastian and spat out some water. "No thanks. I'm not thirsty."

John righted the chair and removed the Dagger of Truth from his coat pocket. He gripped the polished white bone hilt tightly and removed the sheath to reveal its silver coloured trichromiel blade. Engraved with an intricate design of each of the league members' astro sigils, it was spelled so that anyone who was cut by this blade was compelled to speak truthfully until their wound closed.

John sliced Uvall's thigh. "Why are you here?"

Uvall shouted in pain as the effects of the dagger worked instantly. "I was told to watch every league member in North America." He was surprised that he offered the information so freely. "What did you do to me?"

The league members were impressed by how quickly and efficiently it worked, as none of them had seen it in use before.

Conor stepped toward the geist and shouted, "Told by who? Who are you working for?"

Uvall confessed. "Marcus Shea." He struggled against the dagger's power.

At the mention of Marcus' name, Sebastian dug his fingers into the fresh wound on Uvall's leg. In a tone filled with rage, he demanded, "How long has Marcus had you watching us?"

Uvall growled in pain through gritted teeth. He tried in vain to fight the influence of the blade. "Over a year."

Angered that Marcus had been watching them without any of the league members suspecting, Sebastian shouted, "What does he want?"

Unable to lie or keep silent, Uvall laughed. "He's going to replace you all with geist and kill you, one by one. When he has all of your keys, he'll control the portal. Once we take your DNA and replicate you, we can use your keys to open the gates, and from there, we can go to any world where there's a portal. Omm of Eyras was stupid not to remove the ones he didn't want."

Ann laughed. "This geist thinks he can get to other worlds through our portal."

"Marcus said..." Uvall began.

"Marcus," Angeline interrupted. "You haven't learned that Marcus can't be trusted?"

Sebastian needed answers. "Why are you helping Marcus?"

"Marcus promised that if we help him, he would open the portal to our world permanently, so that every last geist can leave the hell we call home."

As he watched their faces, Uvall began to question everything Marcus had promised. Then he remembered that Marcus planned to release Asmodeus.

"How many others are helping him?" John needed to know what they were up against.

Uvall still tried unsuccessfully to resist the blade's power. "He's recruiting more geist every day. He's going to release the most powerful geist from the tomb your league trapped him in. Once Asmodeus is free and we've replicated each of you, Marcus is going to use him to help end your league."

Everyone stood silent for a moment. There had been no mention of Asmodeus for so long, that he seemed to be more of a story than a real being. If Asmodeus was freed from his tomb, the threat level that they faced would increase immeasurably.

"He killed one of your families, but I suppose you know that already. Marcus gave me his knife and told me to get to the house, set off the alarm and wait for the cops," Uvall confessed. "Thing is, I didn't have to trip the alarm. The cops showed up not long after I got there. Death by police wasn't as painful as I thought it would be."

Sebastian now understood what the constable had told him.

Uvall laughed. "I'd love to see their faces when they find my last replicant is just a pile of greasy clothes."

"What are you talking about?" Ann asked.

"Something the league doesn't know. Interesting."

"Why is your replicant a pile of greasy clothes?" John demanded.

Uvall shook his head. "Aah! When a geist's replicated body is killed by anything other than a Soul Dagger, it turns to greasy gunk a few hours after death. Nothing left for anyone to identify."

"Where is Marcus now?" Conor snapped.

Uvall snickered. "He's here. He's been living in a penthouse downtown, close enough to walk to your tattoo shop."

John demanded, "Where is this penthouse?"

"1544 Hillcrest Road. Aah!" He knew that Marcus was going to kill him for revealing so much information.

Sebastian moved to hit him, only to have Ann grab his arm. "Seb, he can't talk if he's got your fist in his mouth. We need more answers."

As he relaxed his fist, Sebastian faced Ann, his teeth clenched. "Marcus needs to die."

Uvall smirked. "Marcus is a patient man. He wants to make you all feel defeated, to keep you thinking you can't win against him. Once you've all given up, he'll take you down, one after the other. I heard he tried a few years ago. He killed someone in one of your families, but you all just kept on going, like the death meant nothing."

John furrowed his brows and thought back. "The only person who was killed in a league family besides Seb's was…" His voice trailed off as he thought of his own mother.

He grabbed Uvall's throat. "Who was it? Who did Marcus have killed?"

"I don't know," Uvall replied indignantly through a cough. "It wasn't me that killed her."

"Her? How did Marcus kill her?" John's was enraged.

Uvall clenched his teeth as he tried to remain silent, but the influence of the blade was just too strong. "He made it look like a car accident. A hit and run."

The league members looked at each other, shocked at this revelation.

With the knowledge that his mother's death was not an accident like he believed, John screamed in anger and with a wave of his hand, the water in a glass on the bar streaked across the restaurant.

John had recently discovered that his ability gave him control over the four elements. He had been privately experimenting with small things - the water in his shower, the flame on his gas stove at home, but found he really had to concentrate in order to be successful. It seemed that his state of mind also played a role in his abilities' performance. Raw emotion, such as the rage coursing through him, seemed to be a prime catalyst.

The intensity of his reaction concerned Ann. She placed her hand on his shoulder. "John, I can feel your power. You haven't had this ability long enough to know what would happen if you lost control."

As John pushed down the rage inside him, he removed his Soul Dagger from his pocket and plunged it into Uvall's replicated heart. The geist went still then gasped; a Soul Dagger shows no mercy to a replicated human vessel. Uvall disintegrated, along with his soul mist, and became nothing more than gritty ash.

Once Uvall had perished, John turned to Sebastian. "What do you know about your uncle?"

"Not much." He leaned against the bar. "Dad rarely spoke of him, just little bits here and there. I knew he existed, but I hadn't met him until…"

Sebastian choked back his grief and continued. "Dad said that he and Marcus had a falling out years ago, Marcus left and they hadn't spoken since. Mom told me a few things, but she didn't say much. Just that she was glad he left."

John knew what had happened, knew why Marcus left; he also knew he had to keep it from Sebastian.

Sebastian continued. "I've seen a few photos of him with my dad and mom, so I knew he was dad's twin. He was an engineer, but other than that, I know as much as any of you."

He heard Ann wince in pain as she placed her hand over her wound. "Hey Ann, why don't you take some of my healing."

"I think I will. Thanks, Seb." She took a seat at the bar.

As Ann began to borrow Sebastian's self-healing ability, he could feel the energy leave his body; it was an intimate connection he could only share with her.

~~~~

John had to inform the rest of the league about Marcus' plans. He walked to Angeline. "Ange, can you set up a conference call with everyone, please? This can't wait."

Once the rest of the league members were up to speed, John said, "Marcus has Seb's key, but he didn't take his ring so he must not know that the rings are what bring out our abilities. We need to make certain he doesn't find out."

John looked at Sebastian. "Once we have Marcus, we need to question him before we bring him to the Immortals."

Sebastian lifted his head slightly and smiled a caustic smile. "I'll try to keep him somewhat conscious until you're done with your questions, but he's mine."

"I want him dead as much as you do, but the Immortals want him alive. We have to let them deal with him."

"They can have what's left of him," Sebastian snapped.

"Fair enough." John turned his attention back to the conference call. "I think that's it. If anyone…"

Ann interrupted. "That's not everything."

John, Sebastian, Angeline, and Conor all looked at Ann with lines of confusion on their faces.

With everyone aware of Asmodeus, Ann felt it was time for the rest of the league to know the secret her bloodline had kept for so many years.

"There's something you all need to know. My bloodline has a secret, a secret that even other league families weren't to know about, unless it was absolutely necessary. With Marcus planning to free Asmodeus, I think that time has come."

As she watched the faces of her friends, she could see the questions running through their minds. She inhaled deeply and exhaled slowly before she began.

"Asmodeus was the most powerful of all the geist, as well as their leader here on Earth. He was a hybrid - part geist, part human, and part demon."

Ann watched as her friends absorbed this revelation. "He was captured and entombed, left to live out his days imprisoned. During that time, my great grandfather was the Taurus league member. He is the one who sealed the tomb...with his blood."

"Oh, love." Angeline placed an arm around Ann's shoulders. "What an awful burden for you to bear alone."

Ann sighed. "There's more."

Angeline sat and looked at Ann. They rarely kept secrets from each other. For Ann to have kept this from her made her realize the gravity of her words.

Ann continued. "Cerra, the high priestess from the Crimson Trad Coven, wrote the spell that helped my great grandfather seal the tomb and ensure that Asmodeus could not get free. The location of his tomb is known only to Taurus league members. That means my mother, my grandfather, and I are the only living people who know where Asmodeus is. My bloodline is charged with guarding his tomb. If Marcus unseals that tomb, we will be facing a far greater threat than Marcus alone could ever be."

As Amber listened through the phone, her thoughts drifted to Sebastian on the floor atop Ann in the Training Arena. He was the just like the others. They all acted like the best of friends, yet rarely made an effort to include her in their plans outside of the league. She never felt as though she was truly one of them. They only needed her because of her DNA.

Marcus was just like her, an outcast. He had everyone in the league shaken up and she began to think that maybe she was meant for something greater than being the keeper of a key. If she were to make a deal with Marcus, one where she could join him and be protected from the other league members, she could gain Marcus' trust. In time, she would control the portal with him. She could think of no reason why he would turn down an offer of help, especially inside help. She was sure he wouldn't dismiss her or make her feel insignificant. He would recognize her true destiny.

John paced in front of the bar, his hands together behind his back as he spoke. "Now that we know where Marcus lives, we can get Seb's key back. I want someone watching his building 24/7 and reporting back until we get that key and get him to the Immortals. This starts now. Who wants the first shift?"

Amber piped up eagerly. "If Angeline will give me the time off, I can take first shift. We've enough staff to handle things in Transcendent. I could get there in just over an hour."

"Oh, absolutely, love," Angeline replied.

John nodded. "Okay, Amber, when you arrive, you are on until midnight, North American time. Angeline, Zayne, and I will make a schedule for the rest of us to take four hour shifts. Switch up if you need to. Since this is the first shift, I will join you for a bit, Amber. I just want to make sure everything goes smoothly."

Amber rolled her eyes and shook her head. *I'm sure if it was Annie you wouldn't need to babysit her.*

"I believe I could help as well, John," Najeeb offered. "Using my ability as a thermalist, I would be able to see if Sebastian's key is indeed in Marcus' home. As our keys are part organic, they give off a rather unique heat signature."

"Sounds good Najeeb, thanks. How long will it take you to get to North America?"

"I can be there in approximately forty-five minutes."

Sebastian stood. "I'll join you as well."

~~~~

Najeeb scanned Marcus' building. "I need a moment to filter out the heat signatures of everything that isn't the key."

He took a few deep breaths. The building had ten floors, so Najeeb knew he would have many heat signatures to sort through before he could pinpoint the astral key, if it were in fact there.

The tenants, their stoves, lights, and plants, as well as anything that emitted heat, had to be disregarded. Najeeb cleared his mind and focused all of his energy on finding the heat signature of Sebastian's key.

After a few moments, he found it. "I see it. It is on the North side of the top unit. It seems to be...wait, someone is leaving that unit."

"It has to be Marcus," John said under his breath. *Finally something in our favour*, he thought. "Let's just make sure it is Marcus."

"The heat signature is most definitely that of a man." Najeeb continued watching whom he believed was Marcus and gave a play-by-play of his movements.

"He seems to be exiting the elevator and walking past vehicles. He must be in the parking garage." He looked up toward the penthouse. "The key is still where I first saw it. He didn't take it with him."

They waited in their car until they saw a vehicle exit the parking garage.

"I'll take this one," Amber said quickly. Her ability, hypertelescopic vision, allowed her to see objects at a great distance with perfect clarity.

Even with the streetlights shining, there was not enough light for the others to be able to confirm whether or not Marcus was in the vehicle.

Amber turned to Sebastian. "He's your dad's identical twin, yeah?"

John looked into his rearview mirror and saw Sebastian's lip turned up in a sneer. "Yes."

At the sound of Sebastian's gruff response, everyone in the car fell silent.

After a few minutes, Marcus exited the parking garage.

Amber knew the others could not see who was driving the vehicle and decided to keep to herself the fact that it was indeed Marcus behind the wheel. *If I didn't know better I would think that I was looking at Jacob*, she thought.

Without any hesitation, she lied. "It is a man, but it's not Marcus."

"Alright, Amber, just sit tight and keep watch," John instructed. He looked at Najeeb. "You're certain there's no one near the key?"

"Absolutely certain."

John turned in the driver's seat. "Seb, are you up for a little B and E?"

"You bet."

John got out of the car and before he shut the door, said, "Amber, if you see Marcus while we're in his place, phone me."

"Will do, John." Amber moved to the driver's seat. She smile outwardly as she thought, *Phone you? I thought I would just holler out the window for you, but you are in charge.*

"Najeeb, stay with Amber until Seb and I are done. If you see anyone heading our way, let me know."

"I will."

John and Sebastian walked to the entrance of the building and entered behind a man texting on his phone. Heads down, they walked to the elevator and once they had entered, John reached in his pocket for his keys, which included his lock picking tools.

Sebastian chuckled. "You have to teach me the fine art of picking a lock sometime."

John looked back at Sebastian and smiled as he worked the lock.

The elevator opened to the penthouse suite. "Quick, quiet and out."

Sebastian knew that if they disturbed any part of the penthouse, Marcus would know they had been there. Despite this, he wanted to break and ruin everything his uncle had.

Without turning to look at John, he replied, "I know what needs to be done."

He spotted his father's katana on the wall and growled.

John loudly whispered, "You can hate him all you want but right now, let's just find your key."

Sebastian turned toward the back wall and saw his key; it sat to the left and slightly behind a decanter of whiskey. Marcus hadn't even bothered to conceal it. He held up the key for John to see. "Let's go."

They slipped out of Marcus' penthouse as quietly as they had slipped in. As they passed the car where Amber kept watch, Sebastian tapped on the hood and opened the door for Najeeb. "You're free to go, Najeeb."

Amber lowered her window. "You've got your key then?"

Sebastian held his key up for her to see.

John looked at Amber. "Phone me if Marcus shows up."

"Of course."

As the three men walked away, John said, "Thanks for your help tonight, Najeeb."

"No problem, my friends. I rather enjoyed the opportunity to use my ability."

~~~~~

In the surveillance vehicle, Amber felt an anger rush through her. "Thank you, Amber. We appreciate your help, Amber. You did great, Amber." She huffed. This made her decision much easier. "If they think they don't need me, I know someone who will."

If joining with Marcus was what it took to get the recognition she knew she deserved, then she was prepared to do just that. As her thoughts bounced between Sebastian and Marcus for nearly an hour, she saw Marcus walk back into the building. "Sorry, John, but I think I'll handle Marcus my way."

Amber hurriedly got out of the car and reached the front door just behind him and put her foot in the doorway so it wouldn't shut and lock. She followed him to the elevator, walked past him as the doors opened, then turned around to face him.

Marcus knew he had been followed since he entered the building. Inside the elevator, he looked at Amber before he turned toward the control panel and inserted his key in the penthouse button.

He knew who this girl was, she was from the European faction of The League of Twelve. Ganga had sent him photos of each of the members she was charged with surveilling.

When the elevator door shut, Amber began. "Marcus. It's nice to finally meet you after hearing so many things about you. Name's Amber."

He raised one eyebrow. "And I thought I would have to find you in order to kill you, yet here you are. Death must be something you are looking forward to. Or is it the foreplay?"

"I wouldn't say I have a death wish. Which brings me to why I'm here. I know what you want and I can help you get it."

"What is it you think you know?" Marcus wondered what this insolent girl could possibly know of his plans.

"I know about Asmodeus. I also know you're planning to have your geist friends replicate every member of the league and take their places. I think I can help you."

The elevator door opened.

Surprised at what Amber said, Marcus stretched his arm out and invited Amber into his home. "You've peaked my interest, little one. Please, come in."

She entered ahead of him and looked around as she walked through his living room. "Nice place, Marcus." She sat on the plush leather couch and ran her hands across the material, noting the quality. Her eyes scanned the living room, impressed with Marcus' taste.

She rose and walked to his bar. After she poured herself a glass of cognac, she turned toward Marcus. "Want one?"

The anger that rose in Marcus was nearly visible.

Amber knew she had the upper hand and that he would soon see that he needed her. It felt good knowing that someone saw her value.

She strolled through the penthouse, ran her finger across the bar, and lifted a small clock from a table. As she continued her scrutiny of Marcus' home, she stopped to examine the katana on the wall. "The league has you under surveillance. I took first watch. You should probably think about leaving because they plan to bring you to the Immortals if they catch you."

Marcus's nostrils flared and he gritted his teeth.

"Annie caught your geist spying on her at Transcendence. He's dead. She called in her boys and they killed him with a Soul Dagger but not before he gave up everything he knew about you. They know what you're planning."

Marcus slammed his fists on the kitchen island. He took a deep breath and turned to face Amber. "So, I've lost Uvall. What is it *you* want?"

"I'm here to offer my services. I can be your eyes and ears inside the league. All I want is your guarantee that I won't be replaced by a geist."

Her drink nearly gone, she walked to the bar to pour herself another. "I keep my key and we work together. I just want to be free of the league."

"Alright." Marcus was intrigued. He walked to Amber, took the glass out of her hand and placed it on the bar. Before he agreed to her terms, he needed her to prove her worth.

"First I want you to bring me something. Something precious to the league. There are two artifacts that I want. Do you know what objects I'm talking about?"

"Artifacts?"

Marcus closed his eyes and rubbed them. "Yes, Amber, artifacts." He began to doubt the abilities of this girl.

"Stone statues. One is in the London antique shop, and the other is kept in the jewelry store in Cairo."

His patience wore thin and through gritted teeth, he asked, "Have you seen them?"

"Yeah, I've seen them. Never knew what the story was behind them, though. What do you need them for?"

He ignored Amber's question, clasped his hands behind his back and began to pace. "If I agree to accept your offer of assistance, what sort of guarantee are you offering? You see, I learned long ago that members of The League of Twelve cannot be trusted to keep their word."

"I can get you one of the artifacts the next time I'm on surveillance duty. Give me your number and I'll ring you up when I have it."

Should Amber attempt any sort of deception, Marcus had no qualms about killing her. He nodded in agreement. "You have yourself a deal."

He scribbled the number of his burner phone on a piece of paper and handed it to Amber.

She picked up her drink and finished it then walked to the elevator. She pushed the button to open the door and just after she entered, she turned, and with a sly smile on her lips, said, "My shift ends at midnight. You'd do well to be gone by then."

As the doors slowly closed, she added, "Oh, and Sebastian got his key back while you were out earlier. You probably should have hidden it better."

Shocked, Marcus watched the elevator doors close. He walked to the far end of his bar and saw that the Cancer key was no longer beside the decanter of whisky.

He snarled. "I will rip his beating heart from his chest when I find him!"

He closed his eyes tightly. There were several homes he had throughout the country that he could use, places the league would never think to look for him.

Marcus poured himself a glass of scotch. Once he had regained his composure, he picked up his cell phone to phone Ganga. She had to take over for Uvall in tracking down Stolas.

Before he dialed her number, he walked to his sofa. His cell phone began to ring. He answered it hesitantly as he did not recognize the number displayed on the screen. "Yes?"

"I know where Stolas is," Nybbas whispered. "Uvall said you would get me the rest of my money."

"And I shall. Meet me behind The Rogue Bistro in twenty minutes."

~~~~

Marcus pulled his coat tight around him as he walked to The Rogue Bistro. Winter seemed to have made an early appearance and he found the wind to be especially biting.

As he approached the alley behind the restaurant, he saw someone pace impatiently and assumed it was the one with whom he was to meet.

Nybbas walked to him. "You bring the money?"

"You will get paid if your information is good."

"The information *is* good! I want my money now!"

"You have two options: One, you give me the information, I get in touch with Stolas, and then I pay you."

"Or?"

"Or two, I slice your throat right here and trap your essence in a discarded olive jar. Take your time. I'm in no rush."

Nybbas could see that Marcus meant what he said. "Stolas left town. Said he's going back to the west coast. A little town called Fayette."

As Marcus walked away, Nybbas added, "So I get my money when you find him, right?"

He stopped, turned around and glared at Nybbas. He did not respond before he turned again to leave the alley. He reached into his pocket and removed his cell phone to see if Kyle had left a message. Finding none, he sent a text. "Any progress, son?"

~~~~

Inside Jayded Ink, Kyle watched as Jayde finished an amazing steampunk clock and rose design on her customer. He found her artistic talent was impressive. His phone signaled an incoming message; it was from his father. He chose not to respond since he had nothing new to tell him.

Jayde stood behind the cash register. "After your deposit of three hundred, the balance is one hundred fifty eight dollars and seventy five cents."

"This is so awesome! Thank you so much!"

"Thank you," Jayde replied. She accepted and counted the cash she was handed. "You know where I am if you want the other arm done."

Her satisfied customer nearly floated out the door.

Kyle leaned against the wall, folded his arms across his chest, and crossed his feet. "I wouldn't be surprised if you had a bunch of that girl's friends in here next week. You would swear you had just told her she won the lottery!"

"Well, I do kinda rock." Jayde's smile was confident.

He walked closer to her. "Since we've known each other for a while now, I believe it's time for me to get my end of our deal."

"Have you made your choice yet?" Jayde thought that he may not be referring to a discount on the price of a tattoo.

As he walked up to her, nearly into her, Jayde felt her breath catch in her throat, a sensation that she was not accustomed to.

Kyle then reached down and lifted a magazine off the table beside her. "I think it was in this book. It's the symbol for Capricorn breaking out of the Earth. If you've got time right now, I've got no plans."

"So you like that astrological stuff?" Jayde was curious and suspicious all at once. There was no way Kyle could know that her family was linked to their astrological sigils in ways he could not even begin to comprehend. It was either coincidence or luck that Kyle was into sigils. "I'm clear for the next three hours."

As they both sat at Jayde's workstation, Kyle rolled up his sleeve. "How long have you been an artist?"

"As far back as I can remember. If you listen to my mother, I was drawing as soon as I could hold a crayon." She smiled while she unwrapped a disposable razor. "Deltoid?"

"Sounds good."

"Do you trust me to draw freehand or would you like me to make a stencil?" She tilted her head slightly downward and looked up at Kyle.

He laughed. "I think I trust your artistic ability."

"Ha! Good answer."

As she wiped Kyle's arm with a sterile alcohol prep pad, she told him more about herself. "Mom is my biggest fan, hands down. I drew on anything and everything when I was young. My parents didn't even mind if I sketched on the wall or the floor."

She chuckled. "My father went so far as to buy a frame and put it around a pencil sketch of a butterfly and the moon I did on the wall beside the staircase. How many kids can say that?"

"I would guess not many." Kyle watched Jayde as she etched masterfully on his arm. He thought Jayde was an amazing girl - gorgeous, talented, with a mind sharp and focused. The time it took Jayde to complete the tattoo seemed like minutes to him.

It was time he let her know that he wanted her. "If I kissed you right now, would that get me tossed out the door?"

Jayde was falling for this guy, hard. She'd had a few boyfriends in the past, but none made her feel the things she felt in that moment. Kyle was easy to talk to and best of all, she didn't scare him like she did so many other guys.

She leaned in and kissed him, long and deep. "Let me lock up."

After she locked the front door, she walked to him, grabbed his hand, and led him to the backroom. She welcomed the assault on her mouth. Kyle's kiss was gentle but forceful, soft yet demanding.

The back door opened and Jayde quickly pulled Kyle behind some stacked boxes and covered his mouth with her hand.

"...not only is he responsible for killing Jacob, Maxine, and Marianne, and nearly killing Seb, but now we find out that Marcus killed Yvette." Ann growled.

As Ann and Angeline walked into the storage closet, Kyle looked at Jayde and whispered, "Someone you know?"

"Yeah, just a couple of family friends," Jayde whispered in reply. She covered Kyle's mouth with hers to get his mind off of what he just heard. When she heard a set of keys unlock the front door, she pulled away from him and placed both hands on his chest. "Wait here."

With Jayde gone, Kyle walked through the back room. He noted shelves along the back wall on which were various bottles of ink and supplies. The large rectangular table in the centre of the room, held a few sketches that seemed unfinished. He knew he didn't have much time so he walked to the storage closet.

When he opened the door, instead of the two family friends, he saw shelves lined with tattoo machines, various office supplies, and sketch pads. He glanced around and noticed that the left corner was bare. His feelings for Jayde had started to deepen and he felt awful sneaking around in her shop without her knowledge, but he had a mission. His father was counting on him.

He examined the wall and realized it was the doorway his father had wanted him to find. His father...he thought surely the Marcus that the two women spoke of couldn't be his father. He'd been told that Sebastian had tried to kill *him*, not the other way around; his father wasn't a murderer.

After he closed the closet door, Kyle walked to Jayde at the front of the store.

Jayde saw him exit the back room. She narrowed her eyes and pursed her mouth before she turned her attention back to her father. "Dad, this is Kyle."

Roy Rivait was a tall man, yet he stood two inches shorter than Kyle. His short brush cut hair gave him the appearance of an army drill sergeant. More often than not, he acted the part where his daughters' boyfriends were concerned.

Kyle extended his hand. "Good to meet you, sir."

"And you. Jayde has told me absolutely nothing about you." Roy suspiciously eyed the young man whose lips were as swollen as his daughter's. "Jayde, why not invite your friend to dinner soon. I'm sure your mother would like to meet him."

"Easy, Dad! We've only seen each other a few times. I'm sure that if we decide to make a thing of...whatever this is, that he'll come around for supper a time or two."

Kyle interjected. "Why wait? I'm always up for a good meal."

Jayde glared at the satisfied look on Kyle's face, but inside, she was glad her father had made the invitation.

He handed her payment for his tattoo before he left. "Thanks again. Just let me know when and where for that dinner invitation."

With Kyle gone, Jayde shouted, "Dammit, Dad! What the hell?"

The corners of Roy's mouth turned up in a sarcastic grin. "What? Don't think that I can't recognize the aftermath of a make out session."

~~~~~

Kyle was no longer sure he was doing the right thing. Could his father be a murderer? What kind of coincidence could it be that his dad had him watching these people and they just happened to mention that a man named Marcus killed four of their friends? Unnerved, these questions ran through his mind as he rode the elevator to his father's home.

He had never questioned his father when he was young and the mere fact that he now doubted him left him feeling disillusioned.

Inside the penthouse, Kyle stopped in front of the katana on the wall. He noticed an engraving on the hilt that read, *To Jacob, with gratitude.*

Marcus entered the living room wearing only a towel, his hair wet. "Son, I wasn't expecting you so soon. Have you been able to locate the door we talked about?"

"I did. I have a question." Kyle stood facing the katana.

"Anything. I'm an open book." Marcus held out his arms, his palms facing upward.

"Why does the hilt read *To Jacob, with gratitude?*"

"My brother gave it to me before he died."

"How did he die?"

"He was murdered in his home by a burglar."

"I thought you hadn't spoken to him since you left, since before I was born."

"Why are you questioning me?" Marcus demanded.

He saw the surprised look on Kyle's face and breathed in deeply to calm himself. He knew he had to keep his son on his side.

"Before he was killed, my brother brought me this blade as a peace offering. I told him to shove it up his ass. He hadn't wanted to be part of my life, hadn't tried to

93

contact me all these years and suddenly he wanted me back in his life? I wanted nothing from him. He told me to keep it. When I found out he was murdered, that katana was the only thing I had to remind me that I ever had a brother."

His father had never been a sentimental man, and Kyle found it hard to believe what he was being told. He decided to reserve judgment for now. "I guess that makes sense."

He turned toward the balcony. "By the way, I did find the door. It's in a storage closet at the back of the tattoo shop."

"I knew you would find it. Oh, and Kyle, I need to be out of town for a few weeks. Feel free to stay here as long as you like." Marcus walked away, satisfied with his son's loyalty. "Phone me day or night if you need me."

9 – FINALLY

Sebastian left the realtor's office and looked at the keys in his hand, ready to begin the next in his life.

After he arranged for a moving truck, he checked the time and called John. "Hey, are you ready for some heavy lifting?"

"We were just waiting for your call. James and I will meet you at the house."

Sebastian phoned Zayne and Angeline next. Not everyone in the league was able to help, but with those who could, he was sure his new place would be set up in record time. He drove to the truck rental company, signed the necessary paperwork, then drove to his family home, unaware that Ganga was not far behind him.

As she parked her vehicle a few houses away from the Shea home, Ganga waited. She knew that Uvall had just been killed and wanted to keep her distance.

She phoned Marcus and let him know that Sebastian was moving out. "I'll tell you where he ends up. And about Stolas, no one can find him. He's not in Fayette anymore."

Marcus looked at the phone in his hand and growled.

~~~~~

Sebastian, Conor, Jayde, Ann, and Angeline worked tirelessly most of the day as they moved Sebastian's belongings into his new home, a condo in a building downtown close to the law firm. When they had finished, they left the moving truck at the Shea home for John, James, Zayne, and Josh to load the bigger items.

Ann and Angeline headed to Transcendence to get some food for the hungry crew and drove past Ganga who sat in a vehicle and watched as they came and went.

Ganga noted that they returned with another league member, one she recognized from London. She settled in for a long night of surveillance.

~~~~~

"I heard there was a party here." Ann smiled as she walked into the condo with a large tray of food. "We have Teriyaki chicken, some salad, dinner rolls and for dessert, macadamia nut cookies with dark and white chocolate."

"As well as some Chivas and a case of beer," Angeline added, as she and Amber entered behind Ann.

"Jayde and I are almost drunk! What were you guys doing?" Conor asked with a slight slur. Even though he could heal his inebriation, sometimes he chose not to.

Jayde raised her beer and clinked her brother's glass. The Rivaits could drink nearly anyone under the table.

Ever since Marcus had returned, everyone in the league felt stressed and tense, especially the North American faction members. This gathering was just what they needed, time spent among friends was a necessary diversion. They ate, drank, and talked about things that had no connection to their league duties.

Sebastian had made certain that his music collection was in one of the first loads brought from the house.

Jayde took control of his stereo once they had set it up. She smiled while she searched through Sebastian's CDs. "A bit old school, but I like your taste in music, Seb!"

Sebastian raised his beer in thanks.

The hours passed quickly. Once the condo looked livable and the last of Sebastian's furniture had been placed in the appropriate rooms, Ann walked to the bedroom at the end of the hallway.

The walls were lined with boxes as well as bedroom furniture. The marble dragon statue sat atop the dresser and a bare mattress was in the middle of the room on the floor.

She entered the room and stepped out onto the balcony and looked out across the city. The sun had just started to set and the sky had begun to darken. She loved this time of day. Everything always seemed so peaceful. The cold breeze felt good to her after having drank so much.

She left the bedroom to rejoin her friends and saw Sebastian at the end of the hall. This handsome man, whom she had always had an attraction to yet never acted on, was now alone with her. She had seen him so many times in the Training Arena, shirtless, his washboard stomach glistening after an intense workout. Many times she had fantasized about running her fingers through his messy hair.

Sebastian's eyes locked with hers and he walked toward her.

"Seb, you know if you need anything, all you have to do is ask. I'll always be here for you." Her voice was low and soothing.

Sebastian stopped, his gaze was fixed on her. "I know, Ann."

He had always been intrigued by Ann. He found her bravery as attractive as her personality and her looks.

For such a petite frame, Ann was tough. She, like all potential league members, had trained in the City of Radiance since she was young, and despite working with food in the restaurant nearly every day, she was physically fit. She had an ivory complexion with long, brown hair that fell in layers to the middle of her back. Her eyes were a striking combination of green and brown.

Many times Sebastian had looked into those eyes and wanted more than friendship from her.

Ann started to walk down the hall toward the living room.

In two wide strides, Sebastian walked to her and softly pinned her against the wall.

She looked up at him but every thought was lost as she stared into his cobalt blue eyes.

With Sebastian's gaze set on her, she felt a fluttering in her belly. He slipped one hand around her waist and placed the other against the wall. He leaned down and kissed her softly; she was receptive as his lips moved across hers.

A few long moments passed before she placed her hands on his chest to push him away. "I don't know if we should be doing this, Seb. The league has to come first for both of us. How could this work?"

He placed his head on her shoulder. "I don't know. I just know what I want."

Her commitment to the league was the same as his but he didn't think it should mean that they had to deny what they felt for each other.

Ann moved to step past him. He grabbed her arm lightly, pulled her back, leaned his head down and whispered, "I need you."

Ann felt her heart beat as though it were trying to break free from her chest. Sebastian had taken her heart years ago but she hadn't believed he felt the same. He was the dedicated lawyer who put his personal life on hold to commit his time to his profession and league training. He was like no man she had ever known and no one had ever come close to making her feel the way that he made her feel.

She gave in to her passion, reached up and held his face in her hands. "And I need you."

He picked her up and kissed her. She wrapped her legs around him. He carried her to his bedroom and shut the door, unaware that Amber had appeared at the end of the hall and witnessed most of what they both thought was a private moment.

That was all it took for Amber to reaffirm that she was no more than an afterthought to Sebastian. She had seen him walk to the hall and thought that if she told him how she felt, he would see that she could make him happy.

Then she saw him with Ann.

Amber walked back to the living room and announced that she had to leave. She was certain that Marcus was her future now.

~~~~

The morning light shone through the bare window. Ann watched Sebastian's chest rise and fall as he slept beside her.

He felt her eyes on him and slowly opened his. "Good morning, gorgeous." He moaned as he rolled her on top of him and kissed her deeply.

She softly whispered, "Good morning."

Sebastian's phone rang and Ann put her head on his shoulder. "It's nothing important, just ignore it." She playfully bit his neck.

He reached for his phone. "It could be something about Marcus."

Ann teased Sebastian with light kisses on his throat and down his chest. He gave in to her and threw his cell phone across the room. As he began to roll himself on top of her, she wrinkled her nose. "You probably should have answered it, Seb. If it's got to do with Marcus we need to know."

With a seductive gleam in her eyes, she added, "Don't make plans for tonight."

Sebastian kissed Ann and got out of bed. He stood and stretched. Ann watched him walk to the far side of the room to retrieve his phone, appreciative of the view.

"It was John." He dialed John's number. "I swear if it's not important I'll...John, this better be important."

John chuckled. "Can you free up your evening?"

Sebastian hung his head and closed his eyes. "Depends. What do you need?"

"I want you, Conor, and I to go pay a visit to Azroth. Conor's good to go, we're just waiting on your answer."

He motioned to Ann, indicating he wanted her to listen. "You want me to go to Solar Flair with you and Conor tonight to see what he knows?"

Ann pouted and mouthed, "That's fine. Just don't be too long."

"I'm in."

"Okay, good. I'll phone you when I'm through with my last appointment."

Ann got up to get dressed while Sebastian was on the phone. While she didn't want to end her time with him, she knew she had food to prepare at the restaurant and she was anxious to tell Angeline what had happened. The intimate details were hers alone, but Angeline was more of a sister than a friend and they kept very few secrets from one another.

"I should head out." She slipped her arms around his waist and rose up on her toes to steal a kiss.

He picked her up and walked back toward the mattress.

"Seb, while I love your idea, we both have somewhere to be. I'm making desserts for the dinner crowd tonight and those pies and cakes won't bake themselves."

He placed Ann back onto the bare mattress, lowered himself on top of her, and whispered, "Ten more minutes."

~~~~

Once she had showered and dressed, Ann walked to the living room to grab her purse. She noticed that someone had cleaned up while she and Sebastian were otherwise occupied. "Hmm, nice."

Inside the elevator, she dug her phone out of her purse and called Angeline. "Ange, meet me at Transcendence. Now."

In her office at the Aemetta Suites, Angeline pulled her phone away from her ear and looked at it. Ann had sounded a bit...different. "Alright, love. I'll leave straight away."

Angeline walked around the front desk to the concierge's stand. "Faith, I will be out for a bit. Please phone Mr. Temple's office to confirm my meeting with him tonight at eight o'clock. If he is not able to keep this appointment, please phone me, otherwise, I will be back in time to meet with him."

Faith had worked for the Flynn family since she was nineteen years old. She twirled a few stray strands of her mid-length black hair.

She smiled and answered, "Will do."

The distance from the Aemetta Suites to Wells' Antiquities, the location that housed the tunnel to the City of Radiance from Europe, was a pleasant fifteen minute walk. Angeline rarely drove as she lived in the largest room on the top floor of the hotel.

Once she arrived in the City, Angeline boarded the nearest Transport Pod and sped to the North American gate. Ann had given no details, no inkling about what the urgent matter was that she wanted to speak about.

In Jayded Ink, Angeline hurried past Jayde and asked, "When can I come in?"

"Tomorrow at 7:00 p.m. I'll come in just for you. I've got a date downtown at 9:00 p.m.," Jayde replied with a devilish grin.

"You're the best, love!" Angeline shouted over her shoulder as she rushed toward the front door. She stopped just before she opened the door, turned, and asked, "Date? With whom?"

"You'll meet him tomorrow if you're still around."

"If I'm still around? I'll let Ann know and we will *both* be here! But right now, I've got to run. Ann has summoned me."

Jayde laughed.

Clouds filled the sky and the wind was cold as Angeline walked to Transcendence. She hoped that Ann had something hot on the stove.

She entered through the front door and headed to the back of the restaurant. On the bar was a bowl of cream of broccoli soup, a glass of water, two shot glasses, and a bottle of honey whiskey.

"My favourite soup! What are we celebrating?" Angeline asked.

"Sit. You're going to want to sit for this."

She narrowed eyes. "Alright, what do you want? My favourite meal, our whiskey...this is not just a celebration. What's going on?"

"Well, I didn't go home last night, for starters."

Angeline smiled. "Oh, really, hmm..."

"Remember when I left Seb's living room and said I was going to look around? I found a balcony off one of the bedrooms. I could see my place from it."

"Oh, Christ, love! Can't you just say that you and Seb have finally slept together?"

"What? What do you mean finally?"

"When you left the living room, Seb was two minutes behind you. After the first fifteen minutes, John realized he wasn't around. I told him he was setting something up in the back and to shut up and have another drink. I had to stop John looking for Seb by pouring him drink after drink!"

"Does anyone else know?"

"Well, when Jayde noticed that you both were missing, she kicked everyone out and she and I tidied a bit before we left."

"You are the best!" Ann reached across the bar and hugged Angeline. "I noticed that someone had cleaned up when I left this morning."

"While I couldn't be happier for you, if you and Seb plan to make this a more...permanent thing, you are going to have to speak with the Council. If I'm not mistaken, there are certain, let's say, guidelines that have to be followed."

Ann pouted. "Nothing is ever simple, is it?"

Angeline grabbed Ann's hands. "If it were, love, we would be bored to tears."

Ann smiled and slapped the bar. "No time like the present, right? Give me a second."

Once she let the day chef know she was leaving, she rounded the bar, grabbed Angeline's hand and pulled her from her barstool.

"Ann!"

The two raced out of the restaurant together.

As they turned toward Jayded Ink, Ann looked at the sky. "Let's hurry. Those clouds aren't looking too friendly."

"I'm meeting Aidan in two hours and I'd rather not look like a soggy kitten! Shall we drive instead?"

"Nope. I'm full of energy that needs to be spent!"

"Well, I'm not," Angeline whined. "Sorry, love, but I refuse to run in these heels!"

"Fine. My jeep is out back."

Angeline flashed Ann her best, sweetest smile. "You're too good to me."

Ann shook her head. They walked through the alley to the rear of Transcendence where her vehicle was parked.

In spite of the chill in the air, Ann rolled down her window and let the wind blow through her hair as she drove.

When they arrived at Jayded Ink, Ann parked beside a red Mustang.

"I do love red," Angeline remarked as she looked at the car.

They watched as an attractive man got out of the Mustang and walked toward the entrance to Jayded Ink. With a smile and wide eyes, they looked at each other and followed Kyle.

He walked to the front door of Jayded Ink and after he opened it, he saw Ann and Angeline headed there as well. He held the door for the two ladies.

"That's lovely of you, thank you," Angeline said.

"My pleasure, ladies," he replied.

Jayde turned to see who Kyle was speaking with. "Oh, hey girls. Ann, Ange, this is Kyle. My dinner date tomorrow night."

Ann leaned close to Angeline and whispered, "Ange, why is this the first I'm hearing about this?"

"I would have gotten to it, but I had other matters on my mind, or have you already forgotten?" Angeline retorted.

"Fine, let's get you to *your* date."

"It's an appointment, love, not a date."

"Tomatoes, potatoes, whatever."

Angeline walked to Jayde and kissed her cheek. "I will see you tomorrow night, my sweet. I cannot tell you how much I am looking forward to this!"

As Ann and Angeline walked to the backroom, Ann looked over her shoulder. "We'll let ourselves out the back once we've got what we need."

"You got it," Jayde replied. "Help yourselves to whatever you like."

"Nice to meet you, Kyle," Angeline sang, a mischievous glint in her eyes.

With a half-smile, Kyle replied, "Yeah, you too."

Once in the backroom, Angeline opened the storage closet, while Ann moved some items around, purposely making noise.

After she opened and closed the back door, Ann joined Angeline and followed her through the door that led to the tunnels.

"Do you think he suspects anything, Ange?"

"I think he wouldn't have noticed if an elephant trod straight through the shop! Did you see the way he looked at Jayde? That poor bloke is completely infatuated!"

Ann put her arm around Angeline's shoulder and sighed. "Just another man falling victim to the charms of our Eyrasine blood."

"On a more somber note, did you notice the slight, pale blue haze around Kyle?"

"I did!" Ann replied. "What's up with that? I know geist can have either black or blue auras, but what Kyle had was really pale blue and not half as large as that of any geist I've ever seen. Honestly, I thought it was just the lighting in the shop. Do you think he's a geist?"

"Well, we are on our way to see the council about you and Seb anyway, so while you are chatting about your love life, I can ask about this. If anyone would know, it would be the council."

~~~~

The Grand Temple was nearly vacant as Ann and Angeline walked to the Council Chambers. The only immortals seated inside were Celeste and Selphia.

While Angeline walked to Selphia, Ann approached Celeste and bowed. "I request your permission to make an inquiry."

Celeste tilted her head slightly to the left. "You may speak."

"Are relationships between two league members permitted?"

Celeste spoke as much with her hands as her voice. "Two league members have, in the past, been united in marriage. There are conditions that must be met, stipulations, should two league members wish to have a sexual relationship."

"So, it *is* allowed? I mean, two league members *can* have a relationship?"

"We understand the needs of mortals, that they require bonds to be made. What we require is that the league continues. The league must remain. You must together come before us. The conditions of such a union will be revealed to you both."

"Thank you, Celeste." Ann bowed again then turned to join Angeline who spoke with Selphia.

Angeline began. "Thank you for granting me permission to speak, Selphia. I would first like to explain what it is I have seen. I was in Jayded Ink with Ann, passing through on our way to the City, when we saw a young man. He had a very pale, very thin, blue haze around him. While I understand what the light blue and black auras indicate, this rather confused us. Can you tell me what this haze means?"

"This is extremely rare, Angeline." Selphia rose to pace.

With her hands held together in front of her, she continued. "As you know, all geist emit an aura that only league members and we Immortals can see. This gift was granted unto you by the spelled rings that you each wear. What you may not know is that there are many different types of auras. The aura you see is dependent on the species with whom a geist procreates. Should a geist and a human create a child, that child would carry aspects of both parents, as all children do. The child would be born in the human form and that part of the child, while weaker than his or her geist half, does affect the aura, making it less vibrant and less radiant. This pale blue, lesser aura that you have described, could result from such a union. In the past, human/geist offspring did not live past their tenth year. The geist essence overpowered the human body and could not escape. Both were destroyed.

"However, three hybrids are known to us that did survive past their tenth year, and of those three, one was killed. His soul mist was unable to leave the body and perished with it."

"Alright. Now, please forgive my lack of understanding, Selphia, but are you saying that geist and humans can produce children together, as well as geist and other species?"

"Yes. Geist have mated with species from many worlds. The only geist you need concern yourself with are those with black auras. The blue auras, whether light in colour, or a pale haze, always indicate a deep seated goodness within the heart."

"Thank you, Selphia." She bowed and turned to see Ann walk toward her.

"Ann, walk with me to my exit," Angeline whispered, as they left the Council Chambers.

"Seb is at Solar Flair with John and Conor tonight, so you've got me for as long as you like."

Ann looked at Angeline and knew instantly that there was something unsettled within her friend. As she listened to her repeat what Selphia had said, she realized that life in the league was getting very complicated, and she feared that it was only going to snowball.

~~~~~

John, Sebastian, and Conor met in front of Solar Flair. Located in the downtown core of Niagara Falls, Solar Flair boasted a large bar and a covered outdoor patio.

They walked through the intricately engraved double front doors. Wooden rafters hung from the high ceiling on chains and created an open, makeshift drop ceiling. A large orb resembling a sun was hung directly in the middle of the club over several round tables.

The three men scanned the bar looking for the owner, Azroth.

Almost six hundred years ago, during a time when his kind were killed without discretion, a geist named Azroth came through the portal. After a few centuries spent as a wanderer in North America, he settled into his life on Earth in the Niagara region. Rather than continue to live in fear of the league finding him, he sought them out and made a deal with their leader. In exchange for being left alone to live out his life peacefully, Azroth agreed to inform the league about any geist who were intrusive in their interactions with humans. His one stipulation was that he would not provide any information on geist who had chosen to live peacefully among humans.

After striking a deal and with the help of league funds, Azroth opened a saloon which eventually became the nightclub Solar Flair.

Azroth, his long, black hair tied back and sporting a soul patch, sat at a corner booth with three beautiful girls.

John, Conor, and Sebastian spotted Azroth and walked toward him with purpose, past a row of window booths and two pool tables.

While Sebastian and Conor had been to Solar Flair as league members with Jacob and had seen the many geist auras around its patrons, this was John's first time. He had been to Solar Flair and met Azroth with his father prior to taking over leadership of the league, however, he had not been able to see geist auras until he wore his league ring. He knew geist auras were either light blue or black in colour, but it was still odd to him to see the blue cloud-like air around Azroth.

Azroth glanced up from his companions. "To what do I owe this honour?"

John looked directly into Azroth's eyes. "We need to talk. In private."

Azroth knew he was obligated to provide whatever help they had come looking for. He waved his hand and dismissed the women beside him. "Shall we go to my office?" He directed the three men to the rear left corner of the bar.

They followed him into his office and John shut the door. "We need you to find some geist for us."

Azroth took a seat behind his large, antique desk. "It's been awhile since I've had you league boys here. Why do you need me now?"

"There are some geist working for Marcus," Sebastian spit out bitterly.

Azroth laughed, placed his forearms on his desk and held his hands together. He leaned forward. "So, Marcus came back. Could these geist could be relatives of his?"

"What are you talking about?" John demanded. "How could Marcus be related to a geist?"

"He married one, boys. Years ago. I can't recall her name." Azroth held out a hand and rubbed his fingers together to indicate he wanted payment.

Sebastian reached behind him for his Soul Dagger and plunged it into the desk, missing Azroth's hand by less than an inch.

"Sweet hell!" Azroth jumped out of his chair. "Okay! Her name was Madeline Walker. That's all I know!" He shook his head. "Hey, listen, you guys came to me! Why shouldn't I get a little something for my troubles?"

With the blade he had just thrust in Azroth's desk still in his hand, Sebastian demanded, "Find the geist that are working for Marcus or next time, deal or not, this dagger will mark more than just your furniture."

He removed most of the blade and scraped the tip across Azroth's desk as he left.

"You owe me a new desk!" Azroth shouted at Sebastian's back.

Sebastian stopped, turned around, and glared at Azroth.

He raised his hands in surrender. "Or we could just forget about it."

"Marcus had Seb's entire family killed. This is personal. Find these geist or he will be back." Conor leaned over the desk and with his face close to Azroth's, added, "The next time we may not be here and, gee, I would really hate to see what he would do if he was alone with you." He tapped the top of Azroth's desk with his fist before he moved to the door.

"Report back to us with anything you find. Anything." John headed out of the office behind Conor and Sebastian.

Azroth leaned back in his chair and breathed a sigh of relief as he watched them leave.

Outside, John leaned against the front door. "I need to tell my father and James what that geist told us in Transcendence. They need to know that my mother's death wasn't an accident." He dreaded this task.

"I didn't tell James while we were helping Seb move in. I wanted to wait until I have both him and my father together. This is going to bring back all the feelings from when we got the call the day she died. An accident was hard enough to deal with but to find out that Marcus had her killed..."

"Want some company?" Conor asked.

Sebastian stayed silent. He didn't feel as though he could offer any comfort to John as his feelings were still raw from his own family's death.

"Thanks, Conor, but I think I should do this alone." John's voice was sombre.

He pulled his cell phone from his pocket and phoned James.

~~~~~

John and James arrived in the City and took a transport pod to their father's apartment, a quaint, stone building with five floors and a beautiful garden in front.

John knocked at the door before he opened it and walked in. "Dad, you home?"

"Yeah, I'm coming. What are you boys doing here at this hour?"

"Sit down, Dad. You too, James."

Confused, both Michael and James sat.

"What is going on, John? Just say whatever it is," James said impatiently.

"There's no easy way to say this. Ann and Angeline caught a geist at Transcendence. We used the Dagger of Truth and he confessed that he had been watching us, every league member, for a while now."

Michael's expression went from curious to unsettled.

"What you don't know is why. Some of them are working for Marcus. The one we caught told us what he's planning to do. He wants to have the geist replicate every league member, steal our keys, and take control of the portal."

Michael folded his arms across his chest. "Marcus is a son of a bitch, but surely he wouldn't do this. Are you sure? How do you know?"

"The geist confessed to everything. The worst part is that he said Marcus had killed someone in the past...and made it look like a hit and run."

Michael's face seemed to drain of all blood. It didn't take long for the shock to turn to a pure, bitter rage. "He killed Yvette? Is that what you're saying?"

Leaning forward, Michael clenched his fists. "My wife is dead and Marcus is the one who killed her?"

"If I find him, he's mine," James shouted angrily as he rose out of his seat.

John began to pace. "James, the Immortals want him alive...and there's more. He's planning to open the tomb of Asmodeus. Ann told us that her family is responsible for guarding his tomb."

As soon as the words left his mouth, John realized he had divulged a league secret.

"James, no one outside of the league knows. We need to keep this between us."

James nodded his head. "Of course, John."

Michael swallowed his anger and offered some advice. "John, talk with Vivian. I think she would be your best bet for any information on Asmodeus."

"We just have to find Marcus before he can release Asmodeus, then he's the Immortals' problem."

"I think I should stay topside for a while, lend a hand where I can," Michael decided. "I'll move back into the house, just until things with Marcus have been settled."

The three men left the apartment. They each felt the same pain and grief they felt so many years ago, as well as a hatred that none of them realized they were capable of.

105

10 – REVELATION

Inside her office, Angeline turned the emerald ring on her finger. She had a proposal prepared that outlined everything Aidan would need to plan a most fabulous party for his employees.

With plush, white sofas and dark wood furniture, Angeline's office made everyone who entered it feel like royalty. Brides felt like princesses and grooms felt like knights in battle-worn armor, who had returned home to their beloved after slaying the dragon. A knight in shining armor was no knight at all, in Angeline's eyes. If he hadn't a scuff or scratch on him, he wasn't worthy of a princess.

All manner of parties had been held at the Aemetta Suites, and in the last few years, Angeline had been the one to plan them. The hotel had been host to foreign dignitaries and international tourists and she often wondered if her being a hyperpolyglot was by design or just chance. Nothing about The League of Twelve seemed random, so it was possible that she was exactly the person she was designed to be.

Faith's voice came over the intercom. "Miss Flynn, Mr. Temple is here."

"I'm on my way."

After a quick check in the large mirror on the wall beside her door, Angeline walked out to greet Aidan. In under one minute, she was at the front desk.

Aidan was leaning against the reception desk. He wore a dark blue suit and a pale blue shirt with its top button undone. She thought of the last time they were together, the feel of his strong arms around her. She inhaled deeply and realized she had been holding her breath.

After exhaling quickly, she walked to him.

Aidan smiled a rather sensual smile. "A pleasure to see you again, Miss Flynn. I am anxious to hear your ideas for my staff party."

"Follow me." She led him toward her office.

"A pleasure," he whispered under his breath. He watched every move of her body as it swayed and glided across the carpeted corridor.

Once they had entered the office and the door shut, he grabbed her arm, turned her to face him, and kissed her passionately.

"Mr. Temple! I had no idea..." Angeline was quickly silenced by Aidan's mouth once more on hers.

"You had every idea." His eyes told her that he wanted more than a presentation.

"While I do love *your* ideas, I've actually had a few of my own with regard to your staff gathering."

Aidan conceded. "We should most definitely deal with the business at hand before dealing with anything else."

He bowed his head. "Please, I would love to hear your ideas."

She straightened her form-fitting, blood red dress and led Aidan to her desk at the far end of her office where she poured two glasses of wine. "I find my clients are always more easily bent to my will with a little wine in their bellies."

Aidan's voice was low and seductive. "I should warn you. I may not be so easily bent."

With her heart pounding in her chest, Angeline sat in the chair behind her desk and began her presentation. "I've selected a colour scheme of silver and copper. Silver and gold have been done to death in my opinion, and you strike me as a man who chooses a path not so well traveled."

He leaned back in the chair and crossed his legs. With his left elbow on the arm of the chair and the back of his hand on his chin, he replied, "And so I am. Please, continue."

As she presented her ideas for menu items, decor, table size, and whatnot, Aidan watched her as a hungry cheetah might watch its prey. He couldn't hear a word she said. The only thing on his mind was how to hurry the meeting along, and how her dress would look in a pile on the floor at her feet.

Angeline smiled sweetly. "I was thinking a nice, white wine with dessert to finish off the meal, before having the band begin. I've drawn up the necessary paperwork on the assumption that you would agree with my choices."

She saw Aidan's mind was not her presentation. "I'll need your importer's license to arrange for the lions the magician will need but other than that, I would say we have everything you need right here."

"Absolutely. Everything sounds fabulous. Whatever you need. I'll make sure....the what?"

He saw her face, her head slightly tilted and both eyebrows raised and realized she knew he hadn't been listening. "I'm sorry but I've had thoughts of you every minute of the day. The wait for this meeting was torturous."

With a dramatic move of her hand, Angeline said, "Lions it is!"

He got up and walked to her, a look of determination on his face. She rose to meet him and they came together as though they had done so for many years.

After a few ardent moments, she moved back a step and straightened Aidan's suit coat. "I believe we should visit the Celestial Ballroom, which I think would be most suitable for your gathering."

He walked to the office door. Once he opened it, he offered her his arm to hold as they strolled to the Celestial Ballroom.

With over three minutes to think as they walked, Angeline wondered how a life with Aidan could be possible. He was the only man who had ever made her want to consider a life outside of the league and she feared it may not be viable. Once again she realized that life was a complicated, fickle little bitch.

"Here it is." She opened the double doors to reveal a spacious room with a stage and full bar.

"The perfect venue. Now, all I require is a date. We can't have the boss show up alone. So, Miss Flynn," Aidan placed his hand over his heart and bowed his head slightly, "would you do me the honour of accompanying me to my staff Christmas party?"

She placed her arms around his neck and smiled. "Why, Mr. Temple, I do believe I will."

~~~~

Ann walked out of the kitchen in Transcendence as John, James, Sebastian, and Conor walked in the front door. "Hey guys, I have Dave cooking up some eggs, bacon and crepes. Have a seat and I'll run back to the kitchen when I'm done here and bring them out with some strawberries."

She looked at Conor on her way. "Grab a jug of orange juice from the mini-fridge behind the bar and I'll bring a carafe of coffee."

"Sure."

Not long after, Ann returned with a large tray and placed it on top of a table. "Eat up boys, I've got some news."

They all moaned before they began to eat.

John closed his eyes. "We have some news of our own."

"Ange and I met Jayde's boyfriend Kyle." She took a bite of her eggs and continued. "We saw a very small, pale blue haze-like aura around him. Ange and I went to see the council and she asked them what it means to have that kind of aura. Selphia said it means he's part human *and* part geist!"

All four men stopped chewing and looked at Ann.

She took another bite. "Selphia also said it's very rare that geist and humans can procreate. She said that there have been human/geist unions in the past, but very few have produced a child and when they did, the child died before reaching the age of ten. The geist essence apparently overpowered the human body and both the physical body and the geist essence died. Since Kyle made it past ten years old, he's definitely unique."

John put his head in his hands and ran his fingers through his hair in exasperation. "This is not good. We went to Solar Flair and spoke with Azroth. He said that Marcus married a geist."

Ann looked up from her meal, a blank look on her face.

With a look of disgust on his face, Sebastian shouted, "No! There is no way I have a geist cousin."

John groaned. "We should keep an eye on Kyle. Watch where he goes and who he sees."

Conor exhaled loudly. "My sister, for one. I'll figure out how to let her know about Kyle."

"I'm going with Ange to get her tattoo done later. We can tell Jayde about Kyle," Ann offered. "It might sound better coming from a friend rather than an overprotective brother."

"Just let her know that I'd like her to find out as much as she can about Kyle and his family. How likely is it that Marcus has had geist watching everyone in the league and now a part geist is getting friendly with Jayde? If he really is Marcus' son, we need to know where his loyalties lie, blue aura or not."

Conor continued eating. "Kyle is coming to my parents' house today at 1:00 p.m. for lunch. I'll keep an eye open for the aura you mentioned, Ann."

If Jayde was dating him, Conor knew Kyle couldn't be all bad. Jayde was very selective about who she allowed in her life and he trusted her judgment. He decided to keep an open mind for the time being.

~~~~

At the Rivait house, Kyle parked in the driveway behind Jayde's Hummer. He turned off his engine and stared at the steering wheel. His feelings for Jayde had deepened over the past few weeks.

He gathered the white and purple calla lily flowers from the seat beside him and walked to the large front door. He pressed the doorbell and was greeted by Jayde's father.

"Kyle." Roy looked at the flowers as he extended his hand. "Good to see you again. Come in."

Kyle accepted Roy's hand and stepped into the foyer. "Good to see you, sir."

The entranceway of the Rivait home was decorated in a contemporary style with hardwood flooring. A curved bench was placed below the winding staircase that led to the upstairs landing. As he passed, Kyle smiled when he saw the framed wall sketch Jayde told him about.

Roy led the way to the library. "So, Kyle, what is it you do for a living?"

"I'm a judo instructor, sir. I recently closed my dojo to move to Niagara Falls. I'm originally from out West."

"I see, and what made you…"

Jayde interjected. "Dad! Kyle doesn't need you grilling him the second he comes through the door!"

She looked at the flowers Kyle held in his hands and unintentionally grimaced. "Are those for me?"

"Actually," he turned to Jayde's mother, Yvonne, who was already seated in the library with Rachel and Conor, "they're for you."

"Thank you, Kyle!" Yvonne rose to accept the flowers. "They're lovely."

Yvonne's shoulder-length reddish brown hair caught the sunlight shining through the windows as she walked to the fireplace and placed the flowers on top of the mantle.

Jayde breathed a sigh of relief. "I guess you really do know me."

Kyle grinned at Jayde's remark and followed her to sit on the sofa at the far end of the library.

As the afternoon progressed, Kyle found that Jayde's family was every bit as amazing as she was. He could see the love, the bond they had with each other. His own family had love, but not like this.

His mother had been a wonderful person who always made him feel loved. However, while he was sure his father loved him, Kyle felt as though it was more like a controlled response to the experiment of fatherhood: give the child love, teach the child, mold the child.

Yvonne took her seat on the sofa directly across from Kyle and Jayde. "What about your family, Kyle? Are they here in Niagara Falls?"

"My father is, but my mother passed away. She would have loved meeting you."

"I'm certain she was a lovely person to have raised such a fine son." Yvonne smiled and folded her hands in her lap. "And your father? What line of work is he in?"

"He's an engineer. While my mother and I stayed home, he would find work in various parts of the country and other countries as well."

Conor watched Kyle throughout the afternoon. He could see the faint, pale blue haze around him and thought that it was odd in its colour and size. He decided that he would reserve judgment and said nothing to Jayde or his parents.

~~~~

Ann and Angeline spoke on the phone as Angeline made her way through the City of Radiance to the North American tunnel. Ann told her what she, John, Sebastian, and Conor had discussed earlier in Transcendence - the possibility that Marcus was Kyle's father.

"How do we tell Jayde that Kyle is part geist, let alone that Marcus could be his father?"

"I have no idea, but I am certain you will think of something," Angeline answered, a mischievous smile on her face.

"Yeah, thanks. How do you tell someone something like this?"

"His aura *is* blue. He's definitely not a bad part geist/human/Eyrasine hybrid...type guy. Oh shite, I'll think of something," Angeline offered.

Outside the front door of Jayded Ink, Ann paced as she and Angeline tried to think of ways to break the news to Jayde.

Jayde opened the door. "You having a private party out here?"

"Just talking with Ange. She's pretty excited about this tattoo."

"I am!" Angeline chimed in as she came into the shop from the backroom.

Jayde placed a pair of latex gloves over her hands. "Okay, park it over on the left bed and turn with whichever side you want me to work on facing up."

Angeline walked to the bed, exaggerating her words as she spoke. "You don't mind if I sleep while you're working, do you, love? I am absolutely knackered!"

"Ha! You really think you'll be able to sleep while I'm poking a bunch of needles into your flesh?" Jayde asked with a half-smile.

While Jayde prepared the ink machine, Angeline took a deep breath. "Before we start, I have something to tell you. It's about your Kyle."

Ann's eyes went wide and she plopped herself on the sofa as she prepared for Jayde's reaction. Jayde was unpredictable and her reaction to this news was sure to be the same or at the very least entertaining.

Jayde became defensive. "Okay, but you've seen him once, right? What could you know about him?"

"Put the ink machine down, love. I am already nervous enough," Angeline whispered as she stood and began to pace.

Jayde put her machine down and crossed her arms. "Just say it. Does he have two wives and dog somewhere up North? Just say it!"

"He's part geist," Angeline blurted as she brought her hand up to cover her mouth.

Jayde's expression went from one of curiosity to that of shock. "Come again."

"He's part geist and part human. You know we see auras, right?" Angeline continued to pace while she kept a good distance between herself and Jayde.

Jayde nodded her head.

Angeline added, "Well, his aura is smaller and a paler shade of blue." She gasped. "Oh God! I should have led with that! His aura is blue! So he's not a bad guy."

Ann chimed in. "Blue auras mean he's got a good heart, Jayde."

"He's a geist. I'm dating a geist." Jayde was stunned.

"But a *good* geist!" Angeline hoped to reassure Jayde.

Jayde rose and paced around the shop, silent. The silence worried Ann and Angeline more than if she had screamed and thrown things.

Angeline walked to Jayde and put a hand on her shoulder. "Kyle is Kyle. He's only part geist. This means that he can't turn to mist and leave his body if he's killed, not that he will be, mind you. Oh my, I'm saying this all wrong. Being only part geist, I wouldn't think that he could control his aging like full blown geist can; I assume he would be stuck in human form and age like humans do. Not that it's a *bad* form. We don't know if he has any kind of ability, but as far as we know he's human with a bit of geist thrown into his gene pool."

"I'm dating a geist," Jayde mumbled. "What am I supposed to do with this?"

"Only part geist, and a *good* geist." Ann crossed her legs and stretched her arms across the back of the sofa. "Maybe he's got a super sex ability. You really owe it to yourself to find out."

As Jayde absorbed this newest hypothetical information, she cast her eyes upward. "Keep talking."

"You have been seeing him for a bit now, right? How does he kiss? Is it a messy, sloppy kind of kiss or is it a melt you down to your toes, hot kind of thing?" Angeline's voice took on a sensual tone.

"After every kiss I'm a puddle." Jayde sank into a chair. "He makes every inch of my body ache and want him even more."

"Okay, so he's hot, he makes you hot and his kisses are melty hot, right?" Ann asked. She raised her eyebrows. "I heard you brought him to meet your mom and dad. Whose idea was that?"

"My dad, who else?" Jayde threw her arms up in the air. "He came by while Kyle was here and we had been making out in the back room. Dad invited him right then and there. He could have been a serial killer and my dad just invites him to lunch!"

Angeline spoke hesitantly. "Maybe we shouldn't have you armed with a bunch of needles today. Especially aimed at my flesh."

"Get your ass back on that table!" Jayde demanded as she pointed to the tattoo bed.

Angeline grimaced. "I have more to tell you."

"Seriously? What?" Jayde shouted, her hands held up with her fingers flexed.

Angeline wasn't sure if she should mention that Marcus may possibly be Kyle's father. "John asked if you knew anything about Kyle's family."

"Not much, actually. I guess now we have a topic of conversation for dinner tonight."

"Shall we reschedule?" Angeline asked, hopeful.

"Huh? Oh, yeah. How am I going to be able to have a good time tonight? Maybe I should cancel."

"No!" Angeline and Ann shouted simultaneously.

"Don't you dare!" Ann commanded. "If he makes you feel all melty, let him make you feel all melty! That doesn't happen all the time...does it?"

"No, it does not." Jayde's voice was stern. "But you guys know I'm an awful liar." After a brief pause, she held up her index finger. "Wait."

She went to the back room and returned with a bottle of Malibu Caribbean Rum and three glasses. "You guys need to help me."

She poured three generous glasses. "I can't do this sober. Not tonight. This, this is just too much to take in."

Angeline raised her glass. "Cheers, love."

Ann and Jayde joined in the toast.

The three of them talked and drank until they had emptied two and a half bottles, with Jayde having the lion's share.

Once they were sufficiently intoxicated, Angeline called Sebastian to pick Ann up. There was no chance that Ann would make it home without passing out on the sidewalk in her current state. However, she hadn't thought about how she herself was going to get home.

Just before Sebastian arrived, Kyle walked into Jayded Ink. The three ladies looked at Kyle, and Angeline slurred, "Kyle, love! You're here! And you're so big!"

With a confused expression, Kyle looked at Jayde, who sat beside two empty bottles of rum. With a laugh and a shake of his head, he said, "I'm guessing our dinner is cancelled."

"Hell no! I'm starving. I have to put some food in my belly to keep all this rum company!" She patted her stomach.

"I had planned on us going to The Rogue Bistro. I read some good reviews about it online last night, but we can head to a greasy burger joint if you think your rum would like that kind of company better."

"My rum wants food. If it's not moving, I'll eat it." Jayde laughed uncontrollably.

"Ah, my kind of girl!" Kyle winked and noted that she had just said to him, exactly what he had said to her the day they first met.

He caught her as she nearly fell out of her chair. Kyle smiled. "Hey, you've got to be careful when you've got a belly full of rum."

The bell on the front door chimed as Sebastian opened it. "Where are the drunk girls?"

Three hands went up.

Kyle looked at Sebastian. "I've got one. Are you here for the other two?"

Sebastian stopped. He could see Kyle's aura and knew who this man was. It took every ounce of self-control he had to refrain from ripping his throat out.

"I'm Sebastian Shea." He was curious as to what Kyle's reaction would be to hearing the Shea name.

Kyle kept his face expressionless. "Kyle." He looked at Sebastian and wondered if he was the man who had tried to murder his father. Nothing made sense anymore. Jayde, Ann, Angeline, they were really great people. He needed to speak with his father. There had to be more to it than just what he was told.

Sebastian looked at Ann. "How about you and I walk Ange home."

"Sure!" Ann replied. She walked to Sebastian, threw her arms around his neck and whispered, "Ange and I are a little bit drunk."

Sebastian smiled and kissed the top of Ann's head. He placed one arm around her waist and led her to the back room. "Let's get Ange home, then we can work on sobering you up."

Sebastian and Ann walked to Angeline and he helped her to her feet.

"Let's go, Ange," he said as he lifted her.

Angeline smiled, her eyes half closed. "Thank you, love."

"We'll let ourselves out the back, if that's OK, Jayde." Sebastian and his two drunk companions walked toward the backroom door.

"Yup. Just lock the door on your way out."

Sebastian nodded.

Once inside the storage closet, Sebastian used his Cancer key to unlock the door.

Ann had lost the effects of most of the rum by borrowing Sebastian's self-healing gift as they walked Angeline to her exit. She realized she had been borrowing Sebastian's energy quite a bit lately and thought that she should probably return the favour, with a special meal, perhaps.

"We'll walk you to your room in the hotel," Sebastian offered. "You wouldn't want one of the guests to recognize you and stop you to have a conversation right now."

"No, I would not." Angeline gasped. "Maybe I need a disguise."

She pulled a pair of sunglasses out of her purse and loudly whispered, "There! Now no one can spot me."

"Where's Conor when you need him? I think Ange could use his healing hands to help her sober up." Ann laughed.

Once Angeline was safely in her suite, Ann and Sebastian began their trip back to Jayded Ink.

Ann felt Sebastian's hand brush up against hers and then take hold of it as they walked from the hotel to Wells' Antiquities.

He looked at her and asked, "You don't mind, do you?"

"No, I don't mind." Ann's heart was soaring.

~~~~

Jayde lowered her window as she and Kyle drove to The Rogue Bistro. The cool night air that blew through the window helped her sober up a bit.

"That was a lot of rum," she said. "I'm starving!"

Kyle chuckled. "We're almost there. Exactly how much did you drink?"

"More than I should have, that's for sure. I just needed something to either give me courage or make me forget."

"Courage?" Kyle was confused. "You are one of the most courageous people I know! I'll never forget the way you tossed that guy out into the street the first day I met you."

"Ha! Well, he deserved it, but I would call that more hot-headed than courageous."

"So, if it wasn't courage, what were you hoping to forget?"

"I am going to need more alcohol if you want me to tell you."

She couldn't remember ever feeling so frightened and uncertain. Kyle had her emotions tied into knots and she was not sure, geist or not, that she wanted them unknotted.

Once they had been seated, Jayde ordered four shots of tequila.

The waitress placed the drinks and two glasses of water on their table. "Are you ready to order?"

"When you walk by and see these shot glasses empty, we will be ready to order," Jayde replied.

"Take your time." The waitress smiled and walked away.

Jayde downed the first shot, shook her head and then did the same with a second. "Okay, I want you to look me dead in the eyes and give me an honest answer to my question. Will you do that for me?"

"Sure, but I've got to say, I don't play games in my relationships, and I'm pretty sure you don't either."

"Alright. First, let me tell you that I have a nasty mix of Native and Irish in me. You may have noticed my temper is easily sparked."

"Maybe a little, yeah."

"You also know I speak my mind which has, on occasion, not worked in my favour, but nonetheless, more often than not, if I think it, I say it." She could feel herself stalling. "First question."

"Fire when ready." Kyle picked up one of the two shot glasses in front of him.

"Are you a geist?"

Kyle started to cough as the tequila hadn't quite found its way down his throat.

"So I'm guessing by your reaction that you know what I'm talking about."

As he drank one of the glasses of water, Kyle hoped he would have a good answer by the time he finished it.

"Would it help if I said I was only part geist?" he replied nervously. He wasn't sure why he was nervous, other than being told his entire life that no one could find out about his mother's geist heritage. Now, this amazing woman had asked him point blank about it.

"Points to you for telling the truth. Did you know who I was before you came into the shop?"

"Yes."

Jayde felt her blood boil. "You know about the...no, you tell me. What do you know? I want to hear all of it."

"I know about The League of Twelve. I know about Eyras. I know about the City of Radiance. I probably know as much as you, since your brother is in the league. Maybe we should go somewhere else to talk about this."

"Yeah, let's go back to the shop. This gets settled tonight." She walked to the front door of the restaurant. Her black combat boots fell heavily upon the floor with each of her steps.

Kyle tossed some money on the table and followed her out. He watched her thrust her palm into the glass door as she continued her angry march to his car.

She stood beside the front passenger door of his car as he walked to her, unlocked it, and opened it for her.

"I can open my own door," she snapped.

"You're welcome."

Kyle sat in the driver's seat and looked at Jayde. Her head was turned away from him.

Once he turned the key in the ignition, Jayde lowered her window. She felt tears well in her eyes and she was not willing to let Kyle see them.

Jayde stared out her window; both she and Kyle were silent. The more than ten minute trip seemed to take only two.

Once she unlocked the back door of the shop and she and Kyle had entered, she turned and kissed him.

Confused, Kyle asked, "Not that I'm complaining, but what was that for?"

"I just had to have one last taste, in case I have to kill you."

Kyle's expression went from surprise to sombre. "Let's hope our talk goes better than you think it will."

Jayde loudly harrumphed as she walked to the door that led into the shop. "I'm joking, of course, but judo instructor or not, I can give you a run for your money, Mr. Kyle Walker. If that's even your name."

"Mostly," he replied.

Jayde stopped walking, turned around and scowled at him. "I've been nothing but honest with you from day one and you didn't even give me your real name? Just get out of here!"

"Please, Jayde, I'll tell you everything just hear me out."

"You've got five minutes and if I were you, I'd stay back because if you're within arm's reach I may very well beat the hell out of you."

"Understood. You may want to sit, though."

Jayde and Kyle walked to the front of the shop and Jayde sat on the arm of the sofa along the back wall.

"Go ahead." She motioned with her hands. Her voice didn't mask her anger.

"My name is Kyle. But my last name isn't Walker. It's Shea."

"Shea? As in Sebastian Shea's what? Brother? Cousin?" She tried to understand how Kyle could possibly be related to Sebastian.

"I guess I would be his cousin...since his father and mine were brothers."

Jayde got off the sofa and paced, wide-eyed. She leaned her head back and closed her eyes. With a smile on her lips, she opened her eyes and slowly said, "Your father is Marcus...Shea?"

She pointed to the front door. "You've got three seconds to get out of my shop."

Kyle crossed his arms and shouted, "Wait a second. You asked for honesty and I gave it to you. I'm not asking you why my cousin tried to kill my father, but if you know, please, enlighten me!"

"What? You think Seb tried to kill Marcus? No, pal, you got it all wrong. Marcus killed Seb's father, his mother, and his sister, and then stabbed Seb and left him for dead! Your father is a monster!"

"No, my dad was attacked by Sebastian. He said he had to defend himself." Kyle didn't want to believe his father was capable of such things.

"Your father is also a liar. Just leave." She pointed toward the door. She felt hurt and angry all at once.

"I'm not leaving. You said we would settle this one way or another tonight, so let's settle it. Do you want to hear my side? What you've said is not what I was told."

Jayde shouted, "I'll bet! Your father fed you a bunch of lies and you just ate them up, like a good little geist."

"Hey, that's enough!" Kyle yelled. "From where I stand it looks like you are the one who was fed the lies. Why would my father lie to me? Did you ever think that maybe it was your family lying to you?"

Kyle didn't want to believe his father would lie to him.

"Do you even know what The League of Twelve is? What they do? The Eyrasines are safe here because of them!"

"Yeah and geist get killed. Doesn't matter what they do, they just get killed."

"They only kill geist that are a threat. There's a way they can tell who's good or who isn't, and all peaceful geist are left to live their lives as long as they don't cause trouble!"

"Really? Then why did my mother have to hide? Why was she always a target?"

"Was she evil? Did she kill people?"

The atmosphere in the room seem to vibrate with negative energy.

"No. But my dad said…"

She interrupted him, her hand up with her palm facing him. "Yeah, stop right there. Your dad said. Just another lie he spoon fed you. If the league wanted her dead, she would be dead. Ask her. See what she has to say."

Kyle's expression turned sombre. "She's already dead."

Jayde sighed and lowered her head. "Kyle, I'm so sorry, I completely forgot. How did she die?"

"She just went to sleep one night and never woke up. Dad and I buried her in an unmarked grave behind our house. He said that if the league knew where she was buried they would…"

Jayde's voice took on a softer tone as she spoke. "Honestly, how could you believe the things he said, Kyle? Did you never question him? From what you know of my

117

family, of Ann and Angeline, of *me*, do you think we're heartless monsters? Kyle, your father has been lying to you your entire life."

"Let me ask you something. How did you know I was part geist?"

"Ann and Angeline told me. They're both league members. They said that you have a good heart and that's the only reason I'm even giving you a chance to explain yourself."

"Okay, so if I'm good, doesn't it stand to reason that my father is as well?"

"Oh no! Your father is a waste of skin!"

"I...I can't do this." He lowered his head and rubbed his face, feeling betrayed. "I'm having a hard time believing that everything my father told me my entire life was a lie."

Jayde walked to Kyle, took his face in her hands and looked directly into his eyes. "Look, I get it. He's your dad and you want to believe him. But Kyle, he's not the man you think he is. I don't know how he managed to trick you into thinking he's the victim, but he's a murderer."

She paused, lowered her hands and removed her cell phone from her pocket. "You know what? I want you to meet some of the league, officially."

"Are you kidding me? Are you sure you're not going to have them kill me?"

"Listen, you already met Ann and Angeline, well, the drunk version of them, and you met Seb when he came to pick them up."

She stopped speaking and opened her mouth. Her eyes narrowed and she gasped. "You knew! You knew who Seb was when you met him!"

"I did, but I thought he was the man who tried to kill my father. Now you've told me that my father killed his family. I just don't know what to think."

"Okay. I told you we were going to settle this tonight and we will."

She dialed Conor's phone number. "Conor pick up John and come to Jayded Ink. Now. I'll explain when you get here."

Next, she dialed Sebastian's number. Once he answered, she asked, "Seb, did you guys drop Ange off yet?"

"Just now. Why?"

"Go back and get her. I need the three of you in Jayded Ink. Conor is on his way to heal Ange's drunk."

She turned to face Kyle. "You're about to meet five of the twelve league members, including the leader, John."

"Great," Kyle replied sarcastically, worry evident on his face.

He pointed to the half bottle of rum that the girls hadn't finished. "Mind if I help myself? I'm not sure I should do this sober."

Kyle drank and paced.

Jayde busied herself tidying the shop while they waited.

Fifteen minutes passed, then Conor, John, and James walked through the backdoor of Jayded Ink. Conor ran through the storage room and shouted, "Jayde! What's wrong?"

"Nothing," she replied, calmly. "I'm just going to need you to sober Ange up when she gets here."

Conor looked at his sister and shook his head. "You had me thinking there was an emergency here."

Kyle said, "Hey, Conor."

"Kyle?" Conor was surprised to see him. "Jayde, what's going on?"

"I'll tell you when everyone else is here. Patience, bro."

John entered the shop with James. "Jayde, what's the…" His sentence trailed off as he saw Kyle's thin, pale blue aura. "I take it this is Kyle?"

"Yes, John, this is Kyle."

Kyle held his hand out to John. "Good to meet you, John."

"Yeah, you too." John shook his hand, unsure of how he should feel.

James walked past Kyle, sizing him up without saying a word. He held up the half bottle of rum. "Is this bottle for anyone in particular, Jayde, or should I get us each a glass?"

"There are some plastic cups in the cupboard over the fridge in the back. Bring a few cups and grab another bottle while you're there."

James walked into the storage room just as Sebastian, Ann, and Angeline came through the door from the tunnels. "Hey, Seb. Ann, take this bottle while I grab some glasses."

"Again? I think I'm done drinking for the night, thanks." She took the bottle with her to the front of the shop.

Sebastian supported Angeline as he followed Ann. "Come on, Ange, just a few more steps to the sofa."

"You're so nice to me, Sebastian," Angeline slurred. "You're so sweet. Did you know that? Do you know that you're a sweet, sweet man?"

"Yeah, I'm a real prince, ya silly drunk. Sit." He eased her onto the sofa.

"Jayde, what's…" Sebastian began as he turned and saw Kyle. "Kyle, you're still here?"

"Yeah, I'm still here. We have a few things to settle, cousin."

Every muscle in Sebastian's body tensed. He looked at Jayde and demanded, "Jayde, what is going on?"

"Conor, please take care of Ange," Jayde said calmly.

Conor walked to Angeline and placed one hand on her head and one on her stomach. "Give me two minutes and she'll be good to go."

Once Angeline was sober, Jayde told them what she and Kyle had discussed.

Sebastian struggled to maintain his composure as Kyle told them what Marcus had said.

"My dad wanted me to get to know a few of you and find out as much as I could. Now that I've come to know Jayde and her family, I'm having trouble believing what he said. I don't know what to think. I just know that you're not the awful people that my dad made you out to be."

John folded his arms. "I'm not surprised. From what I've been told about Marcus, he's not fond of the truth."

Kyle rubbed his eyes. "I spent most of my childhood with my mother since my dad was always taking jobs out of town. Sometimes he would be gone for months at a time. Since she died, I've been pretty much on my own. Dad never settled down into a fatherly role." He felt as though he were baring his soul.

He continued. "I guess from what you're telling me, I'm lucky he wasn't around more to influence me because I'm nothing like the man Jayde described."

He turned toward Sebastian. "So, cousin, if you can tell whether I'm good or bad, tell me. What do you see?"

"Trust isn't given. You have to earn it. Whether you're good or not isn't the issue as far as I'm concerned. Right now your aura shows that you're on the good side of things, but if I ever see you going dark, I will kill you."

"Fair enough. With me, what you see is what you get. I've never changed who I am for anyone and I don't plan on starting now. Not for you or my father."

John asked, "Kyle, what information did Marcus want you to get out of us?"

Kyle hesitated. He didn't want to betray his father, but if there was even a slim chance that he was the monster that these people thought he was, he felt he needed to let them know at least some of what Marcus had planned.

"He wanted me to watch as many of you as I could and let him know when you went to or from the City of Radiance through this shop, as well as where you keep your keys."

Although Marcus had asked Kyle to help him replace the league members, he wasn't ready to share that just yet.

Sebastian walked to Kyle with fists clenched and shouted, "What have you told him?"

"I just told him where the door is. He already knew about it, he just wanted me to find out how it was accessed now that the building is no longer a motorcycle repair shop. That's all I've told him. I haven't even seen any of your keys."

"Your father can't be trusted, Kyle. He killed my family and left me bleeding out on my sister's bedroom floor," Sebastian growled. He lifted his shirt to reveal the two scars from the stab wounds on his left side. "Thanks to the Eyrasines, I healed up pretty quickly but not even their medicines could take away these scars."

Kyle looked at the raised, pinkish marks on Sebastian's side. He then looked from one person to the other. "I have a question for you guys. How can you tell I've got geist in me? Dad said you wouldn't be able to detect my geist half because the human side of me would mask it."

Conor looked at Kyle. He felt sorry for him. "That's not how it works. If you have geist in you, we can see it. Your father lied to you, Kyle."

Sebastian furrowed his brows. "Let me get this straight. Your father sent you to spy on us, knowing that we could tell whether you're a geist or not? Apparently, your father thinks you're expendable."

"So why haven't you killed me?" Kyle spat.

Sebastian moved to hit Kyle.

James jumped in between them with his arms stretched out toward each of them. "Relax! Both of you!"

John and Conor moved toward Sebastian. Each of them grabbed an arm to hold him back.

"This is not the time, Seb," John said sternly.

Jayde walked to Kyle, stood beside him and shouted, "Enough! Ann and Angeline said Kyle has a good heart. Were they wrong?"

She glanced around the room, saw Sebastian, John, and Conor look at each other without speaking. "I asked a question! Answer me!"

"No," Conor replied. "He's okay. He's different from any geist I've ever seen, but I guess that would be because he's got geist mixed with human and Eyrasine."

"Just so you know," Sebastian added, "we don't just kill every geist we see."

John looked Kyle directly in the eyes. "Do you know where your father is?"

"He gave me the keys to his penthouse and said he had to be out of town for a while so, no, I have no idea where he is now." Kyle felt conflicted.

With his eyes still on Kyle, John said, "I need to know where you stand."

"You want to know where I stand?" Kyle asked defensively. "What do you want me to do? What do I have to do to prove to you that my father isn't the monster you think he is?"

Sebastian pointed at Kyle. "Tell you what. Let Marcus know that you and I are good pals and we're going out for dinner together tomorrow night. Seven o'clock, at Transcendence, a double date. You and Jayde, Ann, and I. Tell him you found out that we always keep our keys on us when we're not at home. Let's see what he does with this information."

Ann and Jayde looked at each other, their eyes wide.

"Fine. I'll phone him right now." Kyle pulled his phone from his pocket and dialed.

Marcus answered on the second ring. "Yes?"

"Hey, Dad, I've got some information. I'm in pretty good with a few of the league members now." Kyle looked at Sebastian with a sarcastic smirk. "I found out that they always have their keys on them when they're not home."

"This is good, Kyle! You've done well."

"Tomorrow night I'll be having dinner with Jayde at Transcendence at around 7:00 p.m. Sebastian and his league girlfriend will be joining us."

"Excellent! I knew you wouldn't let me down. In the meantime, enjoy my penthouse. You've earned it." Marcus was pleased with his son.

"I'll let you know how it goes." Kyle ended the call. With his phone back in his pocket, he tilted his head. "I guess we will see tomorrow night what kind of man my dad really is."

"Okay." John formulated a quick plan for the next night. He knew that Marcus was unstable and unpredictable. As he walked slowly through Jayded Ink, he shared his plan. "We're going to keep this small. I'll bring my dad with me. Ann, bring Drew and ask your parents if they mind us using the restaurant for a private dinner tomorrow night. We can't risk having the public walk in if this goes south.

"Ange, let Josh know he's on door duty for this. Conor, phone your parents, see if they can join us as well. We need to have bodies in the restaurant, so Marcus won't suspect anything. Nobody else needs to know about this. We will all meet up tomorrow night, 6:00 p.m. at Transcendence. I'll phone Ethan and have him join us as well, since he will already be here in Niagara Falls."

He looked at Kyle. "We're trusting that you won't let your father know what we're planning."

"I need to know exactly what kind of man my father is. You have my word that I won't speak with him before tomorrow night. I want your word that none of you will kill him if he shows up tomorrow."

"You have my word, Kyle," John replied. He looked around the room at the other league members; his eyes locked with Sebastian's. "No one will kill him tomorrow if he shows up."

John raised one eyebrow. "Tomorrow night is going to be interesting."

11 – BETRAYAL

Ethan settled in for his surveillance shift. He didn't mind the alone time after dealing with the public most of the day in the antique shop. While he loved all things with an historic past, it was the modern era patrons for which he had little tolerance.

The hours passed quickly. His mind wandered to the new flat he had started renting a few months prior. Once he moved out of his parents' home, Ethan lived the life of a free-spirited bachelor. While he entertained the occasional female guest and had the necessary furnishings for a fun-filled evening, he wasn't big on the idea of home decorating, or commitment.

Ethan phoned John when his shift had nearly ended. "Hey, mate, there's been no sign of Marcus for almost a week. I'm thinking he isn't here any longer."

"Yeah, Kyle told us earlier Marcus gave him the keys to his place because he was leaving town, but my gut is telling me otherwise. Damn it! He must have another place here." John checked the list on his phone. "Amber's up after you. Let her know her shift will be the last. I'll phone Angeline and Zayne and let them know. Thanks Ethan."

"Alright, mate. I'll see you later."

Ethan saw Amber walk toward the surveillance car through the side mirror. He rolled down the window. "Here she is now."

Amber leaned in the car window. "Hiya, Ethan. Anything moving about tonight?"

"Lots of blokes, just none of any concern to us. Have fun." He got out of the car and leaned on the door before he closed it. "Almost forgot. Your watch will be the last. Seems Marcus isn't around any longer but one final watch ought to prove that either way, right?"

"I suppose."

"Alright then, I'm off. I've got to see a man about a dog," Ethan said with a wink.

Amber chuckled. "Nice. You do that."

As she watched Ethan walk away, Amber pulled her cell phone out of her purse and phoned Marcus.

~~~~

While Amber began her surveillance shift, a few of the others set the scene at Transcendence. Vivian agreed to take the part of waitress, and Jake's role was to be bartender. Nick, the chef at Transcendent in London, was in the kitchen, while Yvonne and Roy Rivait were seated by the east wall.

John instructed, "Josh, if anyone other than Marcus or a geist tries to get in tonight, tell them the restaurant is closed for a private party."

"Will do, John."

"The rest of us will be seated throughout the restaurant. Remember, we want to find out what Marcus wants. He will most likely send geist in rather than showing up himself. Let's try to keep one alive."

~~~~

While Sebastian, Ann, Jayde, and Kyle prepared for their evening at Transcendence, Marcus arranged to have five geist join his son to persuade Sebastian and Ann to relinquish their keys.

Marcus phoned Ganga.

"Yeah?"

"Ganga, has everyone been given their instructions?" He wanted to be certain that the geist who were going to Transcendence knew that they were not to kill his son.

"I told them what you said," Ganga replied, rolling her eyes.

"Repeat it to me," Marcus commanded.

Ganga sighed. "Go to the restaurant, get two keys that look like metal circles. Whatever happens, don't kill the guy in the picture. That is what I told them when I showed them the picture of your son."

"Did you also instruct them to bring you the keys?"

"Yes. I did. They're going to text me once they have the keys. I told them to meet me at your favourite spot, the alley behind The Rogue Bistro, and that I would pay them when they gave me the keys."

Marcus sighed as he ended the call. He wondered if the geist Ganga had enlisted for this job knew that their lives would be forfeit if they killed his son. He also wondered if these geist would be able to help him in his pursuit to control the portal between Earth and Eyras, as he had eleven seats to fill.

"We will have to see how they do with this first job."

~~~~

In Transcendence, Jayde, Kyle, Ann, and Sebastian ate dinner, had a few drinks and talked while they waited to see who, if anyone, would make an appearance. Much to his surprise, Sebastian found that Kyle was easy to talk to and a rather good conversationalist.

"When did you first get into judo?" Sebastian asked.

Kyle finished off the last bit of his beer and leaned back in his chair. "I was five or six years old when my mother first brought me to the dojo in town. My dad was always away for work and she wanted me to be able to defend myself. She said I was different than the other kids and that some of them wouldn't understand."

"Unless they were in The League of Twelve, no one would be able to tell you were part geist." Ann's eyes were sympathetic.

"When I was young, I wasn't able to control myself like I can now."

Jayde looked surprised. "What do you mean, control yourself?"

"I'll show you some other time. I'm not sure this is something everyone would want to see."

"No," Sebastian said, curiosity in his voice. "Let's see what it is you've been hiding."

"Okay. Just remember, you asked for this."

Kyle looked at Sebastian, studied his features for a moment then morphed his face into that of his cousin. He held the likeness for a few seconds before his face returned to the one with which he had begun the evening.

Almost everyone in the restaurant looked at Kyle with eyes wide. Jayde began to choke on her supper.

"Jayde!" Kyle shouted and patted her back.

Jayde stopped choking and began to laugh. "That was amazing!"

"How can you do that?" Sebastian was both astonished and impressed.

"I'm not sure. As far back as I can remember, I've been able to change my appearance to anything I saw. It doesn't hold for long, but there you have it. The freak that is me."

Just then, Josh let two geist into the restaurant. He signaled to Vivian, who came to the front to seat them.

She grabbed two menus. "Good evening, gentlemen. Table for two?"

"Yes," one of the geist replied.

"Follow me."

She led them to the back of the restaurant and seated them one table away from where Kyle, Jayde, Sebastian, and Ann sat.

Vivian took their drink orders. "Two draught, coming up."

She told Jake what the geist ordered and he poured the beer slowly.

Vivian took the drinks and as she placed them on their table, she said, "I'll be back in a few minutes to take your dinner order."

She saw Josh signal her again and went to the front door. This time, she brought two more geist to the back of the restaurant.

"We're just here for drinks," one of them said.

"Okay, the bartender will be happy to help you."

They seated themselves beside Michael and Ethan who had taken their places on two of the bar stools.

What seemed like less than a minute later, Vivian was once again summoned to the front door. As she walked this geist to a table, he looked around and took in his surroundings.

He recognized Kyle from the photo Ganga had shown him. "Kyle? Geez! I haven't seen you in a long time."

Kyle looked at the geist, confused.

"It's me, Dan. We went to high school together. How ya been?"

Kyle stood to shake his hand. "Good, Dan. How are things? What have you been up to?"

"I've just been taking odd jobs here and there. I'm not big on being tied down," Dan replied with a wink. "What about you? I heard you were some big karate guy now."

"Judo, actually." Kyle knew that this geist could only have known about his connection with martial arts if Marcus had told him.

"Really? I'm more of a boxing kind of guy myself." Dan held up his fists and jabbed at the air in front of him.

"Yeah, I get it. Well it was good seeing you. Enjoy your meal."

"You too, Kyle." Dan walked to the table where the other two geist were seated.

Kyle sat and shook his head. "I don't know him. I've never seen that guy before but I'm sure he's geist."

"He is geist, Kyle." Sebastian said, his expression curious. "And not one of the good ones, but how did you know?"

"I can feel a vibration that other geist give off. All geist can, whether just half like me or full on geist."

"It's fine." Ann shrugged one shoulder. "We were expecting something and now it's here."

"I'm sorry, Kyle." Jayde placed her hand on his. "I know how much you were hoping that nothing would happen tonight."

"It's alright." Kyle felt betrayed. "It's better that I know what kind of man my father really is."

After a few minutes, Dan, along with his two friends, picked up the chairs in which they had been sitting and walked to Kyle. One sat between Kyle and Jayde, and the other between Jayde and Ann. Both geist pointed knives at the women under the table.

Dan placed his chair between Kyle and Sebastian. He leaned back and pointed at the others. "We don't want to make a scene, so if you could just hand over your keys, we will be on our way. My friends have knives pointed at your ladies, so unless you want them hurt, just give us the keys."

Sebastian asked, "What keys?"

Dan turned to Kyle and ignored Sebastian. He placed his arm around the back of Kyle's chair. "Kyle, we were sent to get some keys. Which of your friends has the keys?"

"I've got the keys." Kyle answered. He took his key ring out of his pocket, removed two keys, and placed them in the centre of the table.

The geist with his knife pointed at Jayde, looked at Kyle, angry. "Is this some kind of joke? Marcus said the keys were thick metal circles."

Yvonne and Roy watched the exchange from their table. Roy began to stand and Yvonne put her hand on his arm. "This is their fight, Roy. We have to let them do this."

Roy sighed heavily. "I know, but…"

"If they need us, we can help, but we have to give them a chance to do this on their own." Yvonne was worried, but she knew they had raised their children with the knowledge and skills to be able to handle themselves.

At Kyle's table, one of the geist stood and threw the keys to the floor. He grabbed Kyle's hair and pulled his head back. His knife, no longer pointed at Jayde, was now against Kyle's throat. He spoke directly in Kyle's face. "Listen asshole, if you don't hand over the keys right now I will slice your throat!"

"Just give him your keys," Kyle said, his fists clenched at his sides.

Sebastian slammed his key on the table. "Here. Back away and it's all yours."

Dan grabbed Sebastian's key. "Where's the other key? There's supposed to be two!"

No one spoke.

The geist who held his blade against Kyle's throat pierced his flesh and drew blood.

Jayde saw Kyle flinch. Adrenaline shot through her body and every muscle tensed.

Ann shouted, "Stop! It's in my purse, by my foot."

The geist between Ann and Jayde reached down to retrieve Ann's purse.

Jayde took advantage of the situation and kicked his face.

He was thrust backward and dropped his knife as he brought his hand to his face.

Ann quickly reached down into her purse. With her Soul Dagger in hand, she lunged at the geist and plunged it into the centre of his chest.

The geist with his blade at Kyle's throat spoke through gritted teeth. "Enough! Put the key on the table or you can watch your friend here bleed!"

The geist dropped his knife as he gasped and then disintegrated. No one had seen Ethan as he used his gift of invisibility and took position behind him.

As the two geist seated at the bar got up, John and Drew aimed their guns at them.

"This won't kill you, but I'll bet it will still hurt like hell," Drew said.

One of the geist charged at Drew. He took a bullet to his shoulder but still knocked Drew to the floor.

John shot the other geist from the bar. He aimed to ensure he wouldn't get up, but also wouldn't die and mist out of his body.

Dan watched as his friends turned to ash. He knew he would soon join them and was determined to take someone with him.

He pulled out his blade and lunged at Kyle.

Sebastian moved behind Dan and thrust his Soul Dagger into his side. He watched as his key and a knife landed in the pile of Dan's ash on the floor.

John turned and slammed his fist into the geist who stood over Drew.

The geist hit the floor and was slow to rise. That gave John the opportunity to grab his Soul Dagger from his pocket and stab it into his throat.

One geist remained.

The geist that John had shot managed to get to his feet and staggered toward Sebastian, only to have Conor intervene.

Conor tackled the geist from behind.

John shouted, "Keep that one alive!"

Conor slammed the geist's head into the floor; blood dripped from his mouth and nose.

The geist tried to swing his arm behind himself in a feeble attempt to knock Conor off his back and failed. He saw no other option but to leave the body he inhabited, so he pulled a blade from his belt and thrust it repeatedly into his side.

Angeline ran to the geist and plunged her dagger into his neck.

Conor dropped to the floor as the geist disintegrated beneath him.

"Bloody hell!" Angeline shouted.

"Is everybody alright?" John asked.

Ethan rematerialized and one by one, they began to report that they were unhurt, except for a few cuts and scrapes.

With their last chance at gaining information about Marcus gone, John pounded the nearest table. "Damn it!"

Kyle took his hand away from his chest and looked at the blood on it. As he fell to his knees, Conor and Jayde both rushed to his side.

Conor ripped open Kyle's shirt. He tried to heal him but the wound was too severe. "This is bad. We have to get him to the City if he's going to survive."

Yvonne and Jake reached Kyle at the same time.

Jake brought a generous supply of napkins. "Yvonne, here." He handed her the napkins.

Yvonne placed the napkins over Kyle's wound and applied pressure.

Jayde knelt down beside Kyle and cried. "No, no, no. Kyle, come on!"

Kyle coughed up blood. His eyes were fixed on Jayde's face. She slowly faded from his sight as he lost consciousness.

Conor turned to Jake. "I can't heal him. We have to get him to the City now. Jake, help me get him to my car."

Jayde remained motionless as she stared at Kyle.

She looked at her brother, her face stained with tears and watched as he and Jake lifted Kyle off the floor.

"Ange and I will go ahead to speak with the Immortals," John said, as he and Angeline rushed out of the restaurant.

Conor saw the tears in his sister's eyes, something that was quite rare. "We will get him to the City. He'll make it, Jayde."

"I know." Jayde wiped her face. "I'll drive. You try and stop the bleeding. Please, Conor, I can't lose him."

Sebastian and Ann followed behind the others as they exited the back door that led to the parking lot.

Once Kyle was in the truck with Conor by his side, Jake shut the door.

Jayde hurried to the driver's seat and fumbled with the keys in the ignition. She couldn't stop her hands from trembling.

On their way to Sebastian's car, Ann looked at Jayde. "Seb, I'm going to drive Conor's truck to Jayded Ink. Jayde is in no shape to drive."

"Okay, I'll meet you there," Sebastian replied, as he continued on to his vehicle.

Ann opened the driver's door on Conor's vehicle. "Move over Jayde, I'll drive."

With tears still in her eyes, Jayde didn't argue. She climbed over the centre console and sat in the passenger seat. "Thanks, Ann," she whispered.

Ann turned the key in the ignition and sped to Jayded Ink.

~~~~

In the City of Radiance, the Immortals were waiting for John and Angeline at the west entrance of the Grand Temple.

"We know that the child of Marcus Shea is being brought to us this night," Araton said, as he tilted his head slightly. Araton's psychic abilities allowed him to sense when anyone had thoughts of the Immortals.

"He must be placed in a healing tube immediately upon his arrival if he is to survive. Selphia and Pen-Ming will aid in the child's healing. As he is part geist, his body will require more attention than the Eyrasines alone can provide."

"Thank you, Araton." Angeline and John bowed then walked to the Healing Chambers with Selphia and Pen-Ming.

Selphia looked straight ahead as she walked. "I sense a conflict within you, John. You must put your feelings for Marcus aside, as his child is more of his mother than his father. Araton has foreseen greatness in Kyle, son of Marcus."

"I will try, Selphia." With anger and hatred in his voice, he added, "I'm having trouble getting past the fact that his father had my mother killed and slaughtered Seb's entire family. How do I put that aside?"

Pen-Ming answered. "You must find a way. If you do not, many things that have been foretold, will not come to pass."

John stopped outside the doors as Selphia and Pen-Ming entered and watched as Sebastian and Conor carried Kyle into the Healing Chambers. Jayde and Ann were close behind.

Angeline, still at John's side, saw him look down. She put her hand on his arm and squeezed gently. "You have to know that you can do this, John. It's not enough that the rest of us believe in you, you have to as well."

She kissed his cheek. "Let's get the lad healed, yeah?"

"Yeah," John whispered. He knew that he had a lot of soul searching to do.

~~~~

Kyle sat up quickly, unsure of where he was, only to have Jayde ease him back down.

"Hey, not so fast."

"Where am I?" he asked, confused.

"You're in the Healing Chambers in the City of Radiance."

"What? How did I get here?"

Pen-Ming approached, his hands held out in front of himself. "That, Kyle Shea, is thanks to your friends. Had you not been brought to us, as you are geist as well as human and Eyrasine, your wound surely would have proved fatal."

Kyle didn't blink as he looked at Pen-Ming. The red streak in this extremely tall man's coal black hair and perfectly matching red eyes, rendered him speechless.

Jayde introduced them. "Kyle, this is Pen-Ming, one of the seven immortals that run the City of Radiance."

"Hi." Kyle's voice was barely audible. He found that the forming of words was not easy.

Pen-Ming looked directly into Kyle's eyes. "We have granted you access to our city. We believe your heart to be kind and just, but we are not fools. Knowing that your father is Marcus Shea, that his blood flows through you, we feel we must warn you that any breach of our trust will not be taken lightly."

"Understood," Kyle replied. He struggled to sit up. "I want you to know that I am my own man. My father was never much of an influence in my life and now that I know who he really is, you can trust me to help you stop him."

Pen-Ming tilted his head slightly, glad to hear Kyle say what he had suspected. "Your wound should be sufficiently healed to warrant a short trip through the City, if Miss Rivait would like to accompany you."

Jayde bowed. "I would be happy to. How about it, Kyle?"

She brought a wheelchair to Kyle's bedside. With a wink and a smile, she added, "Do you want to let me push you around a bit?"

"I can walk," Kyle retorted. He then tried to get out of bed and nearly collapsed. "Maybe the chair isn't such a bad idea."

Jayde smiled and helped Kyle into the wheelchair. "That's what I like to hear, the tough guy knowing what's good for him. I'll grab your stuff."

"Shut up and push, woman!" Kyle laughed just before he grabbed at the wound above his heart and groaned.

As they strolled through the Grand Temple, Jayde pointed out the different rooms that the league and their family members used. At the West exit, she pushed his wheelchair into a transport pod and they rose fifteen feet above the crowd. She wanted him to have the best view of what the City had to offer.

"It's almost like a regular city on the surface, but here, they don't use money. If you want something, you ask for it. If someone wants something from you and you have it, you give it. Everyone here cooperates. It's a virtual utopia. There's no crime, no greed and no poverty."

"Are all of these people from Eyras?" Kyle was astounded.

"Most are, but some are part Eyrasine and part human, like me."

Kyle cast his eyes downward, as he thought back to the previous night in Transcendence. "My father sent a bunch of geist and one nearly killed me."

He pounded his fist on the arm of his wheelchair.

"Your father is insane."

"Can you hand me my cell phone, please?"

"Sure," Jayde replied.

"It's time my father knew where he stands with me."

She handed Kyle his cell phone and he dialed Marcus' number.

When Marcus answered, Kyle spoke angrily. "Hey, just thought you should know that your friends, the geist, screwed up at the restaurant and they were all killed. They earned their pay though. One of them stabbed me and if it wasn't for Jayde and the league members that were there, I'd probably be dead. No reason for concern though. They brought me to the City of Radiance and the Immortals treated my wound. Thanks, Dad, you really outdid yourself."

"Kyle, I never wanted you to get hurt. I know you can handle yourself. You must believe me, I would never purposely put you in harm's way."

"Oh, okay, that makes it all better. Lose my number."

Marcus looked at his phone, closed his eyes, and clenched his teeth tightly as Kyle ended the call. "Ungrateful child," he muttered aloud to himself.

As his phone rang in his hand, he saw Amber's name on the display. "Amber," Marcus snapped. He wondered if she had actually managed to get some information for him.

"I'm in a car across the street from your building. I've got your artifact."

Marcus set aside his disappointment in his son and smiled.

On her way through Wells' Antiquities to get to her surveillance duties, Amber had helped herself to the artifact that the European faction had kept safe for so many years. She had seen it many times, but never thought that one day it would prove to be her means of revenge.

She grinned as she thought that the rest of the league had no idea what was coming. She would see to it that they were sorry for making her feel insignificant.

"When will you be round to collect it?" she asked.

"I'll send someone for it. You've done well, little one. I am quite pleased. Have you any information for me yet?"

"Not yet. I know where the other artifact is though. It's in the Jewelry shop in Cairo. We're having a meeting soon and I can phone you when it's done to let you know what the rest of the league is up to."

"Be sure you do." He ended their call.

Marcus immediately phoned Ganga to let her know that the geist had failed to acquire the two astral keys. He then told her to collect the artifact from a young woman in a car parked on the street across from his building. "And Ganga, phone me the minute you have it in your possession and I will let you know where to bring it."

"You bet." Ganga set out toward Marcus' building. The cold wind of North America had Ganga wishing she had chosen a more robust human to replicate.

As she neared the building, Ganga saw four cars parked on the street. "A car, he said. Guess he didn't think that other people would park here too."

The first vehicle she passed had no one inside. The rest, however, had tinted windows. She tried not to look suspicious as she stood beside the next car and knocked on the window. The knock went unanswered.

At the next vehicle, a woman lowered her window. "Can I help you?"

"Marcus sent me to pick something up." Ganga immediately recognized Amber as one of the European league members that she had been assigned to watch.

Amber narrowed her eyes. "He sent a geist?"

"He never said it was a league girl I'd be meeting. Let me see what you've got."

As Amber reached across the passenger seat, Ganga saw a great opportunity. She pulled a blade from her coat pocket and drove it into the back of Amber's neck, penetrating her skull.

Ganga pushed Amber's head and she slumped forward.

She felt around inside the door for the lock release, unlocked the door and got into the back seat.

"Let's get this window up, shall we?" Ganga reached into the front seat. "Wouldn't want anyone to see you lying here all dead in your car." She smiled. She was quite pleased with herself.

Both the artifact and Amber's astral key were in her purse.

Ganga phoned Marcus. *Wonder what Mr. Wonderful will have to say about me not only bringing him this artifact, but a key as well*, she thought to herself with a satisfied smile.

When Marcus answered his phone, still smiling, she said, "I've got your statue, boss, and a little bonus as well."

"Bonus? Ganga, what are you going on about?" Marcus was annoyed.

"The girl who I met with, she was one of the league members you were having me watch in London. I killed her and I got her key."

"Ganga! You moronic fool! That girl was my informant within the league!"

"You never told me that!" Ganga used her best sarcastic tone. "You said you wanted their keys, I got you a key. I thought you would be happy. What do you want me to do now?"

Marcus closed his eyes and tried to calm himself. "Bring the items to the corner of Merchant and Henley. I will meet you there in one hour."

Marcus weighed his options. He couldn't kill Ganga; she was one of the few geist he found most obedient.

~~~~

Angeline awoke with the previous night's events on her mind. The time that was supposed to have been spent in the Nite Cap with the other league members to celebrate Mariam's birthday, had instead been spent in the Healing Chambers with Kyle. She made a mental note to phone Jayde to see how Kyle was faring.

After she showered and dressed for the day, Angeline headed to Transcendent, the Transcendence satellite restaurant in the Aemetta Suites, to get her first cup of coffee. Inside, she saw two of her waitresses look over the duty roster, both with lines of concern on their faces.

"Good morning, ladies. What's troubling you?"

"Miss Flynn, you haven't seen Amber this morning have you? She was supposed to be here over thirty minutes ago." Claire, the head waitress, was not happy.

"No, I haven't. I'll give her a quick ring and see where she is. In the meantime, Claire, please phone one of the other girls and see if they can make it in."

Angeline reached into her purse for her cell phone. She dialed Amber's number and it went directly to voicemail. She left a message. Amber had had the last watch on Marcus' building the previous evening, so she thought perhaps she had spent the night in either Niagara Falls or the City.

After she finished her coffee, Angeline poured another and walked to her office. Something felt off. She phoned Amber again, and again Amber did not answer.

Angeline activated the locator app on her phone. With the message, *Location not found* displayed, Angeline decided to go to North America, as that was the last place Amber was supposed to have been. She phoned Faith as she walked to the Aemetta's front doors. "I'm stepping out for a bit. If anyone needs me, jot it down and I'll see to them straight away once I'm back."

"Will do," Faith replied.

Angeline walked the few blocks to Wells' Antiquities. She hadn't put her astral key away since she found out Marcus had returned; frequent trips to the City seemed to be the norm now.

Once in the City, Angeline phoned John. As he jolted awake, he heard Angeline's voice. "John, have you seen Amber today? She hasn't come into Transcendent yet and she should have been there over an hour ago."

"No, Ange, I haven't. I've got a complicated extraction later this morning, but I can help you track her down when I'm done, if you'd like," he replied through a yawn.

"Bollocks! I'm always forgetting about our time difference. So sorry, love. Go back to sleep. I'll handle this."

Normally, Angeline enjoyed the walk through the City, but today, she boarded the nearest Transport Pod and looked for Amber as she traveled to the North American exit.

Once through Jayded Ink, she stood on the street and tracked Amber's phone. She was unable to locate her in London, which could only mean that Amber wasn't in Europe.

"Brilliant! There you are!" She walked toward Amber's location following the route outlined in the app.

On her way, she realized she was headed to Marcus' building and quickened her pace. At nearly half past two in the morning, the streetlights were brightly lit and Angeline spotted the surveillance car easily. The black tinted windows made it difficult to see inside the vehicle. She tried the door and found it unlocked.

"Amber, are you alright?" She saw Amber sitting with her head back and her eyes closed. When Amber didn't respond, Angeline shook her shoulder gently.

Amber's head fell forward.

The blood on the back of her neck and jacket had Angeline gasp. "Amber!"

She checked for a pulse and was not surprised there was none. She immediately dialed John's number again.

"Angeline, didn't we just have a chat about the time difference thing?"

"She's dead, John. Amber's dead. Someone killed her in the surveillance car."

John jumped out of bed. "I'll be there in ten minutes."

He dressed quickly and sped to Angeline's side. He found her sitting on the curb beside the surveillance car.

"I thought you said Marcus wasn't around any longer. You told me we were done with this surveillance."

"I did. We are. Amber was supposed to be the last one. We should have had him by now. Ange, I'm so sorry."

A single tear escaped from her eye. Angeline rose and pulled her jacket down, straightening it as she steadied herself. "We need to find a replacement. I searched her car and found her Soul Dagger, but I was unable to find her key. I'm assuming whoever killed her took it."

She opened her hand. "I've got her ring."

Angeline had to put her feelings aside. She was responsible for finding someone to take Amber's place. Her next thought, however, was of Edmond and Hannah, Amber's parents. She closed her eyes tightly. "Oh, John, I've got to tell Edmond and Hannah. She was their only child."

"I'll notify the police," John offered. "You should probably stay and give them a statement when they get here."

John quickly formulated a plausible scenario. "I'll phone Ann and have her say Amber was a student from a culinary school in London who was staying with her here on an exchange program. If we need it, I'll get Seb or Drew to draw up some legal paperwork and backdate it. I'll take care of letting the rest of the league know."

He sat beside Angeline as he placed the 911 call. Together they waited as the cold wind blew around them, though neither of them could feel it.

12 – HANNAH'S INDISCRETION

When she arrived at the door that led into the back of the antique shop from the tunnels, Angeline made the call. She tried her best to keep emotion out of her voice. "Edmond, it's Angeline. Can you and Hannah meet me at Wells' Antiquities? I've some news for you."

Edmond wondered what business the European faction leader of the league would have with him. "Is it urgent, dear? Hannah and I were off to lunch with some friends just now."

"I am sorry, but this really shouldn't wait." Angeline ended the call, turned her key in the metal door, and entered the shop.

Hearing the mirror move, Ethan and his sister, Olivia, both turned to the sound.

Olivia wiped her mouth. "Hello, Angeline. Ethan and I were just sneaking a few biscuits Mum brought by. How are things at the Aemetta?"

Angeline looked at the floor. "Amber is dead. She was killed last night. I'm waiting for Edmond and Hannah to meet me here so that I can let them know their only child has died."

Olivia walked to Angeline and placed a hand on her arm. "Oh, Angeline. What happened? What can I do?"

Shocked and angered, Ethan stood, his fists clenched. "Do the others know?"

"John knows. He said he would take care of informing the others. Whoever killed her took her key. It has to be Marcus, Ethan. Who else would take Amber's key?"

Angeline, Ethan, and Olivia walked to the front section of the shop as they heard the bell at the top of the front door ring.

Edmond joked, "So, Miss Flynn, what news have you that has caused us to postpone our luncheon?"

They listened to Angeline recount the events that led to Amber's death. Hannah sobbed uncontrollably while Edmond held her. The blood seemed to drain from Edmond's face and he felt his heart beat hard and fast inside his chest.

Angeline held Amber's ring tightly inside her jacket pocket. "I have her ring and Soul Dagger."

Olivia walked to Hannah to console her, while Angeline took Edmond aside.

She could see the question in his eyes. "Before you ask, her key was not with her."

"Bloody hell."

"Edmond, I hate to ask, but with Marcus wanting all of our keys, we need someone to take Amber's place as soon as possible, someone to fill the Aquarius role for when we do get it back."

Edmond cleared his throat and put aside his grief. He spoke, his voice stoic. "My sister has a son. I will get you the information when I can. Where is Amber? We have to go to her."

"She's at a hospital in Niagara Falls. John stayed with her." Angeline couldn't help but feel as though she had failed. Amber was her responsibility and she had been unable to keep her safe.

~~~~

Not a word was exchanged as Angeline sat across from Edmond and Hannah in the transport pod that sped through the City to the Niagara Falls exit.

Hannah looked at her husband. Seeing his sadness at the loss of his only child, she felt the guilt of her betrayal so long ago resurge.

Once they were through the tunnel, Angeline turned her key in the metal door that led to the back room of Jayded Ink. "John saw to it that we have a car at our disposal."

They walked out the back door into the crisp air. Hannah didn't blink as Edmond led her to the car.

~~~~

The elevator doors opened and Edmond led Hannah out into the hallway. He looked up at the arrow on the sign reading *Morgue*.

Just outside the morgue, John stood waiting. Edmond looked at him as they passed by. No words were exchanged.

Edmond and Hannah continued to the large glass window behind which laid their child's lifeless body. They watched as the attendant lifted the sheet to reveal Amber's face.

Edmond closed his eyes and nodded as confirmation that the lifeless girl beneath the sheet was indeed his daughter.

Hannah stared through the glass that separated her from her daughter for a few moments before her legs buckled beneath her. Edmond felt her falling and gripped her tighter. "Hannah, we should go."

He turned to Angeline. "Can you please arrange to have Hannah brought to your hotel here while I make arrangements for Amber's funeral?"

"I will phone Roberta at the North Metta once we leave and let her know we will be arriving shortly."

John pulled Angeline aside. "Ange, I spoke with the Immortals. Because the police were involved, this is now a murder investigation. They said they would take care of it."

Angeline kept her voice low. "Alright...what? John, we can't have a murder investigation. What do the Immortals plan to do to take care of this?"

"I don't know. I spoke with Pen Ming. He said the police would have their perpetrator in a few hours."

"How is that possible? Have they found Marcus? What the bloody hell is going on, John?"

"They just said they would take care of it. Do what you have to do for Edmond and Hannah. Everything else is being handled. I contacted Josh to let him know there will be another funeral."

John placed his hand on Angeline's arm. "Go, Ange. We've got it under control."

~~~~

The North Metta in Niagara Falls, one of two Aemetta Suites satellite hotels owned by the Flynn family, was the designated league hotel in North America.

Edmond turned to Angeline in the car on the way to the hotel. "I think we should have Amber's funeral here in Niagara Falls, as I would rather not subject her to a trip through the City."

His heart was heavy, but his mind was clear. Hannah was his only priority now.

"Of course, and Edmond, I can have Josh take care of everything for you. You will just need to give your consent at the funeral home. I know how difficult this must be for you. We can see Hannah to the hotel and then continue on to the funeral home."

Edmond patted Angeline's hand. "Thank you, dear."

"I will also speak with Vivian and Jake about having a meal at Transcendence after the funeral. I am certain they will arrange something beautiful, something Amber would have liked, a real proper send off."

~~~~

A few hours before the funeral service, John had sent a text to every league member calling for a meeting the day after Amber's funeral. They needed to search the Central Archives for a new Aquarius member.

The league gathered once again at the funeral home. Anger and revenge were foremost on everyone's mind, though they all tried their best to conceal it from Edmond and Hannah. They were all certain that Marcus had a hand in Amber's death and now they wanted nothing more than to find Marcus and end him once and for all.

Outside, before they entered the funeral home, Ann spoke with John, Angeline, and Zayne. "The police phoned me and asked me about Amber. They let me know that my exchange student was dead. They also said they found who killed her. Is it possible it wasn't Marcus?"

John stood, his hands in his pockets. "No. The Immortals took care of it so that we could have Amber's body released."

"What did they do? How did they take care of it?" Ann asked, confused.

John pursed his lips, irritated. "I asked, Ann. Pen Ming said we didn't need to know."

Zayne interjected. "It's done. We need to deal with Amber's funeral now, not what the Immortals have done."

Together they entered the funeral home. The air seemed to hang heavily in the room as sadness and vengeance mixed in everyone's minds.

Edmond spoke with everyone in attendance. Hannah sat and tried her best to be stoic, to accept the condolences being offered, but her mind was filled with thoughts of Amber's father.

Sebastian stood near the back. He had been in this very room a few weeks prior and could not bring himself to approach Amber's casket. The walls felt as though they would crush him and he found it difficult to breathe. He hurried out the front door to find some air.

Ann was with Hannah when she saw Sebastian exit the room. She excused herself and followed him. She found him outside with his hands against a brick pillar, his head hanging low. She could see his shoulders rise and fall with each breath he took.

She placed her hand on his back. "Seb, we can leave if you need to. I'm sure Edmond and Hannah would understand."

"I'll be fine. I just couldn't…"

"I know." she whispered. She gently rubbed his back before she linked her arm with his and placed her head softly on his shoulder.

Sebastian turned and embraced her. "Let's go back inside."

~~~~

The day of the wake, Transcendence was decorated in a beautiful shade of emerald green to match the colour of the stone in the league ring Amber once wore.

Hannah had phoned Vivian from her room in the North Metta Suites and asked her to make a black forest cake, as it was always Amber's favourite. Vivian displayed it in the centre of the dessert table.

She led Hannah to a chair. "I remember seeing her here as a child. She always ran straight to the candy jar we used to keep on the bar next to the mints."

The two women talked about the past and cried together. Vivian gave Hannah a tight hug as she excused herself to tend to the meal.

Over Vivian's shoulder, Hannah saw a man through the side door window. She recognized him instantly. He looked through the window and locked eyes with her before he moved past the door to wait in the alley.

Hannah turned to her husband. "Edmond, I'm going to step outside for some air. Please make my apologies to anyone who asks after me. I won't be long."

Edmond kissed her cheek. "Of course, dear."

As she exited the side door that led to the alley, Hannah saw him and her pulse began to race. He was every bit as handsome as he had been so many years ago.

Marcus leaned against the building. "Hello Hannah."

Hannah walked to his side. "Why are you here? If anyone inside sees you, they will kill you." Her voice was quiet, yet her anger was evident.

Marcus raised an eyebrow. "They may try."

"Why are you here, Marcus?" Hannah's tear-stained cheeks and swollen eyes concealed the sexual pull she still felt for him.

"I'm here for you, Hannah. Your daughter has died. I thought I could help you work through your grief." Marcus raised his hand to wipe at the tears on Hannah's cheek.

She slapped his hand away. "You need to leave. Now."

He placed his hands in his pockets and walked away from the wall. With his back to Hannah, he confessed. "Hannah, I know who killed Amber."

She turned him to face her. She kept her voice low but it was filled with desperation. "Who was it? Tell me."

"It was someone who works for me. This...person thought they were doing what I had asked but I swear to you, Hannah," Marcus grabbed both of Hannah's arms before he continued, "I gave no instruction to harm Amber."

He released Hannah, placed his hands back in his pockets, and looked down the alley. "They took her key for me."

Marcus turned his head, his chin jutting outward. "You do know that I plan on taking every astral key, don't you?"

"Yes. Edmond told me. I don't think you will be able to."

The look on her face told Marcus that she doubted his abilities. He felt his temper rising.

Hannah continued, "They all know you are after them. Do you really think you stand a chance against the league?"

Marcus gritted his teeth, grabbed Hannah's shoulders, and whispered, "*I know I do.*"

He pushed her aside and walked a few steps away from her. With his back to her, he stopped. "I've got one now, and before long it will be two, then three, then all twelve. They can't stop me."

His arrogance was palpable. He quickly turned, walked back to Hannah, and placed his arms around her. "Come with me."

Hannah struggled in his grip before she broke free. "Leave, Marcus. I will never be with you again."

"If that's what you want, I will go. It's a shame Edmond wasn't in the car with Amber. He could have taken her place." Marcus sneered before he turned to leave the alley.

Hannah felt the anger boiling inside her and grabbed Marcus' arm. She moved to face him. Her tears flowed freely. "She was your child, Marcus! Your man killed *our* child!"

Marcus stood motionless as Hannah pounded on his chest and wept. "She was yours. She was yours."

Marcus remained still for a few moments, his hands clenched into fists while Hannah cried on his shoulder. He pushed Hannah away and walked down the alley behind Transcendence. Had he known Amber was his child, she would not be dead, she would have been by his side helping him seize control of the league with her brother.

Marcus made his way down the alley and decided that after he had killed Ganga's body and trapped her soul mist in a pickle jar, he would kill every league member himself.

They took his daughter from him and he swore he would take everything from them - their astral keys and their families. Once his geist had replaced them, the last thing each of them would see would be his face.

Hannah watched for a few moments as Marcus walked away from her. His casual gait and the fact that he did not look back, told Hannah that she had made the right choice all those years ago when she decided to let Edmond believe that Amber was his child.

Back inside the restaurant, Hannah found Edmond with Angeline and walked toward them.

Edmond handed Angeline a piece of paper. "This is my sister's and nephew's information." He smiled as he thought of his nephew as a young boy. "He always loved training at my shop. He was good, too. Still pops in from time to time. He runs a fancy company now, but still finds the time to visit me. He will make a fine addition to the league, Angeline. A very fine addition."

Angeline saw Hannah and placed a hand on her arm. "Have you eaten? Would you like me to prepare a plate for you?"

"Thank you, love, that would be very nice."

Angeline walked to prepare Hannah's plate and unfolded the piece of paper Edmond had just given her. When she read the names Julia Price-Temple and Aidan Temple, she gasped, pleased and concerned all at once. The man she was beginning to have very strong feelings for would be able to share in her life with the league. This same man, should he accept, would now be put in harm's way.

~~~~

The day after Amber's funeral, Angeline and the rest of her faction entered the Hall of Gates and saw that the others had already arrived. The Central Archives were already initiated, so Angeline announced, "I have a name. Search for Aidan Temple."

Ann looked at Angeline, eyes wide. "Aidan Temple? *The* Aidan Temple?"

"What Aidan Temple? How do you know this Aidan Temple?" Sebastian asked, as much to Ann as to Angeline.

Ann simply watched as Angeline relayed the information. "Edmond's sister, Julia

Price-Temple has a son, Aidan. He is an Aquarius. He is also the CEO of Temple Technologies and the man I have been dating for a while now."

The room fell silent as all eyes turned to Angeline. "Okay," John replied slowly. "So one of us knows Aidan Temple. Let's get us all up to speed. Information on Aidan Temple."

As the Central Archive's 3D holographic screen lit up and began to scroll, everyone looked intently at the information on Aidan Temple, starting with his birth. Everything Edmond knew of his life was displayed.

Angeline felt as though she were betraying Aidan's trust, gaining information that he had yet to share.

John's brow furrowed in curiosity. "Ange, how did you realize Aidan was in a league family?"

"I spoke with Edmond and let him know that with everything going on, I felt it best to fill Amber's seat quickly. Until he gave me a note with Aidan's information on it, I was completely unaware that he was Edmond's nephew."

Angeline hoped her voice didn't betray the array of emotions she felt. Worry, anger, and her own inadequacies with respect to keeping Amber safe were all present inside her.

After everyone had a chance to review Aidan's life history, John shut down the Central Archives and looked from one league member to the next. "Alright, everything checks out. Everyone agree? Let's have a show of hands."

All hands raised. Angeline sighed. "All that remains is council approval. John, Zayne, shall we?"

John addressed the others before he left. "I would like you all to wait here and I will come back to let you know what their decision is. I'm guessing we won't have a problem."

When the three faction leaders walked into the Council Chambers, every member was standing, waiting for them.

The three bowed and before they could speak, Selphia stepped forward. "A decision has been made."

With the paranormal aid of Araton, the councilors had convened earlier that day after Angeline had spoken with Edmond. They unanimously agreed that Aidan was an acceptable replacement for Amber.

Angeline spoke. "You know why we have come. Has Aidan Temple been approved as the next Aquarius member of The League of Twelve?"

Selphia tilted her head slowly and gently to the right, her hands clasped behind her back. "He has." Her words flowed out of her like silk in a gentle breeze and the air around her glowed a radiant shade of violet. "The only potential obstacle will be his willingness to accept the role he is offered. It is a grand responsibility for someone who has not been raised with the knowledge that is held by the rest of the league members.

He will need guidance and training, and as he will be part of the European faction, Angeline, he will be your responsibility. You must see to his transition from the world he knows, to the one that he is to be part of, should he accept."

"I will, Selphia."

"You have the Aquarius ring?"

When Angeline nodded her head, Selphia moved her hands as though she were gently plucking at the strings of a harp. "It must be presented to Aidan Temple by Edmond Price under the next full moon. You have less than two weeks in which time he must make his decision and have the ring's stone reset in a band of his choosing before his Ring Transference can take place."

"Thank you, Selphia." The faction leaders bowed again and turned to leave the Council Chambers.

John looked at Angeline. "Go find Aidan. Zayne and I will let the others know that the council approved him. You don't have much time to make sure he's properly trained before the next full moon."

Angeline snapped. "I am well aware of the time constraints, John."

John looked at Angeline, his eyebrows raised.

She realized the abrasiveness of her words and softened her tone. "Oh, John, I apologize. I'm so twisted inside about this. I am just not sure how Aidan will react to our lifestyle."

"If you like the guy, he's got to be special. Ange, you should really trust your judgment. I do, and so do the others." John hoped his words would alleviate her anxiety. He remembered a time not so long ago when Angeline spoke nearly the same words to him.

She kissed his cheek and thanked him before she made her way to the European exit. As she walked, she thought about how best to approach Aidan with this information and decided that her first call would be to Aidan's mother. Julia Price-Temple had grown up knowing about the league and the City of Radiance, as well as many of its secrets. Angeline believed that Julia had to be the one to tell Aidan that his life would drastically change should he accept the role of Aquarius league member.

Angeline nervously dialed Julia's number. This was not just someone's mother, it was Aidan's mother.

When Julia answered, Angeline took a deep breath and spoke in a voice she normally reserved for her clients. "Julia, this is Angeline Flynn. I believe Edmond let you know that I would be in touch?"

"Yes, Angeline dear, how are you?" Julia's smile was evident in her voice.

"Quite well, thank you. I need a favour. Would you be able to meet me at Transcendent in the Aemetta Suites in one hour?"

"I absolutely can! I am quite eager to speak with you."

~~~~

The Aemetta Suites, a fifteen-story cylindrical hotel constructed of steel and glass, was located near the heart of downtown London and was a pleasant walk from Wells' Antiquities.

Angeline walked across the lobby, past a large marble water fountain that flowed day and night. The hallway on the right just past the front desk led to Angeline's office.

As she continued toward the restaurant, Angeline saw Julia enter the hotel and changed direction to meet her.

Julia walked past the small bistro, just to the left of the revolving front door. She continued toward the restaurant and met up with Angeline between the bistro and Transcendent.

"Mrs. Temple, it's so good to see you. Please, follow me."

"Please, call me Julia."

Angeline led the way to a table at the far end of the restaurant, out of earshot of the other patrons. "I hope you don't mind, Julia, but I've arranged a bottle of champagne for us."

"Not at all, dear. I know you wouldn't remember, but I used to visit the City of Radiance with Edmond when you were just a young girl. You have grown into quite a beautiful woman."

Angeline simply smiled.

Julia continued, "Before we begin, let me just ease your mind. I am quite happy that my son has the opportunity to join The League of Twelve. I was always a bit envious of Edmond when we were younger. His life seemed so exciting and mine so dull in comparison."

She reached across the table and took Angeline's hands. "It is dreadful what happened to Amber. I do hope whoever is responsible is apprehended soon."

"As do I, Mrs. Temple. I don't suppose you've had a chance to speak with Aidan yet, have you?"

"Not yet. He's so very busy with work at Temple Technologies most days and with a new woman in his life. I can phone him now and see if he is available for a chat this afternoon. While I'm at it, I will also ask if he is free for supper tonight so that the three of us can meet and discuss this unique opportunity, if that suits you, dear."

Angeline could see that Aidan's mother was quite proud of everything her son had achieved. "That sounds wonderful, Julia."

She thought that Aidan's reaction to finding out that she was the European faction leader would most definitely be memorable.

After dialing Aidan's phone number, Julia began. "Aidan, how are you, dear?"

"Good, Mum, and you?"

"I'm well, dear. Are you free later this afternoon? There is a rather urgent matter I need to discuss with you."

"Urgent? You're not ill, are you? Dad? Is he not well? I spoke with him just yesterday."

"No, no, we are both fine. The matter we need to discuss is rather unique."

"I can meet you in an hour in my office if that works."

"It does, and Aidan dear, would you join me for supper tonight?"

"Does 7:00 p.m. at the restaurant in the Aemetta Suites fit your schedule, Mum?"

"The restaurant in the Aemetta Suites?" Julia smiled at Angeline. "Why yes, dear, that sounds lovely. I will be at your office shortly."

Julia ended the call with her son and grinned as she looked at Angeline.

The look on Angeline's face hinted that she had something to divulge. She clasped her hands together and placed them on the table in front of her. "When you see Aidan, please do not let him know that I am the European faction leader. I would like to tell him myself. You see, I am the woman he has been spending time with."

"Oh my! Well, his mum finds you utterly delightful. This day has been filled with the best news I have had in quite some time."

~~~~

Julia walked into her son's office and was reminded of the days when the very same office belonged to her husband. "Hello, Aidan dear."

She walked to her son behind his desk and kissed his cheek before she sat. "It is so good to see you looking so healthy."

"You look radiant, as always, Mum."

Aidan looked back at his computer screen and finished composing an email. "I have a meeting in thirty minutes so I am afraid I need you to get right to it."

"Alright. Do you remember that when you were younger, I insisted that you learn martial arts?"

He smiled. "Yes, I do. I also remember not wanting to have any part of it, but in the end, I rather enjoyed it. I still do. How is Uncle Edmond? I haven't seen him for a few weeks now."

"There was a reason, dear, why I pushed you so hard."

As Julia told Aidan about Amber's death and everything she knew about The League of Twelve, the City of Radiance, the Grand Temple, and the people from Eyras, Aidan sat speechless. He was saddened to hear his young cousin had died, yet the fantastic story he was being told made everything he heard seem like a fairy tale.

He had so many questions. He wanted to know everything about this League of Twelve, starting with why he was chosen.

"You, Aidan, are the next Aquarius in our family's bloodline, after your cousin Amber."

"Aquarius? You mean to tell me that this League of Twelve relates to astrological birth signs? How does the circumstance of someone's birth play a part in member selection?"

"That is a question better asked of your faction leader, dear."

She leaned forward on the desk, lowered her head, her eyes looking up at her son. "Aidan, I cannot stress this enough. No one can know about the league. No one. Not now, not ever. Not even your most trusted friend."

"This city, this place, how is it possible?" He ran his fingers through his dark, curly hair, baffled that such a place could actually exist.

"I have been there, dear. It really is rather amazing. The Eyrasine people are much like we are, as we both are part Eyrasine. In the City of Radiance everyone shares everything. It truly is a beautiful place."

After hearing of a city hidden interdimensionally in the centre of the Earth, he did not think he could be shocked by anything else, and he found he was mistaken. Aidan had listened intently, up until he heard his mother say that he shared blood with an alien species.

"Your Uncle Edmond was the Aquarius member of the league years ago. He had passed his ring and key to your cousin Amber and when she died, you, dear, were next in line."

Julia saw the look of confused awe on her son's face. She took Aidan's hands in hers. "Aidan, this is not an obligation. It is your choice whether or not to accept this role being offered, but I will tell you this: your Uncle Edmond was a league member and as his younger sister, I was entitled to visit the City of Radiance, to train in the City's arena, and I had access to many of the wonderful things offered only to league members and members of their immediate families. While I enjoyed them all, I was still quite envious of my brother and his exciting life. I was not able to come and go as I pleased as he was. I was never allowed into the Hall of Gates. I was never granted access to the Armory. These privileges were for league members only. In my opinion dear, this is the opportunity of a lifetime."

Aidan rose and began to pace in his office. "This is so very much to process. I am having a difficult time understanding that these things you are telling me are true, and that you have not simply lost your mind."

Laughing, Julia rose and moved to hug her son. "Aidan, my mind was lost years ago."

She placed her hands on Aidan's arms and begged, "You will still dine with your mother this evening though, won't you dear? The European faction leader has arranged to join us."

"Of course, Mum. I understand. Now that I know someone else will join us, I would not feel right setting you loose on this poor bloke without my supervision."

"Lass, dear. The faction leader is a woman."

"Well then, I should think this lass will thank me for saving her from your utterly mad ways."

"I will see you later, dear," Julia bubbled as she left her son's office. She knew her son quite well and was more than certain that he would be the next Aquarius member in the European faction of The League of Twelve.

After his mother had left his office, Aidan decided that he needed to see Angeline one more time before he made his final decision. It was, as his mother pointed out, an opportunity that comes but once in a select few lives. His decision should be simple, but his feelings for Angeline were not.

He dialed Angeline's office and his call went straight to her voicemail. "Angeline, I need to see you this evening. I will be at your office at 5:00 p.m. I have something I need to tell you."

<center>~~~~</center>

Angeline sat in her office and listened to Aidan's message, knowing that Julia had spoken with him. She wondered what it was he had to tell her. She was certain Julia would have stressed that the league was to be kept secret, that he was to tell no one. As her mind could think of nothing else, one final thought made an ugly appearance: what if he had decided to join the league and no longer wanted her in his life?

"Then it's a bloody good thing I'm going to be his faction leader," she said aloud to herself.

The hours passed quickly as Angeline worked while she waited for Aidan. Hearing a knock at her office door, she walked to it and looked through her peephole. With Marcus running free, there was no telling who it could be.

She opened the door and Aidan entered her office. He grabbed her and kissed her while he shut the door with his foot. The passion in his kiss was potent.

"What have I done to deserve this?" Angeline was surprised and delighted.

"I may have to leave and I want you to know why. I cannot give you any specific details but I need you to know some things."

"Alright, but I may have something I need to tell you as well."

"Please, love, this is one of the most difficult things I have ever had to do," Aidan began, as he turned away from her and paced the room.

He clasped his hands together at his back and continued. "I met with my mother this afternoon and she shared some information with me, information that, should I accept something that is being offered to me, will change my life. I will be meeting my mother tonight for supper to discuss this unique opportunity. Apparently she had been grooming me throughout my childhood in the off chance that this invitation would present itself. I suppose it is a good thing she had done, as I do plan to accept it."

Aidan paused and slowly looked toward Angeline. "I hadn't been certain that I would accept until just now." He felt as though he had just torn his heart from his body.

"Angeline, I am so very sorry." He turned away from her, unaware that she had a rather satisfied look on her face.

"Aidan, I will be joining you and your mother for supper this evening and..."

Before she could finish her sentence, he resumed pacing and interrupted. "You

147

can't. This is not a casual dinner. If I could, I would tell you everything, please know that."

"Aidan, I am the European faction leader."

He stood still as the words she had just spoken sank in. He had thought that he would have to let her go, in order to join The League of Twelve. He walked slowly to her and kissed her deeply.

Angeline laughed. "Aidan! There's more I need to tell you now that you have officially accepted your role with your faction leader."

"Sorry, ma'am, please forgive me. I had thought that in accepting this role I would have to keep secrets from you and I just couldn't have."

"Maybe we should sit, as this may take some time."

Together they walked toward the sofa. Angeline stopped at her refrigerator and removed a bottle of champagne. "This is going to sound like a rehearsed speech, but every faction leader is told certain things that they are to relay to new members in situations such as this."

She popped the cork on the champagne bottle and poured two glasses.

Aidan leaned back into the sofa. "Continue."

She handed him a glass of champagne. "Alright then."

She placed her glass on her desk and began to pace. "This role isn't something to be taken lightly. It is a lifelong commitment and it is dangerous, especially now. Your mother may know some things about the City of Radiance and The League of Twelve, but not nearly half of it.

"There are three factions consisting of four members each. The astrological sign under which each member was born traces back to one of the original twelve kings of the planet Eyras who came to Earth many, many years ago. That is how the positions in the league are determined; the first born child bearing the astrological sign of the current member becomes the next in line to take his or her place."

Aidan watched her pace and absorbed every word.

Angeline held her hand out. "We each wear a league ring. Our faction members here in Europe wear emeralds. In North America, the stones are sapphire; in Africa, they wear diamonds. Everyone with Eyrasine blood is born with an innate ability that only surfaces when they wear a league ring."

Aidan looked at Angeline surprised and curiously hopeful. "You are telling me that once I wear this ring, I will have a supernatural ability?"

"Yes. Each of us has a different ability. My ability allows me to read and understand any language."

Aidan took a long sip of his champagne before he placed his glass on the table. "I imagine that would come in quite handy in your line of work."

Angeline laughed softly. "It does, actually. With my ability, once I have heard or read a language, I retain it and can extrapolate other words from there."

"How will I know what my ability is?" He was anxious to find out what power he had lurking dormant inside him.

Angeline sat on the arm of the sofa and continued. "Every ability is random. Well, almost every ability. The Taurus bloodline are all endowed with the same ability, but we can get into that later. Your ability will develop slowly, over a few days once you have put on your ring. Should you take your ring off, your ability will fade shortly thereafter. If it remains off your finger for more than a few days, your ability would vanish until you placed the ring back on your finger."

"When is it that I will receive this ring?"

Angeline smiled at the anxious anticipation she could see on Aidan's face and hear in his voice. "There is a Ring Transference ceremony of sorts. The current ring holder passes their ring down to the next in their bloodline, who is to become their replacement in the league. In your case, that responsibility falls to Edmond since...Amber has died."

Angeline paused for a moment and closed her eyes, thinking about Amber before she continued. "Edmond will give you your ring on the day of the next full moon."

She moved to sit on the sofa next to Aidan, lowered her head slightly and stressed, "Aidan, these secrets cannot be shared with anyone. Not even your mother. In the league, secrets are what keep us alive so that we can protect others."

She reached up and twirled a lock of Aidan's hair in her fingers with a playful look on her face. "Of course, you can and must tell your faction leader everything. It is a requirement, you see."

Aidan took Angeline's hand in his and rose. He took her in his arms and whispered in her ear, his voice seductive. "I vow to tell you everything. Every little detail of my every move." He positioned himself behind her and began kissing her neck.

She sighed. "Aidan." Reluctantly, she turned around. "Aidan, I've not finished. Please, sit down."

She led him back to the sofa. "On each solstice and equinox, we open a portal for people from Eyras to come to Earth. Once here, they are given a quick look-see by the medics in our Healing Chambers. They are then set up with lodging in the City of Radiance and after a few weeks of adapting to the gravity and customs of Earth, they are given a choice to remain in the City or to travel to the Earth's surface and stay there. However, those who choose to live on Earth must request permission to return to the City, even those of us in the league cannot bring them back to the City unless the Immortals have agreed to it in advance.

"There are rules for which, should they be broken, the consequences are dire. The Immortals are the highest authority in the City of Radiance and while they are fair, they do not tolerate betrayal.

"Anyone arriving in the City for the first time is brought before the Immortals. *You*, as well as your immediate family, will be brought before them. They will know everything about you prior to your meeting. Aidan, in order for you to be considered for the league, the rest of us had to look into your past. *I* had to look into your past. I have seen everything that Edmond recorded about your life since the day you were born. I know what schools you attended, who you dated, everything."

Aidan sat, sombrely considering this information. He knew he had nothing to hide from Angeline. He had no regrets about his past, but knowing that ten other people had looked into his life unnerved him.

"As you now know, Edmond was a league member before he passed his responsibilities to your cousin Amber. Amber died in Niagara Falls and we held her funeral there. Niagara Falls is where the North American faction calls home. Only league members and their immediate families attended."

Angeline looked at the floor as the guilt she felt for not having protected Amber resurfaced. "She was killed while she was performing her league duties. Our league couldn't protect her. We should have been able to keep her safe. *I* should have kept her safe."

He could see the guilt on her face. "Angeline, I am sure you all did everything you could. Amber was always a bit of a selfish child. I am sure that she would not have accepted help even if it were offered to her."

"I am the one who found her, Aidan." A tear slid down her cheek. "She was my responsibility and I didn't keep her safe."

He moved his hands to hers and held them tightly. "Whatever you did or did not do, her death is not your fault."

Angeline lowered her head. "In my mind, I know this, but in my heart...I cannot accept her death. We never bonded like we should have. The league is a family. We all care deeply for each other but with Amber, it was difficult to really get to know her."

Aidan led Angeline to the sofa and together they sat. "Growing up, I spent most of my free time at my Uncle Edmond's martial arts shop. I started going because my mother insisted that I do, but then I came to thoroughly enjoy my time there. I pride myself on being observant, on being able to read people and yet I had no idea who my uncle truly was."

"As for Amber, I can't say I recall seeing her in the shop very often. I remember seeing her at family gatherings, always off on her own, playing or just sitting."

Taking Aidan's face in her hands, Angeline looked directly into his eyes. "I need you to be aware of all the things you will be giving up, Aidan, the friends that you will most likely lose because of the secrets you will be sworn to keep."

He pulled her close. "Do I still get to keep you?"

Angeline placed her arms around Aidan's neck. "Oh, Aidan, you will be wishing me gone before too long. I believe Sebastian, the Cancer member, said some time ago that I am somewhat of a hard ass."

Aidan stood and chuckled. "It seems we have a dinner engagement with my mother. I wonder what she will have to say."

He held his hand out for Angeline. "Well, from what I saw this afternoon during our chat before she met you at your office, I would say that she thoroughly approves of your taste in women."

He feigned disapproval. "Talking with Mum behind my back, are you?"

Walking hand in hand to Transcendent, Angeline thought that despite Marcus' best efforts, the league had never been as strong as it currently was. She knew that with all of them working together, he did not stand a chance of defeating them.

~~~~

Once the meal had concluded, Angeline and Aidan walked together to her office where Angeline called John and informed him that Aidan had officially accepted the Aquarius position in the league. "Now we just have to introduce him to the rest of the league and the Council of Seven. He is clearing his schedule for tomorrow as we speak."

Angeline watched Aidan pace through her office as he spoke with his assistant and lost track of her conversation with John until she heard his voice. "Ange? Are you still there?"

"Yes, yes. I was just saying Aidan is free tomorrow to meet the Council and the others."

"I hope he can free up the next couple of weeks as well. You have a lot to teach him before he gets his ring on the next full moon. That doesn't leave him a lot of time for things like work," John's voice trailed off, "or dating."

Angeline laughed. "I am listening, John, and I will have you know that Mr. Temple's dates are all part of his training. He needs to have a good understanding of what his faction leader is going to expect from him, now doesn't he? Goodbye, John."

Across the room, Aidan sat as he wrapped up his phone call. "If something requiring urgent attention should arise, bring it to my father. If I need to attend to it personally, email the details to me. Thank you."

Ending her call, Angeline turned to Aidan. "I believe we should celebrate."

Pulling her close to him, Aidan agreed. "And celebrate we shall. You see, I know the Event Planner of this posh little hotel and I believe a bottle of champagne is being delivered to her suite very soon."

"Why, Aidan, are you trying to gain favour with your faction leader?" Angeline batted her eyelashes, trying to appear coy.

"I am, Miss Flynn. I plan on gaining many, many favours." He slid his hand down Angeline's arm, took hold of her hand and led her to the elevator that would take them to her suite.

13 – NEW RECRUIT

Across the street from Wells' Antiquities, Aidan furrowed his brow. "I've been in this shop. What has this got to do with your league?"

Angeline smiled coyly. "Our league, Aidan. You have agreed to join us."

Wells' Antiquities was a quaint shop in the heart of downtown London and concealed within it the entrance to the European tunnels that led to the City of Radiance. The Wells family had owned this shop for as long as anyone in London could remember. They specialized in relics from ancient Egypt, Victorian era British heirlooms, and Native North American wares. Aidan himself had purchased an antique gramophone as a gift for his mother.

The staff, made up of Wells family members, were the only ones permitted behind the counters, except of course, members of The League of Twelve, who traveled to the City of Radiance via the door behind the large mirror in the storage room.

When Angeline and Aidan entered the shop, Josh walked to them and extended his hand toward Aidan.

"You must be Aidan Temple. Josh Morrison, Pisces. Welcome to our world!"

"That sounds rather ominous. Is there anything I should know about where we are going? Am I to meet monsters twenty feet tall?"

Ethan snickered. "Today, you're just meeting the Immortals. Though they are tall."

Ethan lifted the wooden half-door, rounded the counter, and extended his hand to introduce himself. "Ethan Wells, Sagittarius. This is my family's shop."

"Good to meet you, Ethan."

Ethan held his arm out toward Olivia and introduced her. "This is my sister, Olivia."

Olivia walked to Aidan, her hand held out for him to take. "Nice to meet you, Aidan."

"And you, Olivia."

Aidan glanced sideways at Ethan. "Now, did I hear you correctly? Immortals?"

Angeline simply smiled and led the way to the tunnel entrance. "Shall we?"

"I'll be here when you return," Olivia said, as she moved off to arrange some new pieces of jewelry.

Aidan followed Angeline into the storage room with Josh and Ethan behind him. He was still trying to rationalize how such a place could exist. As Ethan walked ahead and pulled the mirror aside to reveal a metal door with an odd-shaped keyhole in its centre, Aidan said nothing. All of this was alien, designed by actual aliens, and his technologically curious mind found it quite fascinating.

Angeline removed her key from her purse and held it up for Aidan to see the Capricorn sigil embossed on it.

Each thick, circular astral key was made from the Eyrasine metals trichromiel and biostentium - one inorganic, the other organic, and much the same in colour as steel. Etched in the centre of the key was the key holder's astral sigil, the portion that activated and unlocked the doors that led into and within the City of Radiance.

"This is my Capricorn key. Only I can use this key, as it was linked to my DNA on the day I received it along with my ring. My key is known as the Flynn key. The Price key, once we recover it, will be linked to your DNA, and then be known as the Temple key. While the stones in the rings we wear alter our DNA and grant us our abilities, our keys can detect that alteration and can then only be used by the correct key holder. It's really quite simple."

Aidan ran his hands along the metal door, studying it. "I know simple and this is not it."

Josh nudged Ethan with his elbow. "You think the new guy wants to be alone with the door, yeah?"

Aidan jokingly pressed his cheek against the door. "Oh, but aren't you a lovely door." The others laughed loudly.

Aidan tapped the door. "Alright, I'm good. Shall we see this key in action?"

Angeline obliged. She inserted her key, turned it to align with her Capricorn sigil, pushed it, and then turned her sigil to the top position, explaining each step as she performed it. Once inside, Aidan looked left and right, expecting to see a magnificent...something. Instead, he was greeted with ancient rock tunnels.

He was somewhat disappointed. "Not quite what I expected."

"These are just tunnels." Josh pointed toward the tunnel that led to the City of Radiance. "That is where we want to go." He led the way to the raised platform and with everyone onboard, said, "I've got my key, Ange. I'll get us moving and you might want to hold on to the new guy."

Angeline put her arm around Aidan's waist. "Your first time taking a trip through this tunnel can be somewhat disorienting, even a little nauseating. You can just look at me and that should ground you. If you think you've got the stomach for it though, take a look around as we travel. It really is quite beautiful."

Josh held his key over his head, searching for the stone to activate the platform. Once he saw the stone light up, he said, "And five, four, three, two, one. We're off!"

Aidan held on to Angeline but looked around as they shifted interdimensionally through the tunnel toward the City's entrance. The lights that streamed past seemed to travel faster than anything he had ever seen, yet at the same time, he could see lights that appeared to be standing still. It was an experience unlike any he had ever had.

He pressed his lips to Angeline's and confessed. "I was happy to have you in my world before this, and now, I am so very humbled to be part of yours."

Once the platform reached the end of the tunnel, Josh announced, in his best train conductor's voice, "We have arrived at the City of Radiance. Please watch your step as you disembark and thank you for riding Josh's Magical Platform. Yeah, that was just bad."

The others groaned and then laughed.

Aidan looked at the stone wall in front of them, confused. "A hole in the wall?"

Ethan stepped forward and patted Aidan on the back. "It's a keyhole, mate." He inserted his astral key and the stone wall began to slide back. He then removed his key and the stone wall disappeared into the tunnel wall to reveal a metal door.

"Now, same type of door as in the shop, the key works the same way. I am the Sagittarius key holder, so where Ange turned her key to the Capricorn sigil, I turn mine to the Sagittarius sigil."

The door to the City of Radiance opened and Aidan stood in awe of everything in his sight.

Angeline grabbed Aidan's hand. "This is just the doorway. Let's go all the way in, shall we?"

As Angeline walked onto the balcony, one of the guards spotted Aidan. "Stop! I'm sorry Miss Flynn, but we have orders from the Council of Seven not to let anyone pass if they are not members of The League of Twelve or family members that we recognize."

"I understand, but if you would kindly let the council know that the newest league member, Aidan Temple, has been held up, I would greatly appreciate it."

"Newest league member?" Remembering that Amber had died, the guard cast his eyes downward. "I'm so sorry, Miss Flynn. I forgot about Amber leaving us. Please…" He motioned for them to pass.

Angeline smiled. "It's quite alright. I will be sure to let the council know of your vigilance."

Aidan walked to the rail at the edge of the large balcony and looked down at the circular city. Angeline pointed out the Grand Temple and explained that the Hall of Gates found at its centre was where the league members met when they first entered the City.

Aidan saw more wonderful sights than he had ever seen. He considered himself well traveled, as his position at Temple Technologies required him to visit many cities in the world to conduct business. Now he had been made aware of another world, a world other than the known world, and he felt like a child on Christmas morning.

Despite being situated interdimensionally in the heart of the Earth, the circular city shone with the brilliance of a perpetual sun. Had he not known that he had just traversed a tunnel that began in an antiques shop and ran beneath Stonehenge, Aidan would have been unaware that he was not on the surface of the Earth.

"How is it that this place exists?" He was still in awe.

Angeline hadn't seen anyone experience the City for the first time as an adult and was pleased with Aidan's reaction. "The City was created thousands of years ago by Omm, but we can talk about him later. The temperature here is kept a consistent twenty-four degrees Celsius and the dome above us acts somewhat like a shield as well as a source of energy; it invigorates everything and everyone beneath it."

Just inside the dome, surrounding the City, he saw a large wall that appeared to be made of polished white granite which stood nearly ten feet high.

"Josh, Ethan, you two should take your own pod as Aidan and I will be taking a bit of a tour before we head to the Hall of Gates."

Josh nodded. "Right then. We'll see you two there."

Once Angeline and Aidan had both entered their transport pod and the door had been shut, the feminine disembodied voice of this particular unit requested, "Please state your destination."

Angeline looked at Aidan, who was looking up in the direction from which the voice had originated. "Aidan, just say where you want to go and how quickly, which would be the Grand Temple, east entrance. If a speed is not specified, the pods automatically assume you wish to arrive at your destination as quickly as possible."

Aidan cleared his throat. "Grand Temple, east entrance, mid-range speed."

A few seconds later, the pod rose and headed toward the Grand Temple.

Angeline manually adjusted the pod's speed, slowing it a bit to allow Aidan to take in as much of the City as possible. He looked down as they drifted fifteen feet above the floor in this spectacular city. The people milling about, the gardens, the waterfalls - it was the most breathtaking city he had ever seen.

The buildings seemed to be constructed of a glossy stone embedded with jewels. He saw lush parks, farms, homes, shops, and cafes as they traveled.

"Every need of the City's citizens is met here." Angeline pointed to a three story apartment building. "That is the league apartment building. Every member has their own unit." Nudging Aidan with her shoulder, she added, "Of course, sharing is encouraged."

"Noted." Aidan placed his arm around her.

"In the City of Radiance, there is no need for currency. Everyone lives communally, sharing what they have and taking only what they need. No greed, no theft, no crime at all. Well, actually, it has happened twice, I believe, since the City was built some four thousand years past."

"Two crimes in four thousand years? Although, had you asked me a few months ago if the perfect woman were possible, I would not have believed it. It seems to be my fate to be pleasantly surprised." He rested his lips against the top of Angeline's head and lightly kissed her.

Just before she turned to kiss Aidan, Angeline scolded, "Now, if Josh and Ethan were here with us, I would have to reprimand you, Mr. Temple."

She tilted her head slightly and cast her eyes upward. "If I am remembering correctly, someone had stolen something from the Council Chambers 'round about two hundred years ago."

"And the second?"

"An Eyrasine woman killed her spouse while she was on Earth's surface and fled into the City with a league member, claiming that she was in danger. I'm not certain of the details, but no one knows what happened to her and it was not documented as the rest of the trial was. The only note of it in the record was a single line stating, *The punishment has been enacted.* I remember seeing those words and how they sent a chill through my bones. You see, no matter the crime, a fair trial is held with witnesses and the punishment is carried out by the Immortals if the accused is found guilty. The councilors are the jury, judges and, for lack of a better word, executioners."

Aidan furrowed his brow. "I am not entirely sure I'm prepared to meet these councilors."

Angeline laughed and placed a hand on Aidan's thigh. "They are immortal, they are fair, and they speak honestly. They may not tell you some things, but what they do tell you will always be truthful."

The transport pod slowed and began its descent. Aidan looked at the Grand Temple. "Is there anything in this city that isn't absolutely brilliant?"

"Not really, no." Angeline pointed to the other league members. "There's our welcoming committee."

As they exited the transport pod, Angeline introduced Aidan to the other league members who stood waiting for them. "Aidan, this is our league."

John stepped forward first, his hand extended, and introduced himself. "I'm John Evans, North American faction leader and head of the league."

"John, a pleasure."

Angeline introduced Zayne next. "This is Zayne Nader, African faction leader."

"Good to meet you, Aidan."

"And you, Zayne."

One by one, the other league members introduced themselves.

Ann was the second to last league member to introduce herself. "I'm Ann Johnston. I've heard a bit about you but clearly, not enough."

Lastly, Sebastian possessively put one arm around Ann and extended a hand to Aidan. "Sebastian Shea. Welcome to our little corner of Crazy Town."

John looked at Angeline and Aidan. "We're all going to Transcendent for some breakfast/lunch/whatever meal in the Aemetta. You two care to join us when you're done here? We really should go to The Nite Cap as well, for a proper toast to our newest member."

They looked at each other and after a silent agreement, Angeline replied, "This shouldn't take more than thirty minutes or so, plus travel time. We will meet you there."

As the rest of the league headed to the European exit, Angeline turned to Aidan. "Now that the introductions are out of the way, let's get to the Council of Seven."

She took his hand and began to walk. Aidan, uncertain of what to expect, remained still and Angeline stopped as her arm jerked.

Aidan's heart began to beat faster. "Other than what you have already said, is there anything I should know to prepare?"

"Just follow my lead."

They walked to the Council Chambers. "When we first enter, we bow. I will talk first. Just answer anything that they ask you honestly and try not to be nervous."

She looked at Aidan with her eyes narrowed. "They can smell fear."

Aidan stopped walking.

Angeline began laughing.

"You will pay for that."

"Promises, promises."

They stood at the Council Chamber doors.

"Here we are. Did you bring a gift? They usually expect one." Unable to contain herself, Angeline laughed.

"Stop!" Aidan tried to shake off his nervousness. "Okay, they are just people. I have done this hundreds of times. Never with alien immortal people, but...alright. I can do this."

They walked into the Council Chambers side by side. As Angeline bowed, he bowed.

"I come before you with Aidan Temple, who is to replace Amber Price as Aquarius member in The League of Twelve."

Aidan found himself looking at seven people, each with coal black hair and eyes that perfectly matched a coloured stripe in their hair. They each stood approximately seven feet tall and were dressed in luminescent robes. He could distinguish male from female and noted that they all seemed to be the same approximate age.

His skill in assessing his clients at Temple Technologies faltered as he stood before seven immortal beings.

Each Council member stepped forward one by one as Angeline introduced them to Aidan.

Selphia stepped forward first. The shoulder-length spiral curls of her black hair cascaded around a face of a delicate ivory, showcasing her one curl in a striking shade of violet.

Next, Umabel moved toward Aidan, tilting her head slightly, her short, layered black hair and indigo coloured stripe, framed the coffee-coloured skin of her face.

Araton, with skin the colour of a human Caucasian, and black, fringe-styled hair with its blue streak, spoke first. "I welcome you to our family, Aidan Temple."

He had known that Aidan would replace Amber the moment Angeline read the slip of paper that Edmond handed to her at Amber's wake.

While he normally would not shake hands with anyone, as he could sense their true nature and had, on occasion found it disturbing, he nonetheless moved to shake Aidan's hand. He found that Aidan was not easy to read, that he had a sort of turmoil within him. While he could sense that Aidan would greatly aid the league, he also felt something that he could not quite make sense of.

Celeste saw that Araton felt uneasy and so she moved to Aidan for Angeline to introduce her. She tilted her head slightly downward, the long, curly streak of green hair dangling out of her short, spiked black hair beside her vanilla-coloured face.

Celeste kept her hands clasped behind her as Angeline introduced her.

"Aidan, this is Celeste."

Celeste spoke softly. "Welcome, Aidan."

Aidan bowed slightly. "Thank you, Celeste."

Jael, with his dark brown skin and shoulder-length straight, black hair, looked at Aidan, and silently assessed him; he knew that soon he would test Aidan's skills.

He moved toward Aidan as Angeline introduced him and lowered his head slightly before moving back to join the other immortals. His yellow eyes matched the yellow stripe in his hair and made him look rather formidable.

Raziel was introduced next. His skin, olive in colour, perfectly complimented his black dreadlock hair and single orange dread.

Lastly, Pen-Ming stepped forward as Angeline introduced him.

"Aidan, this is Pen-Ming. He is not only immortal, he is also a skilled surgeon."

Pen-Ming bowed his head slightly and closed his eyes. He wore his long, straight black hair tied back in a ponytail, its red streak prominently displayed.

Aidan bowed his head in greeting.

After the introductions, in a clear, strong voice, Jael spoke. "Aidan Temple, you have accepted a great responsibility. As the guardian of the Aquarius gate, your first priority must always be the league. Being a member of The League of Twelve, you are now part of an elite group who carry many secrets and many burdens."

Jael tilted his head to the side and moved back as Pen-Ming stepped toward Aidan and spoke, his hands clasped together in front of him. "It is imperative you understand that The League of Twelve must endure without the inhabitants of Earth being aware of its existence, save those who mate with its members. Should humans become aware of Eyras, its people, or this city in an alternate dimension at the centre of their world, the damage would be irreparable. It is this secrecy that has kept safe those with Eyrasine blood.

"There have in the past been humans who discovered who we are and were brought before us, in this very room." Pen-Ming motioned to his right. "The decision was unanimous, the judgment just, and the verdict final."

Celeste spoke next. "Your heart is pure. Let it guide you. Your mind is powerful, yet your emotions also play a part in your destiny."

As Celeste stepped back, Selphia wore a look of uncertainty upon her face. "Your mind will be your greatest asset, but it may also prevent you seeing what your heart is attempting to show you."

She turned toward Angeline. "Angeline, you must guide Aidan on his journey through understanding our world. His mind is capable of things that he may not yet understand."

"I will, Selphia. Thank you." When Angeline bowed, Aidan did the same.

Selphia asked Aidan, "Is there anything you would like to say, Aidan Temple?"

Bowing again, Aidan placed his right hand over his heart. "I am honoured to be part of your world, Selphia. I will never take my role as a league member lightly and I will do everything in my power to keep the residents in the City of Radiance, as well as those descended from Eyrasine bloodlines, safe from any harm. Thank you all."

As they bowed one last time, he and Angeline left the Council Chambers as the Immortals turned away from them.

"Now, I understand that the councilors are immortal and I can accept that. The fact that their eye colour is the same as a streak of colour in their hair, however, is beyond what I had imagined."

Angeline took his hand in hers. "Many things that you once believed will now be challenged, but your mind will be opened to some rather fantastic new truths. Now we shall visit the Hall of Gates for a quick peek, make a wee bit of a stop in the laboratory, and then we can join the others. I think we have seen enough for today, yeah?" Angeline winked at Aidan.

Having just met the Immortals, he wanted to be prepared. "Is there something I need to know about those who work in the laboratory?"

"We just need to drop off your mobile phone for a quick adjustment. You may have noticed that as it stands now, it doesn't get a signal here."

Aidan pulled his cell phone from his pocket and looked at the screen; he noted that it did indeed read, *No Service*.

"So these laboratory technicians will modify my mobile phone to work in the centre of the Earth?" Aidan was both curious and fascinated.

"Yes, and they also make an adjustment so that your mobile phone will always register as being located in London. We can't have you in England one minute and then in Niagara Falls accumulating roaming charges an hour later, now can we?"

"Do you think they would mind if I watched them make these adjustments? I would absolutely love to…"

"Sorry, love, that's one thing that is off limits, for now at least. Let's just head to the Hall of Gates for a quick look-see, drop off your mobile phone, and then we can head to The Nite Cap to join the others."

"Yes. I think I could use a drink or ten about now."

Angeline smiled as she led Aidan to the Hall of Gates.

Outside the Capricorn door, she inserted her key. "Place your hand on top of mine."

Aidan complied, and as she turned her key toward her sigil, he felt the vibration of what he could only describe as an electric current running through her hand into his.

He was baffled. "I have no words. I have worked with so many electrical components, technology that the world has yet to see, but this, this is beyond my comprehension. This is metal reacting with metal, reacting to DNA. Maybe I do have the words after all." He had seen so many wondrous things in this one day that he could never have imagined.

Inside the Hall of Gates, Aidan stood in awe yet again as he looked down at the stunning floor and then up at the celestial ceiling. Angeline stood over her sigil, held her astral key over top of it, and Aidan watched as it rose out of the floor atop a cylinder to meet her key. She inserted her key and the Central Archives came to life.

Temple Technologies seemed so small to him in comparison to the wonders in the City of Radiance.

They left the Hall of Gates through the Virgo door and walked to the laboratory to drop off Aidan's cell phone. Aidan took in as much of the laboratory as he could in the short time they were there.

Angeline took his arm. "How about we go get you a drink."

They walked toward the transport pods. "Just another pod ride, tunnel shift, and we are back in London. It will be second nature in no time."

~~~~

Angeline and Aidan walked into the Aemetta Suites and as they neared The Nite Cap, they saw the rest of the league sitting inside at a table.

At The Nite Cap bar, named for Angeline's Capricorn bloodline, Ann poured twelve shots of twenty-five year old Chivas Regal to toast Aidan joining the league. Once everyone had a glass in their hand, she lifted her glass. "To Aidan. May you kick ass with us for a long time."

They all raised their glasses and clinked them together.

"As we have always done in the past, I've got a key to a top floor room for each of you at the concierge stand, in the event that we celebrate more than we plan to. All complimentary, of course."

Aidan had a playful smile on his lips. "Does this mean my bill is clear?"

"From this day forward, you shall have a room without charge and complimentary meals and beverages at any of our fine Aemetta hotels throughout the world. However, I'm afraid your past stay is already on the books and the tax man must be satisfied." Angeline's voice was dramatic.

Ann added, "Transcendence and all satellite restaurants serve league members for free as well. Being a member of The League of Twelve has its perks!" She began to pour more whiskey into each of the empty shot glasses.

John held his glass out for Ann to refill. "You know, my body never knows what time it is anymore. I guess it's a good thing Conor here brought his healing hands."

Conor held his hands up. "I don't leave home without 'em."

As evening became late night in London, Angeline announced that she was turning in.

Ann stretched her arms. "I think I will as well. I've got to be at the restaurant early tomorrow morning. Is Faith at the concierge stand, Ange?"

Angeline's voice sounded sleepy. "She should be, love. Alright, have a good evening/night/morning, everyone!" She and Aidan headed to the elevator.

Once they arrived at Angeline's suite door, Aidan said innocently, "It seems I have neglected to get a room key for myself."

Angeline unlocked her door and pulled Aidan inside her suite. Her voice was low and seductive. "You will not need that key tonight."

~~~~

Waking up next to Angeline, Aidan felt as though he was exactly where he was meant to be. He stroked her hair as he watched her sleep, rousing her.

She opened her eyes and looked at him. "Good morning, Mr. Temple."

She kissed his cheek as she rose to get out of bed. "While I would love nothing more than spending the entire day enjoying your company, I have a couple coming to see me later."

Aidan retrieved his pants from the floor to search through the pockets for his cell phone, then remembered he had left it in the laboratory in the City. "I should probably let my office know that I will be away a bit longer than I had originally planned. I'm certain my father won't mind popping out of retirement for a few weeks to head up his company once again."

While Angeline showered, Aidan used her phone to call Temple Technologies. He considered joining her in the shower but knew that if he did, they may very well never leave her suite.

Across the hall, Sebastian and Ann were getting ready to leave. Ann stood in the bathroom, drying her long hair, while Sebastian watched her from the bed.

"I know you're watching me, Seb." She had a smile on her lips that Sebastian couldn't see.

He rose and walked toward her, grinning. "Does it make you nervous?" His words were more of a challenge than a question.

Ann turned off the blow dryer and saw that he was now directly behind her. She stared at him through the mirror. "No, it makes me realize that we may be later than we anticipated." Her voice was soft and sensual.

She turned around. He picked her up and carried her to the bed. He sat with her straddled in his lap. They fit together like the pieces of a puzzle, natural and tight, as though they were each merely part of one whole.

They could hear doors shutting as some of the others left to begin their days.

Ann pouted. "I suppose we should head out."

Sebastian groaned. He knew they both had responsibilities but his obligations seemed insignificant when he compared them to his feelings for Ann.

He conceded. "Alright." He rose and placed Ann on her feet. As she walked toward the door, Sebastian lightly smacked her backside. "Just know that I'm not done with you yet."

She glanced at him over her shoulder. "Don't I know it."

~~~~

Angeline and Aidan left her suite once they were both ready and saw Sebastian and Ann together across the hall.

Angeline stopped and whispered, "I love those two to bits. It is so good to see them together."

Aidan smiled and took her hand. Together they walked to the elevator, where Ann and Sebastian stood.

"I suppose you two will be in the City for the next little while, eh Ange?" Ann asked.

Angeline placed her hand on Aidan's back. "Yes. Aidan here has yet to see all the wonders offered in the centre of the Earth and I have arranged a bit of a training session as well."

During the walk to the antique shop, Ann and Sebastian talked with Aidan as though they had known him for years, rather than just meeting him the day before. This ease of friendship was something that Angeline had hoped for, and was thrilled to see.

Ethan was in the antique shop when they arrived.

Ann leaned against the counter. "Will you be heading to the City today, Ethan?"

"Not today. I've got boring real world things to take care of." He pointed to the box of newly arrived antiques.

Sebastian placed his arm over Ann's shoulders. "Have fun with that."

Together with Angeline and Aidan, they entered the back room and stepped into the storage closet.

When the platform was activated and the interdimensional ride was underway, Aidan's mind drifted to his youth. As a young boy, Aidan often imagined things beyond scientific possibility and named them after himself, such as the Aidan-Chute; a parachute that once it reached an altitude low enough that radar could no longer detect it, would further unfold and transform into an aircraft, encasing the jumper and allowing him to travel anywhere undetected. Even so, traveling interdimensionally through stone tunnels, on a stone platform, was not something Aidan had ever in his life imagined he would do.

The four friends stepped into the City of Radiance and boarded a transport pod to the West entrance of the Grand Temple. Angeline and Aidan disembarked, while Ann and Sebastian stayed inside to continue on to the North American exit.

"You two have fun." Ann closed the pod door and she and Sebastian headed back to Niagara Falls.

~~~~

Once inside the Grand Temple, Angeline brought Aidan to the Armory. He looked at the ancient weapons, the longswords and staffs. She showed him her Soul Dagger and the Dagger of Truth, which they had recently used on the geist that had attacked Ann in the alley behind Transcendence.

As she retold the story of how she and Ann caught the geist, Aidan watched her, his expression full of wonder. "From the moment I saw you in the Aemetta Suites, I knew there was something fascinating about you, Miss Flynn."

Angeline simply smiled as they continued through the Grand Temple.

Of all the rooms they visited, Aidan was most intrigued by the Forge and the Laboratory. The technology and what seemed like magic, worked together in a way that fascinated him.

They approached the Training Arena. "I hope you are prepared to sweat, Mr. Temple."

He grabbed her hand. "Why, Miss Flynn, how very forward of you!"

She smacked his arm, a stern look on her face. "You are training today, Aidan. I have asked Jael to meet us. There is no one better to instruct you."

"I have been practicing martial arts since I was a child. I am certain I will be able to match skills with Jael."

Angeline smirked. "I think I'll stay and watch for a bit before I head out. I would hate to miss such a match!"

Jael stood in the centre of the Training Arena with a calm look on his face. Aidan looked at him and felt his own confidence begin to waver.

When he first met Jael in the Council Chambers, Aidan had noticed his extreme height. What he had not seen was the enormity of the musculature this immortal being possessed. He could feel the power emanating from Jael and nearly see the self-assurance he exuded.

Intimidation was new to him.

As they stood face to face on the mats, they bowed to one another. Aidan looked directly into Jael's eyes, hoping to gain some understanding of his opponent. The bright yellow windows to Jael's soul, however, revealed nothing new.

Aidan assumed a fighting stance. He attacked with a fast right overhand punch.

Jael easily stepped out of range. Before Aidan could raise his hands in defense, Jael struck with little effort, delivering six quick hand strikes, each landing squarely in the middle of Aidan's chest, knocking him backward.

Aidan lunged forward, swung at Jael and missed, as his target effortlessly moved out of range once again.

Jael quickly struck Aidan with a right punch to his torso, followed by an uppercut to his jaw. His movements were so quick and graceful that it baffled Aidan.

Aidan's body jerked from one direction to the next after each blow, as Jael denied him time enough to counterattack.

With Jael's next strike, two quick punches to Aidan's abdomen and a final palm strike to his chest, Aidan landed on the floor.

He stared up into Jael's eyes. He realized quickly that Jael was a superior fighter but was still surprised that he had put him on the ground so fast and with so little effort. He considered himself a good fighter but after a few minutes with Jael, he was rethinking his abilities.

As he stood up, Jael stepped back, ready to continue.

With a kiai shout, Aidan kicked toward Jael's head. Jael ducked and immediately slid into a leg-sweep, forcing him to the ground once again.

The air rushed out of his lungs in a wheeze as Aidan landed on his back. He quickly rolled backward and up onto his feet.

Aidan punched. Jael blocked. Jael spun and kicked. Aidan twisted to the side.

Aidan blocked as many of the blows as he could, feeling the pain on his face and chest every time he failed.

Aidan was no longer surprised to find himself on the floor again.

After ten humiliating minutes, Aidan turned to Angeline, and breathed heavily. "I don't think you need to stay any longer. I think Jael would prefer we spar alone."

Angeline wrinkled her nose and nodded but did not speak a word as she turned to exit the Training Arena.

Unable to hold her laughter in any longer, it exploded out of her. She turned back to Aidan with a sweet look on her face. "I apologize. It's just that you remind me so very much of myself during my first training with Jael."

Aidan tried to look cross but couldn't help but smile.

"Alright, Jael. Let's go over the blocking techniques, shall we?"

Hour after hour, day after day, Aidan trained. He had thought his body was in rather good shape until he began training with Jael. While Jael's techniques did somewhat resemble a style of martial arts, there were elements of it Aidan had not seen before and he found he was eager to understand them.

~~~~

The day Pen-Ming brought a geist into the Training Arena, Aidan watched as it was willingly killed so that its geist mist could replicate an Eyrasine female. He stood in awe as a new life formed in front of him, witnessing creation was not something he had prepared for.

The world outside of the City of Radiance now seemed so very small to him.

Aidan had decided to stay in the league apartment complex in the City while he was training and on one particular morning, he heard a knock on his door. He opened it and found Angeline dressed in shorts, a short sleeved shirt, a sun hat, and sandals.

"Are we vacationing today?"

Angeline opened her eyes wide and smiled. "We are going jewelry shopping."

"I can hardly believe how much time has passed since I began training. Does time pass slower here in the City?" As the words left his mouth, he remembered his mother telling him that it did indeed pass more slowly than on the Earth.

"You will get the hang of it eventually. But for now, we have an appointment with Mariam in Cairo."

Aidan, still unable to wrap his mind around everything he had recently discovered, shook his head. "The time it takes to travel from London to Cairo is less than most business luncheons."

"You will get used to that as well, love.

"Just as the league hotels and restaurants provide their services at no cost, so does the jewelry shop. Well, there is no cost for your league ring. If you, perhaps, want to buy me a piece of jewelry for no particular reason, that would not be free of charge." She looked at Aidan with the sweetest smile on her lips.

Al-Jawhara, Cairo's finest jewelry shop, was owned and run by the Chahine family. Omar Chahine was a master goldsmith, having been taught by his father and grandfather how to create stunning pieces of jewelry.

Angeline and Aidan entered the storage room in the back left corner of Al-Jawhara and saw Mariam's father adding the final touches to a gold and diamond bracelet shaped to resemble an ankh, the ancient Egyptian symbol of life. He heard the door to the tunnels open, turned, and saw Angeline with a man he assumed was Amber's replacement in The League of Twelve.

Omar rose out of his seat and moved to hug Angeline. "Angeline! How are you today?"

"Wonderful, Mr. Chahine, thank you. This is Aidan Temple, the newest member of our league's European faction."

Omar extended his hand to Aidan in welcome. "Aidan Temple. Good to meet you."

"And you, sir."

As they entered into the front area of the store, Aidan paused, as he absorbed the fact that in such a short time, he had traveled to Egypt. He walked to the store's front entrance and through the double doors. He held the doors open and looked around to confirm that he was indeed in Egypt. He shook his head, fascinated, and headed back into the store.

Aidan stopped and took in the magnificence of Al-Jawhara, which when translated into English, means The Jewel. He glanced up at the ancient Egyptian hieroglyphics carved into the sandstone coloured walls, walked across the white tile flooring with gold crackle glaze, and past the mirrors that lined the lower portion of the walls.

Aidan's eye was caught by a selection of men's watches inside a glass display case, one of several that were arranged in a horseshoe configuration along the walls. Recessed lighting in the ceiling highlighted the jewelry inside the other displays.

Made to look like a part of the store's decor, the stone artifact that had been entrusted to the African faction so long ago, sat inside a glass case with a white gold, ruby, and diamond necklace draped around it. Aidan watched as Angeline stood admiring the necklace, unaware of the artifact's significance.

Mariam entered the store through the front door. "Angeline, Aidan, welcome to Al-Jawhara. I have some pieces to finish in the back, so when you have made your choice, please find me and I will set your stone at once."

Aidan smiled. "Thank you, Mariam. I will do that."

At first glance, Aidan thought his decision would take some time, but once he had spotted the classically styled band, his choice was made.

He pointed to a contemporary band of white gold. "I do believe this band will suit me quite nicely."

"You do have exquisite taste, Mr. Temple."

Aidan walked to the back room door and knocked before he peeked in and said, "I have selected the band, Mariam."

Mariam put her tools down. "Wonderful! Let us have a look."

They walked together to the display case and Aidan pointed to the sleek white gold band with an opening where the emerald could be placed. "I have never been one to wear jewelry, but I believe I will rather enjoy this one."

Mariam accepted the ring that Angeline had just removed from her purse, and closed her eyes for a moment in remembrance of Amber. "I shall have your stone set within one half hour."

Angeline squeezed Mariam's hand. "No rush, Mariam. I will be by tomorrow at this time to pick it up, if that's alright with you."

"Absolutely. I will have it ready."

~~~~

The following day, while Aidan resumed his training with Jael, Angeline traveled to Cairo once more to pick up the ring that Aidan would soon call his own.

Mariam turned when Angeline entered. She stopped what she was doing and held up the ring she had finished for Aidan.

"Thank you, Mariam. It is absolutely stunning!"

"You are very welcome. Please tell Aidan I am happy he has joined us."

"I will. Thank you again."

"Also, please let Edmond know that if he would like, I would be most pleased to set another stone in Amber's ring, as a gift for him."

"I am certain he would appreciate that, Mariam. Thank you. I will tell him."

~~~~

Angeline's next stop was the Price house in London, where Edmond was waiting for her to bring him the ring and Soul Dagger that he would now pass to his nephew.

Angeline walked to the front door and knocked. Edmond answered quickly.

"Edmond." She moved to hug him.

Angeline removed Amber's delicate band from her purse, her heart heavy. "Mariam wanted me to tell you that whenever you are ready, to just come by the shop in Cairo and she can set a regular gemstone in this band for you, if you would like. I would be happy to bring you or Hannah any time."

"Thank you, dear Angeline, and please thank Mariam for me." He twisted the ring on his finger, the one that once housed an emerald league stone and now donned a square cut diamond. "Perhaps Hannah would like to have a keepsake of Amber's time with the league."

He was certain Hannah would cherish anything that had belonged to their daughter.

"I also have something for you that you have not worn in quite some time." Angeline presented him the newly crafted Price ring, which would the following day become the Temple ring.

"I see my nephew has chosen a contemporary setting. Very nice."

He placed what would soon be Aidan's ring on his finger. "A perfect fit!"

Feeling his ability resurge, he sighed. "I had forgotten the feel of my ability. I wonder…"

Having worn the stone in his own ring for so long, his innate ability resurfaced immediately, as though it recognized its wearer.

Edmond closed his eyes and concentrated. Angeline felt a wave of...something...pass over her as she looked around and saw a bird, frozen mid-flight.

She laughed. "Right! You can stop time! Brilliant!"

Time resumed and the birds continued their flight, trees again swayed in the breeze.

"Alas, it does not last long. A few seconds is all I have ever been granted."

"A bit more than the rest of us, though."

"True enough, my dear. True enough. Thank you for giving this old man a thrill he has not experienced in quite some time."

"Edmond! You are not an old man, but I am glad to see you smile."

Angeline reached into her purse and removed Amber's Soul Dagger. She looked at the etching of the Aquarius sigil on its hilt as she handed it to Edmond. "I've always loved the Aquarius sigil, the two wavy lines depicting the two serpents, one good and the other evil and the wisdom to know the difference between the two."

Edmond sighed. "This blade served me well on many an occasion."

Angeline placed her hand on his arm and smiled. "I'm afraid I must go, but I will bring Aidan to you tomorrow evening."

"Of course, dear."

Angeline kissed Edmond's cheek before she turned and walked back to her car.

14 – IMMORTALS

Angeline and Aidan turned into the driveway that led to Edmond's home.

Aidan smiled. "This was my second home as a child. It does somehow seem fitting that such a turning point in my life should take place here."

They walked to the front door and saw Edmond open it as they approached. He gestured toward the back gate while he closed the door behind himself. "Hannah is having a rough go of it today. Some days are better than others, but there are days such as today where the grief takes hold of my wife. If you don't mind, I would rather not have her know you have come."

Angeline looked at Edmond, compassion in her eyes.

Before walking back to her car, she turned to Aidan and whispered, "I look forward to giving you a proper welcome into the league."

The left side of Aidan's mouth curled up in a half smile.

Uncle and nephew walked to the rear of the house.

"Now Aidan, have they told you what this ritual is?"

"I have been told that you and I are the only ones to be present and that I will be able to access an ability that I had not known I possessed." Aidan was anxious to discover what his ability may be.

"Nothing left now except to give you this." Edmond opened his hand and revealed the Aquarius league ring.

With his heart heavy, Edmond confessed. "I had given Amber my ring too soon, but with my health declining despite the help of Eyrasine medicine, I really had no choice. I know that you are more than ready to accept such a heavy responsibility."

Aidan accepted the ring and placed it on his finger. It started to glow as Edmond's ability left him and Aidan's own ability began to surface. "Thank you, Uncle Edmond. I will do everything in my power to be deserving of this honour."

Edmond placed his arm around his nephew's shoulders and together they walked to the front of the house.

Aidan furrowed his brows in questioning surprise; he had prepared himself for something to happen when he placed the league ring on his finger, but was still quite surprised when his mind began to vibrate.

"I have to say, I am rather anxious to find out what ability I have had lurking inside of me my entire life."

Edmond began, "That will happen…"

"Yes, I know, slowly over the next few days. I still can't help but feel impatient."

"The league is lucky to have you, Aidan."

Edmond presented Aidan with what had been Amber's Soul Dagger. "This is now yours. Might I assume Angeline has explained to you what this is?"

"She has. I have seen her Soul Dagger but have not seen it in use."

Aidan opened the six-inch blade and turned it over in his hand. "Such an intricately etched blade, and so very lightweight. Thank you, Uncle."

"I should return to your aunt, but I do wish you all the best with the league, and with Angeline." Edmond winked as he patted Aidan's back.

"Give my best to Aunt Hannah."

Edmond simply nodded, then walked to his front door while Aidan returned to Angeline's car.

He took his seat beside her. "Not as much as I have been these last few days."

"Not as much what, love?"

"Just answering your...you didn't speak, did you?"

"No, no I did not. I was, however, wondering if you were nervous getting your ring."

Excitement rushed through him. "Let's give it another go. Think of something, anything."

With a stern look on her face, Angeline pursed her lips. "I'll have you know that our abilities only work with one another if both parties allow it. I simply was not prepared for an intrusion into my thoughts just now. Although, I did feel a slight tingling in my mind just prior to you answering the question I had not yet asked."

Aidan pleaded, his hands folded as if in prayer. "Please, humour me. Just for now."

"Very well." She crossed her arms in front of herself. *I should flog you for intruding into my thoughts.*

Aidan bowed his head. "I submit myself to be flogged as you see fit."

"Heavens, Aidan! You should not be able to use your ability yet! This is unprecedented! We have got to tell the council. Buckle up, love." Angeline sped out of Edmond's driveway.

The motorway wasn't busy and Angeline made the trip to Wells' Antiquities in record time. They ran through the shop, saying a quick hello and goodbye to Olivia and Nick, her brother, and hurriedly continued to the tunnel entrance in the backroom.

Once in the City of Radiance, they boarded a transport pod and sped to the Grand

Temple. Without waiting for the pod to land, Angeline jumped out and raced to the Council Chambers with Aidan.

Angeline bowed. "Selphia, I apologize for this intrusion, but we have an urgent question."

Araton stepped forward, his hand outstretched, his fingers spread wide. "Aidan Temple, I can feel your energy. You have been given a great gift."

"I was also able to feel your power during our time together." Jael's yellow eyes glowed with concern. "You must be steadfast in your decisions. The path before you is uncertain and your choices must be made with care."

Angeline's expression was filled with worry. "Aidan's ability was not gradual. It manifested the moment he placed his ring on his finger. To my knowledge, this has not happened before. We would like to know what this means."

"The ability within Aidan is unstable. I can feel a great power within him. He must tread lightly and be cautious." Jael was also concerned.

Aidan stood silently, absorbing all of the information that was being shared.

"Is there anything I can do to help him?" Angeline's voice was somewhat panicked. "He is now my responsibility and I do not know what I should do. I need to know what I must do." Angeline felt powerless.

Araton spoke once more. "I will do what I can to aid you, Aidan Temple, but your mind must always remain true. Angeline can guide you, but the final decision will be yours."

"What final decision?" Aidan felt uneasy about his future. "What must I decide?"

Pen-Ming placed his fingertips on his forehead, his eyes closed, his head down. "I cannot see your future and this is what I find most troubling. You must find a way to remain."

After Pen-Ming looked up, he nodded toward Angeline and Aidan to end their conversation. He then led the other members of the Council of Seven to the back of the room where they each took their seat behind the semi-circular table.

Angeline and Aidan bowed before leaving.

As the door to the Council Chambers shut behind them, Aidan rubbed his face. "What am I supposed to do with this information?"

"We will figure it out together. You have eleven people and seven immortals willing to do whatever it takes to help you."

As they walked to the European exit, she could feel Aidan reaching out to her mind, but the thoughts she was having at that moment were not to be shared. The Immortals offered more questions than answers and the uncertainty she felt now had to remain hidden. She felt as though things were beyond her control.

She touched Aidan's arm. "In a few days we have a league training session. I am certain no one would mind if you asked them how they felt when they first spoke with the Council of Seven. I recall them telling me that my choices would affect not only myself, but everyone in the faction I was to lead. It was rather unnerving to say the least."

"Do they always speak in riddles?"

"Yes, actually. If it helps, I have the utmost faith in you. I am more concerned how Sebastian will handle having to ask for permission concerning his love life!"

As he and Angeline continued to their exit, Aidan chuckled. "I think I might rather enjoy watching that. Although...will we not have to do the same?" The thought that he would have to bare his personal feelings and desires to the Council of Seven left him feeling sympathetic toward Sebastian.

~~~~

Once they had showered off another training session, where they trained not only their bodies but practiced with their abilities as well, Sebastian and Ann walked to the Council Chambers to seek permission to continue their relationship.

"What business is it of theirs if we have feelings for each other?" Sebastian was a mixture of nerves and irritation.

"You know as well as I do that we agreed to assume certain responsibilities when we accepted our keys and rings." Even though she had already visited Celeste regarding their relationship, Ann was still nervous. She was also curious as to what stipulations there would be.

"Fine, but I still think our love life should be private. I'm not comfortable talking about...what we do with the Council."

"Suck it up, babe. We got ourselves some begging to do!" Ann patted Sebastian's back.

Inside the Council Chambers, all seven immortals stood, dressed in flowing robes made of the finest luminescent Eyrasine cloth, hemmed with golden embroidery. Each of their robes had a large hood that, when placed over their heads, rendered their faces nearly invisible.

Sebastian felt like a small child preparing to be scolded.

Every member of the Council of Seven, while nearly as old as the planet Eyras itself, had pitch black hair. The different coloured streak in their hair corresponded not only to their eye colour, but also the chakras they embodied.

Ann looked at each of the Immortals. She could sense the power in the silent and graceful dignity they exuded. She had seen drawings of them in battle, wearing armor over top of the form fitted garments that they wore beneath their robes. Not only immortal and all-knowing beings, the Council of Seven were also fierce warriors.

As the seven main chakras in a body represent different aspects of life and emotion, so there were seven council members. Each of the councilors harnessed the energy of all of their chakras, with the most easily accessible energy provided by the chakra that corresponded to their eye and hair streak colour.

The yellow solar plexus chakra, representing power and self-confidence, coursed through Jael. He stood with his arms crossed in front of his chest beside Pen-Ming, who embodied procreation, survival, and lineage. The red root chakra governed Pen-Ming's ability to guide others and knowing this, both Ann and Sebastian hoped he would be forthcoming with his advice and instruction.

Ann's usual nerves of steel had turned to jelly today as she and Sebastian found themselves walking toward the entire Council of Seven. She gripped his hand tightly, hoping to gain some courage.

Sebastian whispered, "Do you feel like you pushed another child on the school playground and you're waiting for the principal to punish you?"

"Absolutely! If I didn't love you so much, I would be running out the door right now!"

Sebastian stopped walking and Ann realized what she had just said.

He let go of her hand and her heart sank. He turned to face her, put his hands on her face, and kissed her.

Ann threw her arms around Sebastian's neck and they kissed each other deeply and tenderly. They both knew that feelings and emotions in anyone with Eyrasine blood were amplified, and that small amounts of energy passed from them into whomever they touched, but neither was prepared for the intensity of what they were feeling.

Celeste smiled as she felt the intensity of emotion flowing through Ann and Sebastian. Her green heart chakra spun at a higher vibration than her other chakras and allowed her to embody emotion, love and relationships. It was this heart chakra that bestowed upon her a mastery over these aspects in those she encountered.

The psychic abilities and willpower of Araton were granted to him through his blue throat chakra. These abilities allowed him to know whenever someone thought of the Immortals. He smiled as he watched Ann and Sebastian. He could sense their minds were solely on each other as they embraced.

Every council member watched as Ann and Sebastian gave each other their hearts.

Jael cleared his throat to return them to reality.

Sebastian bowed his head, his eyes wide. "I apologize."

Ann bowed her head as well, smiled, and whispered, "I don't." She knew she would never regret her feelings for Sebastian.

Raziel's orange sacral chakra allowed his creativity and sexuality to flow and he felt the sexual energy between Ann and Sebastian.

The Council often spoke in vague terms or talked about esoteric mysteries and truths. Ann hoped that today they would speak simply, in a straightforward manner. A simple explanation was all she wanted.

Each of the council members took their seat behind the semi-circular table at the far end of the chamber.

Sebastian stepped forward to ask their permission regarding his involvement with

Ann. He bowed. "Ann and I have come to inquire about any stipulations regarding our relationship with one another."

Umabel, with her indigo third eye chakra most prevalent, encompassed truth and dreams. She stood silent and smiled in the knowledge that Ann's and Sebastian's hearts were steadfast and true.

A few moments of silence passed and then Selphia rose and placed her hands together in front of herself. With her violet crown chakra most active, she represented universal wisdom, unity, and energy. She spoke first. "There is a connection and correspondence between the macrocosm and microcosm. The universe is alive. Everything that has ever been was set in motion with a purpose and an inevitable end. Your paths and choices will play a part in the greater scheme of things."

Selphia's voice sounded as though it were spoken through water.

Ann listened intently, happy that she had not yet heard the word no.

Celeste stepped forward next, her voice strong and loud. "For every action, there is a counteraction. For every choice, there is an option not chosen. Your decision to seek our counsel was a choice. The first moment you touched each other set in motion a future of possibilities. Although rarely, in the past, members of The League of Twelve have joined together. We have all agreed that a union between you, Sebastian Shea, and you, Ann Johnston, is not only approved, it was fated."

Ann and Sebastian looked at each other, each with a smile on their lips and happiness in their eyes.

Celeste took her seat as Pen-Ming rose. "You have long been aware that those with Eyrasine blood have heightened emotions and feel much more deeply than humans. What you may not know, is that once a ring is received and bonds with its wearer, the impulse to procreate begins to grow stronger and does not cease until the required child is born. The pull you feel toward each other is the beginning of what will become your desire for offspring.

"Know this: a union within The League of Twelve unites two sigils. Should such a union continue, it is required to produce two offspring to replace you once you decide to end your time with the league - one born under the same star sign as the father and one sharing that of the mother. Ann, as a child of Taurus, your first child would bear your sign and inherit your ring and key. Sebastian, in your union with Ann, your second child together would be a child of Cancer, destined to inherit your ring and your key. Until these two children are born, your mating would not produce children belonging to any other star sign. Once your obligations to the league have been met, any progeny produced afterward would be your choice. Guard our secrets and raise your offspring well for they shall inherit your legacies."

A silence fell upon the room. As each of the council members bowed their heads, Ann and Sebastian did the same. They thanked the Council for their advice and left.

Sebastian put his arm around her. "It's fate, Ann."

"I can live with that."

They exited the Grand Temple and passed John on his way to the Armory. They walked past without noticing him, lost in their own world.

John looked at them and rather than ask them to join him, decided to let them have their time together.

Inside the Armory, he stood and looked at the weaponry that lined the walls. While he had hoped that leading the league would not be dull, he had not counted on this much excitement. He knew that Marcus was far from finished. If Marcus' goal was to have his geist replicate every league member and take control of the portal, John knew he was surely holed up somewhere planning just how to bring it to fruition.

The league didn't know how many geist were working for him or where they were, and he hoped that Marcus' reach didn't extend beyond North America, into Europe or Africa.

~~~~

At the Cham residence in Cairo, Oriax wore a crisp white linen shirt and navy blue shorts. The pool cleaner he had replicated, now in a metal bin in an alley, had worn these items just a few short hours ago.

As one of the first three geist that Marcus employed in his effort to gain control of the portal, Oriax was not happy that he was stationed in a country with such a hot climate.

He pressed the intercom button beside the massive iron gate at the end of the driveway and heard a woman's sensual voice. "Your name, please."

As his DNA donor's memories hadn't quite taken hold, Oriax referred to the name sewn on to the front of his shirt before he answered. "It is...Samir. I have come to clean the swimming pool."

"Samir! You are early today."

Oriax walked through the gates and saw a plain young woman holding the front door open for him. "I made falafel and some konafah early this morning before Dr. Cham left. I will heat some for you." She stepped aside to allow Oriax in.

He was rather pleased that this woman was willing to attend to his needs, but he had a job to do. He followed her and walked past three large rooms, each containing beautiful sculptures from various world cultures as well as Egyptian artwork.

Must be nice, he thought to himself.

As the young servant woman hurried to the kitchen, Oriax searched one of the rooms. He entered what appeared to be a living room. High walls, each adorned with different styles of artwork, led to an ornately carved ceiling. He looked around the room and noted the various tapestries on another wall.

There were so many vases and boxes and tables that it would have taken Oriax quite a while to search them all for the key Marcus wanted. The only way to buy himself time was to kill the servant girl in the kitchen. First, he needed to know if anyone else was in the house.

175

He exited the living room and walked to the kitchen at the end of the hallway, with the scent of food leading the way. "You are alone here today?"

The servant wiped the kitchen counter. "Yes, the housekeeper will not be here until midday."

He walked to the young woman and pushed her against the wall. She felt a hand on her breast and smiled. She had often wondered if Samir had the same feelings for her as she had for him and was glad to know that he did. However, she didn't notice that Oriax had a knife in his other hand.

He pushed her shoulder against the wall, plunged the knife into her stomach, and turned it.

Between quick gasps for air, she pleaded, "Samir? Please, why are you doing this?"

Oriax released her and she slumped to the floor. He looked at down at her as she looked up. Before he drove the knife into her eye, he smiled. "I am not Samir."

He walked to the kitchen sink to wash his hands before he resumed his search for the key. He was not sure when the family would return, so he knew his search had to be quick.

In the first room just outside of the kitchen, there were so many shelves of books and trinkets that a discreet search was out of the question. One piece of furniture after another turned up nothing.

In the living room, he tore the tapestries from the wall, overturned every chair, and turned every table upside down and did not find the key.

Oriax headed upstairs hoping that his next search would get him the prize he sought. He passed by a large mirror and noticed the blood staining the front of his white shirt. He swore under his breath, removed the shirt and threw it to the floor.

Inside the closest room, he opened the closet doors and grabbed the first shirt he saw. As he buttoned the shirt he glanced around the room.

In the centre of Najeeb's bedroom, a sturdy bed of solid wood was adorned with beautifully embroidered sheets. The far wall was covered with one large bookcase. More books and artifacts than Oriax had ever seen were set upon the various shelves. He tore the mattress from the bed, then moved to the bookcase. He furiously threw the books from the shelves, one after the other, until a trinket box fell. A fair of amount of coins spilled out of it, as well as Najeeb's Leo key.

Oriax huffed. "Finally!" He immediately phoned Marcus with the news. He looked at the key in his hand. "I have one of the keys."

"Good. Now, find your donor's passport and phone me with the information. I will have a ticket to Toronto waiting for you at the airport and a rental car once you arrive. Good work, Oriax. Your reward shall be handsome!"

Oriax left the Cham house smiling and quickly headed to Samir's residence.

~~~~

Najeeb concealed what appeared to be a chunk of diamond in his personal satchel, not wanting the others at the dig site to see it.

After he had finished for the day, he sat in his car and studied the clear stone. The etchings on it were similar to the Eyrasine symbols on the sapphire tablet in the City of Radiance. He returned it to his satchel, and planned to present it to Zayne when next they met.

When Najeeb returned home he parked his car in the garage. His parents weren't home yet, so he stripped down and dove straight into the swimming pool.

After a short swim, he got out of the pool, grabbed a towel from one of the poolside tables, and dried himself. Once he gathered his belongings, he went into the house for some food.

The moment he entered, he saw his home had been ransacked, and his first thought was of his key. He raced upstairs to his bedroom.

As he ascended the stairs, he looked toward his bedroom where he kept his key and was unable to locate its heat signature. His heart pounded hard in his chest.

His books were scattered throughout his room and the mattress had been thrown off his bed. He searched for the trinket box where he kept his key and found it on the floor, open. His key was gone.

Najeeb cursed under his breath and pulled his cell phone from his pocket. Before he phoned the police, he phoned Zayne to let him know what happened.

Zayne then phoned John and Angeline, and yet another meeting was called.

~~~~

Once everyone had gathered in the Hall of Gates, Najeeb frantically paced while he relayed what happened. "My home was ransacked. My key has been stolen and one of our servants has been killed."

"We got mine back, we will get yours." Sebastian's hatred of his uncle was visible on his face.

John was furious. He clenched his fists and gritted his teeth. "Now Marcus has the Aquarius key and the Leo key. He cannot get anymore!"

"I have something." Najeeb pulled the tablet fragment from his satchel. "I found this at a dig site. It shares some markings with the sapphire tablet."

Angeline was intrigued. "May I see it?"

Najeeb nodded and brought the tablet piece to her.

"This is so lightweight!" She examined the fragment but even with her ability, she could not read it.

"I'm going to bring this to the sapphire tablet. I want to compare the etchings." She walked into the Grand Temple through the Libra door, the most direct route to the sapphire tablet.

With the clear fragment held in front of her, Angeline compared the markings. They seemed to be similar, but she could not find any identical symbols. As she raised it toward the light emitted by the dome overhead, she passed it in front of the sapphire tablet and saw the etchings on it scramble.

"What?" She held the piece of clear tablet directly in front of the sapphire stone and a new inscription appeared. It revealed that there were three tablets: one sapphire, one emerald, and one diamond.

Angeline ran back to the Hall of Gates and quickly entered her door. "It must be part of a decrypting tablet!"

John looked puzzled. "What do you mean, decrypting tablet?"

"There is more on the sapphire tablet than just what we can see. I passed this clear piece in front of it and it revealed hidden words. I only read a tiny piece but apparently, there are three tablets, not just one. Emerald and diamond tablets also exist!"

Angeline looked at Ann. "Grab some food and meet me at the sapphire tablet. I would like your help translating the new inscription from Ancient Eyrasine and since we will both be using my, I am going to need to eat."

"I'm on it!"

John walked to his Gemini door and spoke without turning around. "We need to speak with the council, Zayne. Either they withheld this information or they need to know, but something tells me that they are aware of these tablets."

John and Zayne left for the Council Chambers. Once inside they bowed before the Council of Seven as they sat at their semi-circular table.

John began. "Councilors, I have a question. We have become aware of an emerald tablet and have come to possess a fragment of a clear tablet that has revealed hidden text on the sapphire tablet. Is there anything you can tell us about these two new stones?"

Umabel rose and spoke, her voice soft and fluid. "We are aware of these tablets. Gather the others. This matter must be discussed with all."

~~~~

With every league member present in the Council Chambers, Pen-Ming paced throughout the room, his hands gesturing as he relayed the story of the sapphire tablet. The other members of the Council stood beside the covered oblong table on the right hand side of their Chambers.

Pen-Ming began, "When Omm created the City of Radiance, the twelve kings were the first to travel through the portal to Earth. The sapphire tablet that is above the southern entrance inside the Grand Temple, was engraved by two of these twelve kings - Aries King Euan and Taurus King Stephen. In what is known as the Ancient Eyrasine language, they etched the account of their exodus from Eyras to Earth, as directed by King Alexander, so that the history of their journey, and why they had to leave their home, would forever be known.

"When the first two kings had completed their task, Alexander, the son of Omm and Gemini King, along with Cancer King Javan, were charged with etching information that Omm relayed only to them. They were told to find a witch among the humans to aid the Eyrasine enchantress in spelling their engravings, so that they would be hidden from plain sight. The hidden engravings were to be known only to the twelve kings and the Immortals.

"What is not relayed on the sapphire tablet is that before the kings arrived, Omm had assured their survival and prosperity on Earth. He sent through the portal many pieces of Eyrasine technology, materials that were used in forging many of the weapons that you now possess, as well as three tablets.

"The hidden words on the sapphire tablet also speak of the World Tree and its seven branches that lead to the heavens, and its seven roots which lead to the underworlds. The seven branches and seven roots are known to you as the seven tunnels you see when you travel to the City of Radiance from any of your three vestibules on the Earth's surface. Each of these tunnels leads to a heavenly dimension as well as a dimension of the underworld. You travel only one of these tunnels, but the tablet reveals how the other six may be traveled as well. The door through which you enter the City of Radiance, also leads to a dimension of the heavens and one of the underworld, but these cannot be accessed by mortals.

"In a time long past, passage between Earth and the heavens was as commonplace as travel from the Earth's surface to the City of Radiance is now. Eyrasines and Eyrasine/human hybrids were granted access to these heavenly dimensions through the branches of the world tree, the tunnels. Only in the company of a league member, or a member of the Council of Seven, could they travel to these dimensions as a key is required to leave these worlds, as well as enter them."

The league members listened intently. John clenched his teeth as he felt a twinge of anger rise in him. He knew that the Immortals were aware that Marcus was intent on killing every league member. They all knew that the league members needed to be ready for anything, and yet information that could potentially aid them in this fight, had been kept from them.

Pen-Ming continued. "Eyrasines were granted access to the underworlds as well, though very few made this journey. Those who dared enter an underworld were no longer the same beings upon their return. It was then decided that access to the underworlds be denied to all.

"While the heavens were still accessible, evil found its way inside. Once this evil had been destroyed, it was decided that the heavens also be denied.

"The decision was made by Omm, the Immortals, and the League of Twelve at that time, that from that point forward, they alone would have knowledge of how the heavens and the underworlds could be accessed. Not even future members of the league were to know of their existence, unless that knowledge was necessary to safeguard the City of Radiance and the people within it.

"With the help of the Eyrasine enchantress, Aurora, and an earth witch, the astral keys and the dimensional doorways were again spelled to require two keys to be used to access either dimension, so that no one person could enter alone. When polar opposite keys are close together, they are attracted to one another and form a new key. Keys engraved with one of the first six sigils, Aries, Taurus, Gemini, Cancer, Leo or Virgo, on top of their polar opposite keys of the last six sigils, form new keys that can access the heavens.

"Keys of the last six sigils, Libra, Scorpio, Sagittarius, Capricorn, Aquarius and Pisces, atop their polar opposite keys of the first six sigils, form new keys that access the underworlds."

Angeline knew Cancer was her polar opposite and walked to Sebastian. "Seb, put your key next to mine."

As Sebastian's key got close to Angeline's, a magnetic attraction pulled them together.

Each league member stood astonished as the two astral keys combined.

John snapped. "This information should not have been withheld. We need to know everything if we are to protect this city and everyone with Eyrasine blood."

Jael began to walk among the league members. "Your frustration is understood, John."

Pen-Ming moved to stand by the oblong table. "For many years, no beings have entered the heavens or the underworld. If a fragment of the diamond tablet had not been discovered, you would not have the knowledge you now do. It was decreed that the heavens and the underworld were to remain lost to all, lest all be lost."

"What does that mean?" John shrugged his shoulders and raised his hands, palms upward. "What is the all that would be lost?"

Pen-Ming clasped his hands together. "All. The Earth, its galaxy. Eyras, its galaxy, and the very universe itself. Should a great evil access the heavens or escape the underworlds, all would end as Armageddon would begin."

Pen-Ming closed his eyes and a faint, red shimmer surrounded him as he re-centred himself before he continued. "The blue sapphires in the rings worn by Conor, Ann, Sebastian, and you, John, are small fragments of the sapphire tablet. To allow your extraordinary abilities to surface, they were spelled by the same human witch and Eyrasine enchantress that spelled the tablet's hidden markings. Your ring, John, is the only one with a blue star sapphire stone. As you are the leader of The League of Twelve and of Alexander's bloodline, the stone in your ring was kissed by Kaya, wife of Omm, before being sent to Earth with Alexander along with the tablets from which the other stones were cut."

Pen-Ming looked at Najeeb. "The clear fragment that you discovered is but part of a larger diamond tablet. It was used by the kings and a select few of their descendants to decipher the hidden knowledge. It had been etched by Leo King Larsa, Virgo King Rourke, Libra King Desmond, and Scorpio King Cyrus, to reveal the markings on the sapphire and emerald tablets. The marks upon this tablet were carved so deeply and with such great care, that it required these four kings to devote most of their lives to its completion. Four small pieces of this tablet were given to these kings, one to each, and were spelled as the sapphire fragments were.

"We will have the sapphire tablet removed from the wall and brought to our Chambers. Here, you, Angeline and you, Ann, will together discover that which has not been seen for many, many centuries. When all has been revealed, we shall share with you that which you have not known and that of which you must be wary."

As Pen-Ming bowed his head, indicating he had said everything he intended to, Jael resumed his position beside the oblong table and spoke. "You have now become aware of the existence of the emerald tablet, fragments from which are found in the rings of Angeline, Aidan, Josh, and Ethan."

He removed the white cloth from the table behind which the Immortals stood, and revealed a large emerald tablet. Every league member stood in awe at the sight of such a beautiful object.

Sebastian felt his anger rising. "Why has this been kept from us? What secrets does it hold that are so sacred or so dangerous that you felt you had to keep it from us?"

John placed his hand on Sebastian's shoulder, hoping to calm his friend, in spite of sharing his feelings.

Jael answered. "Young Sebastian, the information on this tablet is far more ominous than that of its sapphire brother. Carved by Sagittarius King Lucius and Capricorn King David, the visible inscriptions on it relay spells and incantations, such as those to trap spirits and demons in sacred circles, knowledge needed to forge amulets, as well as the technical schematics necessary to create magical weapons, such as daggers.

"This tablet also contains hidden writings. The words inscribed by Aquarius King Halden and Pisces King Erech, are things that, should they be known outside of the league, would be detrimental to the very existence of the league itself. These etchings reveal the construction of the astral keys, as well as the precise combination of indestructible materials contained in the vests available to each of you. Also hidden are the incantations used to spell the gems in the rings you wear, and how the Soul Daggers you all carry and your Dagger of Truth were forged, as well as one other dagger, known as the Spirit Dagger."

Everyone wondered what the Spirit Dagger was, yet none of them interrupted Jael as he continued walking amongst them as he spoke, his hands now clasped behind his back.

"Once the necessary items had been created, this tablet was no longer needed. After nearly every evil geist had been destroyed, a pact of peace was made between the league and those geist with pure intentions. It was decreed that any geist with an aura of blue, be granted their freedom and no longer pursued by anyone in The League of Twelve.

"In order to prevent any future threats from discovering its visible knowledge, the Council decreed that the emerald tablet was to be forgotten. It was placed in our Chambers and is never left unguarded." Jael tilted his head and turned to Umabel, who spoke next.

Umabel leaned against the emerald tablet and began to relay the history of the diamond tablet. "As for the diamond tablet, its history is much darker than that of either of its siblings. Etched on this tablet is, as you are now aware, a decoding cypher. When held in front of the sapphire or emerald tablet, it reveals their hidden knowledge. The purpose of this tablet was known only to league members and the Council of Seven, or so we believed.

"Many years past, during a time when trust was given freely and the thought of betrayal did not enter our minds, a resident in the City of Radiance became aware of the diamond tablet and absconded with it.

"This resident was captured and brought before the Council. He offered no explanation for his actions and accepted his fate. The decision was unanimous, the punishment just and immediate.

"Without being able to decode the other tablets, the council then decided that the emerald tablet was to be hidden, forgotten, and never spoken of again."

The council members bowed their heads in unison and turned away from the league members.

John held back his feelings of anger. He knew the Immortals needed to be aware that the Leo key had also been taken. "One further thing."

Each of the Immortals stopped and turned to face John.

"The Leo key has been taken and…"

Araton interrupted. "We are aware, John." The Immortals turned away once again.

John bowed. "Thank you." He then moved to leave the Council Chambers.

The rest of the league did the same, except for Angeline. She asked, "Councilors, once we have deciphered the hidden words on the sapphire tablet, may we begin work on the emerald tablet?"

Selphia stopped and turned around. "You may, Angeline, but know this: The visible words on the emerald tablet may be transcribed, but those that you can only see with the aid of the diamond tablet, are never to be written. These hidden words must never leave our chambers."

Selphia turned her back to Angeline and continued to the hallway that led to her personal chamber.

"I understand. Thank you." After she bowed, Angeline turned to leave the room.

Aidan, Sebastian, and Ann waited for Angeline just outside the Council Chambers door.

Angeline approached Aidan with both arms raised. "Welcome to the league, Aidan. Where the fun never stops!"

Ann's stomach growled. "When do you want to start, Ange?"

"I'm ready whenever you are."

Ann placed her hands on her hips. "Hey, why don't the four of us have one last meal together before we have to abandon our boys for the glamorous life of decoding the sapphire tablet?"

Sebastian shrugged. "Sounds good to me. Aidan?"

Aidan's stomach growled in anticipation of food. "I have no plans."

Angeline took Aidan's arm. "Well then, let's get some food. Up above or shall we stay in the City?"

Ann's eyes searched an invisible calendar. "What day is it? Friday! We are going to Transcendence. Mom made a delicious beef tenderloin with red chili sauce and jalapeño cheese and there's a chocolate raspberry torte with my name on it! I'll share, of course, but, yeah, we are heading topside."

~~~~

Ann and Angeline lingered longer than they should have in Transcendence, and opted to begin deciphering the sapphire tablet the following day with fresh minds. They were also looking forward to Zayne's birthday celebration at the Alda Metta in a few days. It would surely be a welcome distraction from league business and remind them all that life still moved forward.

Sebastian and Ann stayed on the surface, while Angeline brought Aidan back to the City of Radiance, so they could return home.

As they approached the European exit, Angeline lowered her head. "Had you not accepted your position in the league, I'm not sure our relationship would have survived. What would you have thought of me being gone so much? Aidan, I am going to be working on these tablets for quite some time. I will understand if even now you..."

He placed his hands on her hips and looked directly into her eyes. "You'll understand if even now I want you more than I had ever thought possible? Well then, that is awfully intuitive of you. And I thought I was the one who could read minds."

"You are an amazing man, Mr. Temple." Angeline sighed and rose up on her toes to kiss him.

Once she had unlocked and opened the door that led into Wells' Antiquities, Angeline gently shoved Aidan inside. "In you go!"

They left the antique shop hand in hand and headed back to the Aemetta Suites.

15 – THE TAURUS SECRET

John walked into Transcendence and found Vivian waiting for him at the bar near the kitchen.

"Have a seat. I've made you some almond pancakes and a cheddar and roasted red pepper frittata." Vivian lifted the silver warming lid from the plate she had prepared for him. "I have a feeling this is going to involve a lot of me talking and a lot of you listening."

"Thanks, Aunt Viv." He inhaled deeply and closed his eyes. "Mmm. This smells amazing. I haven't been doing much eating lately or sleeping."

"And it shows, dear." Vivian's expression showed her concern. She lightly squeezed John's shoulder as she took a seat beside him at the bar.

"So, when you phoned you said you had questions about Asmodeus. Since you asked me, I can only assume that you found out about the Taurus secret."

"Ann told us when we found out that Marcus plans to release him. I need to know everything you can tell me. Anything you know would really help us."

Vivian opened her eyes wide in disbelief. "What do you mean, Marcus plans to release him? He has no way to access the tunnel! He has no way to know where the tomb is!"

"All we know is he thinks he can release him. We don't know Marcus or what he's capable of. I just need to find out as much as I can so we can stop him."

Vivian's first thought was of her daughter. She sighed and put aside her fears. "Marcus has always been a bastard. As for Asmodeus, I only know what my father and grandfather told me, but I hope it will help." Vivian clasped her hands together, rested them on the bar and began to tell John the story behind the Taurus bloodline's secret.

"Back when my father passed his ring to me, he told me that our bloodline was special, that we had a very important task to perform and that no one, not even the other league members, could know about it. I questioned this because I was always told that the league was a family, and that honesty was imperative.

"That night, my grandfather came by and he, my father, and I took a drive to the falls. We sat in that car for hours while my grandfather told me about Asmodeus.

"He started off telling me that he knew what my ability was going to be. He knew because everyone in the Taurus line since the kings first arrived on Earth, was a mimic.

"Apparently, Araton told my grandfather that he was the only one who could take down Asmodeus because of his ability, which, of course, made no sense since his ability relied on others. However, with a little help from Aurora, my grandfather was able to absorb the abilities of *all* of the other league members, at the same time."

John sat in disbelief, his brows furrowed.

"So, Grandpa then told me about a metal tomb that the Eyrasines built that was encased in stone inside the Taurus/Scorpio tunnel. With the help of a geist…"

"A geist helped to entomb Asmodeus?" John found it hard to believe that the Immortals would sanction a geist helping the league.

"He did. I can't recall his name but yes, a geist. Anyway, since Asmodeus was not only geist, but part demon as well as part human, Aurora put an enchantment on the tomb so that each of Asmodeus' essences - geist, demon, and human, would not be able to escape."

"Human essence?"

"His soul. Asmodeus has a geist essence, a demon spirit, and a human soul. To kill him would take the Spirit Dagger and that blade was lost a very long time ago.

"With the help of an Earth witch, a few of the Immortals, a geist, and his friend Jerry, Grandpa was able to get Asmodeus in the tomb.

"The witch, Cerra, I believe, pierced Asmodeus with a triangle pentacle that would keep him paralyzed, not just his body, but his mind as well. She then cut my grandfather's arm and sealed the tomb with his blood. John, she also created a reversal spell."

"Why would she do that? If anyone found it…"

"She belongs to the Crimson Trad Coven. That coven has been bound to The League of Twelve for centuries and they know the consequences of betrayal. Cerra said the reversal spell was necessary so that the universe would remain in balance.

"Once it was done and Asmodeus was secured in his tomb, Araton told my grandfather that he had to kill Jerry. Humans couldn't be allowed to live with the knowledge that he had of the league and Asmodeus. Grandpa killed his best friend."

John knew the league was never to be made known to humans, save those who became life partners with league members, but he didn't know that the repercussion of such knowledge was death.

Vivian continued. "One last thing. Taurus blood sealed the tomb and only Taurus blood can open it. It's Ann's blood they would need to open the tomb. No one else could unseal it. Grandpa said that it took the combined abilities of the league to bring down Asmodeus. You cannot let him get out, John. Keeping him in that tomb and making sure my daughter is safe have to be priorities."

John sighed. "I know, Aunt Viv. I'll talk to Ann about having someone with her until this is over and we'll do everything we can to make sure Asmodeus stays in his tomb. Right now, Marcus has no way to find out where Asmodeus is. We just have to keep it that way."

Vivian knew her daughter, knew she would never agree to a babysitter. "If Ann puts up a fuss over having someone with her…"

John interrupted. "Let me talk to the Immortals. I'm sure they have someone who could covertly watch Ann without disrupting her life too much, someone she can call if she's in trouble."

John ran his hands through his hair. "She's not going to like this."

"It's for her own good, John. Just let her know it's not optional.

"Anyway, where was I? Right, Cerra. A long while back, Cerra's coven used to meet at a little tea shop called Crimson Spark. I believe your father may have contacted the coven a time or two himself. From what I understand, it was the only coven that the league could trust. Witches can be an unpredictable sort but this coven knows better than to betray the league. The Central Archives should have all of the information you need on the coven."

John stood and kissed Vivian. "Thank you, Aunt Viv. This is exactly what I needed. Thanks for the food, too. It was delicious, as always."

Vivian placed her hand on John's shoulder. "You're quite welcome, dear. If you need anything else, you know where I am."

She was confident that John and the league would be able to do what had to be done, but she couldn't help but fear for her daughter's safety.

After leaving Transcendence, John phoned the Immortals to enquire about a protector for Ann and was given the name, Kayla, and a number at which she could be contacted. He set a reminder on his phone to get in touch with Kayla and then phoned Angeline and Zayne. He asked them to meet him in the Hall of Gates to research Cerra and Crimson Spark. Research wasn't his favourite pastime, but he had come to realize that leading The League of Twelve was more work than it was play.

~~~~

Once the three faction leaders were inside the Hall of Gates, John inserted his astral key in his Gemini port and brought the 3D Central Archives to life. He requested any and all information on the coven known as The Crimson Trad.

"If I knew there would be so much information I would have brought coffee! I do love research." Angeline's voice was nearly giddy.

Both John and Zayne groaned.

Zayne smiled sweetly. "And that is why we love you, Ange!"

Angeline chuckled. "Let's get to it, shall we?"

After scrolling through the data for what seemed like an hour, they found the information they were looking for. Selecting the name Cerra VanCleaf led them first to her daughter, Siobhan Zorida, current high priestess of The Crimson Trad, and then to her granddaughter, Maeve Zorida. Siobhan and Maeve together co-owned Crimson Spark.

John looked from Angeline to Zayne. "Same name, same location. I guess we're going to a tea shop."

Angeline removed her cell phone from her purse. "Shall I ring Ann? She should be part of this as well, since it was her family that worked with Cerra."

"Yeah. Let her know the address and have her to meet us there in an hour. I've got something to tell her anyway. While we're here, we might as well see what the archives has on Asmodeus."

While Angeline phoned Ann, John turned his attention back to the holographic screen. "Display all information on Asmodeus."

~~~~

Ann and Sebastian were waiting outside of Crimson Spark when John, Angeline, and Zayne arrived. A cold wind blew around them as they gathered in front of Crimson Spark. Winter still had a strong hold on Niagara Falls.

John got right to business. He looked through the glass window. "This is where Cerra's coven meets. Her daughter, Siobhan, is now the high priestess of The Crimson Trad, and co-owns this tea shop with her daughter, Maeve."

Ann sighed loudly. "I knew the name sounded familiar. I've been here! Ange, this is where I bought that tea I gave you when you landed that big convention."

"Really? It was fantastic!"

"I completely forgot about its connection to the league. I should have asked for a discount!" Ann laughed.

John addressed the others. "Have any of you heard about this coven? Apparently the league has been using their services at least as far back as Ann's grandfather."

Ann glanced upward. "Hmm, I think I remember hearing stories about witches when I was younger."

Geist, witches, and now Asmodeus. John was glad that at least the witches were on his side.

Ann folded her arms in front of herself as she rubbed them in an attempt to fend off the cold winter wind that blew around her. Sebastian saw her trying to warm herself, and wrapped his arms around her. "No need to freeze when I'm around," he whispered in her ear.

She nestled back into his embrace.

"What's up, John?" Ann saw a curious look on John's face.

"I spoke with your mother today, as well as the Immortals, and it turns out that your blood is needed to open Asmodeus' tomb."

The others listened intently.

"We all decided that someone should be close to you at all times."

He saw Ann's expression and before she could protest, he continued, "Not stuck to your side, but someone to stay in your building, on the floor you live on. Someone to be close by in case something were to happen, just until this situation with Asmodeus is dealt with."

Ann stared at John. Her eyes narrowed and she huffed out a breath. "Fine. I don't suppose I have a choice, do I?"

Sebastian chimed in. "I think it's a great idea. I know I would feel better knowing that someone was close by when I wasn't. Marcus isn't above hurting you to get your blood."

Once those words were out of his mouth, Sebastian realized just how much danger Ann was potentially in. "John, we can't let Marcus get her." Sebastian's mind flooded with anger and fear.

Ann shook her head and sighed. "Seb, Marcus doesn't know where the tomb is. He has no way to find out. But if it will make you guys feel better, I guess a servant wouldn't be so bad." The look on her face was playful.

John removed his phone from his pocket and texted Kayla's name and number to Ann. "Set up a speed dial to contact her if you even suspect that someone is looking at you the wrong way."

Ann glanced sideway at John. "Yes, John." Marcus had killed his own brother, so she knew that he would have no qualms about killing her.

John motioned toward the tea shop entrance. "Let's get inside and see what's what."

When the league members walked into Crimson Spark, they found Maeve stocking the shelves with boxes of various teas. Zayne walked to the far right aisle, wanting to be able to see the entire store at a glance. At this point, he trusted no one.

John recognized Maeve from a photo in the Central Archives and walked straight to her. "Maeve Zorida?"

Maeve turned. "Yes, I am Maeve. Welcome to Crimson Spark. What can I help you with?"

"I need information." Since no one else was in the store, John decided to test Maeve's reaction. "What can you tell me about a spell used to entomb Asmodeus?"

Dropping the box she had in her hand, Maeve bent down to pick it up. "Who are you? How do you know about Asmodeus?"

John was satisfied with Maeve's defensive response. "We are members of The League of Twelve. We were told that your coven played a part in sealing Asmodeus' tomb."

Maeve immediately look at John's hand, searching for the ring she knew all league members wore. She exhaled loudly.

"You had me frightened for a moment. It was my grandmother, Cerra, who aided your league. What is it I can do for you?"

Maeve hoped that none of the league members could sense her nerves as she recalled passing information to Marcus.

"Has anyone been here asking for a reversal spell? A spell that would unseal the tomb?" Standing next to Maeve, Ann felt a strange feeling. It was as though her ability were trying to break free from her body.

Maeve became defensive. "No one knows of Asmodeus other than your league and my family. My mother has told me many things about your league, one of them is that we are bound to you, that we must comply if you request our aid but I have not had the pleasure of meeting any of you until today."

"Maeve, have you found the…" Siobhan's sentence stopped short as she came from the back room holding a mug and saw the league members. "I'm sorry, I didn't realize you were with a customer, dear." She turned around to return to the back room.

"Mother, these people are from The League of Twelve."

Zayne then moved to join the others.

"Oh!" Siobhan quickly glanced at each of their hands, noting that they did indeed each wear a league ring. "I haven't seen anyone from The League of Twelve in a very long time. Come, sit. I am Siobhan Zorida."

John had seen Siobhan quickly look at each league member and realized she was verifying their identities by looking for the rings on their fingers, as Maeve did. He was glad to see that they were both cautious and hoped that the trust the league had placed in them was not misplaced.

Siobhan began coughing. "I'm sorry, I haven't been well. Maeve darling, were you able to find the masala chai tea blend?"

Siobhan turned to the league members. "It is quite soothing on a sore throat."

She waved her hand dramatically. "I don't trust all those pills and liquids they have for sale on every corner. Natural herbs are much better than polluting your body with poisons."

Siobhan looked at John with an odd expression. She walked to him and placed her hands on his face. "I know you." Her words were quiet and slow.

Wide-eyed, John looked at Siobhan.

"No, not you." She gasped as she removed her hands from his face "You are the son of Michael, yes?"

"I am."

"You look like your father, such a kind man. Michael came to me for help a few times years ago. So you are now taking his place?"

"Yes." He motioned toward Angeline and Zayne, who stood side by side. "Siobhan, this is Angeline, our European faction leader and Zayne, our African faction leader."

Siobhan walked to them. "So good to meet you."

She grabbed their hands. "You are both very strong. Good strong hands."

Angeline smiled and tilted her head. "Nice to meet you as well, Siobhan."

Zayne remained silent and simply nodded his head in greeting.

Ann stepped forward. "This is Ann. The granddaughter of Eric Turner."

Siobhan hesitated. "Oh, very nice to meet you, Ann." She knew about Asmodeus and Eric Turner. Seeing his descendent made her a bit uncomfortable.

Ann wrinkled her brow. "You too."

"This is Sebastian."

"Sebastian, oh dear. I heard what happened to your family. I am so very sorry for your loss." Siobhan took his hand in hers.

"Thank you." He sensed that she was sincere in what she was saying, but still felt that something was off. The tension in the room was nearly palpable.

Angeline wanted to change the atmosphere in the shop. "Mrs. Zorida, would you mind helping me select some tea for a gentleman friend of mine? He is quite particular and I'm certain he would love something from your shop."

"Absolutely, dear! Come." She held onto Angeline's arm and led her to a specialty aisle.

"So, Maeve," John placed his hands in his pants pockets, "are you certain no one has been asking about Asmodeus?"

"No one. As I said, we are obliged to aid your league when a request is made."

John saw Maeve's business cards on the counter and reached for one. He picked up the pen beside the cash register and wrote his cell phone number on the back. He handed it to Maeve. "If anyone comes in here and so much as says the name Asmodeus, I want you to call me. Will you do that, Maeve?"

The look on John's face told Maeve that there would be trouble if she didn't comply, but the fact that he asked at all meant that he did not know that she was hiding something.

"I will. I shall let my mother know as well. As she mentioned, she has been ill lately but she does come down to help in the shop every now and then. We will phone you if we have anything to tell."

Across the shop, Angeline gushed. "Thank you, Mrs. Zorida. This will be perfect!"

"On the house. A gift, from me to you."

Angeline leaned down and kissed Siobhan on her cheek. "Thank you!"

John walked to the exit and raised his hand. "Thank you again. It was good meeting you both."

Siobhan waved. "And you, all of you."

Maeve walked to the middle aisle to continue stocking the shelf.

Once the league members were outside the store, Sebastian looked at Angeline and frowned. "How can you act so calm with witches, Ange?"

Angeline laughed. "They're just people with special skills. We all have special skills and you don't find that spooky, do you?"

"No, but we're," Sebastian groaned and narrowed his eyes. "Alright. We're descendants of beings from another planet. Point taken."

Ann looked contemplative. "I never really thought about it, but we are all part alien."

Angeline furrowed her brow and placed her hands on her hips. "Come to think of it, I do believe I am quite offended by the notion of these humans thinking aliens are grey with large heads, big eyes, and skinny little limbs!"

Zayne had lines of concern on his face. "Sebastian may have a point. The minute I walked into that store, I felt uneasy, as though the very air was filled with a negative energy."

Ann's expression was one of suspicion. "I agree. Maeve was kind of creepy. I felt some bad vibes coming from her."

Angeline jumped to Siobhan's defense. "I found Siobhan to be rather sweet. She's just an old woman who just happens to have a deep connection with nature."

Zayne still felt uneasy. "How much do we know about Maeve Zorida? Can we trust her?"

John was convinced that Zayne was jumping to conclusions. "She's in Cerra's coven and she is her granddaughter as well. The Crimson Trad has a history with us and I can't imagine that they would want to jeopardize it."

Zayne couldn't shake his suspicions. "Maeve is not Cerra. She has not proven her worth to us."

~~~~

Later that evening, John, Sebastian, and Conor went to Solar Flair.

Inside his office, Azroth was quite forthcoming. He told them his informant said there were two geist working with Marcus, one called Ganga and another whose name he did not know. "My informant pointed out Ganga last night and I just happened to hear a part of her conversation." He hinted that he wanted cash to continue.

Sebastian growled. "I swear, Azroth, if I see you rub your fingers together, I will end you!"

Azroth raised his hands defensively. "Fine, fine, take it easy. Times are tough. I just thought that maybe you would be a little more appreciative of my hard work."

Conor placed his hands on Azroth's desk. "Leaning on your bar and pouring drinks is not hard work. I've taken an oath to do no harm, but I'm pretty sure it doesn't pertain to geist."

"Sheesh! Alright, already. As I was saying, I hung around and listened to this Ganga as she was talking about how Marcus wanted her to get something from a league member who was switching sides to prove that she was no longer one of the league's lackeys."

John narrowed his eyes and growled. "No one in the league would work with Marcus. Your informant is wrong."

Sebastian pulled his Soul Dagger from behind his back. "Or maybe Azroth here isn't too keen on staying alive anymore."

Azroth held one hand up and placed the other over his heart. "Guys, I swear, if I had recorded the whole thing you wouldn't get a better version!"

He feared that one of these men would make good on their threats. "On my very existence, I promise you that I'm speaking the truth. Shall I continue?"

John placed his hand on the back of Azroth's chair and leaned toward him. "Yes, continue, but know this. If I find out you're lying to me, you will be begging me to kill you by the time I'm through with you."

Azroth raised both hands in submission. "Understood, chief. I hear you loud and clear."

John leaned against the wall with his arms folded firmly on his chest as Azroth continued.

"So, Ganga said this league member was just a kid, and that she thought about letting her live, but changed her mind and stabbed her." He mimicked a stabbing motion and sound. "Right in the back of her neck. She was so sure that Marcus was going to be happy about her killing this little girl as well as getting him a key.

"I was going to phone you once I finished my paperwork, but here you are."

John, Conor, and Sebastian looked at each other. They knew who Azroth was speaking about.

Azroth's voice turned acerbic. "So now, Ganga is trying to recruit more geist to help Marcus because apparently you all killed one of the geist he had on his payroll."

John knew he needed to get the Aquarius key back and no longer cared about the morality of the method. "Let your customers know that you know someone who will pay good money for any info on Marcus' whereabouts. There's a bonus in it for you if we find him."

"Bonus?" Azroth was intrigued.

John removed a few bills from his pocket and tossed them at Azroth. "Here. For today's information." He turned and quickly left the office.

Conor and Sebastian followed John out the door.

"It's Amber who betrayed us. That geist, Ganga, killed Amber." John walked down the street to his car and punched the top of a mailbox. "We need everyone in the Hall of Gates. Now."

"I'll take care of getting everyone there." Conor reached for his phone as they each got into their cars and sped toward Jayded Ink.

"Send a text message to group titled, League." When his phone requested the content of his message Conor said, "Meeting now. Urgent. Stop whatever you're doing and get to the Hall of Gates as soon as possible."

John paced inside the Hall of Gates, unable to calm himself. "How long was Amber working with Marcus before she died? Or rather, before she was killed? How much did she tell him?"

Conor tried to reassure John. "This is not on you. Amber did this all on her own. We will probably never know why."

Sebastian shook his head. "I can't believe this. Amber was kind of a loner, but I always thought she was a good kid."

Angeline and Aidan hurried into the Hall of Gates. She looked at Conor. "What is going on? I can't recall ever getting such an urgent message."

John paced. "I'm going to wait until everyone's here. It's a total snafu, Ange."

Angeline looked at Aidan and opened her thoughts to him. In her mind, she said, *I've never seen John look so upset before. I'm quite worried about what he's going to say.*

Aidan replied with his thoughts as he gently squeezed Angeline's hand. *Whatever it is, we will handle it. I know I'm rather new to this, but I've a feeling that this group is rather invincible together when they've got a mind to be.*

Josh and Ethan arrived next. "Planning my birthday bash, John?" Ethan joked.

"No, but I'm sure we will all want a drink or two after you hear what I have to say."

Ann entered the Hall of Gates next. "What's up? Why the urgent text, Conor?"

"We're waiting until everyone's here."

Ann walked to Sebastian and whispered, "John doesn't look quite calm. Is there anything I should prepare for?"

"Nope. There's nothing any of us can do about it now."

Once the African faction arrived, John let the league know what Azroth had said. "One of the geist working for Marcus was meeting with Amber the night she was killed. Amber was going to give the geist something to prove she was no longer one of us. That geist killed Amber and took her key. Amber betrayed us."

Everyone in the room stood silent. They were all shocked that a member of the league would betray them.

Angeline shook her head and narrowed her eyes. "No, that's not possible."

She let go of Aidan's hand and placed her hand over her mouth. "How could I not have known?"

Her self-doubt turned to frustration and then anger. "I left her to fend for herself when I should have been there guiding her. I...no! This is not on me!" Angeline then realized that Amber's offers to take so many shifts watching Marcus' building was a means to an end for her.

"She knew exactly what she was doing. I swear if she weren't dead I would make her wish she were!"

She looked at Aidan and saw he was furious as well. She couldn't hide the look of disgust and disdain on her face. "Aidan, I know that she was your cousin but this betrayal is immeasurable!"

"You do not need to justify your words to me, Angeline. I am so very sorry she's done this. I have no idea how I will tell Edmond." Aidan dreaded the task.

Angeline placed her hand on Aidan's arm. "You won't, love, I will. Amber was my responsibility and I owe it to Edmond to tell him." She cast her eyes downward.

"Right, well, unless you object, I would like to accompany you."

Aidan looked from John to the other league members, his expression sombre. "Amber was never a team player, even as a child. She always went her own way, avoiding the rest of the family at any gathering we had. I didn't know her well, but I know that right now, I am ashamed that she and I share blood."

John looked from one face to another. "There's something else I need to mention. I spoke with Aunt Viv and she said that our Soul Daggers alone cannot kill Asmodeus. As you know, a geist essence only dies when the host body it inhabits dies as well. Since Asmodeus is a demon, our Soul Daggers aren't going to do anything more than piss him off. She also mentioned the Spirit Dagger. She said that it could kill anything - demon, angel, geist, literally anything, but she also said that it was lost a long time ago. Guys, we need to make sure he stays in that tomb."

~~~~

During the next few days, John found it difficult to work at the dental clinic with so many league-related issues on his mind. He was glad to hear that Kayla had met Ann and that she had moved into Ann's building.

The day finally arrived where he and the other two faction leaders were to meet with the Council of Seven and plan what needed to be done to safeguard against the current threats they were facing.

John walked with Angeline and Zayne toward the Council Chambers. "How did Edmond take the news about Amber, Ange?"

"About as well as expected."

Zayne glanced at Angeline. "I imagine it wasn't an easy thing for them to hear. The shame they must feel has to be immense."

The three faction leaders entered the Council Chambers. After they bowed and greeted the councilors, Araton rose and spoke first.

"Omm is now aware that the Aquarius and Leo keys are no longer in your possession. Their absence presents a threat and it is expected that your best efforts will be put forth in the search for these keys. Should you not have the Leo and Aquarius keys at the time of the Winter Solstice, it is imperative that you inform us."

Araton tilted his head and looked toward Pen-Ming who spoke next.

Pen-Ming pointed to three chairs arranged around a large, round table. "Please, sit."

With the faction leaders seated before them, Pen-Ming began. "We have decided that everyone in the League of Twelve must be protected from the threat that is posed by the demon hybrid Asmodeus. The enchantress Aurora has been tasked with casting a protection spell over each of your rings."

"When are we to have our rings spelled?" Angeline asked.

"Once Aurora has prepared everything she needs, we will meet on the following new moon." Pen-Ming tilted his head, walked to his seat around the semi-circular table, and closed his eyes in meditation.

The three faction leaders bowed and left the Council Chambers.

~~~~

On the day of the new moon, every league member and each of the councilors were present in the Council Chambers. The Eyrasine enchantress, Aurora, had set up her altar in a special room in preparation for spelling the league rings.

Aurora wore a hooded ceremonial robe made of a lightweight cotton in a shimmering shade of blue. She covered her altar with a large white cloth and placed a silver bowl at its centre. All of the items necessary for the enchantment were placed around the bowl.

On either end of the altar, she placed two blue candles and two white candles. She ignited their wicks with a wave of her hand. To the right of the silver bowl, Aurora placed her grimoire and lit incense oil to fill the room with the scent of sage.

She addressed the league members. "Please, place your rings inside the bowl."

The bowl was passed and one by one, each of the league members placed their rings inside.

Aurora took the bowl, placed it at the centre of her altar, and began her incantation. She held both hands over the bowl as she spoke and once she had finished, the rings began to shake.

She moved her hands upward and a large flash of white light encompassed the rings inside the bowl. As the light began to fade, small flecks of black floated downward from the ceiling and seemed to disappear as they neared the rings. The spell took a relatively short time and when she had finished, Aurora walked to each league member and had them remove their ring from the bowl.

As they placed their rings on their fingers, they each felt a wave of energy flow through their bodies. This energy traveled up their arms and up and down their spines and felt similar to the feeling they each had when their abilities surfaced but somehow, it was more intense.

"As long as your ring stays on your finger, a geist will not be able to take your DNA, nor will a demon be able to possess you. They are now protection amulets. Never take them off," Aurora warned.

"While the geist protection is permanent, the protection against demonic possession will fade. Your rings must be enchanted with each new lunar cycle. Before the end of every following new moon, I will summon you to me to have this enchantment on your rings renewed. This must continue until the demon Asmodeus is vanquished."

Aurora tidied her altar as the league members left her room. Once they were gone, she fell to the floor, as this spell required so much intense energy and effort that it left her feeling lightheaded and weak.

John looked at his ring. "I guess the only thing left to do is test them out. Angeline, Zayne, how do you feel about a night out at Solar Flair? We can see if Azroth has someone willing to mist out for us."

Zayne scowled. "Willing or unwilling, it sounds good to me."

Angeline turned to Aidan, kissed him and smiled. "Duty calls."

~~~~~

The excursion to Solar Flair took a relatively short amount of time.

As he walked to Jayded Ink with Angeline and Zayne after having a geist try and fail to replicate them, John dialed Ann's number, and hit the speaker button. "Ann, are you able to meet us at Jayded Ink right now? I would like you to show Ange, Zayne, and I the Taurus tunnel."

"On my way." She wiped her hands on her apron and turned to wave goodbye to her mother in the kitchen at Transcendence.

As she left the restaurant, she asked, "Did the new spell on the rings work?"

John smirked. "Like a charm."

"Oh, John." Angeline shook her head and rolled her eyes. "That was really bad."

Ann and the three faction leaders burst into laughter.

16 – TRANSCENDENCE

In Jayded Ink, Ann sat on the sofa near the back wall and flipped through one of Jayde's tattoo magazines while she waited for the faction leaders to arrive. She stood as she saw John, Angeline, and Zayne walk through the front door.

"See ya later, Jayde." Ann moved to join the three faction leaders and together they headed to the tunnel entrance.

Angeline smiled as she walked past. "I still want to come back for that tattoo, Jayde."

"Let me know when and I'll make sure there's rum!" Jayde's voice was deep and husky.

Ann and Angeline looked at Jayde, and shouted, "No!"

The three women laughed loudly.

John and Zayne looked at the girls, and then at each other.

Zayne raised his eyebrows. "Do I want to know?"

John shook his head. "Let's just keep walking, Zayne."

Once inside the tunnel entrance, Ann headed left. "This way." She led her friends to the Taurus/Scorpio tunnel, and pointed to the faint sigils above the tunnel opening.

Ann walked in first. "The tomb is about fifteen feet in on the left."

Once they arrived at the tomb's location, Ann pointed to a nearly invisible marking on the wall. "This small Taurus sigil indicates the tomb's location."

She knocked on the wall. "Solid rock. There's an enchanted veil that Cerra put up so that no one would know the tomb is here. This wall doesn't really exist. If a witch were to release the veil, the wall would disappear. Asmodeus is literally ten feet away from us right now."

Zayne folded his arms. "If anyone were to find the tomb, they would need a witch, and the right spell to get inside. Is that correct?"

Ann nodded. "That's right."

John felt a wave of relief pass over him. "This is actually good news. Marcus would have to be working with the Crimson Trad and we know they would never betray us. Looks like we're done."

As they walked out of the tunnel, Angeline grimaced. "Is there really no way to kill him, Ann?"

Ann shrugged. "Just the Spirit Dagger but it was lost a long time ago."

John stopped in front of the exit and checked his watch. "I need to get in touch with James." He felt guilty that his brother had to cover his patients for him. "He's been working past our usual hours nearly every night, so that I can take care of league business. If I don't get back to work soon my patients won't be mine much longer."

Angeline sighed. "I, too, should head back and actually do some work. This is a busy time of year for the Aemetta and although mum has been handling things, I do feel bad that she's been working more than she would like."

She turned to Ann. "We still need to get together to decipher the tablets. Let me know when you're up for it, Ann, alright?"

"You bet."

She smiled a mischievous smile. "Right now, I'm going to see what Seb's up to. I'll see you guys later." She unlocked the door that led into Jayded Ink and dialed Sebastian's number. She kept the door open for John to follow her.

Zayne chimed in. "I have responsibilities that must be tended to as well."

He looked at Angeline and held his arm out for her to take. "Shall we?"

"Yes, let's shall," was her reply as she accepted his arm.

John turned to Angeline and Zayne who had headed to the tunnel that leads to the City of Radiance. "I'll see you two next time."

Angeline yawned. "Yeah, next time."

John walked past Ann into the back of Jayded Ink. "Thanks, Ann."

Ann nodded and mouthed, "I'm going to head out back."

Ann walked to the rear exit as John walked to the front door past Jayde.

"We're all set here, Jayde. Have a good night."

"You bet. You too, John." Jayde followed him to the front door to lock it before she headed to the back room to leave.

John phoned James as he walked to his car. "Hey little brother, how are things at the clinic?"

"Busy, but Rachel's been a godsend. I may just have to steal her from you, John!" James winked at Rachel.

"Ha! There's enough of me to go around," she replied and then grimaced. "Err, let me rephrase that."

James smiled. "We're just closing up. Do you plan on coming in tomorrow, John?" Once the office door was locked, he and Rachel headed toward the elevator.

"I do, barring any league emergencies."

James sighed in relief. He didn't want John to know that the clinic had been brutally hectic the last few days. "Okay then, I'll see you at home later tonight."

"You will. I'm headed there now. Bye."

James' stomach growled. "I think I forgot to eat today. Want to head to Transcendence for a bite?"

"Sure, as long as you're buying."

James bowed. "Of course, m'lady. You were amazing today, by the way. I would not have stayed sane with all of those patients if it weren't for you."

Rachel flipped her hair comically. "Just another day."

They both laughed.

The elevator doors began to close and Rachel looked up at James. "Maybe we should discuss a raise over a few drinks as well."

~~~~~

Ann sat in her car behind Jayded Ink. "Hey Seb, want to meet me at Transcendence?"

Sebastian entered the parking garage beneath the law firm and walked to his car. "Sure. I just wrapped up a few things at the firm and I could use a bite."

"Great. I'll have a plate waiting for you."

He smiled. "You're too good to me."

Ann laughed. "Don't you forget it either!"

Sebastian ended the call, smiled to himself, and drove to the exit. Just as he turned left, he saw an accident blocking the street.

"Really?"

He made a u-turn and opted for the side street route to Transcendence, then a delivery truck stopped directly in front of him. "Are you kidding me? What is going on today?"

He turned right and headed down an alley only to find that a car was blocking his way.

"No. I am *not* turning around!" He pressed his horn and lowered the window. "Come on, pal, move it!"

Sebastian watched as a man in a dark toque and winter coat turned at the sound of his horn. It took less than a second for him to realize that the man was Marcus.

Without thinking, Sebastian shifted his car into park and threw the door open. He walked with purpose toward Marcus. "Marcus!"

Marcus stood prepared for yet another round with his nephew.

Sebastian wasted no time in attacking Marcus. He punched at his uncle's face, first with his right hand, then with his left. His punches continued relentlessly.

Sebastian fought like a man possessed. He intended to end Marcus.

He swung again and again, with every other blow connecting.

Marcus swung and landed a few punches on Sebastian's jaw and stomach.

Sebastian screamed, as every ounce of his strength and hatred followed his fists toward Marcus.

Marcus managed to push him away.

Sebastian then spun and kicked, slamming his heel in Marcus' ribcage. He watched as Marcus bent backward over the hood of his car.

Marcus could no longer fight back.

Sebastian punched, again and again, until he heard a female voice behind him shout, "Oh my god! What are you doing?"

He stopped and turned. Fists clenched at his sides, he looked at the petite woman in front of him. Before he could react to the fact that she was geist, she stabbed her switchblade into the top of his thigh, repeatedly. Sebastian howled in pain and punched the side of Ganga's head.

She landed hard on the ground.

Unnoticed, Calob helped Marcus into the front passenger seat, then rounded the car and approached Sebastian from behind. As Sebastian reached for the blade in his thigh, Calob pushed him to the ground and kicked him.

Ganga had enough time to get to her feet and get in the driver's seat of Marcus' car.

Ganga shouted, "Calob! Get in the car!"

Calob kicked Sebastian one last time before he hurried into the back seat.

As Ganga drove out of the alley, Marcus held his ribcage, certain that a few bones were broken. He programmed his GPS. "Drive, Ganga. Quickly."

~~~~

Snow lightly fell as James and Rachel walked through the parking lot. James walked behind Rachel and scanned their surroundings. He felt something brush against his hand. He saw nothing, no one.

Something felt off.

"Let's take my car, Rachel. I can drop you off here after we eat. Sound good?"

"Sounds good."

He walked ahead and opened the car door for her.

She spoke in an exaggerated southern drawl. "A gentleman, as well as a professional. Why, Mr. Evans, I would never have guessed."

James chuckled. "Smartass. Don't let that sarcasm drip onto my baby. I just had her detailed."

"All kidding aside, I do like your taste in cars. Jayde was looking at Chargers before she fell in love with her Hummer."

"This, my dear Rachel, is not simply a Charger. It is a fully loaded Hellcat. Respect the ride."

"Forgive me. What's her name?"

James placed his hand over his heart. "My baby needs a special name. Maybe I should name her Rachel." He furrowed his brow and tilted his head. "She's as sassy as you are."

"Ha ha. Just drive."

In the trees behind the dental clinic parking lot, Phen, Uvall's replacement, hovered in mist form among the trees that lined the alley. He watched, as Ganga instructed, and saw James and Rachel leave. He made a mental note of their names before he left.

~~~~

As they drove to Transcendence, Rachel realized that the feelings she had for James were quickly rising to the surface. She was attracted to his quiet confidence, and her attention was often drawn to the intensity of his dark brown, nearly black eyes.

In the restaurant, Rachel untied her blonde hair. She felt less than attractive. *I have been with him all day and now I'm self-conscious*?

She ordered after the server seated them. "I'll have a margarita. Salted glass, please."

"Rum and coke for me. Who's in the kitchen tonight?"

The server recognized James. "Vivian and Dave. Ann was here for a while but she left. I'll be back in a bit with your drinks."

James and Rachel talked and laughed through the entire meal.

Once their plates had been cleared, James found the courage to ask out. "Are you going to attend the league Christmas party this year?"

"I think so."

"Would you want to go together? Like a real date, sort of thing?"

Rachel's heart began to beat faster. "You don't think it would be weird? We've known each other for so long and I work with you, actually I work *for* you."

At Rachel's comment, James felt like he had just overstepped. "It was just a thought."

Rachel looked down at her drink, her fourth drink. "You know what? I think I'd like that. We're kind of limited to who we can trust so, why not?"

As James and Rachel left Transcendence through the front exit, Ann walked in through the back door. She prepared a plate for Sebastian and placed it under the warming lights in the kitchen.

Her phone rang in her purse and she looked at the display. She saw Sebastian's name and furrowed her brow.

"Seb? Where are you?"

He breathed heavily. "I'm behind the restaurant."

She hurried to the back of the kitchen and out the door. She found Sebastian seated in his car, door open, his head against the steering wheel.

"Seb?" She walked toward him.

Her eyes opened wide at the sight of Sebastian's bloodied face. "What happened?"

"Marcus. I had him."

Ann's eyes quickly scanned the alley. "Marcus? Where?"

"There was an accident on my way here and I ended up going down an alley. He was there, right in front of me. I would have killed him, if his geist hadn't stabbed me."

Sebastian placed his hand over the wound on his thigh. "I had him!"

Her eyes followed his hand. "Geez, Seb!"

She took a deep breath and gently lifted his hand. "How bad is it? Can you heal it yourself?"

After she examined his wound, she was certain he would need stitches.

"I don't know. I think so."

"Move over."

Sebastian snapped, "I'll be fine."

"Move. Over." Her voice was commanding.

He wasn't healing as fast as he would have liked and so he complied.

Ann pushed the phone button on his steering wheel. "Call Conor."

Conor answered on the first ring. "Seb. What can I do for you?"

It was Ann who replied. "Where are you? Seb was stabbed."

"Stabbed? What's going on?"

"Where are you? He needs stitches."

"I'm at home. I have sutures here. I'll meet you at the front door."

~~~~

After Sebastian's run-in with Marcus, all of the league members searched for days, trying to find him or any geist that worked for him. The North American faction frequented Solar Flair and questioned many geist yet were still no closer to finding Marcus or the missing keys.

Each night they scoured news reports for any incidents that could possibly be geist related but had no success. Marcus seemed to have vanished.

In London, Angeline contacted Nellmar, the geist owner of The Sky Clock Pub who, like Azroth, had made a pact with The League of Twelve to provide information on malevolent geist. She had nothing to report.

Zayne had also contacted his faction's geist informant, Rayanatar, owner of Lotus of the Nile Bar and Lounge in Cairo. He also had nothing to share.

The loss of the keys and knowing that Marcus could still be in the area kept them on high alert as they tried to find peace during the holidays.

~~~~

As the league's Christmas party neared, Vivian, Jake, Ann, Nick, and a few of the restaurant servers worked tirelessly for two days. They transformed Transcendence into a Christmas wonderland. Decorations in white and gold were hung around the entire restaurant. Festive garland bordered both bars and was looped around the chandeliers. Vivian had purchased and hung Christmas stockings for each league member with their names embroidered on them. Inside were her favourite chocolates and a small bottle of Chivas Regal, gifts from herself and Jake.

~~~~

Outside of Transcendence, Phen wrapped his mist around a street lamp and watched as the league members and their families entered the restaurant.

He had watched Ann and her family but had not gained any information he felt was worth mentioning to Ganga. However, once she told him that Ann was vital to their plans, he made a point to watch her more closely. He went so far as to enter the restaurant as they prepared for the Christmas party.

Phen stretched his mist thin and hugged the bottom of the walls as he found his way to the kitchen. Once inside, he blended in with the steam coming out of a pot and listened.

The party was held at noon to accommodate the European and African factions and shortly after, people started to arrive. Soon the room was filled with league members and their brothers and sisters.

"That's it for us." Vivian and Jake headed out to let the younger crowd enjoy their party.

Ann walked to her parents and kissed them both. "Thank you. You've really outdone yourselves."

Jake hugged his daughter. "It's our way of giving back to The League of Twelve."

"Let's go." Vivian took his hand and together they left the restaurant through the front doors.

They passed Angeline and Aidan who were the last to arrive with Angeline's sisters, Katherine and Margaret, and Aidan's sisters, Lexi and Lily.

Throughout the afternoon, Phen watched. Some people paired off and some stayed in groups. Having spent more time among the league members than he wanted, he left. He found a DNA donor and while still in mist form, he hurried to Ganga to report.

Lexi and Lily, Aidan's sisters, danced a while before sitting with their brother and Angeline at a table where they sat with John, Ann, and Sebastian. Both girls were tall and slender with straight brown hair and striking green eyes.

Aidan stood and introduced his identical twin sisters.

Lexi, the more forward sister, had taken the seat beside John and flirted shamelessly.

Sebastian looked at Lily who seemed rather out of her element and decided to strike up a conversation. "My father was an identical twin. His brother left home before I was born, so I never got to see them together. I often wondered what it was like for my dad being separated from his twin."

Lily looked up to see Lexi and John were headed toward the bar together.

"I can tell you that it's almost like being half of one person. There were times when Lexi would injure herself and I would feel a pain for no apparent reason, and then come to learn that she had hurt herself. It is an odd feeling, but having only lived life as a twin, I don't know any different."

"Is the connection emotional as well?" Sebastian wanted to know just how deep the connection may have been between his father and Marcus.

"It has been with Lexi and I." She suddenly felt a wave of embarrassment as she recalled a moment when Lexi had been intimate with a man and she felt her sister's lustful feelings.

Lily reached for a glass of water on the table, as Lexi and John approached with a tray of various shots.

John placed the tray on the table. "Grab a shot. Let's have a toast to friends, family, and friends who have become family."

They each selected one of the shots and raised them high. "Cheers!"

As Olivia left the dance floor, she bumped into Conor and noted the mistletoe above their heads. "It is tradition, after all." She rose up on her toes and kissed him.

She thought he looked rather dashing in his white, button down shirt.

"We could dance, if you would like." He was normally shy, especially with women, unless he was in his element, the hospital. As a physician, he was highly skilled and quite intelligent; as a man around women, he was an awkward boy.

"That we could." She took his hand and walked to the dance floor. "I'm afraid I've had more alcohol than I really should have."

"I could help with that." Conor placed his hands on either side of her head.

She looked up into his pale blue eyes and felt her intoxication fade. "That's rather amazing. It's somewhat tingly."

Conor's smiled. "Glad to be of help."

Across the room, Jayde and Kyle sat with James and Rachel. Kyle spoke about his dojo on the West coast and his difficulty in finding a reasonably priced rental unit in Niagara Falls where he could open another.

While Kyle spoke, Rachel's curiosity peaked; she had never met a geist and was quite curious. "So, you're geist. What's that like?"

"I'm part geist, human, and Eyrasine." He was sufficiently inebriated and wasn't shy about showing her his morphing ability. He studied her face and duplicated it on his own.

"Oh, wow!" Rachel was amazed.

"Is that not absolutely wicked?" Jayde was both impressed and proud.

Kyle laughed. "I can't believe I have lived my entire life fearing The League of Twelve and trying to hide who I was in case I ran into anyone from the league. Now, here I am, being accepted for who I am, with no hesitation."

James raised his glass. "To Kyle. A year ago, if anyone told me I would be at a party with a part geist, I wouldn't have believed it. Here's to a year full of surprises."

They clinked their glasses together. Despite the recent tragedies, everyone was determined to have a good time.

Zayne and his brother, Jibril, stood at the DJ stand.

John spoke briefly with them before he addressed the room. "I have a few things I would like to say. First, Merry Christmas. What I have to say next is a bit more business than pleasure."

After a chorus of boos from his audience, John raised a hand and laughed. "Now, it's not *that* bad. There are just a few things that need to be said.

"Our league is a new league. The old way of running things won't work anymore. With everything that's hit us recently, we can't afford to keep secrets from each other. Our league will work openly, cooperatively, and honestly; a brotherhood and sisterhood united by bloodlines!"

He raised his glass. "To us!"

Everyone lifted their glasses. "To us!"

"Lastly, there will be no more quarterly meetings. The league will now meet once a month, on the first Saturday of each month, 7:00 a.m. North American time, in the Hall of Gates.

"And now, I'll turn the floor over to Angeline."

Together, Angeline and Aidan stood. "First off, Happy Christmas to you all! I would like to officially introduce Aidan Temple, the new Aquarius league member."

Aidan stepped forward. "Thank you." He reached into his pocket. "I've prepared a speech..."

As everyone moaned loudly, he raised his hands. "Kidding! I'm kidding! I would just like to say that I'm honoured to be part of this incredible group of people."

With a wink, he added, "Next round is on me, alright?"

Zayne stepped forward as Angeline and Aidan sat.

"We have some happy news from Cairo. Mariam."

Mariam rose with Sameer, her left hand held out in front of her displaying a gorgeous diamond and ruby ring on her finger. "Sameer and I are engaged to be married and of course, you are all invited, though we have yet to set a date."

Applause and well wishes rang throughout the restaurant.

Next, Conor stood. He motioned toward Jayde. "You all know my baby sister Jayde, the amazing artist whose medium of choice is ink and her canvas, human flesh."

He had to pause as everyone cheered. "Okay, okay, we all know she's a rockstar tattoo artist. Anyway, she's here tonight with her boyfriend."

He looked at Jayde, inquisitive. "Is it alright to call him your boyfriend?"

She chuckled. "Yeah, yeah, just get to your point."

"Like I was saying, she's here with her boyfriend. Kyle Shea."

The room fell silent.

"No, he is not Seb's brother, but he is his cousin. Before I say anything more, I just want to say, Kyle, in spite of your parentage, I think you're a pretty great guy. As long as you don't break my sister's heart, you can keep yours in your chest." He winked and raised his glass.

The room erupted with laughter.

Kyle raised his bottle of beer. "Thanks, but I'm pretty sure she'd be able to rip my heart out herself!"

Conor continued. "Anyway, as Seb's cousin, you probably realize that his father is Marcus Shea. That said, you all know that he wouldn't be here without being a good man, so I give you, Kyle Shea."

Whoops and applause rang out.

Kyle smiled. He stood and bowed his head slightly. "It's great to meet you all. I'm honoured to be included in this exceptional group."

After Kyle sat, John spoke once again. "That was one hell of an introduction there, Conor!"

He raised his hand as though he were taking an oath in a courtroom. "Just a bit more business, then I'll let you all party in peace, I promise."

"In order for this league to function properly, we all have to work together. By all, I mean not just the league members, but everyone here, our brothers and sisters. You are all important. You cover for us when we have to leave our jobs, you make excuses to our patients and customers and coworkers. Our families make sure things run smoothly, so that we can be free to deal with all of the threats that we face from geist and others trying to harm, or even kill us."

John looked at Kyle and smiled. "Present company excepted."

Kyle raised his beer.

John continued. "We have to count on you to share the burden of the secrets that we have to keep. Guys, our allegiance isn't just to the planet we live on, but to Eyras as well. If Joe Public ever found out about the City of Radiance or what we do and what we are, life as we know it would end pretty quickly.

"With our new transparency and accountability, keeping League secrets is more important than ever, and the consequence of betrayal is greater.

"The Council of Seven stand as the governing body in the City of Radiance and it is their obligation to enact punishment. Betrayal is not an option. We all know Amber betrayed us and in doing so, she was killed, not by the council, but by her accomplices. I would like to add how lucky she was that she didn't have to face their judgment.

"That's it for business. So, now that I've sobered you all up, enjoy the rest of your night!" John raised his glass. He hoped he hadn't sounded too harsh, but also hoped he made his point.

He walked behind Jibril and picked up a box of gifts he had for everyone in the league. Inside were two shirts for each of the other eleven league members, made from dybiokemex, a light breathable Eyrasine material, and sewn by Aurora herself. Each of the shirts were made to mold to their wearer's form and act almost like a second skin. They were also spelled to prevent any weapons from penetrating them, magickal or otherwise.

John placed the box on the floor and opened it. He walked to each of his fellow league members and handed them their gift, along with a card explaining the purpose of the spelled shirts. With the threats they now faced, John and Aurora had brainstormed and together decided that discreet clothing to protect each of the league members was more practical than the clunky vests that were provided to them.

As Angeline opened her gift, Aidan checked his watch. "I believe it's time for you and I to leave."

Angeline held up a shirt and noticed that on one shoulder was an embroidered endless knot, the City's symbol of unity, on the other was her astro sigil in emerald green. "Very nice, John."

Angeline and Aidan stood. She raised her voice. "Excuse me everyone. Aidan and I will be leaving now, as I have an early appointment with a rather difficult client in the morning." She rolled her eyes.

"It was wonderful seeing everyone tonight. I do hope you will all be able to make it to the Aemetta for our New Year's Eve party. We have been working tirelessly for months planning an evening that won't be forgotten!"

On their way to the back door, Angeline stopped to speak with Josh. "Would you be able to see our sisters home later? I don't think they're quite ready to leave yet."

Josh grinned. "Of course."

"Thank you, love!"

Aidan whispered, "Should we warn Josh about Lexi?"

"I'm fairly certain Josh can handle her quite nicely."

In spite of all of the bad things that had happened lately, everyone was able to find some joy that night.

~~~~

The Winter Solstice arrived and as the Leo and Aquarius keys had still not been recovered, the league was unable to open the portal.

John, Angeline, and Zayne spoke with the Immortals.

Selphia informed the faction leaders that it had been determined that, should they not have the keys in their possession when the Spring Equinox arrived, alternate arrangements would be made, as foregoing another portal opening was not an option.

Between the Christmas and New Year's Eve parties, life for the league members remained quiet. There were neither attacks on anyone in the league, nor geist causing trouble, nor any leads on Marcus' whereabouts. They suspected that Marcus was secluded somewhere, recuperating from his altercation with Sebastian. They also knew he wasn't done yet.

Angeline and Ann made time to work on deciphering the sapphire tablet and planned to reveal their findings at the next scheduled league meeting. Sebastian spent his holiday with Ann's family.

Vivian was quite pleased that Ann and Sebastian seemed so happy together. She remembered how difficult it was for her and Jake when their relationship first began. Vivian had had to take great precautions while dating men who did not belong to a league family. Once she met Jake, however, she knew he would be the one human who could handle the truth and the secrets that she had to keep from him. She soon came to find out that he had a secret of his own.

John made a point of checking in with Zayne, Angeline, and Kayla regularly throughout the holidays. He knew that something could go wrong at any moment and that gave him little peace.

Now that league members could no longer be replicated by geist, his mind drifted to how they could protect their families. If geist became aware that they couldn't replicate anyone in the league, he wondered what would prevent them from stealing the DNA from someone in their families.

John pulled his cell phone from his pocket. "Send a group message to Angeline and Zayne. Let your people know we need to meet. Hall of Gates in two hours."

~~~~

With everyone in attendance, John addressed the league. "I know there hasn't been anything happening with geist or Marcus lately, but we still haven't found the missing keys and we can't afford to let our guard down. Marcus doesn't know that the astral keys will not work without our rings because he didn't take Amber's.

"While we are protected from geist replication, our families are not. We need to find a way to prevent the geist from being able to steal their DNA as well. Has anyone got any suggestions?"

"We had our rings spelled, so why not get family rings made?" Mariam suggested.

"That's one option. I know James isn't big on jewelry, but I suppose he would wear a ring if he had to. Anything else?"

Conor chimed in. "What about ink?"

John furrowed his brows. "Ink?"

Conor offered further explanation. "What if we had some ink spelled and then had Jayde tattoo everyone in our families? It's permanent, can't be lost or forgotten, and it can be done on any part of the body."

The others considered this option. Many nodded and seemed to like it.

Ink proved to be the most popular option. "With a show of hands, all in favour?"

Every hand raised. "Tattoos, it is."

Angeline addressed the room. "Ann and I have a report on the sapphire tablet. We've managed to decipher the hidden information and stored it in the Central Archives. It is just as the Immortals said, it mentions the World Tree, the tunnels, and universal laws. Some are the same as the laws written for the City of Radiance but there are a few others as well, which I can only assume are meant for the heavens and underworlds. And it also speaks of how the polar opposite keys come together.

"Each of the newly formed keys can only open the door in the tunnel meant for the combined sigils. What I mean to say is that mine and Seb's keys together can only open the door in the tunnel with the Capricorn and Cancer sigils lock. Am I making sense?"

John began to pace. "I think we get it, Ange. Since Marcus has both the Leo and Aquarius keys, if they somehow come together, he's going to see that they form a new key. If he also manages to have a geist replicate Najeeb or Aidan, that would give him access to the heaven or underworld in those tunnels. Perfect!"

He ran his hands through his hair.

Ann walked to John and placed her hand on his shoulder. "Hey, we'll get the keys back. Marcus can't use them anyway, and don't forget, our rings are now spelled to protect us from geist replication."

John exhaled loudly. "Valid point."

"There's more," Angeline announced. "It also speaks of the three tablets. We know that the stones in our rings are pieces of the tablets and that they bond with our DNA; the hidden etchings reveal why that is. The stones in our rings are alive, which also means…"

Zayne interrupted. "The tablets are alive."

Many eyebrows raised.

"Yes. And this is the reason those etchings were hidden. If anyone with Eyrasine blood were to realize that a piece of these tablets could bring out an innate ability within them, well, need I say more?"

John paced throughout the Hall of Gates. "We just have to make sure Marcus doesn't find out. You know what? I'm going to pay Azroth another visit, see if he has any new information."

"I'll join you," Sebastian said. "I love watching Azroth play tough guy in front of his customers and then tuck his tail between his legs at the sight of us."

Ann wrinkled her nose. "I'd love to see that."

"Alright, whoever wants to go, meet us at the West exit in 5 minutes." John headed out of the Hall of Gates.

~~~~

"No, no, no!" Zayne shouted. "We are *not* waiting in a line outside of Azroth's bar."

John looked at Zayne out of the corner of his eye and tipped his head back slightly. "Follow me."

He walked to the bouncer who stepped aside. "Mr. Evans, you and your friends can go right in."

"Thank you."

Once inside, Aidan looked at John as the band played loudly. He shouted, "It always pays to know the doorman."

Aidan glanced around the room, noting the many blue and few black auras around the patrons. As the geist danced and moved, Aidan narrowed his eyes in a feeble attempt to shield them from the intensity of the auras in such a dark room.

Dalila spoke, her voice raised. "I had no idea Azroth held concerts here! I can barely hear my own thoughts!"

"Once we find him and get what we need, we can go," John shouted. "But this band isn't half bad."

Azroth spotted the league members moments after they entered. He whispered under his breath, "What do they want now?"

With his arms outstretched, he walked to them. "John, Conor, Sebastian and...friends. What brings you to my little corner of the universe?"

"One question." John leaned closer to Azroth.

Azroth sighed. "Maybe we should take this to my office. Follow me."

They walked behind Azroth to the back left corner of the bar and once inside with the door shut, John got right to business. "Anything new to report on Marcus or his geist?"

"Is that all?" Azroth eased himself into the chair behind his desk, relieved.

"Sheesh! You had me scared half to death! And no, nothing has happened. The last time we spoke was the last time anyone has mentioned Marcus or Asmodeus or anything league related in the least."

He got up. "So if that'll be…"

"Not so fast." Sebastian pushed Azroth back into his chair and shouted, "You mean to tell me that nothing has happened for weeks? You expect us to believe that?"

"On my life, I swear it!" Azroth shouted back.

Aidan walked around Azroth and stood behind his chair.

Azroth looked Aidan up and down. "Just who are you anyway?"

"Aidan Temple. I'm the new guy."

Azroth pursed his lips. "Hey, I have an idea, why don't you guys go pick on Nell or Ray? I'm sure they would *love* a visit!"

"We're more interested in you right now, Azroth." Ann snapped.

John glanced at Zayne. They had recently contacted both Nellmar and Rayanatar.

Zayne nodded. "Marcus is in Niagara Falls, Azroth. That's *your* territory."

"Well, I have nothing new to tell you. Marcus vanished. *Poof!* He's just gone. If I had anything to tell you, I would have let you know.

"In the meantime, please, stay and enjoy yourselves. Here." Azroth opened the top drawer of his desk. He removed a few wristbands that allowed them free drinks for the night.

"Show these to the bartender and you can drink free all night. Just please, no killing my customers tonight, alright? Some of them are spending like mad at the bar!"

17 – NEW YEAR'S EVE

The past few months had been a time of change for everyone in the league, some of it pleasant and some the extreme opposite. Since the Christmas party at Transcendence, there had been a period of peace on all three continents, but they all knew full well it wouldn't last.

The league members met with their dates or escorts at the Nite Cap to have a private celebration for Angeline's birthday, after which, they headed to the Grand Ballroom for the New Year's Eve party.

Prior to meeting everyone in the bar, Aidan knocked on Angeline's suite door to accompany her to the party. When she opened the door, Aidan lost the ability to speak.

She wore a stunning silver dress with an emerald green sash at her waist, and an elegant, flowing skirt that was cut higher in the front than in the back. Aidan thought Angeline looked absolutely breathtaking.

He pulled her to him and kissed her hungrily. "We could always make excuses and stay here all night."

His eyes told her that he was rather serious.

"Oh, no." Angeline lightly pushed Aidan back. "We are not missing my birthday gathering, nor the incredible New Year's Eve party that I spent months organizing!"

He reached into his inside breast pocket, and pulled out a box wrapped in the finest emerald green wrapping Mariam's store had to offer. "Would you like your birthday gift now, or would you prefer to wait until we are in the pub downstairs?"

He held the box just out of her reach.

Angeline turned as though to walk away. "Hmm…I'm not sure. I guess it depends on what it is."

She turned to face him. "What is in that pretty box?"

"Turn around." He said, his voice both commanding and seductive.

Angeline complied.

He stood behind her with his arms outstretched, the box held in front of her.

She opened it, and gasped at its contents.

Aidan removed a delicate diamond and emerald necklace and placed it around Angeline's neck.

"Oh, Aidan."

He saw a mix of emotions on her face. "I know that with you being my faction leader, our relationship may seem inappropriate, but just know that I will do whatever I can to make this work."

He stood at her side and presented his arm for Angeline to take. "Why don't we go join the others?"

~~~~~

In the Nite Cap, John had poured shots to toast Angeline's birthday upon her arrival.

"I would like to make a toast." John held his shot glass in front of him. "To Angeline. Friend, leader, and all around amazing person."

They each raised their glass and drank.

Angeline smiled. "As a token of my friendship, I've left a basket filled with various goodies in each of your rooms.

"Now, let's get to the ballroom, shall we?"

~~~~~

The Aemetta Suites shone in brilliant shades of red and silver. The staff, guided by Angeline, her mother, and her sister, had the lobby and the Grand Ballroom looking like a fairy tale wonderland.

The New Year's Eve tickets had been sold out for over a month, and the hotel bustled with activity as the guests began to arrive.

Angeline and Aidan stood just inside the doorway of the Grand Ballroom. They watched as servers, carrying trays of champagne and hors d'oeuvres, walked among the guests.

She turned to him. "I would like to make certain everything is as it should be, before we take our seats."

"No rush, love." He took her hand in his as they walked about the room.

She glanced at each of the fifty tables which had been arranged in a split circle around the ballroom. On each table, the silver candle was lit inside the clear hurricane vase surrounded by a centrepiece of red and white roses. Two complimentary bottles of wine, one red and one white, were placed on the tables as well, and Angeline ticked off the checklist in her mind.

She then looked up and noted that above the dance floor in the centre of the room, balloons and streamers hung in a net, waiting to fall at the stroke of midnight.

Inside the doors, in the left corner, was a thirty-foot Christmas tree, decorated in sapphire blue, emerald green, and white. A matching tree stood kitty-corner across the room in the far right corner. Angeline smiled.

A disc jockey had set up his equipment beside the stage where a live band would be performing later in the evening.

The floor-to-ceiling windows along the far back wall of the ballroom provided a spectacular view of lightly falling snow, and a bright, waning gibbous moon. Angeline was pleased.

Ann and Sebastian chose a table near the windows, and Angeline and Aidan walked to join them. "Can we get you ladies something to drink?" Sebastian offered.

"Surprise us." Angeline was prepared to have an unforgettable evening. She took a seat beside Ann and poured two glasses of red wine. They watched as the dapper gentlemen and their elegant dates entered the Grand Ballroom.

Ann's gaze wandered the room and she saw Sebastian next to the bar as he spoke with Aidan. She leaned into Angeline and sighed. "Our boys are hot, Ange."

Angeline raised her glass with a look of wanting. "Yes, they are."

They clinked their glasses together and watched their dates with pleasure.

~~~~

As soon as the meal was finished and cleared, dessert trays were brought out to once again fill the tables. Elegant pastries, chocolates, and confections from around the globe were offered.

Aidan noticed that John and Lexi had become quite comfortable in each other's company as they danced together. He leaned close to Angeline. "Were John any other man, I think I would have to intervene."

Angeline laughed. "Your sister is perfectly capable of handling herself." She held her hand out to Aidan. "I do believe we should be dancing as well."

"Any excuse to hold me, isn't that right?" His expression was playful as he led the way to the dance floor.

As they danced, Angeline looked at John and Lexi. "They look rather good together, don't they? It seems that this has been a year of new beginnings as well as, well, everything else that we won't discuss this evening."

Angeline scanned the ballroom. She was content. "Look at everyone having such a wonderful time. This party has always been a favourite of mine, not just because my birthday happens to fall on the same day as the world's largest party each year, but everyone looking forward to a fresh start with a new year makes me feel so hopeful. The extra security at each of the entrances also helps put my mind at ease."

"Even knowing what we know?" Since joining the league, Aidan hadn't experienced much down-time, and he wondered what the next year would hold.

"In spite of it."

~~~~

In an apartment on the outskirts of Niagara Falls, Marcus sat with a glass of wine in his hand as he reviewed the information he had obtained from Maeve regarding Asmodeus. He cleared his throat and felt a twinge of pain in his side. His broken ribs were nearly healed, and he planned to spend more time at his newly acquired property, to ensure that the work being done met his standards. He was in no hurry.

He sipped his wine slowly. He was certain that the league must have thought he abandoned his mission, that Sebastian thought that he had beaten him into giving up. He still had two of their keys and he knew they would come for them sooner or later.

"They would have to find me first."

Once he had freed Asmodeus and partnered with him, he knew the league would not stand a chance. Together, they would prove to be an unstoppable force.

~~~~

Angeline and Aidan returned to their table. Just after they sat, Angeline's phone rang. The display read, *Nell*, and the smile dropped from her face. Phone in hand, she leaned toward Aidan. "I've got to take this, love."

Aidan rose with Angeline. "I'll have a drink ready for you when you return."

She kissed his cheek and walked to the ballroom exit. "Nell." She could scarcely make out Nell's words. "I need to get somewhere quiet, I can't hear you."

Behind the bar in The Sky Clock Pub, Nell rolled her eyes.

Angeline neared her office. "Nell, what do you need?"

"I've got a situation. I had a bloke in here saying that there were geist catching humans, replicating 'em, and making 'em fight themselves in an alley. I thought you'd want to know before the bobbies get there."

"What? Are you certain? This isn't just drunk rantings?"

"No. He's one of mine. This bloke's true to his word."

"I'll be there soon." Angeline sighed.

"Oi! It's not happening here. I'll text you the location."

"Thank you, Nell."

Nell sent the text to Angeline while mumbling to herself, "If it was happening here, I'd have bloody well dealt with it myself. I've been doing this long before you came along."

In her office, Angeline sat and sent an urgent text to the other league members, instructing them to meet her there. She hoped they weren't too inebriated, but knew that Conor could help them sober up if they were.

One by one, the other league members entered her office. She explained the situation and together they left to take care of it.

"And here I thought my birthday would be relaxing," Angeline joked as they rode the elevator to the car park.

"I've sent the location to each of your phones. Ethan, Josh, did you both bring your vehicles?"

Josh answered. "We did."

"Alright. Four of us in each car. We'll meet there."

~~~~

They parked their cars near the alley and approached it from both ends, having coordinated during the ride.

Concealed behind a large trash bin, John took the lead. He looked down the alley and counted nine black auras, more geist than they were led to believe were involved. He watched as a dark grey mist brushed against a man who stood surrounded by geist.

With Angeline, Aidan, and Mariam beside him, John watched the geist replicate the man who looked on in horror at the sight of his own body forming in front of him, while he begged for his wife to be spared. The woman watched from the side of the alley in tears, as another geist held her.

"Kill me, but let her go!" the man shouted.

One geist stepped forward. "Tell ya what. You win your fight, and I'll let her go. You lose, and I kill her."

John looked at the circle of geist that surrounded the three humans. He saw a man and a woman held at knifepoint by geist near the edge of the circle, and a man in the centre about to fight his replicant.

Angeline remained calm, but inside, she was anxious. "This is it, John. This is our first big fight. We've got abilities. Let's put them to use, yeah?"

Mariam stood beside Angeline. "I will position myself behind the wall, near the geist that is holding the woman. I can come through the wall and use my Soul Dagger before he knows I'm there."

John nodded. "Sounds good. Aidan, can you find out what the others are planning to do?"

"I've just had Ethan say he would handle the geist holding the man closest to him, and that Josh would provide a distraction, so that the rest of us can get close enough to dagger the others."

Aidan's eyes darted back and forth, as he read the thoughts of each league member across the alley. "Ann will take care of as many as she can mimicking Ethan's ability, and Dalila said she would surround the circle of geist with her clones. Sebastian and Conor will stay at their end to make sure no geist get past. Conor has said he will tend to the humans if we can get them to him."

Aidan was both exhilarated and nervous for his first fight with geist.

John looked at Mariam. "Alright, Mariam, get into position."

He turned to Aidan. "Tell Josh to start his distraction, something to make them look anywhere but at us, then tell Dalila to surround the geist with her clones. Once the distraction is in place, we all move in."

"I'll let them know."

"Tell them that Zev will be here soon."

"Who?" Aidan asked.

"Just tell them."

Aidan nodded.

John phoned Zev, the head of the Eyrasine Extraction Team, to deal with the hostages.

At the other end of the alley, Josh looked at the others. "Has Aidan filled you in on the plan?"

They each nodded.

Josh focused his energy and created a swarm of ravens high over the geist in the alley. When one of the geist looked up, Josh had one of the birds fall to the ground, then another, and another. Soon all of the geist were looking at the birds, and didn't see the other league members had moved toward them.

From within the wall, Mariam emerged behind one of the geist, and thrust her Soul Dagger into his neck, turning him to ash.

Another geist turned and saw his cohort eliminated. He had just enough time to let go of the man he held before Ethan used his Soul Dagger to slit his throat.

Dalila directed her energy, formed ten clones of herself, and positioned them a few feet behind each of the geist in the outer circle. A few geist wielded knives and swiped at the clones. Ann, now invisible, moved closer. While one of the geist was distracted with a clone, she easily daggered him.

After he watched his friends turn to ash, one geist pulled a gun from his pocket and waved it, as he frantically tried to find a target.

Zayne saw the gun and channeled his energy. He caused the geist to point his gun upward, away from the other league members and the humans, then threw his Soul Dagger. It landed squarely in the geist's forehead. He then hurried to his dagger, pulled it from the pile of ash, and turned to find another geist to eliminate.

Conor ran to assess the hostages as they ran toward him. Together, he and Sebastian saw the hostages to safety.

Conor quickly examined the two frightened people. "Help is coming."

In the centre of the alley, a man and his geist replicant looked at John, Angeline, and Aidan.

John focused his mind on the ground beneath the geist, and caused it to open, dropping him into a hole nearly five feet deep. He ran to the geist as Angeline and Aidan ran to the frightened man.

While Angeline hurriedly escorted the man to Conor at the far end of the alley, Aidan charged at another geist, his Soul Dagger ready. They circled each other. The geist lunged forward as he swiped at Aidan.

Aidan jumped and kicked the knife out of the geist's hand. Before he could turn to run, Ethan had stabbed him from behind.

Ethan appeared and smiled. "You're welcome, mate."

Aidan felt adrenaline race through him. "This lifestyle will take some adjusting to."

He turned and saw two other geist fall to ash, one after the other, as Ann stabbed them.

Ann reappeared but hadn't seen the geist behind her. Aidan, however, had. He shouted, "Ann! Get down!"

As Ann dropped to the ground, Aidan threw his dagger. It found its mark in the geist's chest.

Ann stood up. "Thanks!"

Sebastian, who had watched from the end of the alley, let out a heavy breath as Ann walked toward him.

With no geist left in the alley, the league members met at the far end, where Conor examined the cuts on one man's face.

Zev arrived in an ambulance to take care of the humans. None of them knew what would become of these people, but they knew the Immortals would take care of them.

Two other Eyrasines exited the ambulance with Zev, and escorted the humans into the back. They removed three masks attached to a tank that read, *Oxygen*.

Zev placed a mask over the woman's face. "Take a few deep breaths. You're going to be just fine."

He exited the ambulance while the two others strapped the now unconscious people into their seats to transport them to the Immortals in the City of Radiance.

Angeline walked to Aidan. "That was Zev, Paidi, and Dax. They are the Eyrasine Extraction Team that deal with any humans who witness things that they should not know about. They also help us make a quick escape, should we need it."

"It seems I still have much to learn. What hospital will those people be taken to?"

"They won't. They will be transported to the City and once they've been tended to, they will be taken before the Immortals. What happens after that, well, I suppose we will find out soon enough."

He looked at her and saw blood on the shoulder of her dress. "Are you injured?"

"No, I don't believe so." She scanned her arms. "That's not my blood. We should probably go get cleaned up."

Angeline addressed the others. "It seems that our New Year has started off with a different sort of bang than we had anticipated. As I said, Faith has room keys for each of you at the Aemetta. I will phone her and have her meet us near the back service elevator with some sleepwear for each of you, assuming you will be staying."

They all headed out of the alley as Rafe, Selah, and Ruby entered.

Aidan looked at Angeline, confused. "And who are these three?"

"They are members of the Forensics Team. We certainly are keeping them busy."

He placed his arm around her shoulders and together they walked to her car.

18 – INNATE ABILITIES

The Immortals had hoped that each league member would have at least a year to practice and perfect their skills, however, Marcus Shea had altered that timetable. The Immortals agreed that between his threats and the recent geist activity in London, they needed to hone their abilities quickly.

In the Training Arena, Araton addressed the league members. "You must not only train your bodies, you all have abilities that must be honed as well. As time passes, and you become more proficient in the use of your abilities, you will find that the amount of energy you need to expend will decrease. Utilizing your gifts will become second nature, and you will be able to sustain them for extended periods of time."

He turned to Ann. "You, Ann, have the most difficult task of all, as you must learn to control the abilities of each your friends. Your training will not be easy."

She whispered under her breath, "Nothing ever is."

Araton continued. "You will find that mimicking the abilities of the others will require you to absorb great amounts of their energy. When your energy learns to recognize and mimic that of your friends, you will begin to need less of their energy. Once those connections have been solidified, you will use your own energy, which will benefit you both."

"Alright. Where should I start?"

John walked past Ann toward the Hydration Station. "With me."

Araton tilted his head. "Go with John. His ability requires focus and concentration that you must not only learn, but master."

John walked back toward Ann after he grabbed a cup from the Hydration Station. "We can start with water. Let's go to the pool."

He continued to the Current Pool with Ann following behind.

She knew how to mimic Sebastian's ability, lord knows she had done it enough, but she was anxious to try out John's. *I still need to do something for Seb to repay those favours*, she thought to herself.

Inside the Current Pool area, John dipped the cup into the water. "Water is the easiest of the four elements to control. My guess would be it's because our bodies contain so much of it."

"Okay, so what do I do first?" Ann was eager to begin.

"Most people think water is harmless. We drink it, swim in it, bathe in it, but it is also water that erodes rock."

"Yeah, but I don't think we have hundreds of years to wear down Marcus."

John laughed. "True enough, but in the clinic, we use water to clean people's teeth. When it's concentrated on one small area it can do a lot of damage."

He harnessed his ability and concentrated his energy. With a wave of his hand, he lifted the water out of the cup, shaped it into a needle and directed it toward a towel that was hung over a chair.

"So, you shot a water bullet at a towel?"

"Go look at the towel."

She tilted her head and furrowed her brow before she walked to the other end of the pool. She wondered why he wanted her to look at a wet towel.

As she got within a few feet of the towel, she could see a hole the size of a nickel in it, and she was quite excited. "Are you kidding me? That is amazing! I have to try that."

She ran back toward John.

He cupped his hands around his mouth and imitated a voice over a loudspeaker. "No running in the pool area!"

With a smirk on his lips, he shifted the water under Ann's feet. She landed on her backside.

Ann laughed. "John!"

He smiled. "I couldn't resist."

She got to her feet. "So, how does this work?"

"It takes a lot of concentration, but it gets easier the more you practice."

He filled the cup again and set it down on the floor. Ann watched intently as John lifted the water out of the cup and swirled it in the air twenty five feet above their heads.

He directed the water around the room. "I want you to stop the water from moving."

Ann rolled her head and stretched her neck. "Alright, just concentrate. I can do this."

She held her hands up and saw the water headed directly for her. "It's not stopping, John!"

"Concentrate. Clear your mind and think only about what you are doing. It's either concentrate or get soaked."

Ann's arms dropped to her sides and she glared at John. "You wouldn't!"

"Only you can stop it, Ann."

She concentrated and focused every ounce of her ability. She raised her arms as the water was directly above her and made it stop. "I did it!"

Concentrating fully on the water, she directed it upward.

"That's really good."

"Thanks." She was rather proud of herself.

She lost her concentration and the water sped downward toward her. Mere seconds before it splashed to the floor, she jumped out of the way. "That was close!"

"Next, we have," he pulled a lighter from his pocket and lit it, "fire!"

"Okay, I'm ready." Ann flexed and straightened her fingers.

John sparked the lighter and directed the flame to rise over the pool. "I'm going to give you control once you think you're ready."

"Alright." She concentrated and found fire much harder to control. "Why is fire more difficult?"

John furrowed his brow and thought. "I'm not sure, but I think it would be because it's natural to fear fire, whereas water is something we deal with every day."

"True enough."

"Have you got it?" He was beginning to feel lightheaded.

She stared at the flame above the pool and focused her energy on it. "Yes. I've got it. Let go."

John dropped his arms. He sat in the closest chair and watched as Ann held the flame suspended above the pool. As she made it move, he felt dizzy. "I think that's enough for today."

Ann broke her concentration and the flame fizzled out.

John walked to the exit and felt as though he had given blood. "I guess this is how Seb feels when you heal yourself with his ability."

"Yeah, sorry about that. I need to drain some of your energy to use your ability, but like Araton said, the more we practice, the less it will take." Ann wrinkled her nose innocently. "Although, that took more than I thought it would."

John reached up, stretched his arms, and moaned. "That's alright. I'll just head to the Healing Chambers and see if someone can give me a massage after I grab a bite to eat."

"Ha! You do that! That was really fun. Thanks."

"It is. I'll see you later."

Ann looked through the window between the Current Pool and the rest of the arena to find her next teacher. She walked through the door and straight to Zayne.

She put her hand on his shoulder. "Care to train me in the art of puppet mastery?"

"I prefer the term Marionettist, but sure. Just be warned, it takes a lot of focus to control someone else's movements."

"John said I would have to really concentrate to get his ability down, but I think I did pretty well for my first time out. I'm a rather fast learner." Ann stretched her arms.

"First, I think you should know what it feels like to have your muscle movements in someone else's control."

Zayne focused his energy and lifted both of Ann's arms above her head.

Ann felt a tingling inside of her as Zayne took control of her body. "Okay, I get it. Now stop."

"Not yet." He next made Ann drop to her knees and bow at his feet.

"I swear Zayne, if you do not let me up right now, I will kick you so hard you'll see stars, moons, *and* planets!"

He laughed and released his hold on Ann's muscles.

"That made me feel totally helpless! All kidding aside, Zayne, your ability really screws with the mind, as well as the body."

"Maybe you are a quick study. When I have used my ability on someone, I could see the fear and confusion in their eyes. Anyway, back to your training. First we need a willing test subject."

As he scanned the arena, he decided that Sebastian would do quite nicely as Ann's marionette. "See if Seb is willing to help you out."

"Seb! Can we borrow you for a quick minute?" Ann tried to sound sweet.

Sebastian heard Ann shout his name. He knew that she was practicing with the abilities of the others and hung his head as he realized he was her chosen victim. "Sorry, can't hear you!"

Ann and Zayne both laughed loudly.

Ann pleaded. "Come on, Seb, I need to practice!"

Sebastian walked toward Ann slowly. He stood in front of her and looked directly into her eyes. "Be kind. That's all I ask."

A smile formed on Ann's lips. "I can't believe you even felt the need to mention such a thing, Mr. Shea! I...I...I'm not sure if I'm hurt," her eyes narrowed and her voice became stern, "or angry."

Sebastian moaned.

Zayne smiled, as he sat and opened his bag of carrot sticks. "And...begin."

Ann took the chair beside Zayne, while Sebastian moved ten feet or so away from her. She focused all of her mind on absorbing Zayne's ability and directed her energy toward Sebastian. His right hand raised and then lowered.

"Okay, I think I get the basic mechanics." Ann felt confident.

Zayne instructed, "Try to get him to punch the air in front of himself."

Ann concentrated and Sebastian's hand formed a fist and thrust upward.

"Am I fighting a bird? What the hell are you doing?"

"Sorry!" Ann quietly giggled.

She looked at Zayne. "How do I direct his arm to go where I want it to? I mean, I had him make a fist easy enough, but I was thinking about punching out in front of him and, well, you saw what happened."

"When I was first learning to control my skills, I would make the movements with my own body as well. I found it easier than just thinking about it. My body knew what I wanted to do and since I was controlling the other person, they did as well. Does that make sense?"

"Yeah, actually, it does. Let me try again."

Sebastian pleaded, "Am I done yet? I'd like to...do some other things."

"Not yet, I just want to try one more thing. It won't hurt, I promise."

"Not physically, anyway. What this is going to do to his ego though, that's anyone's guess!" Zayne smirked and popped another carrot stick in his mouth.

Ann cracked her knuckles. "Okay, Ann, focus. Jab, jab, uppercut." She made the motions and watched as Sebastian did the same.

She jumped to her feet and spun around. "I did it! Yeah!"

She wasn't aware that Sebastian was jumping as well. Zayne laughed so hard he nearly choked on his carrots.

Sebastian shouted, "Ann! Stop!"

She continued to jump and turned around to see Sebastian was as well. She ran to him and he ran to her. They stopped just short of crashing into each other.

The others in the Training Arena stopped what they were doing to watch the show. Some of them laughed as they watched Sebastian jump and run in sync with Ann.

"What do I do, Zayne?"

"I should have made a video of this. No one is going to believe me!" Zayne laughed.

Ann and Sebastian both shouted. "Zayne!"

"Just think of something else, something that requires your attention and concentration. What have you got planned for today?"

"I told Mom I would go shopping for new pie plates with her. The ones she has are past their prime."

She placed her hands on her hips. "Now, I have pies on my mind!"

Sebastian shook his head as he felt Ann's control of his muscles subside. "That was rather disturbing. Not having control over my own body is *not* a good feeling."

"What do you say, teacher. Am I a good student or what?" Ann was proud of her accomplishment.

"You are. Well done, Ann." Zayne stood up only to find that he needed to sit a bit longer.

"I've got to say, you sure sucked the energy out of me! Next time I'll eat something more substantial than carrots before I let you tap me."

"Thanks, Zayne. I really enjoyed that. Remember though, the more we practice together, the less energy I'll have to take from you. Can I get you anything to eat?"

"No, I'll be fine." Zayne closed his eyes and relaxed.

Sebastian asked, "Zayne, would you like a protein shake? I'm headed that way to make myself one."

"No, thanks. I'm just going to sit here awhile." Zayne kept his eyes closed.

Sebastian put his arm around Ann's shoulders. "Would you like a protein shake?"

"Actually, I'd love one. Thanks, Seb. Raspberry and pomegranate, please."

"Coming right up!" Sebastian lightly smacked Ann's behind before he headed to the Hydration Station.

As she watched him walk away, Ann wondered why it had taken so long for them to get together. They were completely in sync with each other.

Ann had a hard time deciding whose ability she would like to try next. She had used both Ethan's and Conor's abilities in the past, and had once watched as Josh used his gift as an Hallucinist to make Angeline believe a large, hairy spider ran toward her. At least until Angeline's scream broke Josh's concentration. In retrospect, she was certain that Josh felt it was worth it, despite having his faction leader dress him down in the middle of the City.

Ann looked around the arena for another teacher and caught sight of Drew with Jayde and Kyle.

~~~~

Drew folded his arms. "Show me that again, Kyle. Slower this time."

Kyle narrowed his eyes. "You just like seeing Jayde toss me to floor!"

Drew smiled. "Well, yeah, but I would like to see the way she positioned her hips to flip you like that. I mean, Jayde has always been strong, but you aren't a small guy!"

Jayde winked and flexed her muscles. "I'm always happy to help."

Kyle held onto the sleeves of Jayde's shirt, between her shoulders and elbows, while Jayde placed her right hand on Kyle's shoulder and her left hand on his right arm.

She stepped forward with her right foot and placed it directly in front of Kyle's left foot. She removed her hand from his shoulder, placed her arm around his neck, and as she turned her body counterclockwise, she forced her right hip into Kyle's abdomen. Once Kyle was behind her, she kicked her right foot backward into his shin, bent her knees, and flipped him over her body.

"Alright, I think I've got it. Kyle. You willing to land on your ass for me, too?" Drew chuckled.

Kyle glanced sideways at Drew. "Yeah, why not."

Drew executed the move nearly as well as Jayde.

James and Rachel took off their boxing gloves and moved to join them.

"Is it Kick Kyle's Ass Day?" James smiled.

Kyle smirked . "It could be Kick James' Ass Day, if you'd like to take a turn."

James laughed. "That's alright."

He put his arm around Rachel's shoulders. "We've just finished up a sparring session and we're headed to the sauna."

~~~~

Ann shouted from across the arena. "Nicely done, little brother."

She turned to Dalila. "I remember seeing your replicants in the alley. They seemed so real."

"That would be because I don't just project images of myself, for a few moments, the replicants are solid objects."

"Are you kidding me? So it's more like you clone yourself?"

"It is, but it also takes a lot of energy. Whenever I've come here to practice, I ate a lot of high carbohydrate foods beforehand, things like almonds, blueberries, and bananas. I've had a good lunch, so I should be alright if I sit while you practice.

"The first thing I do is imagine myself filling with something, just like filling a balloon with air. I get fuller and fuller and finally, I release bits."

"Alright, so I'm filling up and then I let some out." Ann nodded her head. "Ready when you are."

"Take your time, just don't take too much of my energy on your first try."

Ann concentrated and could feel herself filling with Dalila's energy. "I can feel it! You know, everyone's energy feels different when it's flowing through me. Yours feels really powerful."

"Why, thank you." Dalila smiled sweetly. "Alright, slow down and try to release some. Concentrate on where you want to place your replicants."

Ann looked at the chair beside Dalila and released some of the energy she had absorbed. Suddenly, a replicant of herself stood beside Dalila with its legs through the chair.

Ann grimaced. "Oh, I guess I should have put her somewhere without furniture in the way, huh?"

The two women laughed.

"Yes, that would have been better. If your opponent sees your legs going through a chair, I am fairly certain it wouldn't take long to realize it isn't real."

"One more time. I've got this."

Dalila began to feel weak and hoped that the lunch she ate would sustain her, though she didn't let Ann know.

With one last focus of her mind, Ann tapped into Dalila's energy and absorbed more than she had intended to. When she began releasing replicants, ten had appeared before she realized that Dalila had collapsed.

Ann shouted. "Medic! We need a medic!" She was in full blown panic mode.

She knelt and tapped Dalila's face. "Come on. Wake up. I'm so sorry. Wake up!"

Conor rushed to Dalila's side and placed his hands over her. He managed to rouse her but found that it took a lot of his energy. "What happened, Ann?"

"I was trying out her ability and I guess I took too much of her energy. Is she going to be alright, Conor?"

"She'll be fine, but I think you're stronger than you realize, Ann. It took a lot of my energy just for Dalila to open her eyes. I can only imagine what you took from her."

Dalila moaned. "Can I please have some water and something to eat?"

Nearly in tears, Ann knelt beside her friend. "I'm so sorry Dalila. I didn't mean to take so much."

Dalila managed to sit up and placed her hand on Ann's shoulder. "It's alright, Ann. I just wasn't ready for how much energy you would need to take. It was as though someone quickly drained every drop of blood from my body."

Conor returned with some food and a large protein shake for Dalila. "Once your energy level is back up, I'll check your vitals. We don't want you heading out into the Egyptian sun light-headed."

"Thank you, Conor." Dalila gulped down the protein shake.

Ann helped her into a chair. "I'll stay with her Conor. When she's finished her shake and food, I'll find you to check on her."

She turned toward Dalila. "I'm going to be by your side until your energy returns."

Dalila smiled and nodded before she closed her eyes and rested her head on the back of her chair.

Ann felt somewhat guilty for taking so much of her friends' energy. She felt incredibly powerful with their energy inside her, still resonating in her veins, while the three of them were left drained and weak.

19 – ENCHANTED INK

Ann arrived at Jayded Ink with Vivian, Jake, and Drew. She had arranged for them to receive their protection tattoos first thing in the morning, as they each had a busy day planned. While they took turns seated at Jayde's workstation, Josh and Ethan arrived with their families from London.

Both Ethan and Ann were good artists and after a quick lesson in the fine art of tattooing, they were ready to help.

Jayde picked up a bottle of the enchanted ink. "This is the first time I've ever used spelled ink."

"It will be our first time working with any kind of ink in a tattoo machine. With the three of us working, this shouldn't take very long." Ann was eager to begin.

Jayde placed the bottle of ink on her workstation. "That's the idea. The Immortals said we only need to use enough ink to cover the surface of a dime for it to be effective. If someone wants something bigger, we can let them know they'll have to come back another day and I'll finish it up for them."

Ann turned to Ethan with a smirk on her lips. "Ready to put your artistic talent to work, Ethan?"

"I am. I've never worked with needles, but I'm always up for a challenge."

"I'm just glad that you two caught on so quickly. I would need more than a day to get all of the league families inked by myself, so thank you." Jayde's words were sincere.

The African Faction families arrived, as Josh left to escort his and Ethan's family home.

Ann leaned close to Jayde. "And here's our next set of brave souls."

Wardah, Dalila's mother, looked around the shop. "All three of you work here?"

"No, still just me." Jayde pointed to Ann and Ethan. "It's just that these two have the art gene and they were willing to help me get you all protected quicker."

Wardah rubbed her arms, a worried look on her face. "This geist business is just awful. Why is it they have come about now? Everything was so quiet, so peaceful."

Ann knew that the truth would only serve to scare her. She wrinkled her nose. "It's just a precaution, really. There have been so many coming through, that we just want to make sure that you all get to keep all of your DNA."

She winked. "Besides, we don't want two of Sameer running around, now do we? Have a seat Mrs. Saliba and I'll get started on your tattoo."

When they had finished with the African Faction families, Jayde cleaned the three ink machines while Ethan and Ann sat on the couch, flipping through tattoo magazines.

"I guess we're just waiting on Angeline's and Aidan's families to come in." Ann felt somewhat impatient.

Ethan asked, "Are your parents stopping by today as well, Jayde?"

"No, I inked them at home last night. I figured it was easier to get them out of the way first, since I live with them. I got Rachel and James done this morning. I would have done Rachel last night as well, but she didn't come home." Jayde raised an eyebrow and smirked.

"Ooh!" Ethan nudged Ann with his elbow. "Attaboy, James!"

Ann laughed. She checked her watch, she furrowed her brows. "Ange said she and Aidan would be here by now. I wonder what's keeping them?"

"Nothing, love!" Angeline and Aidan walked into the shop from the back room with their families.

Jayde pointed to the workstations. "Three of you can sit at the ink stations and we'll get started. It shouldn't take long. You guys are the last bunch to arrive and then we are done."

Lexi looked around the shop while Jayde outlined a beautiful rose on her wrist that looked as though it had just begun to open.

"Ann, is John planning to pop in today?" Lexi didn't bother to sound casual.

"I don't think so. He has no reason, he doesn't need to get the tattoo." She hoped Lexi wasn't too disappointed.

Lexi pouted as Jayde finished her tattoo. "I would hate to have made a trip to North America without seeing that handsome dentist."

Ann looked at Angeline. Their eyes were wide and both of them smirked.

Lily then took the seat in front of Ann and asked for a small treble clef to be tattooed into her left wrist.

As she cleaned Lily's wrist, Ann leaned close to Angeline, who had pulled a chair up next to hers. "John needs to have someone to make him realize there's more to life than just the league and work."

"Cheers to that."

Aidan looked at his sister with brotherly concern. He knew that she had most likely already planned out exactly what she intended to do. "Just behave, Lexi."

She laughed. "Don't I always?" Her eyes hinted mischief.

Angeline interjected before Aidan could disagree. "Turn left once you're out the door, go two blocks, and the clinic is right there. You'll see the large sign out front of the building with a section reading, Dr. M. Evans, DDS and Associates."

Lexi smiled sweetly. "Thank you, Angeline!"

Aidan glared at Angeline.

"What? I'm sure John can handle himself and from what I've seen, I am more than certain Lexi can."

"That is what I'm afraid of." Aidan rubbed his face.

Angeline took hold of his arm. "Shall we head to Transcendence for a bite to eat, Aidan? I believe our families are in good hands here."

"Alright. I believe I could use a pint or two right about now."

Theresa watched as her daughter and Aidan headed out the front door, arm in arm, and her heart was happy.

As soon as Jayde had covered her tattoo and given her the care instructions, Lexi walked to the front door and turned to face the others. "Wish me luck!"

~~~~~

Lexi easily persuaded John to take her to lunch. As they entered Transcendence, they heard Vivian speaking loudly, "Your money is no good here. Now, get out of here with that food before it gets cold!"

Kyle placed both hands atop the bar. "I can't just take this without giving you something. Let me give you…"

Vivian interrupted. "No! There are hungry people waiting for you and if I know Jayde, which I do, she is going to want what I've packed in there. Go!"

John offered some advice. "I would listen to her, Kyle. Aunt Viv won't let any of us pay for anything. Just accept defeat and go."

"Alright." Kyle narrowed his eyes in mock anger as he lifted the bags. "But this isn't over!"

"Okay, dear." Vivian waved to Kyle as she walked to John.

She kissed his cheek. "John, what can I get for you and…"

Lexi offered Vivian her hand. "Lexi Temple, ma'am. Very nice to meet you."

"Aidan's sister! Oh, how lovely to meet you! Call me Aunt Viv, everyone does."

~~~~~

Kyle walked into Jayded Ink carrying two large bags of food. He knew that Jayde hadn't scheduled time to eat between appointments. "I thought you three would probably need some food about now."

"Is he not sweet? And the guy knows food!" Jayde was ravenous.

Kyle walked to her kissed her, then turned to Ann. "Your mother wouldn't let me pay for any of this. I'd like to get her a gift, but I don't really know her that well. What do you think she would like, Ann?"

Ann narrowed her eyes and looked directly at Kyle. "Your mother must have been an awesome lady because you sure didn't get all that sweetness from your father."

"She really was. I wish you guys could have met her."

Jayde introduced Kyle to Angeline's parents.

"A pleasure to meet you, Kyle." George Flynn shook his hand.

Kyle offered his hand to Theresa next, who sat across from Ann. "I've met your daughter. She really looks like you, Mrs. Flynn."

Theresa gushed, "Why thank you, Kyle. I'll take that as a rather generous compliment."

"As it was intended, Mrs. Flynn."

Jayde continued. "And you remember Angeline's sisters, Kate and Margaret."

"I do remember. Good to see you both again."

Margaret turned to Jayde and mouthed, *Nice!*

Jayde laughed. "Thanks, I think so."

"What's that, Jayde?" George was oblivious to the silent communication.

Jayde looked up innocently. "Nothing, Mr. Flynn."

George turned his attention to Kyle. "So, I understand your father is Marcus Shea. Where is that old bastard these days?"

"Dad!" Kate shouted, embarrassed. "Must you always be so forward and rude?"

She looked at Kyle. "Please forgive my father, Kyle. He's not yet been properly trained in the fine art of being polite."

"I'm simply asking a question." George was always blunt and outspoken.

Theresa placed her hand over her eyes and shook her head. Her husband always tested people, sized them up by the way they reacted in certain situations. This was one of the qualities that had made him so successful in the hotel industry, but also one that lost him a few friends.

"It's alright, Kate." Kyle turned to George. "I honestly don't know where he is. Marcus is my father, but he wasn't much of one. Apparently, he felt that his wanderlust was more important than his wife and child."

Jayde found herself in one of her rare speechless moments. She thought that Kyle handled that rather ignorant remark with the finesse of a bomb defuser.

Once she found her voice, Jayde looked directly at George. "Trust me, Mr. Flynn, if Kyle was anything like his father, he wouldn't be here."

George held his hands up in surrender. "Say no more. If Kyle suits you, Jayde, I'm sure he's a really good chap."

Theresa leaned in toward her husband. "You really must learn to control yourself, love. Your mouth may earn you respect among your industry peers, but outside of that circle, your wit isn't always appreciated."

George Flynn knew that his wife was right. "Kyle, I do apologize. I seldom think before I speak. Please, I am dreadfully sorry if I have offended you."

Kyle raised one eyebrow. "I suppose it's something I have to get used to. My father was apparently a stellar bastard and I just have to deal with it."

He looked at Jayde and winked. "Rum definitely helps, though."

Jayde and Ann laughed.

"You are certainly a good match for our Jayde, Kyle Shea." Theresa was pleased that the tone in Jayded Ink had returned to a friendlier one.

~~~~~

Logan Scott arrived in Niagara Falls and, unfamiliar with the city, found himself lost. His GPS system had decided that it would crash with his destination a mere fifteen minutes away. He got out of his truck and decided to walk until he found someone he could ask for directions to his motel. That's when he came across Jayded Ink.

He tried the door only to find it locked and assumed that one of the people inside had forgotten to unlock for the day. He knocked at the door. "Hello?"

"Read the sign. We're closed." Jayde shouted.

"I can see you working inside. I just have a question. Can you let me in?"

"I said we're closed. If I have to stop what I'm doing, your question will be how long will my arm be in a cast!" Jayde retorted.

George leaned toward his wife. "I do believe Kyle will have his hands full with our Jayde."

Kyle looked out front and saw Logan. Under his breath he whispered, "Logan?"

He walked to the door and unlocked.

"Kyle?" The two men hugged each other. "What the hell are you doing here?"

"I've been here since September of last year. What are you doing here is the better question." Kyle was surprised to see his old friend.

Logan looked around the room and saw the others staring at him, with the exception of Jayde. "Who's the chick that won't look at me?"

Kyle laughed. He knew Jayde wasn't concerned with what anyone thought of her. Logan was no exception. "She's the one that told you the shop is closed. Jayde!"

"Busy, Kyle. Give me a minute. Mr. Fussy Pants here won't stop moving!" She winked at Angeline's father while she covered his tattoo.

George whined. "Well, it hurts, Jayde."

Jayde couldn't help but laugh. "I'm sorry, it was just too tempting. Really." She cleared her voice and continued in her best British accent. "I do apologize if I've offended you."

Ethan and Kate snickered at the conversation around them as he tattooed the back of her right shoulder.

"It seems I have been properly put in my place." George ceded.

He turned to Kyle and once again offered his sincerest apologies. "I will make every effort to carefully select my words before speaking in the future."

Theresa whispered to Jayde. "It seems you've given my husband a bit more than he bargained for when we came through your door. I should have brought him to you years ago!"

Jayde chuckled. "Any time, Mrs. Flynn, any time. Just head out the back door. The others are there waiting for you."

Theresa kissed Jayde's cheek. "Thank you again, dear." With a gleam in her eye, she looked at her daughter. "Are you staying here, Kate?"

"No. I'll head back with you."

Ethan and Ann watched Logan carefully, as they could both see the full blue aura around him.

Ethan asked, "Kyle, who's your friend?"

Kyle placed his hand on Logan's back. "This is Logan. He and I grew up together out West."

He walked toward Jayde and continued, "We were inseparable up until I left...when my mom died. This guy and I were like brothers for something like fifteen years. My mom and his were best friends."

"Good to meet you, Logan." Jayde had a cocky look on her face as she added, "But we're still closed."

Logan laughed. "I can see why Kyle likes you."

Ann walked to Kyle. "Can I speak to you in the back room? It will just take a minute."

"It's alright, Ann. Logan knows all about The League of Twelve."

Logan's eyes went wide. "What the hell, Kyle!"

"Mate, we know you're a geist." Ethan hoped to calm the now frightened Logan. "Name's Ethan Wells. Good to meet ya."

Jayde put her head on her work station. "Another one?" She groaned.

"Maybe you should grab what's left of that rum, Kyle. It looks like your friend could use a drink...or four!" Ann laughed.

"What is so funny? You all just scared the hell out of me!" Logan sank into the couch.

"Maybe you and I should go somewhere and I'll fill you in." Kyle wanted to put his friend at ease.

"Yeah, sounds good." Logan stood and backed up toward the front door. He didn't want to turn his back to anyone in the room.

Kyle walked with Logan to the front door. "They know I'm part geist and I'm not dead."

Logan followed Kyle out to the back of the shop. "You drive, Kyle. I think I'm going to need more than few drinks!"

~~~~

After the waitress took their drink orders in a small bar not far from Jayded Ink, Kyle and Logan talked and reminisced about their youth.

"I still can't believe that you're over seven hundred years old. You act like you're a teenager most days." Kyle chuckled.

Logan replied in an old man's voice. "Shut it, whipper snapper!"

"What is it that brought you here, Logan? I never thought you would leave home."

"Do you remember that our neighbourhood was mostly geist families?"

"Yeah, it was great not having to worry that someone would hurt my mother and I, like every time we went into town. I wish I had known back then that the league only killed geist that were evil."

"I know that's what they say, but how do we really know? What's to stop them from just dusting every geist they see? I don't know if I'm willing to take that chance. Looks like you are though, since you're hanging out with them. How did that happen?"

"Jayde. Her brother is in the League. Trust me, they're good people. I don't know how, but they said that they knew that I'm not a bad guy, which is true, of course. I mean, I'm awesome!"

The two men laughed.

Kyle saw that Logan had started to relax. He caught the waitress' attention as she passed. "Two more beers, please.

"Look, as long as you don't cause trouble and just live your life, you don't have to worry about the league. Jayde told me that years ago, the league made a pact with the geist that they wouldn't hunt any who just wanted to live peacefully here on Earth, and up until recently, it's worked out just fine."

"What do you mean, recently?" Logan no longer felt relaxed.

"It's a long story, but I'll just say that it starts with my father not being the man I thought he was."

After their meal was done, Kyle drove Logan back to his vehicle near Jayded Ink.

He parked his car and gave Logan directions to his motel. "It was great seeing you again. How long are you in town?"

"I'm not sure. I just know that I'm not going back. Our nice little neighbourhood has been overrun by a gang of geist terrorizing everyone. It would be nice if we could get some of your league buddies out there to thin the herd a bit."

Logan looked sideways at Kyle. "These guys have been forcing people out of their homes and taking them over. The local cops can't do anything either. You remember how far it is to the main city, right?"

"Yeah, I'm sure that by the time the police get there, there's nothing they can do and the bastards are gone." Kyle shook his head as he looked down. He knew so many good people, good geist, that lived a quiet life back home and to hear that the few rotten ones had taken over made him mad.

"Exactly!" Logan threw his hands in the air. "I told them to get out while they still could, but some of them had nowhere to go even if they wanted to. All I know is I couldn't stay after…"

Kyle recognized the grief on Logan's face. He wore that same look when his mother had died. "What happened, Logan?"

"After you left, this girl Holly showed up. She heard about our group of geist and wanted to join us. She was part geist, like you. Long story short, the bastards killed her."

"I'm sorry, Logan." Kyle placed a hand on his friend's shoulder.

"The couple that raised me passed away not long after you left, so after Holly died, there was nothing to keep me there. I just packed my truck with a few things, some clothes, and left. I was saving money to pay for our wedding and a decent honeymoon. Holly wanted to go to Hawaii. You would have liked her, Kyle."

Logan and Kyle got out of the car.

Logan walked to his truck and slapped the hood. "Do you know any place around here where a geist could shoot some pool? Preferably somewhere far from The League of Twelve. I know you said they don't kill every geist they see anymore, but for my first night in town, I'd rather not take any chances."

"Yeah, I know just the place."

~~~~

Kyle and Logan stood outside of Solar Flair. "It's run by a geist named Azroth. I came here a few times when I first arrived. He'll cheat you if you're not counting your change, but overall, he's a pretty decent guy."

Logan's eyes opened wide. "Are you serious? Azroth? If it's who I think it is, he and I used to run together a long time ago."

He peered inside the bar through one of the front windows and saw Azroth. "I can't believe it. It is him! He hasn't seen this body yet. Oh man, this is going to be fun!"

A tall man with a slim, fit build, Logan looked much different than he did when he and Azroth knew one another. His former body was older and much heavier with a full beard and moustache.

As they entered Solar Flair, they saw Azroth wipe the bar.

They each sat on a stool as Azroth looked up. "What can I get you, boys?"

Logan leaned one elbow on the bar. "Give me a mug of your best ale and two rum chasers, barkeep. And don't be stingy!"

"No. No! Logan Scott?" Azroth was surprised to see the old friend he used to serve in his tavern a few hundred years ago. "You are still using that name?"

"The one and only!"

Azroth rounded the bar to hug Logan. "I figured you'd end up in a younger body one day, but this," He pointed both hands at Logan, "this is just sad!"

Logan punched Azroth's shoulder and laughed. "Shut up, dickhead! I thought you would be a girl by now, sissy bitch! I see you kept your geist name. That's awfully bold of you!"

"Yeah, well, the taxman knows me as Az Roth, and everyone else calls me Roth."

233

Happy to see a friendly face, Azroth lightly punched Logan's arm. "Same old Logan. Good to know some things never change. Listen, whatever you guys want, it's on the house...within reason." He rounded the bar. "What can I get for you, guys?"

While Logan gave his drink order, Azroth's attention was on the front door as John and Sebastian walked in.

Azroth turned to his bartender. "Hey, Matt, get these two whatever they want, on the house."

He came out from behind the bar and patted Logan's shoulder. "It was really good to see you again, Logan. Come by anytime."

He turned his attention back to John and Sebastian. "Hey boys, back so soon? Let's take this to my office."

Sebastian whispered to John, "What is Kyle doing here? And who is that geist he's with?"

"Don't know and right now, don't care." He wanted to get the meeting with Azroth done. "We can deal with them when we're finished with Azroth."

Sebastian knew that John felt the weight of his responsibilities getting heavier every day. He also knew that John's role as leader came with a hefty price tag, sacrificing the majority of his personal life and any chance for normalcy.

Inside Azroth's office, John got right to business. "What news have you got?"

Azroth sat and put his feet on top of his desk. "Well, since the last time I saw you, what," he raised his voice and continued, "three weeks ago?"

He scratched his head and used his best sarcastic tone. "Let me think. Umm, right, nothing!"

Sebastian pounded both fists on the desk. "Three weeks and nothing? Not good enough!"

"Everything is the same as before although, I haven't seen Ganga for a while."

He leaned forward. "I'm sticking my neck out for you guys and all I get in return is a deep scratch on my desk and you guys up in my face! If Marcus found out what I was doing, I would need a new body every day! I've been checking with everyone I can trust and no one knows where Marcus is. Trust me!"

John took a deep breath to steady himself. He was at the limit of his patience with Azroth. "Look, anything you heard could mean something. What have your customers been talking about?"

"Well, there is one thing." Azroth wanted to get paid again but saw the look on Sebastian's face and decided that he had better not raise that issue just yet.

"I told you, no one knows where he is, and that's true. Now, I don't know if Marcus is doing this himself or sending someone, but, I mean if I was him, I wouldn't do it myself. I mean..."

John shouted through gritted teeth. "Spit. It. Out!"

"Okay! A rather large man was here saying the same things Ganga was saying. Said he knew a guy that was willing to pay for all kinds of odd jobs and they would get half up front and half when the job was finished. This guy hands out a paper with a number and leaves."

"Who is this large man? Have you seen him before?"

"No, he just showed up here a couple of times. I'm good with faces and he's not a regular here."

Azroth tilted his head downward. "I'm thinking it *is* Ganga and she misted out of her girly body and picked this guy, or she's sending other people in her place. Whoever it is, they aren't here often and they don't stay long. He just offers quick cash to anyone who's willing to do the work, no questions asked."

Logan nudged Kyle. "What is the league doing with Azroth?"

"How do you know they're in the league?" Kyle was surprised that Logan could identify them.

"The rings. It's not often you see two men both wearing sapphire rings! They've been wearing them for as long as I can remember."

"I've met those two. They're pretty good guys."

Logan rubbed his face. "This is going to take some getting used to. I haven't seen anyone from The League of Twelve in a few hundred years and today I see four!"

John and Sebastian walked out of Azroth's office, straight to Kyle.

Kyle made the introductions. "John, Sebastian, this is Logan Scott. He and I grew up together out West. Well, I say grew up, but what I mean is he found himself in a four-year-old's body and kept it."

Logan smiled but couldn't mask the concern on his face. John offered his hand and Logan took it in his own.

"Good to meet you Logan. And yes, we know you're a geist."

Sebastian offered his hand next. "Sebastian Shea."

Logan's eyes were still opened wide and his brows furrowed together. "Shea? Umm...Kyle?"

"He's my cousin, Logan. His father was my uncle and my father killed him. It's a long story that I don't want to get into right now." Kyle was weary of discussing Marcus.

He addressed John and Sebastian. "Logan knows Azroth from a few hundred years ago. Apparently, he ran a tavern back then."

"How old are you, Logan?" John wondered if he might somehow be useful.

Logan simply stared at John, silent, fear evident in his eyes.

"Would you be willing to help us out once in a while? Maybe fill in some blanks for us?"

Logan hesitated. "That depends on what you mean by help."

"Just let us know when you see any geist looking to cause trouble, or if we have questions about things that happened in the past, maybe you could shed some light on it for us. We wouldn't expect you do this for free, either."

"I guess having The League of Twelve owe me a favour wouldn't be such a bad thing." Logan thought about the geist back home that terrorized his neighbourhood. "For now, I could use some cash since I'm new in town and don't have a job yet."

"I might be able to help you out." Kyle had hired Logan to teach in his dojo out west and he was certain Logan wouldn't mind being a judo instructor again once he had opened his dojo in Niagara Falls.

20 – MAP OF THE UNIVERSE

"Dr. Cham! Dr. Cham! We have found diamonds!"

Najeeb hurried to his feet. "Where, cousin? Show me!" He could barely contain his excitement. Once he had completely unearthed the second piece of the diamond tablet, he placed it in his satchel and sat to review his calculations, factoring in the location.

Najeeb was elated. "The circular pattern calculations were correct, Olivia!"

Olivia ran to join him.

The daylight had begun to give way to dusk. "Dr. Cham! Come quickly! We found more diamonds!"

"This is fantastic!" Najeeb couldn't believe his luck.

Once they were a safe distance from the workers at the dig site, Najeeb and Olivia arranged the two diamond tablet pieces to see how they might fit together. "We now have three pieces! It seems that these two form the right hand side. Do you see how they both have rounded corners, Olivia?"

"I do! Najeeb! This is wonderful!" She hugged him.

"We must get these back to the City."

They walked back to the tent and Najeeb placed his satchel on a table. He grabbed the megaphone and made an announcement in Egyptian.

Olivia was curious as to what was said. "What does that mean, Dr. Cham?"

"Hmm? Oh, I told everyone that we are done working for today and to come back tomorrow morning. You and I must get back to the City now. Come."

On their way to Al-Jawhara, Najeeb phoned Zayne. "Zayne, we have found more pieces of the diamond tablet."

~~~~

After he received the call from Zayne, John phoned Angeline and filled her in. "Can you meet us in the City? I'm on my way there now."

"How exciting! I've just got a few things to finish then I can leave. I will have

Aidan with me as well, as he's here waiting to take me to supper. I'm certain he won't mind going to the City for a bit to see those two pieces of the diamond tablet."

"He wouldn't mind one bit!" Aidan spoke loudly, so that John could hear him.

John chuckled. "Great! I'll see you both in the City."

"Ann and Seb are at Transcendence right now waiting for Aidan and I. I'll phone Ann and let her know what we're doing. Shall I invite her and Seb?"

"No, let them have their night. Thanks, Ange. See you there." John ended the call and headed to Jayded Ink.

~~~~

In Jayded Ink, Kyle sat on the sofa and watched Jayde finish a rather intricate steampunk tattoo on a young woman's shoulder. He had arrived in time to see the last fifteen minutes of this design being etched into her flesh.

Jayde scolded her customer. "Lucy, you need to sit still. I'm closing up in ten minutes, whether I'm done with you or not."

"I'm sorry, Jayde. I dislocated that shoulder last month and I didn't think it would still be sore. I'll be still, I promise."

"I'd listen to her, if I were you." Kyle stretched his arms along the back of the sofa. "I saw her heave a big guy out of here a few months ago."

Jayde laughed loudly. "I forgot about that!"

John walked to the front door of Jayded Ink and heard laughter. He raised an eyebrow before he entered. "What did Kyle do now?" he joked.

Kyle put both hands up. "Hey, I was just telling the story of the day Jayde and I met."

John thought for a moment, then furrowed his brows. "I don't even want to know."

He paused near Kyle. "Can I talk to you in the back for a minute?"

"Sure." Kyle followed John.

Once in the backroom, John shut the door. "I don't have a lot of time, so I'll be blunt. Would you be willing to help us find out where Marcus is?"

"I told you, I'm done with him. I can't believe anything that comes out of his mouth."

"I know, but we need to find out where he is. He's got two astral keys and we need them back."

"And you're willing to kill him to get them, right? If you're asking me to kill him, I won't. I can't."

"We won't kill him. The Immortals want Marcus alive. He has to be held accountable for his actions."

Kyle walked away from John. He had been told that his father murdered three people. He knew that his father sent geist to take Sebastian's and Ann's keys and they had nearly killed him. This decision should be easy, but he found that he still had an inkling of hope left that his father could be redeemed.

After a short internal debate, he concluded that the hope he held onto was just not enough to outweigh the heinous things Marcus had done. He turned back to John and exhaled loudly. "If it means I can finally be done with him and leave the past in the past, I will help you."

"Thanks. You're a good guy, Kyle."

John headed to the door that would take him to the City of Radiance.

~~~~~

Inside the Hall of Gates, Zayne and Najeeb sat on the floor and studied one of the diamond tablet pieces. Najeeb looked up and saw John walk through the Gemini door. "John!"

"Hey, Najeeb." John walked to stand beside him, placed his hands in his pockets, and looked down at the tablet. "What have we got?"

"These two pieces fit together! It's incredible!"

John could see the childlike excitement on Najeeb's face.

"I'm quite anxious to have Angeline translate these writings."

Angeline and Aidan walked into the Hall of Gates together.

"Angeline! I was just saying that I wished you were here to translate the writings on these two fragments of the diamond tablet!"

"I am well, Najeeb, and how are you?" Angeline retorted with a hint of sarcasm.

"Oh, I am sorry." Najeeb apologized and stood to greet her and Aidan.

Angeline smiled. "I'm teasing you, Najeeb! Let's see those diamond pieces you've found, shall we?"

Najeeb handed one fragment to Angeline and he held the other.

"Obviously, they are decoders like the other piece, but they look different. Let me see." She pulled one piece away from the other. "Oh! What was that?"

"What was what?" John asked.

Angeline held onto the fragment Najeeb had in his hands and they put the two pieces together. She saw a line form for a brief instant. "Did any of you see that?"

"See what, Ange?" John questioned.

"Watch as I pull the pieces apart."

"It all looks the same to me." Zayne was confused as to what Angeline could have seen.

"I don't see any difference either, love." Aidan looked closely at the tablet pieces.

John's curiosity nearly turned to impatience. "What are you seeing?"

"It's as though a few extra lines and squiggles are added when the two pieces are together. We need the third piece."

Before she turned to exit through her Capricorn door, Angeline saw Ann and Sebastian walk into the Hall of Gates.

John also saw them and looked surprised.

Ann rolled her eyes. "Did you really think we wouldn't come, John?"

John lifted one corner of his mouth and shook his head in response.

"We're taking the diamond fragments to the council. There's something odd about these pieces!" Angeline hurried out the door toward the Council Chambers.

Ann and Sebastian looked at each other and together, moved to follow Angeline.

With the others close behind her, Angeline entered the Council Chambers and bowed before the full council. "I ask that we have access to the diamond fragment you have been safeguarding here, as Najeeb has discovered two more pieces."

"You have now found half of the tablet." Jael tapped his fingertips together. "We have waited for this day a very long time, unsure of how to proceed when it came."

Umabel walked to the back of the room and through the door that led to the council members' personal living quarters. In under a minute, she emerged with the fragment of the tablet that the councilors had been keeping.

She tilted her head slightly to the right. "There is much for you to discover."

Angeline indicated that she would like to try to put the pieces together. "May we?"

Selphia nodded her head, took the diamond fragment from Umabel, then handed it to John.

Angeline stood with Ann beside her. "Zayne, Seb, would you mind holding the pieces together with the one John is holding, so we can get a better look?"

They obliged and moved to either side of John.

Angeline stepped back. "Can you hold them out a bit, so they catch the light, please?"

When they did as instructed, Angeline gasped. "Oh my! Ann! Do you see it? These pieces *do* fit together!"

"They do!"

"Umm, that's not all Ange." John had both eyebrows raised as he noticed the lines that came together on the back side.

"What?" Angeline moved to see the back of the tablet. "Blimey! It's a map!"

Selphia walked to Angeline, her hands held in front of herself. "It is a map of the universe. This map was etched when the twelve kings from Eyras had first settled on Earth."

John pursed his lips in anger. "Another piece of information you withheld from us! With everything going on, don't you think we should know as much as we can? How can we be expected to safeguard the portal, Eyrasines, and humans, if we don't have the knowledge to do it?"

Pen-Ming held his hands together behind him. "I understand your anger. But you must understand that we are responsible for your safety. While you must protect the humans and Eyrasines, we seven are charged with protecting you twelve, with ensuring you have the knowledge you need to protect yourselves. We were unaware that young Amber's life was in peril. Had we ensured that Amber was made aware of the consequences of betrayal, she would not have placed herself in such a situation."

The room became dark and Pen-Ming emitted an aura in an ominous shade of deep, blood red. "You twelve are the most inquisitive group we have encountered in many centuries. Your thirst for knowledge and answers are beyond that which we have come to expect."

John closed his eyes and breathed deeply. "Is there anything else that you have kept from us that would help us in fighting Marcus and Asmodeus? I really think that we need to be armed with as much knowledge as we can get."

Selphia spoke next. "As it has always been, you are given information as you require it. Too much knowledge can be as detrimental as too little. You must trust us, John, as you always have."

"Actually, we seem to be fine without your help!" No sooner had the words been spoken, John regretted them.

He closed his eyes and shook his head. "Forgive me, but I'm having a difficult time understanding how knowing something could hurt us. We are currently facing two threats and I cannot lead properly without as much knowledge as possible."

"You have been thrown into a situation of great turmoil and must do your best. No one can ask more of you than that. We trust in you, John, as you must trust in yourself." Selphia turned and walked away.

"Kyle has agreed to help us but as of right now, we don't know where Marcus is or what he is planning. I guess we will just work with what we've got and hope for the best. Thank you."

John bowed and left the Council Chambers ahead of the others.

~~~~

Marcus held the Spirit Dagger. He knew that this blade would give him an advantage when he released Asmodeus from his tomb the night of the next full moon.

The Spirit Dagger, together with a Soul Dagger, was all that Marcus believed was needed to kill Asmodeus and that was how he planned to keep the demon in line. Once he obtained more astral keys, he would need to find an expendable geist to procure a Soul Dagger for him.

After he poured himself a drink, Marcus recalled the day he acquired the Spirit Dagger.

He had returned home from an engineering conference, settled in, then sat to speak with his wife, Madeline.

He removed the dagger from his inside jacket pocket. "Do you recognize this blade?"

Madeline gasped. "Where did you find this?"

"So I take it you know what this is."

"That blade is older than I am. It belongs to the League of Twelve. I was told it can kill demons, even angels."

"Hmm, I suppose the league would want it back then." He did not intend to return it.

"If they managed to lose it, maybe I should be the one to keep it. Maybe they don't deserve such power if they can't even…"

Madeline shouted, "Marcus! Have you ever come across a demon? Because I have! They are not something you want to toy with. Bury it, throw it in the lake, I don't care what you do with it, just get it out of my house."

She told him that if word were to reach a demon that he had a knife that could kill them, no one he knew or loved would be safe.

Marcus' cell phone rang and brought him back to the present. He looked at the display and saw his son's name. "Kyle, this is a pleasant surprise."

"I know what I said, but I also know you are the only family I have. I think we should talk."

Even with Jayde beside him on the sofa, his hand in hers, Kyle found the conversation with his father to be more difficult than he was prepared for.

This woman had accepted him, as is. She talked with him, yelled at him, but in the end, she stayed beside him. Marcus had always seemed to do his best to be away from him. Things were now so much clearer than they had been.

"I am so glad to hear you say this, Kyle. My schedule is wide open. When do you want to meet? We can dine at my favourite restaurant, The Rogue Bistro. They have a table they keep reserved for me. We could go now, if you'd like."

Kyle had taken Jayde to The Rogue Bistro the night she found out that he was part geist. He didn't want any part of his time with Jayde to be associated with his father and this information left a bitter taste in his mouth.

"So I guess you're back you're back in town. What about your place?"

"I just got back and thought that you would like to have my penthouse to yourself, so I've opted to stay at another one of my properties and oversee some renovations. Now is not really a good time to entertain."

Kyle shook his head. "Fine. What about Solar Flair? I was there with Logan recently. Do you remember Logan?"

Marcus tried to remember, but he had no idea who Kyle's friends were when he was young. "Ah, yes, Logan. Is he visiting?"

He hoped his interest in his son's friend would gain him favour.

"He's here for good. I told him I was going to open a dojo here and offered him a job."

Marcus remembered that Madeline had insisted Kyle learn martials arts for self-defense, just in case the league didn't honour their pact with peaceful geist.

"So, Solar Flair? I can be there in an hour."

Marcus knew that Ganga recruited geist for him from Solar Flair. He preferred to stay far away from that bar. "Oh, but Kyle, have you been to The Rogue Bistro? The food is exquisite!"

"I'm not the fancy food type. What about the little diner near your old place?"

Marcus grimaced. "That sounds delightful. You don't mind if I bring a few friends, do you? Just in case someone from the league finds it necessary to interrupt our father/son time."

Kyle closed his eyes. "Bring whoever you want."

"I will see you there in one hour."

Kyle ended the call and shook his head. "I need to phone John."

He rubbed his face. "How can my father act like everything's fine? He sent me to the league, knowing they can tell I'm part geist, and then his flunkies nearly killed me. I feel dirty just knowing he and I share blood!"

"John can wait." Jayde got up and straddled his lap. "Let's try to clean you up a bit."

She assaulted his mouth with hers.

Kyle stood and Jayde's legs wrapped around him as he brought her to the backroom. He laid her on the work table and stared into her piercing green eyes. "Why me? Why do you still want me knowing everything you do about me?"

Jayde sat up and took Kyle's hands in hers. "I've always been strong. I've always had a hot temper and for as long as I can remember, if I think something, it usually ends up finding its way out of my mouth. You didn't run. That makes you special."

Without another word, Kyle kissed her. As Jayde reached to unbutton Kyle's pants, the bell on the front door rang.

Maeve had been out for a walk and strolled past Jayded Ink. She could sense magick coming from the shop and decided an impromptu visit was in order.

Jayde buried her face in Kyle's shoulder and moaned. She stood and fixed her hair, which Kyle had been running his fingers through moments before.

"Give me a minute," Jayde shouted to the person who had entered the shop.

"Take your time, I'll just look around," Maeve replied.

Kyle kissed Jayde. "We are not done."

"Don't I know it!" She smacked his backside before she headed to the front to deal with the woman who had interrupted what would have been amazing sex.

"What can I help you with?"

"I was passing by and saw the designs on your wall. I have been wanting a tattoo but could never seem to find one that would suit me." Maeve had actually never thought of getting a tattoo but needed to spend more time in the shop to figure out where the magick she sensed came from.

"You don't have to choose an image that's been done before, you can make your own or we can design one together."

"I did not know that!" As she moved around the shop, Maeve could feel the magick follow her. She then realized it came from the woman who walked beside her.

"I'll have to come back with an image. I own a tea shop not far from here. Crimson Spark. Do you know it?"

"Sure. I've passed by your place quite a few times." She wrinkled her nose. "I'm not much of a tea drinker, so I've never stopped in."

Maeve felt the strongest magick near the workstation. She wondered if this woman dabbled in witchcraft. "My name is Maeve Zorida." She extended her hand and hoped to gain further understanding of the magick she sensed through physical contact.

She accepted Maeve's hand. "Jayde."

Maeve sensed no more than she had already felt.

"Thank you. You have given me quite a bit to think about."

"No problem." She handed Maeve one of her business cards.

"If you decide you would like to have something done today, just call and I'll see what I can do. I've got a few hours between appointments this afternoon where I could squeeze you in. She followed Maeve to the front door and hung a sign, *Back In 15 Minutes.*

"It was nice to meet you Jayde, and I am certain I will be back soon."

She held up Jayde's business card. "I will check my schedule, once I'm back in my shop and see when I can make it back."

"Thanks. I look forward to hearing from you." She hoped Maeve would hurry up and get out of her shop.

With Maeve gone, Jayde locked the door and quickly made her way to the backroom where she found Kyle asleep in a chair.

She walked to him with purpose. "Oh, no."

She woke him as she kissed his neck. He responded quickly and lifted her to once again place her on the table. No words were exchanged as they undressed each other.

~~~~

Marcus stood just inside the front door of Crimson Spark as Maeve appeared from the backroom. She looked around wide-eyed, saw one customer with her mother, and quickly walked toward Marcus.

"Why are you here?"

"I need your services. Shall we go to your workshop? Or shall I let you know what I need right here?"

Maeve grabbed Marcus' arm and led him to the backroom. "What do you want?"

He removed the amulet from around his neck. "I want this spelled to protect me from demonic possession. You can do such a thing, can't you, Maeve?"

She sneered. Until she had read Cerra's grimoire, Maeve was not aware that such a spell existed. With the help of the Eyrasine enchantress, Cerra had created a spell that would protect her as she helped entomb Asmodeus. This spell, however, had to be performed again on every new moon to maintain the enchantment.

"Bring it here."

Once all of the ingredients were ready, she walked to Marcus and held a small bowl and a knife. "I'll need a few drops of your blood."

Marcus took the knife from her and cut the palm of his hand. His blood dripped into the bowl as he stared into her eyes.

"Come back in thirty minutes and your amulet will be ready."

"No, Maeve. I will stay right here while you perform your witchery. That amulet is far too precious to me to let it out of my sight."

"Sit and get comfortable then. This is not a quick spell. Do not speak so much as a single word or I will need to start the ritual over." She walked to the door that led into the shop and shut it as she looked at her mother. She locked the door and walked back to her work table to begin.

Marcus watched her as she removed her clothing and put on a long, red, hooded robe.

She lit some sage and waved it around herself as she chanted words of protection.

He was fascinated at the complexity of witchcraft. He had always assumed that a witch was born with the innate ability of magick, much like every Eyrasine was born with an innate ability that was only realized by members of The League of Twelve.

As he watched Maeve, however, he discerned that she must have studied for many years to be able to perform such feats of mysticism. He grew impatient.

"Did you know that your amulet has been spelled before?"

"Yes. I assume this will cover your services for today?" He threw five hundred dollars on her work table.

"It will." She quickly picked up the money before Marcus changed his mind.

"Your amulet will protect you now until the next new moon. You will need to have your amulet spelled on every following new moon to maintain the enchantment." She handed him his amulet.

Marcus narrowed his eyes and stared silently at Maeve. He walked toward her as she backed toward the rear door. She did not want him to walk through the store because she knew her mother would sense the blood magick in his amulet.

"It seems that we were destined to work together, Maeve. I will return on the day of every new moon until my association with Asmodeus has ended. I expect you to make yourself available to me as necessary to renew this enchantment."

Maeve backed into the rear door, then opened it.

Marcus smiled. "I look forward to working with you again."

She smiled sarcastically at him and shut the door, once he was through it. She didn't trust Marcus and didn't know what to expect from Asmodeus, and so she knew she had to do whatever was necessary to protect herself. She quickly walked back to her work table to prepare more of the ingredients, so that she could spell her own amulet.

"Damn ass of a man!"

Maeve removed her robe and put her clothes back on. She wanted to get her own amulet spelled and her bags packed, so that she could leave town the moment she was through with Marcus.

After she prepared the ingredients for her spell, she selected a picture of a circle interlaced triquetra, the symbol of her coven, to have tattooed on the upper portion of her back. She wanted to find out more about the magick in the tattoo shop and decided there was no better way than to get a tattoo herself.

She gathered her purse and coat and walked the few blocks back to Jayded Ink. Inside, she handed Jayde the picture she wanted.

"That shouldn't take more than forty five minutes to an hour." Jayde took the photo to the backroom. There, she copied it onto a template.

"For something this size, the cost will be three hundred dollars after taxes, cash up front."

Maeve handed Jayde three hundred and twenty dollars and waved her hand. "Keep the change. Is the cost the same regardless of ink colour? If so, I would like to have my tattoo etched in crimson red."

"Same price, no matter what colour. Where were you thinking of having it done?"

"The upper portion of my back, between my shoulder blades."

"Would you prefer to lie down or sit up while I work?"

"I think I'll sit."

"Alright. Jayde placed the portable room divider in front of one of her work stations. "Just have a seat behind the divider. There are gowns in the top drawer of the white stand. Take your shirt off and put one of those on if you'd like. I'll be right back with the red ink."

Maeve walked through the shop and tried to sense the magick she felt earlier. She couldn't sense anything.

After she returned to the workstation, she removed her shirt and opted to forego the gown. She didn't feel anything until Jayde had returned and sat behind her to begin. Unable to sense the same potency of magick she had earlier, Maeve wondered where the magick originated.

The time passed fairly quickly as Maeve and Jayde discussed various topics, from Crimson Spark and the teas they sell, to the photos of tattoos on the walls inside Jayded Ink.

Once she had finished, Jayde reached for the clear covering and medical tape. "Just need to cover this and we are done."

She handed Maeve an information sheet. "Everything you need to know to protect the tattoo while your skin heals is on this sheet. You have a one month guarantee. If you're not happy for any reason, I will change anything within reason on your ink free of charge. After one month, the cost is yours."

She handed Maeve a hand-held mirror and positioned her in front of a long mirror, so she could see her tattoo.

"This is better than I imagined it would be!"

"Glad you like it. I aim to please."

Jayde stapled her business card to Maeve's receipt. "If you find you want any more ink, give me a call and we can set up an appointment. The shop hours are on the back of my card."

Once Maeve was gone, Jayde phoned Kyle. "Hey, are you planning on coming back to the shop anytime soon?"

"I was just about to phone you."

"Then get your sweet ass back here and we can continue the conversation we started earlier."

Kyle smiled. "I'll be there in ten minutes."

~~~~~

Kyle approached Jayded Ink and saw the sign, *Back In 30 Minutes*. He smiled and walked in. "Jayde?"

"Backroom! Lock the door."

He walked to the backroom with his cell phone in his hand. "I need to phone John first. I talked with my..." He fell silent as he saw Jayde wrapped in nothing but a white sheet.

"John can wait." She stood and the sheet fell to the floor.

Kyle had never seen a woman as amazing as Jayde. She was talented, gorgeous, her body was everything any man could ever want, and she was his.

He moved to her and they came together. He laid her on the couch and removed his shirt as she removed his belt. Kyle was certain his future was with Jayde.

~~~~~

Kyle walked to the front door of the shop to remove the sign from the door. "John asked me to find out where my father is but as usual, everything about him is difficult. He wouldn't tell me where he was staying and he didn't show when we were supposed to meet. John and Conor showed up for nothing."

"You are not your father. You have to quit beating yourself up over things he's done."

He walked to her and kissed her deeply. "How did this happen? It's like I walked into a movie of someone else's life. Things like this don't happen to me."

She wrapped her arms around his neck. "Get used to it. My life isn't exactly normal, as you've seen. The league and everything that's been happening lately, needing tattoos to protect us from geist...present company excepted."

Her smile was playful.

Kyle put his arms around Jayde and pulled her close. "You're the only non-geist person I've ever dated and been comfortable with just being myself. As long as you'll have me, I'm yours."

21 – TRIBULATION AND TRIUMPH

Oriax parked his vehicle across the street from Al-Jawhara a few minutes before the Cairo jewelry store was due to close, and watched. The only people inside were Mariam and an older man and he knew that once they were gone, the store would be vacant. He was glad that the temperature went down with the sun, as he had not acclimated to the warmer temperatures in Cairo.

Marcus had texted him a picture of the artifact that Amber had taken from the London antique store, and he had noted its brother's location on a few of his previous visits. A stone statue in a jewelry shop was rather conspicuous.

Omar Chahine turned off the lights and locked up before he and his daughter left.

Oriax waited ten minutes to be certain no one would interrupt him before he reached down and picked up a crowbar from the floor of his van. He walked to the back entrance of the store, scanned his surroundings, then picked the lock. Once the door was open, he knew he didn't have much time to take the artifact before the alarm would sound.

With his face concealed by a scarf, he headed straight for the artifact in the showcase; they had never moved it. This job was much easier than Oriax had thought it would be, and much quicker than retrieving the other league member's key.

He smashed a few of the displays and took as much jewelry as he could fit in his pockets, then exited the building through the back door before the alarm sounded. Calmly he walked to his car and phoned Marcus as he slowly drove away. "I've got it."

"Excellent! Does your current host body have a passport?"

"I have been living in this body for quite a while now. I have the passport with me." He was insulted that Marcus felt it necessary to ask. He gave Marcus his host's full legal name and waited for any further instructions.

"Go straight to the airport. I will have a ticket waiting for you." Marcus ended the call. He placed his cell phone in his pocket and walked out onto the balcony of his new condo, where he had been staying since the league discovered his penthouse. It wasn't as large as his penthouse downtown, but then it was never meant to be his main living space.

He looked up at the full moon in the night sky and deeply inhaled the frigid air. His plan to eliminate everyone in the league and control the portal would soon come to fruition.

When Kyle brought two league members to meet with him at the diner, Marcus knew his son had turned against him. He hoped the geist and the witch would prove more loyal. He reached into his pocket for his cell phone and phoned Maeve.

She answered the call hesitantly. "This is Maeve."

"Prepare whatever you need to perform the spell to open the tomb. Tomorrow night we free Asmodeus. Be ready to leave as soon as I phone you."

"Where am I to meet you?" Maeve was anxious to have her business with Marcus concluded.

"Behind a shop called Jayded Ink downtown. Do you know where it is?"

Maeve realized that what she had sensed in Jayded Ink the day before had been a foreshadowing. "I know where that is, but first I need you to help me. The league cannot be able to trace any of this back to me. My coven is the only one that knows about the league's connection to Asmodeus and they know my coven played a part in his entombment."

"What would you like me to do?" Marcus' tone was condescending.

"Arrange for someone to break into Crimson Spark and take some things, break things, and toss papers about. I need to have the league believe that someone other than one of my coven could have helped you."

"I will send someone tonight. Will that suffice?"

"That will do nicely, thank you." She knew Marcus could easily kill her but she also knew that he needed her. She was the only one who could open the tomb; she had the upper hand. The minute her work with him was done, she planned to leave the country and never look back.

She picked up her grandmother's grimoire to take with her, before she locked up the shop and headed upstairs. She needed to keep Cerra's secrets safe.

~~~~

Marcus dialed Ganga's number. When she answered, Marcus heard a man's voice instead of the female one he knew. "Who is this?"

"It's me, boss. I got tired of the scrawny girl body and upgraded." Ganga flexed the muscles of his latest form, a tall, fit man.

Marcus shook his head and sighed. "Starting immediately, I want you to have three geist watching Drew Johnston, and you and two others watching Ann. Tomorrow night we release Asmodeus."

"You got it." He now had eleven geist recruited. Ganga found it difficult to recruit geist willing to help as they all knew The League of Twelve had Soul Daggers, the only weapon on Earth that could end their existence. Those he did manage to enlist were told to be in Solar Flair every day between 6:00 p.m. and 8:00 p.m. to wait for him to approach them with a job offer.

"So, what can I tell them you're paying for this job?" Ganga was curious himself.

"Tell them that they will each receive five hundred dollars for the surveillance and an additional one thousand dollars each to bring me the one they're watching, where and when I call. Alive."

Ganga's mouth opened wide in astonishment. "I wish I had five extras of myself to do this job! You sure? That's a lot of cash!"

"Yes, Ganga, I'm sure." Marcus closed his eyes and shook his head. "Get it done!"

"I'm on it." Ganga wasn't too impressed by Marcus but he did like his money, and he seemed to have a lot of it.

Before he ended their call, Marcus had one last instruction. "One more thing, have one of your geist break into Crimson Spark tonight. Tell him to take some papers and books from the back room and throw things around. I want it to look like a break in. Have them bring you what they take."

"The tea shop? I thought the witch was working with us?"

Marcus exhaled. "Just get it done! This job pays five hundred dollars as well."

"I can do that myself." Ganga was ready to take as much of Marcus' cash as he could.

"No, Ganga, I want you watching Ann. Have someone else break into the tea shop." Marcus rubbed his eyes and wondered how his intelligent, beautiful wife Madeline could have possibly been of the same species as Ganga.

Before Ganga could utter another word, Marcus ended the call.

Ganga phoned Nybbas with the offer to break into Crimson Spark. "Hey, it's Ganga. You want five hundred dollars for a quick job?"

"Ganga? I thought you were a girl! Who is this?"

"It's me moron! I traded in the florist for a bigger model. So, do you want an easy five hundred dollars, or not?"

"Five hundred? How easy?" Nybbas wanted the money but knew it was a lot for an easy job.

Ganga spoke matter-of-factly. "Break into a tea shop, steal some papers and books, and bring it all back to me. Easy in, easy out."

"When?"

"Any time tonight. It has to be done before the owners open up tomorrow morning."

"Am I supposed to take tea?"

Ganga laughed. "All Marcus said was to take some papers and books, throw things around, and leave. He doesn't care what papers or books, just a few that you can carry. If you want some tea, help yourself."

"Okay." Nybbas felt uneasy. His current form was that of a tall man with a medium build and bright orange hair. He had chosen this form as it seemed to stand out and he wanted to be unique among his geist friends.

"Is there any kind of alarm system on the place? Any cameras?" He ran his hands through his hair.

"Probably. Just wear a hat and keep your head down. Trust me. This is easy cash!" Ganga ended the call before Nybbas could change his mind.

~~~~~

Ganga phoned Marcus. "Everything is in place. The tea shop will be robbed later tonight. I have three of us watching Drew, and myself and two others watching Ann. Phen said that he would take care of Ann's bodyguard."

Marcus raised his eyebrows in surprise then furrowed them in anger. "What bodyguard? Who is Phen?"

"Uvall's replacement. This guy, he doesn't care about losing lifespan every time he mists out. He's been in and out of bodies, watching and listening to everyone I pointed out to him. He even managed to get in a few houses in mist form and they didn't see him."

Marcus growled. "Why is this the first I'm hearing about this?"

"What? All he ever told me was that the girl had a bodyguard and John's brother is hot for Conor's sister. Nothing you would be interested in. I would tell you."

"Stay on them. I will phone you when I want you to grab Ann and Drew. If Phen gives you any further information, I want it relayed to me immediately."

~~~~~

Marcus awoke the next morning to a phone call from Maeve. She informed him that her store was trashed beyond recognition.

She was livid. "Your man ruined my entire store! The spells that were taken cannot be replaced and I want them back! You can keep the damn tea!"

"You asked for a break in and gave no instructions as to what was to be taken or destroyed. I will have someone meet you behind The Rogue Bistro in an hour to return your property. Keep your phone with you today. I expect you to be ready at a moment's notice."

Maeve looked around her shop, glad in the knowledge that she would soon be free of Marcus. "When we are through tonight, I expect the rest of my payment."

"You will have it as long as you fulfill your part of our bargain."

Maeve snapped. "I'll be ready when you call." She phoned the police to report the break in and while she waited for them to arrive, she cast a spell of anonymity on the cloak she would wear later that night.

Marcus knew he needed this witch but he also knew he could not trust her. He phoned Ganga. He did not want to leave anything to chance. "Have your friend that broke into the tea shop meet the owner behind The Rogue Bistro in one hour to return her goods. After their meeting, I want him to follow her discreetly and watch her. If the witch goes anywhere, I want to know."

As Ganga agreed to Marcus' latest demand, their conversation was cut short by a call from Oriax.

Marcus terminated the call with Ganga and answered Oriax. "Yes?"

Oriax said, "My plane just landed. I can be in Niagara Falls in about two hours."

"Call me as soon as you arrive in Niagara Falls."

With Oriax on his way, Marcus phoned Ganga again to continue their conversation. "Do you have everyone in place?"

"Yes. I have three pairs of eyes on Ann and three on her brother." Ganga was pleased with himself.

"If you lose sight of either one of them, phone me immediately. Get them to me alive and on time tonight and you will be handsomely rewarded."

Ganga pulled the phone away from his ear, surprised at how much money Marcus was throwing around. "They'll be there. I'll make sure of it."

As soon as his call with Marcus was done, Ganga phoned Eligor, one of the geist he had arranged to watch Drew. He wanted to be certain that he and the other geist knew that neither Ann, nor her brother, was to be killed.

~~~~~

Transcendence was alive with people. Vivian looked at her two children as they finished their meals. She rested her elbow on the bar and smiled. "It's so rare to have both of you here at the same time."

Ann and Drew were always close growing up but when Ann entered university ahead of her brother, their lives took different directions.

Drew placed both hands on top of the bar on either side of his plate. "Well, I hate to break up the happy, but I need to get home. I am somewhat drained. A woman came into the office today, yelling at me about her husband cheating on her. She wasn't happy when I told her that I was not a family lawyer, but if she wanted to incorporate, I'd be happy to help her."

Ann laughed. "Did she hit you?"

Drew popped the last bit of his meal into his mouth. "I didn't wait around to give her the chance. I brought her to Gary Caoilin. I'm expecting to find a nasty note on my desk tomorrow morning."

Vivian and Ann both laughed. Drew rounded the bar and kissed his mother. "Thanks for the meal, Mom."

"Wait! Let me give you something for lunch tomorrow." Vivian disappeared into the kitchen and within a few minutes, returned with a large bag filled with a variety of food that she had prepared for her son.

He took the bag from his mother with a look of astonishment on his face. "How much do you think I eat for lunch?"

"Just take it. I like to know my children are eating something besides chips and burgers."

"Alright." Drew knew it was pointless to argue with his mother. "I'll see you both later."

~~~~

Just before Drew reached his building's entrance, he realized he had left the food in his car and headed back to retrieve it. The freezing temperatures over the last few days had covered the parking lot with ice and Drew slipped on the light snow that covered it. He grumbled as he carefully made his way to his car. "It would be nice if they could clear this lot once in a while."

The three newest geist recruits, Eligor, Sallos, and Ravon, had followed Drew home from Transcendence. Eligor drove their vehicle into the apartment's lot and parked right beside Drew's car. He soaked a cloth in chloroform, as each of the geist exited the vehicle and walked toward Drew. He moved closer to Drew, looked down and purposely bumped into him. "Sorry, man."

"No worries." Drew thought nothing of the encounter and continued to his car.

Eligor quickly turned around and was able to subdue Drew from behind with the cloth held over his nose and mouth.

Sallos and Ravon took position on either side of Drew and helped Eligor to restrain him as the chloroform took effect.

Drew had little time to realize what had happened before he lost consciousness.

After they tossed Drew in the trunk of their car, they bound his hands and feet before they closed it and drove to Jayded Ink.

Eligor turned to Sallos. "Let Ganga know we got him. Tell him we're on our way to the tattoo shop."

~~~~

Ganga smiled when he received the call. He phoned Marcus. "We've got the brother. I'm just waiting for the girl to leave. I'll phone you again once we have her."

"Ganga, you are certainly proving your worth tonight! I will be waiting." As so many things fell into place so easily, Marcus smiled. He believed that the universe was working in his favour.

Ganga turned to Calob and Botis, his two accomplices, and pointed to Ann's Porsche. "That's her car. We follow her when she leaves and wait for Phen's call. Got it?"

Both geist nodded.

Ganga hadn't selected these two for their intellect, but for the strong bodies they had chosen to replicate. In spite of being a petite woman, Ann was strong and agile, and would surely put up a good fight.

Calob nudged Botis. "Here she comes."

They watched as she loaded her car with a box full of food.

Vivian came out of the restaurant with a bottle of wine. "Wait! This one will go well with that roast."

"Thanks, Mom." Ann smiled and kissed her mother.

As she drove, she pressed the phone button in her car. "Call Sebastian."

Sebastian answered, his voice low and deep. "Ann. I was just thinking about you."

"Hey, why don't you come by my place in a couple hours? I'm just leaving the restaurant and I have everything I need to make you a meal you won't soon forget."

Sebastian got up from his couch and headed to the front door. He picked up his jacket on the way. "I can be there in five minutes."

Ann laughed. "I need a couple of hours to get everything ready."

Sebastian grunted. "Alright. Two hours."

Ann whispered seductively. "Bye, Seb."

She drove home. "Just you wait, Mr. Shea. Just you wait."

~~~~

Ann entered her condo and placed the box of food on her kitchen table. She moved to her living room and turned on the stereo.

After she prepared the meal and placed the roast in the oven, she decided that a quick shower was in order. She headed to her bedroom where she stripped down to her undergarments before she selected a black spaghetti strap tank top and low rise yoga pants to wear after her shower.

She placed the clothes on the bathroom counter before she entered the shower. Her eyes closed as the warm water flowed over her body. She thought about Sebastian. He made her happier than she ever thought any man could. The fact that he was hers made it seem more like a dream than reality.

~~~~

After they watched Ann enter the underground parking lot, the three geist waited in the cold shadows nearly twenty minutes before they were able to enter the building.

Ganga's phone rang. "What?"

Phen closed the lid on the steel trash bin behind the apartment. "The bodyguard is gone."

Ganga smiled and turned to Calob and Botis. "Follow me."

The geist entered behind a blonde woman on her phone.

Ganga held the door open and instructed Botis to find Ann's unit number. "The name is Johnston."

Botis, the larger of the two, looked at the directory listing. "Unit 1004."

They waited for the elevator and rode it to the ninth floor. From there, they climbed the stairs to the tenth floor, scanned the hallway through the landing's window and found it empty.

Ganga opened the door and the three geist headed to Ann's unit. They listened at Ann's door and heard loud music.

Ganga looked down the hall. "Pick the lock, Calob."

It took Calob under five seconds to get Ann's door unlocked. He turned the handle and smiled; the door chain was not latched.

~~~~

With the noise of the blow dryer, the music, and her own singing, Ann didn't notice that three geist had entered her condo. As she flipped her hair to one side, she saw Ganga's reflection in the mirror. She was unaware that two more geist stood just outside the bathroom door.

She continued to sing as she gripped her blow dryer tighter to use as a weapon.

The moment she stepped out of the bathroom, Calob grabbed her arm and quickly threw her to the floor.

From the bedroom, Ganga heard the commotion, changed direction and walked toward them.

Ann quickly got to her feet and turned to face her attackers. She knew they were geist but with so many of them, her best chance to get out alive was to try to talk her way out, rather than fight. "What do you want?"

Ganga moved closer to Ann and looked her up and down. "I can see why the boss wants you. You are a pretty little package, aren't you?"

"Who are you working for?" Ann thought of Marcus.

Ganga walked away from her.

She looked between the two geist who stood in front of her and watched Ganga enter her living room and empty the contents of her purse onto the coffee table. Both her key ring and her astral key were in plain view.

"You don't need to know." Ganga searched through the items on the coffee table, picked up the keys, and placed them in his pocket as Ann watched.

She knew she had to make a decision, forfeit her astral key or forfeit her life.

The other geist turned to watch Ganga, and she saw an opportunity to get away. She ran between them and headed for the front door, only to be stopped as Ganga threw a lamp at her. It hit the top of her back and she fell forward.

Ann scrambled to her feet and ran into the foyer as Ganga lunged at her. Her head hit the wall and she fell back to the floor. She quickly jumped to her feet, turned around and stood face to face with Ganga. She punched his face. Her league ring scratched his nose and blood trailed down his cheek.

Angered, Ganga grabbed her arms, threw her back to the floor, and straddled her. He sat on her stomach, placed both hands around her throat, and squeezed.

She kicked her legs and punched at him.

Ganga turned to Calob. "Get the bottle and rag out of my pocket!"

Calob ran to him. He poured the chloroform onto the cloth and held it over Ann's mouth and nose. She struggled but the chloroform worked quickly and left her helpless before she lost consciousness.

Ganga wiped the blood from his face with the back of his hand before he bound Ann's hands and feet. He turned his head. "Botis, stay behind and find her league knife. Marcus said she has dagger with fancy markings on it. And shut that damn music off!"

Botis pulled the stereo's plug from the wall before he searched for Ann's Soul Dagger.

Ganga threw Ann over his shoulder. "Get that blanket off the couch, cover her and we'll take her down the stairs."

He could smell the food Ann had cooking. "Shut the oven off! We don't need to trigger the fire alarm. And Botis, when you're done leave the building and wait for my call."

Ganga looked at Calob and clenched his teeth. "Should I get the door?"

Calob stood confused. Then it clicked. "Oh. No, I got it."

Ganga scoffed and shook his head.

The two geist walked quickly to the stairwell and hurried down to the main floor. They exited through the back door that led to the parking lot. The cold, dark night kept the parking lot void of people as Ganga and Calob placed Ann's body in the trunk of their car and drove away.

On the way to Jayded Ink, Ganga phoned Marcus. "We have the girl and we're heading to the tattoo shop now."

Marcus was pleased. "I will meet you there."

He phoned Maeve. "Go to the back door of Jayded Ink now. It's time."

"I'll be there shortly." Maeve grabbed her dagger and the unsealing spell and placed them in her satchel. She donned her cloak and left the tea shop, unaware that she was being watched.

The light dusting of snow on the ground served to illuminate the dark night. Maeve kept her head down and the hood of her cloak up as she walked to her car. Her conscience warned her to stay away from Marcus, to renege on her deal with him, but she knew that her life would surely be forfeit should she fail to honour her part of his plan.

She got into her car and drove to Jayded Ink.

When Maeve was close to her destination, she saw three men outside of a car parked in the designated meeting area. She weighed her options and chose to remain in her car until Marcus arrived. One minute turned to ten before she finally saw Marcus.

She saw one of the men open the trunk of their vehicle, and watched as Marcus peered inside and then quickly shut it. With the hood of her cloak still pulled, Maeve grabbed her satchel, exited her car, and walked cautiously to Marcus.

As Marcus watched her approach, he couldn't see her face. "Maeve?"

"Yes, Marcus. I've concealed my face and altered my voice. I don't need anyone recognizing me and risk having the league find out that I'm helping you." Her voice was sharp. "Can we get this done now?"

"We are waiting for one more guest...and I believe she's here now." He motioned toward the vehicle that Ganga drove into the lot.

Ganga parked directly in front of the back door.

Maeve's heart raced as she watched Ganga and Calob walk to the trunk of their vehicle and remove Ann, as the other three took a man from their trunk.

"I know the woman, but who is the man?" Maeve was nervous.

"Well, Maeve, the woman is the one whose blood we need and the man is her brother. He is our insurance policy. Should the woman refuse to play nicely, her brother will be the one to suffer." Marcus' voice hinted at annoyance.

He turned toward the door. "Who has the key?"

Calob walked to the door with Ann's keys in his hand and held them out to Marcus.

"No, no." Marcus backed away from the keys. He then gestured toward the locked door. "Please."

Calob tried key after key until he found the correct one and smiled as he heard the lock disengage. He opened the door and held it as Marcus entered first.

Marcus switched on the lights just inside the door and glanced around the room to confirm that there were no security cameras. Kyle had mentioned that he didn't see any, but Marcus was no longer certain he could trust his son. Satisfied, he walked to the storage closet and opened the door. He saw the door that would lead him to the tunnels, the same door he had been through many times in his youth.

Calob and Ganga then entered through the backdoor and dropped Ann onto the cold, tiled floor.

Eligor, Sallos, and Ravon followed suit and dropped Drew next to his sister.

Maeve came in last. She watched silently.

Marcus demanded, "Who has the astral key?"

Calob stepped forward. His facial expression was blank as he held up the Taurus key. "This?"

"Yes. That." Marcus cast his eyes upwards. "Now wake her up. I want her conscious for this next part."

Ganga slapped Ann's face, but she remained motionless. He slapped her again, and she slowly opened her eyes.

When she realized that both her wrists and feet were bound, she glared up at the geist who stood over her. She turned her head and saw her brother next to her, unconscious, with his hands and feet tied as well. Marcus stood beside him.

Ann looked at her brother. "Drew!"

She turned her attention to Marcus and growled. "Let him go!"

Marcus walked toward her. "Ah, but you see Ann, he is the reason that I know you will help me."

He reached down, pulled Ann to her feet, and held her tightly from behind. He whispered in her ear, "Now, I need you to hold your key and unlock this door for me."

"I would rather die than help you!"

"Such a noble sacrifice."

Marcus moved his hands to Ann's waist, picked her up, and placed her in front of Ganga. "Hold her."

Ganga complied.

Marcus then walked to Drew, a knife in his hand. "However, would you sacrifice your brother's life?"

Ann watched Marcus crouch down beside her brother, open his jacket, and place the tip of his blade on Drew's chest. As he slowly pulled the blade downward, the knife sliced through his shirt and penetrated deep into his skin.

Drew awoke screaming.

Ann struggled in Ganga's grip and he threw her to the floor. "Stop! I'll do whatever you want, just leave him alone!"

Drew frantically looked around the room and saw Ann on the floor not far from him.

He snarled. "Don't give them what they want, Ann. They're going to kill us anyway."

Marcus looked at Ganga. "Get her up!"

He pointed at Drew. "Calob, keep him quiet!"

Calob took a cloth from the shelf, placed it inside Drew's mouth, and tied it around his head.

Marcus then took Ann's astral key from Calob and placed it in her bound hands before he dragged her to the door.

When she tried to resist, he slammed her head into the doorframe. "Open the door!"

He grabbed her hand and forced her key into the lock. With years of experience watching his father unlock the door, he expertly inserted the key, turned it to Ann's Taurus sigil and aligned it.

Ganga watched with a smile on his lips.

Ann thought of resisting, but knew Marcus would not hesitate to kill her brother. Her thoughts then turned to Sebastian. The dream evening she had planned had turned into a surreal nightmare. She wondered if Sebastian had been to her apartment yet and had started searching for her.

~~~~

Still inside Ann's apartment, Botis walked to the kitchen and turned off the stove. The smell of the roast cooking was too much for him to resist and decided he would help himself to her supper. He took it out of the oven and placed it on the kitchen table, before he walked to the fridge and got himself a beer to enjoy with the meal she had intended for Sebastian.

With his belly full, he walked through the apartment to find the folding knife.

In the bedroom, he kicked the clothes on her floor and felt something hard connect with his foot. He reached down and pulled her Soul Dagger out of a pocket in her pants. "This must be it."

He put the dagger in his pocket and left the bedroom, unaware that Sebastian had just exited the elevator and approached Ann's apartment. As he opened the door to leave, he came face to face with Sebastian.

Sebastian expected to see Ann, so the sight of a geist standing in her doorway took him by surprise.

Botis tried to close the door quickly, but Sebastian brought his hands up and kept it from shutting. They both pushed against the door in a battle of strength and determination.

Sebastian then rammed his shoulder against the door and knocked Botis off balance.

As he backed away from Sebastian, he reached in his pocket and removed the Soul Dagger he had picked up.

Sebastian moved to punch him, then the dagger in his hand. He unsheathed his own Soul Dagger as Botis threw Ann's blade at him.

The blade missed Sebastian by mere inches.

Botis backed away from him and ran to the kitchen. He picked up the knife he had used for his meal and ran to the far side of the kitchen island.

Sebastian was incensed. "Where is she? What did you do with Ann?"

"I don't know any Ann."

He threw the knife in his hand at Sebastian. Furiously, he pulled knife after knife out of the wooden knife block and threw each of them at Sebastian.

Sebastian managed to dodge a few knives and raised his arms to block others. One made contact and cut his forearm.

Botis picked up one of the barstools and threw it at Sebastian. This gave him enough time to run to the balcony and throw himself over the rail. He knew that his essence would survive the fall, even though his replicated body would not.

Sebastian screamed in anger. His next thought was of Ann.

"Ann! Ann!" Sebastian ran through the apartment looking for her. He phoned John as he searched for a towel to wrap around his bloodied arm, which had already begun to heal.

John answered on the second ring. "Seb, I was just on the phone with..."

"John! Ann's gone!" Sebastian paced the room, panicked.

"What do you mean she's gone?"

"I showed up at her apartment and a geist opened her door. He had her Soul Dagger and she's not here. I just talked to her two hours ago. She was waiting for me."

"Maybe she got out. Is her phone still there? Did you try phoning her?"

"Her apartment is a mess. Her cell phone is on the coffee table. Someone took her!"

"I'll phone Ange, maybe she's heard from her. Seb, you call Kayla." He had an uneasy feeling deep in his gut as Mariam had also just informed him that the jewelry store had been broken into.

"Why would she leave without her phone? John, something happened."

"Just phone Kayla. I'll phone you back after I've talked with Ange." He ended the call with Sebastian and quickly dialed Angeline.

"Hello, John. Aidan and I are currently on our way to...well, that's really not your concern, now is it?" Angeline laughed.

John began to feel nearly as concerned as Sebastian. "Ange, have you heard from Ann?"

"No." Her stomach knotted at the tone of John's voice. "The last time I spoke with her, she said she was working tonight in the restaurant and then having Seb go to her place for supper."

"Seb is at her apartment now. He said there was a geist there and Ann's gone. Her phone is still there, but she's missing."

Angeline touched Aidan's arm to get his attention, fear in her eyes. "Ann's missing? Have you spoken with Drew? Has he seen her?"

"Ann's missing? I'll phone Drew," Aidan offered.

"I haven't talked with Drew and I don't want to call Aunt Viv yet, not until we know something." His uneasy feeling had turned to a fearful worry.

Aidan now shared their concern, as the call to Drew went straight to voicemail. "Angeline, he didn't answer."

"We're about twenty minutes' drive away from Wells' but we're coming to North America. Where are you, John?"

"I'm at the clinic. I'll meet you at Jayded Ink." He hurried out of the dental clinic toward the stairs.

"I'll have Aidan try to connect with her on our way. John, she could be anywhere. If Marcus has done anything to her…"

She paused and closed her eyes for a moment to regain her composure. "I'll let you know when Aidan finds her."

22 – ASMODEUS

Marcus grinned when the door that led to the tunnels opened. He led the way, while the others followed, dragging Ann and Drew. Maeve kept a few paces behind.

Calob looked up at the light crystals in the ceiling that illuminated as they walked. He looked at Ravon, who simply shrugged. When they had first come through the tunnels in mist form, their essence hadn't been enough to trigger the crystals to brighten the passageway.

Marcus turned around, reached down, grabbed Ann's hair and pulled her head back. "Which one?"

Ann spat in his face.

Marcus stared into her eyes. "Slice his throat."

Ravon pulled Drew to his knees and held a knife to his throat. The blade began to pierce Drew's skin, and he winced in pain as blood dripped down his neck.

Ann screamed, "Stop!"

"Which tunnel?"

Ann sighed and closed her eyes. "It's the second tunnel on the left." She hung her head, knowing that she had to help Marcus or watch her brother die.

Marcus walked toward the Taurus/Scorpio tunnel, dragging Ann behind him.

She reached up, her wrists still bound, and held her hair, hoping to reduce the pain. "How far down?"

Ann hissed. "About fifteen feet in, there's a mark on the left wall above the tomb entrance."

Marcus spotted the sigil on the wall. "Bring the brother!"

Ravon and Calob took hold of Drew's feet and dragged him toward Marcus.

Drew twisted and tried to kick at the two geist holding his feet.

Calob sneered. "Enough!" He kicked Drew's side.

Maeve stayed back. She wanted to keep everyone in sight.

She had read about these tunnels many times in her grandmother's grimoire, but had never seen them herself. She looked behind her, curious as to where the other tunnels might lead.

Marcus looked at Maeve, raised both eyebrows, and gestured toward the wall.

Maeve walked to the wall. She cut into her palm and traced the sigil with her blood. With her palms held outward toward the wall, she chanted her spell.

She repeated the final phrase three times. "Lift the veil, reveal to me, that which I cannot see."

When she had finished, she lowered her arms; the wall vanished and the entranceway was revealed.

The small room held nothing more than the stone tomb, inside which was Asmodeus.

Maeve looked at the top of the tomb and saw a five-point star pentagram seal carved in its centre. She placed a candle on each point, lit them in a counterclockwise sequence, and began the unsealing spell.

Marcus watched intently as Maeve chanted.

"Now I need her blood." Though no one could see her face, Maeve glanced toward Ann and felt conflicted. While she was betraying The League of Twelve, she also enjoyed the powerful energy this spell channeled.

Across the tomb, Marcus brought Ann to her feet and held her from behind. Maeve reached out and pulled Ann's hands over the centre of the pentagram.

Ann pulled back, trying to resist.

"Uh, uh, uh." Marcus tilted his head slightly. "Comply or your dear brother will pay for your obstinance."

Ann stopped struggling. Silent tears escaped her eyes and slid down her cheeks as she willingly held her hands toward Maeve.

Holding her double-edged knife in her hand, Maeve placed it between Ann's palms. She held Ann's hands together and slowly slid the blade between them. As Maeve sliced both of Ann's palms, she squeezed them, allowing her blood to drip onto the seal.

Ann screamed in agony as she watched her blood flow out of her palms and pool into the centre of the pentagram. She gasped when she saw the blood disappear into the tomb. She began to sway in Marcus' arms as more and more blood left her body.

Suddenly, she heard something in her mind and realized it was Aidan trying to reach her.

~~~~

Angeline and Aidan sped down the motorway. "Aidan, have you found Ann?" Angeline asked, her deep concern evident in her voice.

Aidan concentrated on Ann, searching for her, but couldn't make a connection. Frustrated, he exhaled loudly. "I can't. Wherever she is, she must not be awake. I've tried reaching you before while you were sleeping and I couldn't."

"Oh, Aidan! We have to find her!" Angeline feared the worst.

"We will find her, Angeline." He grabbed her hand as he continued down the motorway.

While he drove, he continued to search for Ann's mind.

He finally heard her. "Angeline! I've found her! She's alive."

Angeline let out the breath she hadn't realized she was holding. She faced Aidan and squeezed his hand. "Where is she, Aidan?"

Aidan focused his mind and spoke with Ann telepathically. *"Ann, where are you?"*

"I'm in the Taurus/Scorpio tunnel with Marcus. He's opening Asmodeus' tomb. Drew is on the floor. I don't know if he's alive. They're using my blood!"

~~~~

Marcus dropped Ann to the floor and retrieved the artifacts from his inside jacket pocket.

Maeve pointed to the centre of the tomb. "Place the artifacts inside the pentagram. They were also sealed by Cerra."

After she smeared some of Ann's blood onto the artifacts, she quietly chanted a few words and then said, "You must now break the stones to reveal the metal keys hidden inside."

Marcus exhaled loudly, and then smashed the artifacts against the side of the tomb. "Clever of them to hide these keys in stone."

"The key with the Taurus sigil is placed in the north end of the tomb and the key with the Scorpio sigil is placed in the south end."

Once Marcus had inserted and turned both keys, the tomb's seal was broken. Particles of dust scattered from the edges between the tomb and its lid.

Marcus turned to the geist waiting in the tunnel. "Remove the lid."

Eligor remained in the tunnel outside the tomb entrance and stood guard over Drew as the other four geist approached the tomb. They pushed the lid off and let it fall to the floor.

The stench that came from inside the tomb was noxious.

Ganga winced in disgust at the odour.

Marcus covered his nose and mouth with his hand and peered inside. He looked upon the frail, desiccated body of Asmodeus. "Take him!"

Sallos and Calob picked up the fragile body and carried it down the tunnel to the exit.

Marcus picked Ann up off the floor and positioned her over his shoulder. He looked at Ganga as he stepped over Drew's body. "Kill him."

Ann screamed. "No!" She tried to struggle and Marcus threw her to the ground. He reached down and smashed her head against the tomb, before he dragged her through the tunnel once again. Ann's shirt slid up her torso and her back scraped against the dirt floor, tearing her flesh.

She reached out to Aidan before she lost consciousness. *He's dragging me down the tunnel. Marcus…*

Ganga handed his knife to Ravon and huffed. "Make it quick."

Ravon walked to Drew, knelt down, and plunged the knife into the right side of his chest.

Drew screamed through his gag, then watched as Ravon walked away to join the others.

~~~~

Maeve stopped Marcus just before he entered the storage room at Jayded Ink. "There is one other thing you may wish to know."

Marcus hissed through gritted teeth. "Please, Maeve. What bit of information have you withheld?"

"Not withheld, so much as unwilling to share with those currently in our company." She glanced toward the geist.

He turned to Calob and Sallos, who carried Asmodeus to the back exit. "Wait here."

He grabbed Maeve's arm and led her away from the others.

Maeve began, "When Asmodeus was set in his tomb, Cerra had placed an object in his flesh that would ensure he remained unable to move while he rotted in his prison. Chanting an immobility spell, she pressed a pentacle in the shape of a pyramid into his flesh at the base of his neck. It bonds with whomever it pierces, regardless of their species or form. This pentacle was once part of the sword that Asmodeus wielded so long ago. It was made by the Creators Of All Things."

"The Creators?" Marcus was intrigued. "I must have this pentacle."

Marcus walked directly to Asmodeus to examine the back of his neck for the pentacle.

Not finding it, he growled. "Where is it? Where is it, witch?"

Maeve looked at Marcus with contempt. "If it is not in his neck, it must have fallen off as he shriveled in his tomb. But there is more you should know."

Marcus turned, grabbed both of Maeve's arms and shook her. "Tell me. Now!"

Maeve struggled out of Marcus' grip and glared at him before she continued. "Once the pentacle pierced Asmodeus' flesh, it rendered him paralyzed. Cerra had spelled it so that he could be easily controlled, and the spell ensured that he would be unable to free himself from his tomb. This paralysis also numbed his mind. It was written in Cerra's grimoire that this mind paralysis would prevent Asmodeus from contacting any other demons."

Marcus absorbed this information and knew that such an object would be beneficial to him should the demon prove less than cooperative.

Maeve walked away from Marcus to stand in front of the door. "We have been here long enough. If any of the league come through, I do not want to be here."

Marcus also knew that the longer they lingered, the chance that a league member would enter the tunnels increased, but he also wanted the pentacle.

"Eligor! Go back to the tomb. Look for a pentacle in the shape of a pyramid and bring it to me!" Marcus assumed that even geist mist could bond with the ancient pentacle.

Ganga took hold of Asmodeus' feet. "Calob, go with him."

He looked at Marcus. "Better to have two sets of eyes looking for it, right?"

Marcus glanced sideways at Ganga before he turned his attention to Maeve. "Is it possible that geist mist can carry this pentacle?"

"From what I read of it, it takes on the characteristics of whatever it bonds with. So yes, I believe it can."

Marcus walked toward the exit, stopped, and looked over his shoulder at Eligor and Calob. "Once we leave, you will both need to be in mist form to get out. Join us at the barn when you have the pentacle in your possession. Do not leave this tunnel without it."

Eligor and Calob looked at each other and then at Marcus, confused. "We can't carry anything while we're mist."

Maeve chimed in. "This object will stay with you while you are in mist form. First you must pierce yourself with it, make it a part of your flesh, so that your soul mist will be able to fuse with it. Then you must kill yourself immediately because it will not take long for your physical body to become paralyzed."

Marcus wondered how Maeve knew so much about this pentacle, yet had never seen it. "How can you know this?"

Maeve blinked slowly and placed a hand on her hip. Her voice was confident. "It was written in Cerra's grimoire, which is now mine. You see, my grandmother was a seer as well as a witch. When she held an object, it revealed its past to her."

"If you are lying to me, witch…"

Maeve interrupted. "I am not. You may want to inform your geist that he shouldn't take form until he is with you at your barn, otherwise his new body will become paralyzed as it is forming. You wouldn't want someone else to find the pentacle, now would you?"

As the two geist headed down the tunnel to search for the pentacle, Marcus pulled Ann to her feet and smacked her face to rouse her.

When she opened her eyes, he put her astral key in her bleeding hands one last time to open the door that led into Jayded Ink.

Ann howled in agony as Marcus pushed her key into the open wounds on her palms to open the door, and again when he withdrew it, before he let her fall to the floor.

Marcus stood in the doorway, keeping it open as Ganga and Sallos carried Asmodeus through it. He then turned to Ravon and wiped Ann's blood from her key onto his shirt. "You get the honour of being the first to replicate a member of the league, Ravon."

Marcus removed the knife that he had in his back pocket and plunged it into Ravon's heart.

Ravon groaned and fell to the floor. His essence escaped the replicated body he had been inhabiting, and he tried to steal Ann's DNA. Uncertain as to why he was unsuccessful, Ravon tried again. Still unable to replicate her, Ravon moved to Maeve and took some of her DNA.

Ravon's soul mist began to take form. The grey mist changed from a translucent haze to an opaque fog. The fog thickened further as it began forming a replicant of Maeve's body, finishing in only a few minutes.

"I couldn't do it!" Ravon exclaimed, once his shape had formed. "I couldn't take her DNA!"

"How is that possible?" Marcus reached down and cleaned his knife using the shirt on Ravon's former body. He looked at the replica of Maeve, unclothed in front of him. "Cover yourself!"

"You must also cover your face as we leave." Maeve ordered. "You are wearing my body!"

Once Ravon had removed his former host's clothing and put them on his new body, Marcus pointed at the form on the floor. "Take this replicant shell out of here and throw it in the car!"

Ravon looked from his previous body to Marcus. "I think I'm going to need help moving my old form wearing the witch's body."

"I'll grab its feet. We need to leave," Maeve spat. She was anxious to put this evening behind her.

Marcus rubbed his eyes. "Just get him in one of the cars."

Ravon pulled his hood up, concealing most of his new face.

Knowing that Ann's mother was also a viable Taurus DNA donor should he require it, Marcus saw no need to keep Ann alive. He walked to Ann and placed her astral key in his pocket. He knelt down and slowly pierced her side with his blade.

As she gasped, he whispered, "Thank you, Ann. You played your part perfectly."

He stood up and looked at Ann's torn and bleeding body. He smirked and turned to walk through the door into the storage closet, knowing that he was yet another step closer to his goal of controlling the portal.

Marcus quickly made his way to the exit. "You all know where to go." Without turning around, he walked through the door into the cold night. "I was clearly the superior choice for Cancer league member and now their mistake will cost them everything."

~~~~

"We're coming for you, Ann. Stay with me."

"Aidan, he's dragging me down the tunnel. Marcus..."

He lost the connection with Ann as she lost consciousness.

Aidan pressed down hard on his gas pedal. "She's hurt but she is alive. She said Drew is lying on the floor and she doesn't know whether or not he is alive."

He didn't mention that his connection to Ann had ended abruptly.

"We need Conor." Angeline reached in her purse for her phone.

"There's more. Marcus has opened Asmodeus' tomb. Ann is in the tunnels with him right now."

Angeline pleaded, "Hurry, Aidan!"

Conor answered his cell phone after seeing Angeline's name on the display. "Hey, Ange, what can I do for you?"

"Conor! Get to Jayded Ink now! Ann and Drew are hurt. Marcus is there. Aidan and I are on our way! Hurry!"

"Angeline? What are you talking about? Ann and Drew are hurt?" Conor could hear the panic in her voice.

"Marcus has her. She's in the North American tunnels with him. She said Drew is there as well and she doesn't know whether or not he's alive. Please, Conor, hurry!"

"I'm at Transcendent. I can be at the Wells' gateway shortly." He left the restaurant and ran to Wells' Antiquities.

Angeline phoned John. "Aidan connected with Ann. She's alive. She's in the tunnels. John, Marcus has her. She said he was opening Asmodeus' tomb."

John hung his head. "I'll let Seb know."

The immensity of the situation found its way to his fist and he punched the wall inside the stairwell. He quickly dialed Sebastian's number as he exited the stairwell, ran out the back door to his car, and composed himself.

Sebastian answered immediately. "Did you find her, John? Kayla isn't answering."

"Seb, Aidan was able to reach Ann. She's in the tunnels with Marcus. Seb...he opened Asmodeus' tomb."

Sebastian ran out of Ann's apartment and down the stairwell. His first thought was of Ann, hoping beyond all hope that she was alright. His next thought, however, was of Marcus. Since the day Marcus killed his family, Sebastian knew that he would be the one to end his life. He had come close not long ago and knew that the next time he encountered him, he would make certain that Marcus suffered immeasurable agony before he begged him to end his life.

~~~~

Sebastian pulled into the parking lot behind Jayded Ink and saw John's car. He ran to the back door and fumbled with the lock as he hurriedly tried to get inside. He pushed the door open and charged straight for the door that led to the tunnels.

His hands were shaking as he inserted his astral key. Knowing Ann was on the other side, the simple action of opening the tunnel door, something he had done so many times, seemed to take an eternity. He impatiently waited for the door to slide down and saw John on the floor next to Ann, trying to revive her.

He fell to his knees beside her, terrified. There was so much blood.

John leaned back on his knees. "She's alive, but I can't get her to open her eyes."

Sebastian picked Ann up, held her tightly, and rocked her back and forth in his arms. "Please wake up. Ann, please wake up."

His mind drifted to his mother; he had pleaded for her to wake up as well. He was not going to let Ann die.

Conor, Angeline, and Aidan arrived from the City of Radiance and rushed to their friends.

Looking up, Sebastian cried, "I can't heal her, Conor! I can't wake her up!"

Conor knelt down beside Ann and checked for a pulse. "She's alive, but her pulse is weak."

"Where is Marcus?" Angeline asked.

John rose quickly, his eyes wide open, and said, "The other tunnels. They could be hiding at the end of any of the tunnels. We need to check them."

Angeline asked, "Asmodeus? Is he…"

"Check the other tunnels!" John shouted, he rushed down the Taurus/Scorpio tunnel.

Conor placed his hands on Ann's head and her wounded side, and began to heal her. His energy drained quickly but she slowly began to open her eyes.

Ann blinked a few times to focus on the face in front of her. As the haze of unconsciousness faded from her eyes, she saw Conor.

"Drew is in the Taurus/Scorpio tunnel. He's in bad shape. I'll be alright, go to him." Her voice was weak and her breathing was shallow.

Sebastian pleaded. "Ann, take my healing."

"Seb…" Ann's voice was faint and she tried without success to absorb his self-healing energy before she lost consciousness again.

Angeline emerged from the Leo/Aquarius tunnel, walked to Ann, and sat on the floor beside her to remove the ropes from around her wrists and feet. She looked up at Conor. "Find Drew."

Aidan offered to go with Conor. Together, the two men ran down the Taurus/Scorpio tunnel. They found Drew bound, a knife protruding from his chest, with John kneeling beside him.

"He's alive, but just barely," John said. He rose and walked to the entranceway of Asmodeus' tomb. He was gone.

Conor knelt down and put his hands beside the knife in Drew's chest to begin healing him. "We got this, John. Go."

John ran out of the tunnel to continue searching for Marcus.

Angeline saw John exit the tunnel and shouted, "I've searched every tunnel except Aries/Libra."

In the Taurus/Scorpio Tunnel, Aidan removed the bindings from Drew's wrists and feet.

Drew's eyes opened and he gasped, before the pain overtook him and he again lost consciousness.

Aidan stood, walked to the rectangular stone tomb and peered inside, unaware that Calob and Eligor were concealed behind it.

Conor swore under his breath. "Let's get Drew out of here."

Aidan turned to leave and heard something in his mind, something he didn't recognize. He pulled his soul dagger from his pocket and spun. The two geist attacked. He fell to the ground, but not before he pierced one of them. Eligor perished on top of him. He covered Aidan's face and body with his ash remains, as Calob backed away.

Conor heard commotion from inside the tomb and, still holding onto Drew, yelled, "Aidan! What are you doing? What's going on?"

Aidan stood and wiped the geist dust from his face before scanning the room for the other geist. "I'm handling it! Stay with Drew!"

Calob stood across the room. He held up the pentacle for Aidan to see, and smirked. "Wish I could stay, but..."

Before Aidan could reach him, Calob forced the tip of the pentacle into his neck, and with his other hand, quickly slit his own throat.

Aidan charged at the geist, his Soul Dagger gripped tightly, only to stop when he saw the geist kill himself.

Calob sputtered until his body fell dead onto the ground. His soul mist flew past Aidan to exit the tunnels and join Marcus, carrying the pentacle within itself.

Aidan went back to Conor. "There were two geist in there. I killed one and one turned to mist. Conor, the tomb is empty."

"Let's just get Drew out of here."

Together they carried Drew back through the tunnel. Conor healed him along the way as much as he could, knowing he wouldn't survive unless they got him to the Healing Chambers.

Conor and Aidan approached the tunnel entrance as Sebastian boarded the transport pad with Ann in his arms.

Sebastian whispered softly, his mouth against Ann's cheek. "I can't lose you, too."

The last one to board the transport pad, John activated the stone to set it on its way to the City. As he looked down at hands stained with yet another friend's blood, he recalled his dream of Ann months before. It had been more than just a dream. John clenched his fists and growled through gritted teeth.

Conor again tried to heal Ann, but his energy had been drained trying to stabilize Drew.

Aidan's expression was sombre. "There were two geist hidden behind the tomb. I killed one and the other had something in his hand; a triangular medallion of sorts. He killed himself and as his mist flew past me, I saw the object floating within it. If they were willing to die for it, it has to mean something."

Conor shook his head and exhaled loudly. "I've never heard that a geist can mist out with anything."

John and Angeline looked at each other. They both felt overwhelmed and wondered what their next move should be. The league had not faced such a formidable threat since the last time Asmodeus walked the Earth.

Angeline put her hand on John's shoulder. "We need to speak with the council. They may know what this medallion is."

John nodded in agreement, but didn't speak. The weight of responsibility now felt as though it would crush him.

Angeline looked toward Aidan. "Any detail you can remember will help."

He saw Angeline struggle to maintain her composure and pulled her close. "You do not always have to be the strong one."

Angeline looked up at Aidan. "We can't lose them."

As the friends stood in silence, the transport pad continued toward the City of Radiance, while both Ann and Drew drifted in and out of consciousness.

The League of Twelve

ARIES   Conor Rivait. April 16. Physician.
           Transference Healer.

TAURUS   Ann Johnston. May 14. Chef.
           Mimic.

GEMINI   John Evans. June 11. Dentist.
           Elementalist.

CANCER   Sebastian Shea. July 9. Lawyer.
           Self-Healer.

LEO   Najeeb Cham. August 7. Archeologist.
           Thermalist.

VIRGO   Dalila Saliba. September 8. Nurse.
           Replicator.

LIBRA   Mariam Chahine. October 13. Jeweler.
           Intangent.

SCORPIO   Zayne Nader. November 15. Engineer.
           Marionettist.

SAGITTARIUS Ethan Wells. December 4. Antique Store Owner.
           Invisibilist.

CAPRICORN   Angeline Flynn. December 31. Hotel Event Planner.
           Hyperpolyglot.

AQUARIUS   Amber Price. January 31. Waitress.
           Hypertelescopist.

PISCES   Josh Morrison. March 7. Funeral Director.
           Hallucinist.

League Families

North American Faction

RIVAIT Family - Tattoo Shop. Jayded Ink.
ARIES Bloodline. Aries ring passed from Yvonne to Conor.
Dr. Yvonne Rivait - Aries. April 5. Surgeon.
Roy Rivait - Gemini - May 31. Entrepreneur.
Dr. Conor Rivait - Aries. April 16. Physician.
Jayde Rivait -Taurus. April 26. Tattoo Artist.
Rachel Rivait - Cancer. June 28. Dental Hygienist.

JOHNSTON Family - **Niagara Falls. Restaurant. Transcendence.**
Niagara Falls. North Metta Suites Restaurant.
Transcendency.
London. Aemetta Suites Restaurant. Transcendent.
Cairo. Alda Metta Suites Restaurant. Transcended.
TAURUS Bloodline. Taurus ring passed from Vivian to Ann.
Jake Johnston - Scorpio. November 7. Owner and Manager.
Vivian Turner - Johnston - Taurus. April 30. Chef and Owner.
Ann Johnston - Taurus. May 14. Chef.
Drew Johnston - Pisces. February 23. Lawyer.

EVANS Family - Dental Clinic. Dr. M. Evans, DDS and Associates.
GEMINI Bloodline. Gemini Ring passed from Michael to John.
Dr. Michael Evans - Gemini. May 23. Dentist/Clinic Owner.
Yvette Evans - Cancer. July 3. Social Worker. Deceased.
Dr. John Evans - Gemini. June 11. Dentist.
Dr. James Evans - Scorpio. November 8. Dentist.

SHEA Family - Law Firm. Shea and Partners, LLP.

CANCER Bloodline. Cancer ring passed from Jacob to Sebastian.

Jacob Shea - Cancer. June 24. CEO/Senior Partner.

Maxine Shea - Sagittarius. November 27. Secretary.

Sebastian Shea - Cancer. July 9. Lawyer.

Marianne Shea - Libra. October 2. Student.

SHEA Family - Extended.

CANCER Bloodline.

Marcus Shea - Cancer. June 24. Robotics Engineer.

Madeline Shea - Scorpio. November 9. Secretary.

Kyle Shea - Capricorn. January 15. Judo Instructor.

African Faction

CHAM Family

LEO Bloodline. Leo ring passed from Hayat to Najeeb.

Shareef Cham - Sagittarius. November 30. Museum Registrar.

Hayat Cham - Leo. July 25. Museum Curator.

Dr. Najeeb Cham - Leo. August 7. Archeologist.

Walid Cham - Aquarius. February 5. Museum Tourist Guide.

SALIBA Family

VIRGO Bloodline. Virgo ring passed from Youssef to Dalila.

Youssef Saliba - Virgo. August 28. Pharmacist.

Wardah Saliba - Capricorn. December 23. Housewife.

Dalila Saliba - Virgo. September 8. Nurse.

Sameer Saliba - Aries. March 25. Accountant.

CHAHINE Family - Jewelry Store. Al-Jawhara (The Jewel).

LIBRA Bloodline. Libra ring passed from Yasmeen to Mariam.

Omar Chahine - Scorpio. October 27. Goldsmith/Owner.

Yasmeen Chahine - Libra. September 29. Accountant.

Mariam Chahine - Libra. October 13. Jeweler.

Layla Chahine - Pisces. March 3. Office worker.

NADER Family - Engineering Firm. Al-Nahda (Progress).

SCORPIO Bloodline. Scorpio ring passed from Khalil to Zayne.

Khalil Nader - Scorpio. October 31. Engineer/Owner.

Maya Nader - Taurus. May 4. Stewardess.

Zayne Nader - Scorpio. November 15. Engineer.

Jibril Nader - Cancer. July 1. Chef.

European Faction

WELLS Family - Antique Store. Wells' Antiquities.
SAGITTARIUS Bloodline. Sagittarius ring passed from Sabrina to Ethan.
Joseph Wells - Taurus. May 15. Co-Owner.
Sabrina Wells - Sagittarius. November 28. Clerk.
Ethan Wells - Sagittarius. December 4. Co-Owner.
Olivia Wells - Virgo. August 26. Purchaser.
Nicholas Wells - Aquarius. January 22. Chef.

FLYNN Family -   London. Hotel. Aemetta Suites Luxury Hotels.
Niagara Falls. Hotel. North Metta Suites.
Cairo. Hotel. Alda Metta Suites.
CAPRICORN Bloodline. Capricorn ring passed from Alexander to Angeline.
Alexander Flynn - Capricorn. January 7. Hotel Owner.
Theresa Flynn - Libra. October 5. Accountant.
Angeline Flynn - Capricorn. December 31. Event Planner.
Katherine Flynn - Scorpio. November 6. Purchaser.
Margaret Flynn - Pisces. February 27. Student.

PRICE Family
AQUARIUS Bloodline. Aquarius ring passed from Edmond to Amber.
Edmond Price - Aquarius. February 2. Martial Arts Shop Owner.
Hannah Price - Leo. July 27. Secretary.
Amber Price - Aquarius. January 31. Waitress.

MORRISON Family - Morrison Funeral Services
PISCES Bloodline. Pisces ring passed from Diana to Josh.
Christopher Morrison - Capricorn. January 9. Embalmer/Co-Owner.
Diana Morrison - Pisces. February 25. Funeral Coordinator/Co-Owner.
Josh Morrison - Pisces. March 7. Funeral Director.
Faith Morrison - Scorpio. November 11. Concierge.

TEMPLE Family - Temple Technologies.
Charles Temple - Pisces. March 3. Retired CEO.
Julia Price-Temple - Virgo. September 4. Engineer.
Aidan Temple – Aquarius. February 14. CEO.
Lexi Temple - Leo. August 11. Laboratory technician.
Lily Temple - Leo. August 11. Cosmetologist.

Acknowledgements

~~~~

A tremendous amount of gratitude to:

The Fishfish, Matthews, Naklie, and St. Andrews families
for their love and support throughout our journey.

Our dedicated Piscean editor, proofreader, and friend, Jennafer Simpson,
without whose brilliant mind and tireless eyes this book would not have been possible.

Our Capricornian friend Yvette McKenzie
who never tired of the multiple readings.

Our Geminian friend Marybeth Molyneaux
who read our manuscript in its earliest stages.

Our Sagittarian and Cancerean friends, Susan Del Col and Brian Atkins, for their input.

Sarah at Mirador Publishing for bringing our world to light.

CPSIA information can be obtained
at www.ICGtesting.com
Printed in the USA
LVOW08s0807240418
574507LV00002B/19/P